THE DISTANCE BETWEEN US

One February afternoon, Stella sees a man walking towards her on a London pavement. She hasn't seen his face for many years, but she instantly recognises him. Or thinks she does. At exactly the same moment, on the other side of the world, Jake is realising that the crowd around him, celebrating Chinese New Year, is about to turn dangerous. They know nothing of one another's existence, but both Stella and Jake flee their lives: Jake in search of a place so remote it doesn't appear on any map, and Stella for a destination in Scotland, the significance of which only her sister, Nina, will understand.

THE DISTANCE BETWEEN US

The Distance Between Us

by

Maggie O'Farrell

Magna Large Print Books
Long Preston, North Yorkshire,
BD23 4ND, England.

British Library Cataloguing in Publication Data.

O'Farrell, Maggie
The distance between us.

A catalogue record of this book is
available from the British Library

ISBN 0-7505-2211-9

First published in Great Britain in 2004 by Review
An imprint of Headline Book Publishing

Published in Large Print 2004 by arrangement with
Headline Book Publishing Ltd.

Magna Large Print is an imprint of Library Magna Books Ltd.

Printed and bound in Great Britain by
T.J. (International) Ltd., Cornwall, PL28 8RW

for Will

I do know that lives can change overnight, though it usually takes much longer than that to comprehend what has happened, to sense that we have changed direction

Jay McInerney

I came to these places … to claim kin with them, to be guided by them

Geoff Dyer

She was my liegeman, my alter ego, my double; we could not do without one another

Simone de Beauvoir,
on her sister

part one

He wakes to find himself splayed like a starfish across the bed, his mind running at full tilt. On the other side of the room, the fan turns towards him then turns away, as if offended. Somewhere beside him, the pages of a book flutter, reel and divide. The apartment is filled with an inky light and flashes of neon scissor the ceiling. Late evening.

'Shit,' he says, and raises his head with a jerk. Something soft yet integral between his shoulder blades stretches and tears like wet paper. Swearing and reaching round to feel for the point of pain, Jake stumbles to his feet and skates in his socks over the wooden tiles to the bathroom.

His face in the mirror is a shock. The creases and pleats of the bedsheet have left reddened lines over his cheek and temple, giving his skin a peculiar, raw look. His hair stands up as if he's been electrocuted, and appears to have grown. How had he managed to fall asleep? He'd been reading, head propped up on his hands, and the last thing he remembered was the man in his book descending a rope ladder into a disused well. Jake glances at his watch. Ten past ten. He's already late.

A moth blunders into his face, then

ricochets into the mirror, the faint powder on its wings leaving a mottled mark, a ghost of itself, on the glass. Jake stands back for a moment, watching it, tracking its course through the air, then snaps his cupped palms at it. Misses. The moth, sensing danger, spirals upwards towards the light but Jake aims again and this time he gets it, its delicate, confused body knocking at the cage of his hands.

He nudges the lever with his elbow and pushes at the window. The roar of the street, nineteen floors below, rises up to meet him. Jake leans out over the strings of washing and opening his hands, tosses the moth upwards. It falls for a second, turning over, disoriented, then recovers and, catching a hot thermal draught from an air-conditioning unit down below, flitters into invisibility.

Jake slams the window shut. He rattles through the flat, collecting wallet, keys, jacket, pulling on his shoes, left in a heap by the door. The lift takes an age to come and when it does, it stinks of sweat and stale air. In the entrance hall, the janitor is sitting on a stool beside the door. Above him are the frilled red and gold decorations of Chinese New Year – a fat-cheeked child with tar-black hair rides astride a pink pig.

'*Gung hei fat choi*,' Jake says, as he passes.

The man's face cracks into a gap-toothed grin. '*Gung hei fat choi*, Jik-ah!' He slaps Jake on the shoulder, making his skin prickle and sting like sunburn.

Outside, taxis splinter the light of the road's puddles and an underground train shakes the pavement. Jake tilts his head to look up at the building tops. The year is turning from ox to tiger. When he was a child, he used to imagine the year at the stroke of midnight as a strange mutant creature, caught in half-metamorphosis.

He moves away from his building, almost crashing into a diminutive elderly woman pushing at the handle of a cart laden with collapsed cardboard boxes. Jake sidesteps her and heads south, past the basketball courts, a small red kerbside shrine with a bouquet of spent joss sticks, past men sitting in a *yum chai* shop, mah-jong tiles clicking on the tables between them, past serried rows of draped motorbikes, intricate webs of bamboo scaffolding, past restaurant tanks where doomed fish are stretching out their gills, searching for oxygen in the cloudy water.

But Jake doesn't see any of this. He is looking up at the darkening clouds, humming as he walks, his thin-soled sneakers moving over the pavement. The air swings with incense, firecracker smoke, and the amniotic salinity of the harbour.

The bus isn't coming. Stella pulls her scarf

closer round her throat and stands on tiptoe to gaze down the line of traffic. Cars, cars, taxis, motorbikes, the odd cyclist, cars, more cars. But no bus. She looks up at the screen that is supposed to tell her how long she has to wait. It's blank.

She separates her coat sleeve from her glove to check her watch. She's on an afternoon shift today and she's going to be late if she waits any longer. Stella stands for a moment, thinking. Is it better to stay and wait for a bus that will come eventually or to start walking and get there just a little bit late? She could get the Tube but that's a ten-minute walk from here and might be delayed as well. She'll walk. It's probably the quickest way, now.

With a brief glance over her shoulder to make sure the bus still isn't coming, Stella sets off. The street is cold, unusually cold for this time of year, the ground sharp, gilded with frost that cracks underfoot. The sky is an uncertain grey, crazy-paved with leafless branches.

She's back in London for several weeks – no more than that, she hopes – working on a late-night radio show. She has a flat here, a bedsit on the edge of Kennington, but usually rents it out while she goes off to different places. A month in Paris, a stint in Moscow, half a year in Helsinki. She's not sure where she'll go next – Rome, maybe,

Madrid, Copenhagen. Stella doesn't like staying in one place.

She marches north, towards the Thames, her breath steaming, her body inappropriately warm inside the layers of clothing. As she takes her first steps on Waterloo Bridge, the city begins to split in two, the river opening out to her. The bridge was built entirely by women, she read somewhere once, during the Second World War. It's deserted today. Cars swoop past, heading north, but on both sides the pavements stretch out, empty.

At the crossroads, Jake leaps on to the backboard of a rattling tram just as it's pulling away. The downstairs, murky and dim, is crammed – people filling the seats and clinging to the ceiling rails. An old man in a vest and faded trousers is nearest Jake, a birdcage held on his lap. From its pendulum perch, the bird regards Jake sideways with the tiny black beads of its eyes. The heads of the two Westerners on the tram sway above those of the Chinese.

Jake thunders up the wooden stairs. He takes the seat right at the front, leaning his head out of the window, facing into the speeding breeze, and watches the cluttered, neon-scribbled buildings of Wanchai slide into the slick concrete-and-mirror edifice of the huge shopping complex.

Jake's hair is dark and his skin can turn to

almost the same shade as his friend Hing Tai's if he stays in the sun long enough, but his eyes are the colour of deep water. He has a British passport, a British mother and, somewhere, a British father. But Jake has never seen Britain, or his father, and has never been anywhere near Europe.

Stella sees a solitary figure, far away, at the other end of the bridge, heading towards her. A man. Shrunk down by distance. She could raise her hand and encircle him with a finger and thumb. As if pulled towards each other by a string, they walk and walk and walk. He becomes more defined: tall, hulking, wearing a green jacket.

Stella looks out over the river, where the huge wheel is sequined with lights and people small as insects swarm along the South Bank. She swings the beam of her vision back to the bridge, to where she's heading, and the shock is so great she almost stumbles. She has to grip the wall with her hand to stop herself falling and her heart trips and stutters, as if unsure how to continue.

Stella stares down at the brown, twisting water of the river, then back at the man. He is closer again and Stella wonders if he will just carry on getting bigger and bigger until he is looming over her, vast and terrible as a brockenspectre. He is looking straight at her now, his hands jammed into his pockets.

She cannot believe it, she really cannot. He has that swollen, white-pink skin, the same dense fuzz of red hair, and the eyes pitted deep into the flesh of the face.

It's as if time has buckled back on itself, as if the years have swallowed themselves. Stella can feel the clammy give that skin would have beneath her grip, and the peculiar, damp animal smell of his hair. The man is coming towards her now, close, so close she could touch him, and a scream hovers somewhere at the base of her throat.

'You all right, doll?'

Her gloved fingers tighten on the rail. He is Scottish. Just as she had known he would be. Stella nods, still looking at the river, its surface muscled like the backs of serpents.

'You sure?' He is standing just out of view. Stella can't breathe, seems unable to stretch open her lungs for air. 'You don't look it.'

She nods again. She doesn't want him to hear her speak, to hear her voice. She has to get away. Without looking at him, she starts to move off, pulling herself along by the railing. She has to pass quite close to him and she can feel the movement of his breath on her hair as he says, 'If you're sure, then,' and it makes her shake, makes her flesh shrink around her. ''Bye for now,' he says.

Stella swivels her head to see him go. That same lumbering gait, his feet splayed, the massive shoulders hunched. He turns round once. Pauses for a second. Then carries on. 'Bye for now.

Two trucks thunder past in quick succession, making the air churn. She breaks into a stumbling run, her coat flapping and tugging behind her, the city buildings veering ahead. A sharp, dragging ache has started up in her chest, as if something with teeth and claws is trying to fight its way out of her. She trips, her palms and knees meeting the pavement, and before she scrambles up, she looks behind her.

He's vanished. The bridge stretches away from her, domed, curving and deserted.

She drags herself to her feet. Grit and dirt smudge her palms. Her hair is wet with tears and sticks to her face in the cutting February wind. She looks up and down the street, unsure of what she is seeking.

Coming towards her on the other side of the road, she sees the lighted oblong of a taxi sign. She darts into the traffic, one arm raised above her head. A car screeches and swerves. 'Please stop,' she mutters to herself, her eyes fixed on the light speeding towards her, 'please.'

The taxi slows and pulls up. Stella runs towards it, opens the door and climbs inside.

Jake clatters down the stairs as the tram

does its double-corner-swing into Central. He likes feeling the swooping, shuttling change of direction beneath him, likes to be standing for that bit when you have to brace yourself against the contrary motion. He drops down to the road in front of the weighty, jagged structure of the bank and cuts through, under the black glass of the building where empty escalators are humming, churning round, transporting nobody up and down.

He toils up the steep incline of Lan Kwai Fong, threading his way through the already thick crowd. The cobbled road is lined with bars and clubs, all filled with Westerners who work in the legal offices, newspapers, schools, radio stations, IT departments of Hong Kong Island, and return each night by ferry to their flats on Lamma or Lantau, stopping off here to tank down some alcohol and meet their friends. Jake never usually comes here, but Mel and her crowd like it.

Jake often thinks of Hong Kong as a kind of overflow pipe for Europe. The people who come here have left their homes and their families for a reason, and not usually one they ever disclose. They're all in varying degrees of separation, or running away from something, or in search of an elusive element that might complete them. Or at least hoping the feeling that something is missing from their lives won't pursue them over the ocean. If you go far enough you might never catch up with yourself.

At the top of the hill, Jake turns left into the Iso-Bar. It is filled with icy, over-conditioned air and hordes of people, drinks in hand, packed close together. He scans the crowds, searching for Mel. Suddenly she is there, right in front of him. Their eyes haven't yet met but she is printing a kiss on his face in lipstick and turning her head towards her friends. 'I told you he'd be late, didn't I? Didn't I say he'd be late?' Her face swims before him in the murky gloom. She has her light, fine, almost colourless hair pulled into a ponytail high on the back of her head and her hands are fastened behind his back.

'I'm sorry, I fell asleep,' Jake yells over the music. 'I don't know how. One minute I was reading and the next I–'

'You must have been tired.' She smiles up at him.

'Yes.'

He extracts himself from her embrace to say hello to the others. They nod and smile at him, raising their glasses, and Lucy, Mel's best friend, gives him a brief, distracted kiss before turning back to the man she's talking to. Someone gives Jake a tall glass, slippery with condensation.

'We're going to Lantau tomorrow,' Mel is shouting over the noise, leaning towards one of her colleagues, her fingers hooked into Jake's arm, 'to see the Buddha. Jake wants to go hiking in the hills.'

'Are you going with him?' the colleague asks, amused.

'Yes.' Mel nods and glances his way. 'If he'll have me. She squeezes his arm. 'I thought I should give it a go, you know.'

'But you hate that kind of thing!'

Nina places the phone on the floor next to her and dials the code for London, then the number. There is a short pause before the pulsing purr of a distant ringing.

She waits, frowning, picking apart one of the sandwiches Richard made for her that morning, extracting the silvery half-moons of onion. He knows she doesn't eat raw onion. Then there's the gasp of electronic ether before the hiss of a voicemail recording: *Hi, you've reached Stella Gilmore in Production. I'm either away from my desk or on another–*

Nina hangs up, reassembles her sandwich and puts a corner of it into her mouth.

'Twelve minutes to go!' Lucy exclaims, peering at her watch. 'And we all turn from chickens to pigs!'

Mel turns to Jake, a slight anxiety on her face. 'Is that right, Jake?'

'Ox to tiger,' he murmurs, 'and it's not

really us it's–'

'Let's go to that bar down the road!' Lucy is saying. 'The one with the DJ. Come on, let's go!'

They toss back their drinks and head for the door. Outside, the air is tepid and a thin, fine veil of drizzle brushes their faces. The street is packed, a sea of heads bobbing and rippling between them and the buildings opposite. Jake has to flatten himself against the wall to let a group of Japanese boys go past. Lucy stumbles on the raised kerb, falling against him. On his other side, Mel grips his hand. Across the street, a gang of Brits are singing 'Auld Lang Syne'.

In an office in London, a mobile phone starts to ring. The sound is muffled, as if the phone is underneath a coat or a folder or a bag. It makes several people in cubicles around it turn their heads, listening, wondering. Then they realise it isn't theirs and turn away again.

The girl who shares an office with Stella pulls the headphones down from her ears and looks across at Stella's desk. The chair is tilted away from the computer. Where Stella should be there is just a view through to the uneven chimneys and blackened, rain-polished roofs of Regent Street.

Should she answer it? Stella quite often forgets to take it home with her. It's rung several times in the past hour or so. Someone must be anxious to get hold of her. The phone stops, as abruptly as it began. The girl pulls the headphones back into place. She'll tell Stella when she gets in.

The noise of the street rises, as if someone's turned up the volume. People are shouting and laughing and yelling. A man just in front of Jake is brandishing a small, fragile paper dragon, its teeth bared, its nostrils trailing fire. Jake starts pushing his way through the throng of bodies, in the direction of the bar, Mel just behind him, in his wake, Lucy behind her. The others have melted into the swell. More and more people are streaming out of doors to join the thick current of people. Jake is hit and buffeted by shoulders, elbows, hips, feet. He twists his head and looks up the street. Is it any less crowded there? No. Heads are appearing, flowing in from adjoining lanes, and D'Aguilar Street is blocked half-way down by a police barrier. He feels his heart accelerating inside him, falling over itself, and he clutches Mel's fingers.

Everyone is shoving and pushing. Jake forgets how selfish people become in a situation like this. Three men all wearing red party hats elbow their way past, one treading on his foot, grinding the bones against the pavement. More and more bodies are pouring like water into the street. Jake feels very warm all of a sudden. He turns one way and then the other, unable to decide what they should do, which way they should go. Mel is saying something to him and as he turns to hear her, he stumbles and nearly goes down. He grabs for the nearest thing – the coat of a woman standing to his left – and drags himself up again. The woman gives him a quick, panicked glare but turns away silently when Jake apologises. The crowd is pressing nearer, closing in on his ribcage.

'I don't like this,' Mel says. 'Jake, I don't like it.'

'I know,' he says. 'Let's try–'

His words are snatched away from him because several things happen at once, and very fast.

Behind them, a man carrying several bottles of beer trips and falls forward. The bottles burst from his fingers and drop to the ground. The glass explodes and beer fans out over the cobbles, a frothing, dark, slippery stain. Jake pushes back into the dense pack of bodies on the pavement, dragging Mel with him. There is a sudden wild surge from up the hill. Jake sees the beer-bottle man go under. Then Lucy slips, pulling away from them, vanishing, the crowd closing over her head.

Francesca is in the garden, bending over the echium she bought in a nursery in Arran, which, she's just noticed, is beginning to be blackened by frost. Francesca hates frost, hates it more than the sticky-footed greenfly which in summer swarm up her roses, more than the orange-frilled slugs that tear their way through her nasturtiums. She can't ever kill slugs, though. The thought of poisoning them with noxious chemicals or sprinkling them with salt is too much, too cruel.

She shivers and pulls Archie's cardigan more tightly round her. The Edinburgh sky above her droops, low and soft as the belly of a goose. The cold today has the metallic tang of snow.

Her body responds to the electronic trilling before her mind. She's straightened up and turned towards the house before she's realised what it is. The telephone. The new telephone that Stella bought her.

She picks it up and presses a button at random, but the trilling doesn't stop. Francesca sighs, reaches for her glasses, looped around her neck on a chain, and peers at the buttons more closely. There is one with a minute picture of a telephone receiver on it. Maybe that was it.

'Hello?' she says tentatively, expectantly.

'Have you still not worked out how to answer that phone?'

It's Nina, she's pretty sure. They sound

quite similar on the phone and neither of them ever seems to think they need to identify themselves. ‘Of course I have,’ Francesca lies, playing for time. They’d be offended if she got the wrong one. ‘I was in the garden, that’s all.’

‘Oh.’ There’s a pause in which Francesca hears the suck and drag of a cigarette. Definitely Nina, then. ‘How are you, anyway?’

‘Oh, fine. You know, busy. Your dad’s gone to Munich.’

‘What for?’

‘I’m not sure. A conference, I think.’

‘Look,’ Nina announces, ‘I can’t talk now. I’ve got an appointment in five minutes. I was just wondering if you’d spoken to Stella today.’

‘Stella?’ Francesca repeats, thinking. Stella is the one she doesn’t have to worry about. ‘No.’

‘When did you last speak to her?’

‘Last week. I think. Or maybe the week before.’

‘But not today?’

‘No. Why?’

‘No reason. I just can’t get hold of her. I’ve left messages and she hasn’t called me back.’ Nina takes another drag of her cigarette. ‘She’s disappeared.’

Francesca often feels at a slight disadvantage when faced with the relationship between her two daughters. It’s always seemed too private, too elliptical for her to comprehend. She brightens with an idea. 'Maybe she's taken the day off or–'

'She would have told me,' Nina interjects.

Francesca doesn't know what to say. But diversionary tactics have always worked best with Nina so she asks, 'Why don't you come over later? There might be a good film on TV. I'll make you dinner.'

'OK,' Nina concedes. 'Perhaps.'

Mel is screaming Lucy's name over and over, and fighting against Jake's grasp. The crowd seethes with yells and sweat and the hot stench of beer. Jake struggles to keep hold of Mel while pushing forward to find Lucy. Then there is another great heave and surge, and Jake feels the ground drop away from his feet, and they are carried by a current of bodies away from Lucy, towards the window of a bar where people are dancing to music only they can hear. Jake is jostled up against the cold grain of a wall. Mel has been snatched away from him. He fights his way round, pushing his elbows into surrounding flesh to create space to breathe, kicking his feet against the wall. His lungs feel red hot, airless and compressed.

'Mel!' he shouts. 'Melanie!' But he can't even hear his own voice over the noise. A blond man with a beard is pressed up against his back and a Filipina girl is clinging to his jacket sleeve, sobbing rhythmically. 'Mel!' he yells again, trying to twist round.

The crowd rushes again, in a different direction, downhill, sweeping him along, and Jake feels something beneath his shoes, something soft and yielding. A body? A sharp jag of panic crosses his chest and he tries to look down but he is wedged between a screaming teenager with hennaed hair and a woman with wide, staring eyes. Jake looks into them and sees the black stretch of the pupils, the way her head is lolling on her neck, the slackened jaw.

Jake thrashes his legs beneath him and tilts his head back, gasping to draw breath. Drizzle feathers his face. High above, the sky domes over them, black, depthless and impassive, brittled with silver. He can hear the thin wail of sirens, far away. He can hear the tearing screams of the teenager next to him, tailing off to a whimper. The blurred, metallic words of someone somewhere over a Tannoy, telling them in two languages to keep calm, stop pushing, keep calm. Different currents of music from the bars around them. The distant crackle of the harbour fireworks. The rushing, thudding trip-trip of his blood against his ears. The terrible silence of the woman with the staring eyes.

By four thirty, the girl who shares the office with Stella is annoyed. She and Stella still have to sort out a guest for next week's show; one of them is supposed to have read a book, or part of a book, and written the interview questions for James; PRs keep on phoning, pushing their clients for appearances on the show, and the girl, Maxine, doesn't have the time to edit this week's interview while answering the calls. Where thc hell is she?

The production phone rings. She snatches it up. 'Hello, *James Karl Show*, this is–'

'Maxine,' a quiet but offhand voice, 'sorry, it's–'

'Nina,' Maxine cuts in, even more annoyed now. Stella's sister. She'd recognise that voice anywhere. She rings about twenty times a day, and usually about absolutely nothing. Maxine and another woman who works on the show have a joke that Stella's sister can't make a cup of tea without asking Stella first.

'She's not here,' Maxine snaps.

'I gathered that,' Nina snaps back. 'Do you know where she is?'

'I wish I did. She was supposed to be in by one, but she hasn't turned up.'

'Where was she this morning?'

'I don't know.'

'Was she meeting anyone?'

'I've no idea.'

'What time did she leave last night?'

Maxine sighs. The last thing she needs right now is Stella's loopy sister giving her the third degree. 'Nina, I'm actually really up against it here and–'

'What time did she leave?' Nina repeats.

'For God's sake,' Maxine mutters. 'I don't know ... twelve thirty. One a.m. maybe. It would have been after the show finished.'

Maxine hears the flick of Nina's lighter.

'Can I take a message?' Maxine enquires, twirling a pen round and round her fingers. She has to get back to that interview – James will go mad if it's not finished by five. She waves to another woman through the glass partition in another office. The woman is motioning drinking, asking her if she wants a coffee. Maxine signals yes and gives her a thumbs-up.

'No,' Nina is saying, 'no message,' and hangs up.

'Goodbye to you too,' Maxine mutters to the empty cubicle.

He is caught in a surge again, carried this time uphill, the pressure around him increasing until he can no longer draw breath. The scene in front of him dissolves and blurs, and a deep pain is spreading from his shoulder down his back. The important thing is not to fall, he is telling himself, over and over, to stay upright, not to go under. His ribcage creaks and strains, there seems to be no oxygen getting to any of his body, his limbs are numb and prickling, and Jake feels sure that this is it, his time is now, that nothing and no one could withstand this, and his mind is flat and calm and heavy as molten lead.

Suddenly he is cannoned into the back of a man who turns round angrily. 'Oi, do you mind?'

The man turns back to his companions. Jake stares at them. They are drinking and chatting. He has come up against a section of the crowd who don't know, who are still caught up in the change to the Year of the Tiger.

The man with whom he collided is saying, 'I mean, what would you do if a client took you to one of those places with flattened pigs' heads in the window?'

The woman beside him cackles, throwing back her head. 'When in Rome!' she shrieks, and they all laugh.

Around him, he feels a sudden release. Bodies fall away from him. It's as if a membrane has been punctured: the currents of people start draining away. His legs buckle like melted plastic, and the cobbles come up to meet him. He crouches there, gagging and coughing for breath, trying to suck air down into his bruised lungs, aware of people standing around him, staring, murmuring. It seems very quiet all of a sudden.

Jake raises his head and looks down the street.

Nina drops into Richard's surgery on her way home over the Meadows, striding past his row of patients, past the receptionist (who never speaks to Nina because Nina once accidentally called her a fat cow at the annual surgery party), and up to his door.

Richard is putting some funny equipment made of steel and black tubing back into its box. 'Hello, beautiful,' he says, when he sees her, and kisses her forehead, which Nina hates but doesn't want to have a row about now. 'What are you doing here?'

'Came to see you.' Nina sits herself down on the examination couch and crosses her legs.

'How nice,' he says, but she catches him throwing a swift glance towards the clock.

'I'm worried about Stella,' she says.

'Oh?' He is shuffling pages together on his desk, looking at something on his computer screen.

'She's gone AWOL.'

He is writing something on one of the papers. 'AWOL?' he repeats – his trick to reassure her that he's listening. 'But she's always doing that, isn't she? It's an integral part of the ... the Stella package.'

'What is?'

'The vanishing act.' Richard glances up. Nina sees him put down his pen, sees him reminding himself to tread carefully when talking about her sister. In the early days of their relationship – years ago now – she'd hurled a tin-opener at his head when he'd asked if she didn't think Stella was just a little bit flighty.

'But she always tells me first. I...' she shrugs uneasily '...I've just got this feeling that something's happened.'

Richard comes towards her. 'I'm sure she's fine,' he says, stroking her cheek. 'When was it you last heard from her?'

'Last night,' Nina says, then regrets it. She sees his mouth twitch, sees the diagnosis 'hysterical' crossing his mind. 'But I've left her loads of messages since then.'

'She'll turn up,' he says soothingly. 'She's probably just busy, don't you think?'

Nina doesn't answer. She reclines on the examination couch, her spike heels snagging in the paper cover. Richard's palm lands on her hip. She can feel the heat of it through the thin material of her skirt.

'Maybe you need an examination,' he says, his fingers beginning to hitch up her hem, the callus on his thumb snagging on her stockings.

Nina stares at the ceiling above her, listens to the rustle of the paper that covers the couch, the leaping second hand of the clock on the wall, Richard's breathing.

'No,' she says, sitting up and pulling down her skirt. 'I have to find Stella.'

Jake stands next to a melamine desk, his right hand clutching his left arm. The ache in his shoulder is overwhelming, drilling, rooted, and the arm dangles at an angle, turned away from him, as if it belongs to somebody else. Something is bleeding at the side of his face. He has to keep wiping it away, tiger-striping his sleeve. Nurses, orderlies and paramedics swirl around him, busy, electrified.

Jake leans over the desk again. 'Melanie Harker,' he says to the receptionist. 'Is she here?'

'Please take a seat,' she says, without looking at him. 'The doctor will see you soon.'

'I don't want a doctor,' he says, 'I have to find her.' The white light from the overhead strips is making his eyes smart. 'How about Lucy Riddell? Is she here?'

The receptionist fixes him with a glare. 'Please take a seat.'

If he moves his head too quickly, the walls and corridors see-saw around him. He grips the peeling edge of the desk for balance. His hand is shaking like an old man's. He is still struck by the ease with which his lungs swell and deflate, swell and deflate. He feels he will never get over this.

The white flash of a doctor flits past the double doors into a perpendicular corridor. Jake moves after him, propping himself up on the wall as he walks.

‘Excuse me,’ he says, stumbling down the corridor, sliding along the shiny pale green paint, ‘excuse me.’

The doctor gives him a quick side-glance but hurries on.

‘M’goi, m’goi,’ Jake switches to Cantonese, *‘gau meng ah.* I’m trying to find Melanie Harker. Is she here?’

The doctor stops in his tracks and stares at him, attentive now, shocked, as people always are, by a *gweilo* speaking Cantonese. ‘Melanie Harker,’ the doctor repeats, still staring at him. ‘Yes. She’s here. I saw her earlier. She is...’ He stops ‘Are you a relative?’

‘No ... yes...’ Jake attempts to formulate an explanation. He fills the seemingly massive capacity of his lungs from the endless supply of air around them. ‘She’s my ... my girlfriend. Her family are in Britain,’ he manages. ‘Norfolk,’ he adds, without knowing why.

The doctor, a man with grey circles of fatigue under his eyes, looks him over. ‘Have you been seen?’

‘No,’ Jake shakes his head impatiently, ‘but I’m fine. I need to know–’

‘You don’t look fine,’ the doctor says, fishes a slender torch from his coat pocket and shines it into Jake’s eyes. When he touches his left arm, Jake flinches, hot pain arrowing down his arm. ‘You’ll need an X-ray for that,' the doctor says. 'It's broken. And you're in shock. You'll stay here tonight. *Neihih ming m ming ah?*'

'*Ngor ming*. But when can I–'

'Melanie Harker,' the doctor interrupts, 'is in a critical condition. She's in Intensive Care.'

Jakes stares at a light fixed to the wall. A fly has got trapped inside it and is battering against the white, opaque glass. It feels as if the movement and the noise are inside his head. He opens his mouth to ask a question, but can't quite think what it is.

'I'll see if you can visit her,' the doctor says, more gently.

Stella sits on the floor, her back against the door of the flat, her coat still wrapped round her. Everything in this room seems unfamiliar. Did she buy that picture on the wall, the vase, those books? Do they belong to her? Is this her life, or someone else's? Was it her who spent a whole weekend stripping and waxing these floorboards, a mask over her face? Why had she done that? What was it for?

Beyond the thick green stalk of an amaryllis, Stella catches sight of herself in the mirror. Her face seems bloodless, and it stands out, stark, from her hair. She has the long-boned hands of her father, the green eyes and dark hair of her mother, and, she was surprised to discover recently when she found an ancient, browning photograph in her grandparents' flat, the face of a great-great-aunt from Isernia. A mish-mash, a collision of genes.

The phone rings again, making her jump, making her look away from herself. She plucks at the interlocked stitches of her gloves. It rings four, five, six times, then the answerphone clicks on and she hears her sister's voice, unspooling into the silence.

Stella bows her head, covers her ears.

Mel seems drained of colour. Her skin is so pale that she sinks, like some camouflaging animal, into the magnesium-white sheets and walls. Machines sigh and blip around her. Somewhere overhead the air-conditioning hums.

'Mel?' Jake curls his fingers around hers. They feel dry and cold, a loose collection of bones. On her other hand is a grey plastic clip, like crocodile jaws. 'Mel, it's me,' he whispers.

Her eyes slide under their lids, marbled with violet, then her lashes part. It takes her a while to focus on him. Her mouth opens, but nothing comes out. He sees her inhale and swallow. Everything seems to take her so long and so much effort. He wants to tell her that it doesn't matter, that she doesn't need to speak, but she is saying his name on an outward breath and her hand twitches beneath his. Then she is mouthing something he cannot hear.

'What was that?' he whispers, leaning closer. She doesn't smell as she usually does. Underneath the starched antiseptic tang of the hospital there is a sour, queer scent, like something left too long in the dark.

'Lucy,' Mel whispers. 'Lucy.'

Jake looks away as he says, 'She's not here.' He finds lying hard, has never been very good at it. He's always afraid that the truth is obvious, that it's readable on his face, as if projected on to it. Lucy is lying in the morgue, several floors below Mel's bed. 'She was taken to another hospital,' he invents quickly. 'Queen Mary. In Happy Valley.'

Mel's eyes travel over him, over the plaster cast on his arm, the sling on his shoulder, the vivid bruises blooming on his face. 'Are you OK?' The words come out jerkily, separated, as if in different sentences.

'Fine.' He nods. 'It's just a fracture. And a dislocated shoulder. But it's fine. How are you feeling?'

Her head moves on the pillow and she sighs, misting the oxygen mask. Jake sees tears spreading into river deltas at the corners of her eyes. Her mouth moves again.

He bends over her and touches his lips to

her cheek, smoothing damp hair away from her forehead. 'What was that?' he says.

'I'm scared,' he hears. He is leaning over her, so close that he can see her tongue forming the words. 'Jake, I don't want to...' Her eyes swivel until they find his. 'I don't want to die–'

'You're not going to,' he gets out, before he realises that she hasn't finished, that she is saying:

'–without having married you.'

Jake, crouched around her on a bed in Intensive Care, blinks. He is about to say, 'What?' but stops himself. He heard her. It's such a bizarre thing for her to come out with that a very distant part of him wants to laugh. Surely she can't mean that. 'Mel,' he begins, unsure of what he wants to say, what he should say. What do you say to something like that? To a girl you've only known for four months?

'I don't want... I can't bear the thought,' her voice rises like a leaf on the wind, 'of dying without being ... tied to you.' She is sobbing now, and people are running around them, feet hurrying against the tiles. 'I can't bear it without...'

A nurse is readjusting the mask over Mel's face. Mel is struggling against her, trying to speak more, but the doctor is there, fiddling with a machine, telling her to shush, to please lie back.

'Maybe...' Jake tries again but he can't seem to order his thoughts. He would give anything just to be able to lie down for a minute, to shut his eyes against the violence of the lights, to stretch out on some starched sheets, for one of these nurses to tell him what he should do. 'Maybe we should see how you are tomorrow,' he says. He is aware of how lame these words sound and he catches her look of dismay.

'You know, she isn't going to last the night,' the doctor, standing to Jake's right, says in Cantonese, gentle but emphatic.

Jake turns to look at him. The pain in his arm and shoulder judders and twists. It suddenly seems incredibly hot in here. He looks back at Mel. Her eyes blaze and glitter behind the mask.

'I'm sorry,' the doctor says.

Stella is shivering cold, her flesh studded with bumps, her teeth chattering. The heating's not on. Earlier, she'd leant across and snapped on the light. Above her, the bulb burns yellow. She has no idea what time it is. The building and, indeed, the whole city seem to have disappeared, dissolved around her, receded into the night. The phone rang twice more, and fell silent. The people next door had their television up very loud. But that's stopped too now. It's as if the lit box of this room hovers, alone and solitary, in dark space.

Stella shuts her eyes, tight. There must be some way to stop this dominating her existence. How many times has this happened to her? How often does she glimpse him in the face of a stranger, on the street, in a train, in a bar, in a lift, across a shop? These sightings mar her life like sinkholes, the ground around them eroding, precarious.

Stella stands up quickly. Her vision blurs and wanes from the sudden movement, her joints aching. A small, winged creature flutters round her head briefly, then circles up to the light. She stands watching it for a moment and it's then that the idea appears in her head. It reaches her from some external place, like lightning hitting a conductor, and as soon as she thinks it, she's made the decision.

She jerks into action, an over-wound toy, moving through her flat, collecting things: clothes, a jacket, a map, her compass, wallet, some books. She pulls a bag from the top of a cupboard and shoves the heap of things into it, yanking the zip closed.

The priest is someone who knows Hing Tai. He greets Jake as Jik-ah, tells him he is sorry for his troubles. An unsmiling nurse with a white cone hat perched on top of her thick black perm acts as a witness. As the first light of the Year of the Tiger soaks into the little room, Jake lays one hand on Mel's and another on the black leather of a book he doesn't believe in and says I will, I will, I do, I will.

A frost is forming as she unlocks her car. She has to sit for several minutes, hot air blasting through the dashboard, until the starbursts of ice have dissolved from her windscreen.

The keys to the flat she slides into an envelope, addressed to a friend. As she drives out of the fringes of London, she pulls up near a postbox and pushes the envelope into its wide red mouth.

She is surprised by how many cars are out on the streets in the middle of the night. At a motorway sign saying 'Scotland, The North' she pushes her foot down on the accelerator and almost smiles.

part two

Stella is sliding a knife along the seal of an envelope. The paper, a heavy-grade cream, gives and separates, the edges fraying like lint. As she inserts her fingers, easing out the letter, the building shudders around her.

She looks up. A pair of precisely laced hiking boots is descending the stairs. Stella watches them for a moment, then drops the letter, slips off the chair and wedges herself behind a tall, spike-leafed plant balanced on its own special stand. She's served breakfast, cleaned up the kitchen, taken two booking enquiries already this morning, and she doesn't really feel like getting into idle conversation with a guest.

The man from room four lopes through Reception, dressed as if about to take part in a polar expedition, a pair of binoculars swinging from his neck. When he reaches the front door he extends his head out, tortoise-like, holding up his palm to check the weather. His other hand, Stella sees, is busy scratching one of his buttocks. She wrinkles her nose and a strangled giggle escapes her, which bounces around the deserted hotel reception like a ping-pong ball.

The man stops scratching and looks round. Stella holds her breath, her mind racing through possible explanations of what she might be doing crammed behind a pot plant. He doesn't see her. Her neck is beginning to ache from being crunched like this but she can't exactly reappear now.

When she hears the slam of the front door, Stella unfolds her body and stretches, her arms held long above her head, her vertebrae shifting and clicking all the way down her back. She sits down in the chair again and picks up the letter, smoothing it against the desk with the heel of her hand, flattening the loops and dashes of her mother's handwriting.

Her mother's always written with a fountain pen. Stella knows where she keeps it – in the smallest drawer on the right-hand side of the bureau – and she knows exactly what her mother would have looked like as she dipped the moulded, fragile nib into the wet mouth of the ink bottle. She can picture her as surely as seeing her own face in a mirror: blutting out the air pocket from the rubber pipette in a stream of bubbles, drawing ink up into the pen like blood into a syringe. Francesca would then cross her ankles under her, set a sheet of paper on the blotter, which lay squarely in the middle of the desk under the bay window, and making a peculiar motioning gesture, like a conductor silencing an orchestra, she'd have leant forward, pressed her pen to the blemishless white and begun: *Dearest Stella.*

Stella glances down the pages: *your father and I*, she sees. Then: *trying hard to understand why you've done this*. She skips a few lines ... *don't see how anyone could just throw in a job, a very good job, in London* ... she turns over ... *such a strange thing to do...*

Stella looks up, away from the pages, and through the window. It's possible to see right across the valley from here – through the trees, which toss and stir in the breeze, along where the burn winds its way through patches of marsh, patches of peat, and to the cluttered houses of the village beyond. The day is bright, the sky scudding with fast-moving clouds. The reflective surface of the loch is pleated, made restless in the wind. Behind the hotel, the terrain gets rockier, wilder, the ground lifting and steepening towards the mountains, fast-moving rivers cutting their way through rock. Stella doesn't look out of those windows much.

She turns back to the staircase, lined with gilt-framed oil paintings in soupy, dark colours. A man with abundant side-whiskers glowers at her, a shut-eyed hare slung by its heels over his shoulder. A cross-eyed child of indeterminate gender in a tam-o'-shanter poses next to a harp. The moth-eaten deer's head at the top of the stairs, Stella notices, is slightly skewed.

The letter is still held between her fingers.

All best and love, it ends. Then the flattened loops of her mother's signature. *All best and love.*

Stella scuffs her sandals together, the buckles snagging. Her fingers are tucked beneath her thighs. She chews the final, greasy mouthful of sausage and gulps it down. Her plate is empty now, apart from the beans. Everything else gone. She's eaten round them very carefully, banking them up on the rim, making sure that nothing else touched them.

At a right-angle to her, around the four-sided table, her grandmother is leaning on her elbows and saying something about side-plates. Opposite, Nina slices her food into equal, geometric shapes, her eyes lowered. Whenever their mother has to work during the week, their grandmother – their Scottish grandmother, their father's mother – comes to look after them. 'Who else would cook your dinner?' she asks, in the kind of question that Stella knows doesn't require an answer. Under the table, the cat weaves invisibly through ankles and chair legs, fur sleeking against their shins.

Stella puts her knife and fork together, a mismatched pair, as stealthily and noiselessly as she can. The fork end makes a minuscule click against the china, but maybe no one heard it, maybe no one will notice.

'But, Archie, surely there are colleagues who can help you with...' Stella hears her grandmother's voice trail into silence. She keeps her eyes trained on the repetitive pleats of her school skirt. She is aware of the height of her grandmother towering next to her and she's aware that she's looking at her. Or, more specifically, her plate.

'Are you not eating your broad beans, dear?' Her grandmother's voice is melodious, studiedly offhand.

Stella's father grows the beans in the vegetable patch so disapproved of by the other people in their tenement, who prefer roses and cyclamen. Stella loves to pick them, to disentangle and pull the swollen lengths of the pods from the mass of wreathing leaves; she loves to split them open and find the perfect rows of beans bedded down in the silvery fur. But boiled by Granny Gilmore for a good twenty minutes and spooned on to a plate, they have metamorphosed: a puckered, toughened hide clings close to twin halves that squeak against your teeth. The taste is sickly, cloying and dry. She cannot eat them, she cannot, she really cannot.

'I don't want them,' Stella says.

'Pardon?' Granny Gilmore says, still achingly polite.

'Maybe–' her father interrupts, low, but Stella sees a quick gesture from her that silences him.

'Come on,' Granny Gilmore leans across, picks up her fork and nudges three of the green shapes on to it, 'just try them. You might like them.'

Stella presses her lips together and leans back into her chair as the fork looms towards her.

'Open your mouth.'

The waxy, compost smell of them is reaching her nose. She shakes her head.

'Stella, open your mouth.'

She stares fixedly at the three beans before her. Could she? But she imagines the feel of their chill solidity on the damp warmth of her tongue, the sore ache of the salivary glands in the back corners of her mouth working to digest them: her throat closes just as her stomach heaves up. She gags, coughing. Her grandmother must have seized the opportunity of her lips opening because metal is clashing against her teeth and her mouth is jammed full of rubbery, green shapes.

Stella retches, her mouth swilling with acrid liquid, and the beans shoot out on to the tablecloth. She sobs and clamps her hands like a portcullis over her face.

'Well,' her grandmother puts down the fork with a clash, 'I'm not prepared to have a battle about this. You're to sit there until you've eaten what's on your plate.' She scoops the regurgitated beans back on to Stella's plate. 'And those as well. All of it.'

Stella hears her father mutter something.

'Archie,' her grandmother warns, 'she has to learn.'

Through the slits in her fingers, Stella sees her grandmother clear away the plates, her father pouring more water into Nina's glass. After it gets dark, their mother will come back from the café, smelling of cigarettes and suds and coffee, bringing a carton of *gelato di cioccolata* for her and *gelato di fragola* for Nina. It's getting hot behind the shield of her hands and her arms are aching but she won't take them down. She watches them leave the table, one by one. Nina gives her a swift, unreadable glance as she goes.

Stella peels her hands away from her face. The house is quiet around her. She can see her grandmother, sitting on a chair in the garden, reading a paper. A radio is playing somewhere. Footsteps in the room above. Everyone feels very far away. The striped back of the cat faces her from the windowsill. No use. The cat won't eat beans. She doesn't look at her plate. She has no intention of eating them.

Then, behind her, a door sighs open. Stella doesn't turn round. She is wondering if it's Granny Gilmore. Back to save her? Or back to scold her? But it's Nina, tiptoeing across the carpet on shoeless feet. Stella gazes at her, her face stiff with dried tears. Her sister holds a finger, as straight and definite as an exclamation mark, against her lips.

Nina leans forward, stretching out her hand, and picks up the fork. She stabs the beans, one by one, right through their hearts. She opens her mouth and the fork disappears into it. Stella sees it come out again, clean and silver. Nina chews, quickly and concentratedly, and swallows. Once. Twice. Then she grins, puts down the fork and flits away, out of the room.

Before there was anything, there was Nina. Stella is sure her face is the first thing she ever saw, or ever remembers seeing. Their mother tells them that Nina spent all day hanging over the bars of Stella's cot.

For a long time, Stella couldn't tell the difference between them. She thought Nina was her or that she was Nina or that they were one person, one being. For years, she believed the blood that pumped through their veins was in some way connected, that if she cut herself she might very easily see crimson seeping from a part of Nina's body.

But she has a clear memory of, one day, Nina lifting her up to the mirror in the bedroom they shared until Stella left home – even though she was younger, she left first. It was a hot day. They were both in shorts, so it must have been summer. Festival time, maybe. She has an idea that she could hear the droning hum of faraway aeroplanes, streaking the skies above the city, and the gentle murmur of a crowd at some event on the Meadows. But she might have imagined that since.

Nina hooked her hands under Stella's armpits and clutched Stella to her. Her skin against Stella's hurt, like the wring of a Chinese burn. It took Nina a great deal of effort to lift her from the ground – even then Stella was catching up on her in height – and Nina had to strain and heave.

Stella saw the curve of a second forehead rise into the silver square of the mirror and suddenly there were two faces in the glassy, reversed world ahead of her. It was a shock. They were almost the same, but not quite. Nina's was narrower, sharper, her hair, in the forked tongue of summer sun slanting in from the high window, ever so slightly fox-coloured.

There is no sky here. Just a depthless, grey-white miasma. Jake stares up into it for a while, at the black cut-outs of birds streaking through it. Then he wheels round, the wind plastering his hair into his eyes, and looks towards the village, indistinct with mist as if dissolving into air. The clustered buildings, stuccoed with brown-black pebbles, are huddled together against the low, persistent wind, the tall cone of the windmill standing above them, its immense sails stuck into a giant black X, as if warning him away.

He shivers in his borrowed clothes. Ever since he arrived in this country he's been unable to get warm.

A restless tea-coloured wave turns and turns back on itself on the brown shingle. A bird with a curved beak scuttles up the beach, wings folded to its body. Further out to sea, a piece of flotsam heaves up and down on an invisible swell. He stares out at the horizon, barely discernible: grey sky, grey sea. This place feels to him like the edge of the world.

He thrusts his hands deep into his pockets, turns and walks back up the beach, through the scrubby marsh and the tall, restless reeds. As he passes underneath the mill sails, they are vibrating in the wind with the high-pitched whine of a mosquito.

He vaults over the garden fence, remembering too late that the wet grass always soaks through his shoes. Why do they bother to have fences, ostensibly to keep people out, which are so low a child could climb over them? He makes his way down the side passage of the house, past the trees, which are being slowly espaliered, branches pulled and trained back with wire frames. He can't look at those trees without feeling a kind of sympathetic ache in his shoulders.

His shoes are sodden and squelching by the time he reaches the kitchen. He bends over, yanks them off and hurls them towards the big, boiling stove thing in the corner. What's it called again? It looks like a steam engine. It's a funny word. Aga. That's it. Aga.

He pulls open the tiny freezer compartment and crams cracking, steaming oblongs of ice into a glass, which he then fills with water. He reaches up to a shelf for a bowl and pours cereal into it.

Barefoot, he climbs the stairs, the tray held in front of him. Florence bloody Nightingale. He should get himself a lamp. In the bedroom, light glows like a furnace behind the flowered curtains. He puts the tray down on the bedside table. The duvet is pulled up high, covering the pillow, covering the chrysalis form of a body.

Jake sits on the edge of the bed, the mattress bouncing from his weight. Nothing. No movement. No acknowledgement. He leans forward and tweaks down the top of the duvet. 'Hey,' he murmurs. 'You awake?'

Her hands, pressed together as if for prayer, are slid between her face and the pillow. Is she still asleep? No. Her eyes open slowly and she looks up at him.

'I brought you breakfast.'

He helps her to sit up, arranging pillows behind her, placing the tray on her lap.

'You're so good to me.' She smiles at him, high spots of colour in her cheeks. From the heat of the room? Or does she have a temperature? Perhaps he should check. 'I don't know what I'd do without you.'

Her hand rests on his for a moment before Jake stands and moves to the window. He pulls back the curtains and peers out.

'Jake,' her voice is low, teasing, 'have you put ice in the water again?'

He turns. 'Oh. I might have.'

She shakes her head. 'We don't need ice, now that we're in a place with a normal climate.'

'Sorry.' He folds his arms. 'Force of habit.'

Mel stirs the cereal, then lifts a minuscule amount to her mouth.

'How did you sleep?' he asks.

'Not great.' She pulls a face. 'But I'm OK.'

He doesn't say that he lay awake most of the night, listening to the way she breathes when asleep, with a tiny, shrill whistle on each exhalation. *Wife*, his mind hisses at him, *this is your wife*. He turns back to the window and grips the sill, staring out at the row of cottages, the wind-bent trees, the coiling wet road, the undulating sea, the flat estuarial mud, as if he's never seen them before. What is he doing here? How did he get here? Between them, the ice shrinks in its glass.

Jake knows the story backwards, and sometimes used to tell it to himself that way when he was a child, beginning with the fact of his own existence and working back, like a genealogist.

His mother, Caroline, decided to leave Britain and join the wave of people dropping out of their lives and going on the road to travel east. London was grey, wet and cold, and when the man who shared her bed listed the attractions of India, there wasn't a great deal her room's damp-scarred walls and temperamental gas fire seemed to have going for them. Her parents hadn't spoken to her for months, but she phoned her brother to tell him of her plans and he said the family would consider her dead if she went. After putting down the phone, she called the man to say, yes, she was coming, so please save a place for her.

It amazes Jake how young she was – much younger than he is now – when she packed up her entire life and left in a VW camper-van with three men and another woman. They drove into Europe, through France, through Turkey, through Iran, into Afghanistan. In Herat, they shed the other woman, one of the men, and gained a German, a cat and a parrot. In Kabul, they shed Caroline. 'Irreconcilable differences,' she used to sigh when Jake asked her why. She carried on alone, hitching her way into Pakistan.

In Islamabad she was sitting beside a road with her pack and 'the biggest bunch of bananas you've ever seen'. A man on a motorbike stopped and offered her a ride. 'He had black hair,' Caroline would tell him, smiling, 'tied back in a ponytail,' she would let her fingers stray through Jake's hair, 'lovely blue eyes – just like yours – and a beautiful deep voice. Scottish. It was the accent that did it for me.'

He was called Tom, that much she could tell him, but she never knew his last name – 'You didn't really ask questions like that then' – and as they chugged their way through Pakistan, into India, through Amritsar and up to Dharmsala he told her about the commune he'd started, somewhere in the Highlands, near Aviemore, in a place called Kildoune. 'It worked really well, apparently – not like a lot of them. He loved it so much he talked about it all the time.'

They separated in Delhi. They had spent three weeks together. 'Tom wanted to go into an ashram and I didn't – I was headed for Nepal.' Two days after she'd waved goodbye and watched him being swallowed into a seething crowd in a Delhi street, she realised she was pregnant. At this point in the story, she would look guilty and say, in a kind of singsong, rhyming chant: 'By Kathmandu I knew I was having you.'

She washed up in Hong Kong, a place

she'd never imagined for herself, seven months pregnant, with six US dollars sheaved into themselves in her back pocket. She told herself she'd stay for three months – enough time to have the baby, earn some cash and buy a ticket out of there. She had this image in her head, of her wandering out into the world with a baby on her hip.

She found a job teaching English, and somewhere to live: a one-bedroomed apartment on the nineteenth floor in the middle of the red-light district in Wanchai. 'As many floors as my age,' she would say, 'which was a sign that something was right.' She braided her hair into a plait, slid her feet into her only pair of shoes and took the escalator to Mid Levels to teach the well-fed children of ex-pats. She discovered that she was good at teaching, that she liked it: 'I'd never been good at anything before.'

When the baby was born, she called him Jake Kildoune, after the only concrete thing she knew about his father. She wanted to give him a new name, a name no one else had. Calling him after a place would, she decided, tether him to the world and not to people, would free him for ever from the stranglehold of family.

She told herself that she'd stay for a few months longer, earn a bit more cash, let the baby settle, at least until he was weaned. Mrs Yee on the floor below minded Jake during the day: this they had worked out in the lobby while waiting for the lift to descend, with hand gestures and a Cantonese–English phrasebook. Mrs Yee had a son, Hing Tai, the same age as Jake; she said two was no different from one and, besides, the coloured eyes and white-soft skin of this baby fascinated her. Also – and this she hadn't told Caroline – she'd felt terribly sorry for this lonely *gweilo* with her long, floaty clothes and her long, floaty hair and a tiny baby strapped to her back.

There seemed nothing to return to the UK for. Caroline's family held true to their word. She wrote aerogrammes, letters, cards, but nothing ever came back. She decided she'd stay for a bit longer, then a bit longer, then perhaps a little more, just until she'd saved some money, and one day she turned round and Jake was sixteen, feet propped up on the kitchen table, reading a book, the radio on full volume, cracking the striped pods of sunflower seeds and scattering them to the floor. She would eventually leave five years later, when she hooked up with a man closer to Jake's age than her own and moved to New Zealand with him. Jake would carry on living in the flat he was born in. It would take him months to get used to the space.

Everything in Jake's world had two names, an English one and a Cantonese one, even himself: he was Jake to his mother and the white people he knew, and something that sounded like Jik-ah to the Chinese. Mrs Yee always spoke Cantonese with him, his mother English, so he grew up thinking it was normal for the world to have a double meaning.

The Hong Kong Chinese have a name for those who have become too assimilated with the pale-skinned colonialists: a banana, they'll spit, yellow on the outside, white on the inside! Jake has never known what this meant for him, born and raised in Hong Kong, speaking English and Cantonese, educated in the school for rich European children where his mother taught, but going back down the hill each night to a narrow apartment block. His classmates called him Chinky, laughed at the Chinese comics they found in his bag, pulled the corners of their eyes into slits when they saw him coming. He spent hours in his childhood trying to think of something that was white on the outside but yellow in the middle. What was the opposite of a banana?

He went to his mother who was lying under the ceiling fan, writing a letter. 'What's white on the outside but yellow on the inside?' he asked, damp fingers clutching the bedsheet.

She looked up, smiling, as if it was the first line of a riddle or a joke and she was ready for the punchline. Jake watched her smile fade like cloth left too long in the sun. She thought rapidly and concentratedly, biting her lip. They remained like that for some time, her silent and him standing beside the bed, waiting.

'An egg,' she said eventually. 'A boiled egg.'

He ate boiled eggs for his dinner for a whole week. His mother never said anything. Every night she would ask, 'What would you like for tea, Jakey?' and he would say, 'A boiled egg.' 'OK,' she would reply and go into the kitchen and place two in a pan of water. She ran them under the tap afterwards so that they would be cool enough for him to dissect, pick off every bit of shell, cup in his palm the slippery grey-white flesh, dense and hard as an eyeball. The crystallised yolk was always perfectly circular, might sometimes still be warm, still liquid, a soft yellow heart.

Sometimes he hears people who don't know him mutter, '*Gweilo*,' behind his back – foreign devil, walking ghost. If he's in the mood, he'll turn and give them a reply in flawless, tone-perfect Cantonese. Other times he won't.

They were filming a scene on one of the winding, hidden stone staircases that run like spines up the centres of buildings. A beautiful but lonely female assassin was finally meeting her biggest rival – a beautiful but lonely male assassin. Jake cast his eyes over the set. Everything was ready: the lighting, cameras, crew, makeup, actors, continuity, the director. The leading woman was just touching the end of her cigarette with a sputtering yellow match-flame when the peculiar, muffled sound of an electronic voice started up behind a wall somewhere, grinding and continuous.

The director, Chen, shouted, 'Cut,' the actors shifted impatiently from their marks, and the crew raised their eyes to the slanted ceiling, the sweating walls, listening.

'Where's it coming from?' Chen snatched off his cap. Everyone turned their heads, first one way then the other, trying to locate the sound.

'What is it?' Chen shouted, and turned, as he did in all moments of crisis, to Jake.

Jake put down his clipboard. 'I'll go and find out.' He pushed his way through the fire door and stepped from the hot, graffitied dark of the stairwell into a tiled corridor. The strip-lighting in the corridor hummed as he walked, his head cocked to one side, listening. Everything else was silent – no TVs, no radios, no gasps and exclamations of distant sex, no rumbles of conversation came from behind the row of closed doors. Jake ran his hands over the speckled concrete walls, pressing his ear to them like a doctor in search of a heartbeat. A security camera winked from the ceiling.

The corridor bent away from itself and Jake arrived in a cul-de-sac with two lifts, their steel doors shut. In a square black screen above them, flickering red numbers rose and fell, rose and fell. The noise was louder here.

Jake leant towards one of the apartment doors. The noise subsided. He stepped towards the other: the noise was clearer and sank into distinct words. He listened for a moment. A recorded voice saying something about a cat who walks alone. Jake frowned, then smiled. He recognised the words from a story his mother used to read him. Who on earth stays at home listening to recordings of English children's stories in the middle of the afternoon?

He reached his hand through the metal door grille, pressed the buzzer and waited, turning to watch the lift numbers flicker and settle. Behind him, the door sucked open and he turned again to see a white woman holding a small Chinese boy by the hand.

They looked at him, the boy with wide eyes and the girl from under her fringe.

'I'm really sorry to bother you,' Jake began. Why was she staring at him like that? Had he met her before? No, he didn't think so. 'I'm with a film crew, we're filming in the stairwell, and we were just wondering if you could possibly turn off your tape-recorder – just for half an hour or so.' He shrugged awkwardly. 'Maybe more. Would you mind?'

The woman's gaze flicked from one side of his face to the other, as if she couldn't decide which to settle on. 'My tape-recorder?'

'Yes.' He nodded. 'We can hear it through the wall, you see.'

'Oh.' She pushed at her hair. Jake was surprised to see the red stain of a blush creeping up from the neck of her shirt. 'Well ... I'm giving a lesson,' she indicated the boy. 'It won't be long though. Another ten minutes.'

'Ten minutes? OK. That should be fine. Sorry again for disturbing you.'

'Miss Mel,' the boy whispered, pulling at her arm. 'Miss Mel?'

'Be quiet a moment,' she said, still looking at Jake, 'please.'

'You be good for your teacher,' Jake said to him, in Cantonese. 'Thanks,' he said to Mel. ''Bye.'

They both stared after him as he left.

She came out into the stairwell twice that day to put out rubbish. The next day, when they were filming in the lobby, she walked past four times in an hour. On the third day, she phoned the film company and left two very hesitant messages on his voicemail – the receptionist said, giggling, that she'd asked for 'the guy with the blue eyes'. The fourth day, the entire crew was teasing him about his persistent admirer: 'Hey, it's your stalker, Jik-ah,' the soundman shouted, whenever she happened to walk past. When they finished that evening, he waited for her outside the building, more to try to stop her turning up on set than anything else. He was also curious about this woman who made her desire so clear, who seemed so unswervable in pursuing what she wanted. He took her in the vertiginous tram up to the Peak, where they watched the Star Ferry stitching the black water of the harbour with light.

Francesca is planting bulbs, her knees pressing dents into the damp lawn edge. The soil in the new garden is thick and dark. It has rained and rained for weeks, and the ground feels sodden between her fingers. Each of her nails is crescented with black. She presses a dense root tangle into the hole, then packs earth on top of it. She has to do this quickly: her mother will be here in half an hour and if she sees her bending over in the garden she'll shriek her head off about the *poverina bambina*. She's been in this country for forty years, but still hasn't mastered the language. Francesca has always had to be the linguistic filter between her parents and the world – writing letters, making phonecalls, translating rent demands, tax forms, bills, prescriptions.

The tight drum-curve of her belly rests on her thighs, the feet of the child pressed up against her lungs. This baby is different from the first. It can go for hours in utter, almost eerie stillness without moving a hand or a limb, then something will wake it – a noise, a peristaltic gurgle, the rumbling echo of a cough, Francesca never knows – and it flips into manic, vehement action, somersaulting, punching, flailing, as if grappling with an invisible assailant. With her first baby, Francesca felt all along that she knew her, that she almost recognised her when she was handed to her, bloodied and dripping and compressed, but with this one she has no idea what she's getting. It could be anyone.

Somewhere behind her is Nina. Francesca can hear her panting, the shuffle of her small unformed feet through the grass. A hot hand grips Francesca's shoulder and a strand of her hair, and Nina appears, flushed and purposeful, a doll dangled by its foot in her hand.

'Hello.' Francesca circles her daughter with an arm and presses a kiss into the creases of her neck. Nina staggers backwards in surprise, thrown off-balance by this sudden rush of affection. 'What are you up to?'

Nina frowns. 'Messy,' she admonishes, pointing at Francesca's hands, stained with the garden.

'It's only mud,' she says, 'look, it feels

nice,' and tries to press Nina's fingers to her own. She doesn't want her to grow up fastidious, fussy.

Nina snatches away her hand. 'No-no-no-no-no,' she wails, 'messy.'

'OK, OK. I'm sorry.' The sight of her daughter's affronted, indignant face makes her want to laugh, but she bites her lip. 'Sorry,' she says again, more seriously.

Nina is surveying her, assessing, critical, her wide green eyes travelling over Francesca's face, hair, shoulders and neck, coming to rest on the swelling beneath her shirt. Francesca doesn't breathe, but waits, tense and ready. She hasn't mentioned the pregnancy to Nina yet: a child-psychologist friend of Archie's told her to wait until Nina asks. Is she going to ask? Is she? Oh, please, ask.

Nina's eyes flick to her mother's face, then back again. 'What's that?' Nina enquires, in her high, reedy voice.

Francesca's spine straightens and lengthens towards the spring sun above them, as if an invisible thread is pulling her upright. She's had this rehearsed for months and is now so excited the words are tumbling around her mouth like bubbles in champagne. She breathes in through her nose and out through her mouth, like they teach her in antenatal classes.

'It's a baby,' she says, beginning the first

words of the speech she has down pat, because she wants these sisters to be happy, to love each other, more than anything she has ever wanted in her whole life, and because she knows that whatever she says in the next few seconds will impact through Nina's and this unborn child's life for ever. 'For Nina,' she adds.

Nina leans closer, her hand gripping the collar of Francesca s shirt. Francesca feels the baby shudder and flex, arching its back as if waking from a long sleep.

'For Nina?' Nina repeats.

'Yes.' Francesca swallows, nervous. She presses the back of her hand to her cheek. Pregnancy makes her feel hot and full. 'For you. It's going to be your sister. When she's born she's going to be very small, like this.' Francesca holds her hands apart like a fisherman measuring a fantasy catch. She speaks slowly, watching Nina's face. 'And we're going to have to look after her, you and me, because she's not going to know how to do anything. She won't know how to feed herself, or dress herself or–'

'A sister,' Nina says, and Francesca realises she's never said the word before. 'For Nina.'

Francesca nods, takes Nina's hand in hers and presses it to the hard, dense dome of her stomach. 'Let's see if we can feel her moving.'

They wait. A lawnmower roars and belches in the garden over the wall. The tune of an ice-cream van unwinds somewhere out on the road. Nina looks unconvinced. Come on, Francesca wills the baby, just this once. She pictures it as she saw it first in the grey, soupy fuzz of the scanning screen, floating upside-down, a trapeze artist in freefall. There is a flash of movement, a twist, a snake shrugging off a skin.

Nina's face is stretched, disbelieving, like a traveller who's just been told that the earth is flat after all.

Stella lies on her front, resting her chin on her knuckles. If she narrows her eyes to a certain point, the sun makes prisms of her eyelashes, lining the edges of her vision with jewels. At the top of the garden her mother sits with Evie on a rug. Evie is her mother's friend. They talk together in low, laughy voices, drink wine and sometimes Evie combs out her mother's hair with her fingers. With just one word, Evie can make her mother throw back her head and laugh so that her throat is long and tears wet her face.

Evie has hair the colour of gold– 'Dyed, of course,' her father says, in a way Stella always thinks shows he doesn't like Evie very much. Her fingernails, like candied hard petals, can be lilac, pink, frosted white or glaring scarlet. She wears lacy cardigans with buttons that strain over her breasts, lots of clanking necklaces and high red shoes that she lets Stella try on sometimes and shuffle around the kitchen. 'A child after my own heart,' she announces, when Stella does this. Stella pictures Evie's heart as pulsing, dense as a pincushion, covered in thick, plush velvet. She can't imagine why she might be after it or want it, or what she would do with it if she got it.

Evie has her own words for evcrything. She calls her mother 'Cesca'. Stella and Nina are 'darling' or 'Franette One' and 'Franette Two'. Cigarettes are 'ciggies', wine 'drinkies'. Stella's father is 'Himself'. Definitely with a capital H.

She is Nina's godmother and every year on her birthday, Nina receives a package with spangling paper and ribbon curled in ringlets, which means it was wrapped up in a shop, not at home. Inside is a pair of shoes or a feather-adorned hairslide or a necklace or a bag crusted with glass beads. If it's a dress, Stella will get to wear it, eventually, a year or two later (Evie always buys big – 'I never know what size children are, darling!'), bleached by washing, but still beautiful, still desirable, still Evie's.

Right now, Evie is leaning against Francesca on the blanket while they watch

Nina, who is dressed in a leotard with sequins like the interlapped scales on a fish – an Evie present that Stella is waiting for. Nina, who has recently been told by her ballet teacher that she is double-jointed, is performing the splits, her legs folding out from under her like the struts on a deck-chair. Francesca doesn't usually let Nina perform in front of visitors– 'Not now, Nina' – but for some reason Evie is an exception.

'Darling,' Evie's voice floats down the garden, 'it looks like *agony*. Can you do it the other way, I wonder?'

Evie is English, her mother told her, when Stella asked why her voice was funny.

'She's so like you, Cesca, it's *eerie*.'

Eerie. Eerie. Agony. Eerie. Stella likes Evie's words. She likes the shapes they push her mouth into, the weight of them on her tongue.

'Where is Franette Two?' Evie calls. 'Can she entertain us with contortionist gymnastics as well?'

The air is swirled full of airborne seeds, slow as moths, and the tang of Evie's Turkish cigarettes. Stella is aware of the soil beneath her, the hardness of it, the way it presses up into her body, holding her there on the crust of the earth.

'No,' Stella hears her mother answer quickly, 'but she's good at other things.

Aren't you, Stella?' she calls.

There is a pause in which Stella senses Evie sensing her mistake.

'Of course she is.'

At the other end of the garden, she sees Evie pass her cigarette into her other hand and hold out her arm. 'Darling Stella, come and give Evie a cuddle. You are very good at cuddling, I know.'

Jake trudges along the road, laden with shopping bags. Mel's mother, Annabel – a woman with the same mild grey eyes as Mel – asked him if he would mind going to the shop, and Jake had jumped at the chance. One of the worst things about this insane situation he's got himself into is that he has nothing to do. No purpose in life. No definite idea about how he's supposed to spend his time. Other than to dance attendance on Mel.

Jake shudders inside Mel's father's coat. This is mad. He has to do something about it. It cannot go on. He feels as if he's been buried alive.

He doesn't like the word 'homesick', doesn't feel it does justice to what it's supposed to describe. He prefers the long, pulling, mournful vowels of the German word, *Heimweh*. For him, it's not just a mild case of nausea – he feels flattened, steamrollered, horrified, miserable, disjointed, desperate.

It's as if he's the wrong species for this place: there's not enough sun, the air doesn't have the right ratios of gases, everything is too spread out, too sprawling, and he can barely understand what people are saying to him. He never realised how much he thought in Cantonese. Maybe it's because he's never been to Britain before, but he's never felt so cut off, so far away from Hong Kong and everything he knows and everything he likes and everything that makes up his life and him.

What really disquiets him is that this is the country his mother is from – and his father, for that matter – the country stamped on the outside of his own passport, and he has never felt so alien. He cannot get over that everyone here is *white*. He has never in his life been in a crowd of people where all the faces are pale. He cannot understand why people here don't stare at him, why they don't give him more than a cursory glance when he passes them in the street, why they don't stand stock-still and gape at him, because he feels like an extraterrestrial. The idea that he looks just like them shocks him more than anything else.

He has found that he cannot think about the apartment he's lived in all his life. He cannot think about the feel of the hot wooden tiles under his feet, the rattle of the faulty air-conditioning unit, the aluminium window-frame, which doesn't quite fit, the buzz of the electric mosquito repeller, the discoloured patch on the ceiling above his bed, where the people in the floor above him had a leaking shower. Sometimes, still, he wakes and wonders for a split second where he is.

He stops on the corner outside the church to swap round the bags. He's packed them badly and one is heavier than the other, making him lopsided. An immense car the colour of forests swoops past him, spraying grit against his trousers. In the churchyard, a large black and white bird hops from gravestone to gravestone. Jake watches it, the shopping at his feet.

He is going to have to talk to Mel at some point. Why not now? This cannot go on. He presses his fingertips into the sides of his skull. It seems to him a problem so unusual, so unaccountable, that there is nothing to relate it to, to explain it. Is it worse to talk to Mel now, when her health is still fragile, or to wait until she's better? Jake doesn't know – doesn't have any idea. He spends endless nights awake, cogitating his way around this question, while a tickertape machine somewhere in his head prints the same words over and over again: I never loved you, I have to leave, I never loved you.

Jake is seventeen and walking through a wet

market in Wanchai when Leah spots him. The paleness of his skin and his height draw her eye from a long way off: she looks all the way through the low red lamps, the banks of star fruit, the crowds of raven-haired people, the wooden stalls stacked with oozing carcasses and slit-bodied fish – and fixes him at the centre of her gaze.

She watches him buy a slab of beancurd at one stall, a dangerously spiked durian at another. The Chinese boy with him chats constantly, gesticulating. The white boy doesn't say much back, she notices, just nods. He moves with a kind of grace, a loping, even stride.

As they near her, she runs a finger over an eyebrow, pulls her blouse straight and steps into the aisle, blocking their way. They both pull up short. The Chinese boy is wary, she sees, but the other scans her face as if wondering whether he knows her. 'Maybe,' she says, addressing them in English, 'you could help me.'

They glance at each other. The white boy shifts the leaking skin of the beancurd into his other hand. 'Sure,' he says, frowning.

Leah suppresses a smile. She loves boys at this age – fresh from their mothers, untainted, not cynical, not worldly. They are like molluscs without their shells. The sickly, opiate scent of the durian spirals towards her.

‘I want to buy some fruit,’ she gesticulates at the stall behind them, ‘but am having a few language difficulties.’

She hopes he’ll ask his local friend to help and then she’ll be able to talk to him. But she is astonished when the blue-eyed white boy speaks to the toothless stallholder in the jerked, hacking sounds of their language. The friend adds a few monosyllabic rejoinders. Mangoes and papayas and lychees are produced, wrapped in unreadable newspaper parcels.

Outside on the pavement, the light is white and level, the heat almost audible – Leah imagines it would make a hissing sound, like air escaping from a tyre. She stands with her arms weighed down by the fruit she didn’t really want. Sweat is crawling down her back like ants. The boy is in front of her, about to leave, his friend lurking behind him.

Leah is thirty-three, a film producer from LA, with one minor hit, three flops and two divorces on her resumé, in Hong Kong for several months working on a production. She always wears co-ordinating underwear, lipgloss and a ring on each finger. She likes piercing the seal on new jars of coffee with the end of a spoon, and the smell of the underside of men’s wrists. She is very good at packing suitcases, matching colours, soothing difficult actresses, and persuading financiers – especially male – to sign large cheques. She likes the way her hair grows away from her brow in a peak. She doesn't eat carbohydrate, squid or processed sugar. She has a manicure once a week and a hair colour once a month. She once stole a jazz album from a friend she didn't like.

She holds out her business card. 'You should call me. Come for a swim in my hotel pool.'

The boy blushes furiously as he takes it. Part of her is certain he will call, part is certain he won't.

Mel's medication is laid out on the kitchen table, Jake picks up the bottles one by one, extracting the pills and dropping them into his palm. He's going to talk to her. Right now. After she's taken her pills. He can't put it off any longer. He is turning to make his way down the hall when Mel's parents appear on the threshold. 'Hi,' Jake says, realising they are all standing disconcertingly close, crammed between the table and the door.

'Jake.' Annabel moves towards him as if she is going to embrace him, her arms outstretched, but at the last moment she seems to change her mind. Her arms fall back to her sides and she stands before him. 'Andrew and I,' she begins, taking his hand in both of hers, 'wanted to talk to you.'

'Right,' Jake says, and forces himself to smile at them. He can feel the pills warming up in his other hand.

'In private.'

'OK.'

'We wanted,' Annabel exchanges a pleased glance with her husband, 'to give Melanie a present.'

'A present?'

'A surprise,' Andrew says.

'A wedding,' Annabel says.

Jake is speechless. Mel's pills are melting in his grasp and her parents are both beaming at him, as if they expect him to hug them.

'But...' He gropes for something between what he should say and what he wants to say. 'But ... but we're already married,' is what comes out of him.

'We know that.' Annabel laughs. 'But we thought it would be nice if ... that you might like to do it properly. Now that you're back.'

'We feel,' Andrew begins, clearing his throat, 'that it might be something for Melanie to,' his hand circles in the air, 'look forward to. Work towards.'

'Something to get better for,' Annabel explains, peering at his face. 'She doesn't know anything about this yet.'

'We were wondering if you'd like to ask her,' Andrew says.

There is a pause.

'Or tell her,' Annabel amends.

There is another pause. Jakes stares at them blankly. They appear to be waiting for him to say something. Did they ask him a question? He can't remember.

'It is a present from us,' Annabel says hastily, clutching at his arm. 'From Andrew and me.'

'We'd be paying for everything.' Andrew leans towards him as he says this. 'Don't you worry about that.'

Jake realises he has to say something. 'That's very kind of you.' His voice sounds thin and unrecognisable. 'I think perhaps ... maybe I should ... we should...' He tries again: 'I might need to have a think about it.'

'Of course,' Andrew says.

'Naturally,' Annabel agrees.

Leah's hotel was the oldest and most famous in Hong Kong. Jake had never been inside it. He'd seen it, of course, from the outside – it was hard to miss, sitting as it did in colonial, chiselled-stone assurance on the waterfront in Tsim Sha Tsui. He'd heard his schoolmates talking about it: how it had two helipads on the roof, how for afternoon tea you got an immense tier of cakes, that a live orchestra played in the lobby, that it made its own chocolates, that there was a barman who had been taught how to make a certain cocktail by Clark Gable himself.

Jake hid himself behind a pillar in the gold-ceilinged entrance hall, fingering the clammy leaves of a pot plant. This was a side of the city he didn't know about: marble floors, chandeliers, white women in hats drinking tea from bone china, uniformed lackeys opening the door. A boy of about his age in a bellboy's suit passed by and gave him a suspicious, sidelong look.

'Are you going to stand there all day or are you going to sit down and have some coffee?'

He turned. Leah was sitting at a table five feet away, a cigarette held in the V of her fingers, thighs crossed, a waiter pouring dark liquid into her cup. She motioned towards the chair next to her.

He told her about the school he went to on the Peak, about Hing Tai, about how he had never been to America but that he'd always wanted to go to New York. She said she thought he would love New York because everybody did. LA, she said, was more of an acquired taste. He told her about his mother travelling the world and how he didn't know his father. 'Your mother,' she said, drawing smoke into her lungs, 'sounds like a very brave lady.'

They went swimming in the pool on the hotel roof. He could see all the way over the harbour, beyond Wanchai to the Peak and, in the other direction, all the way to the immense, mist-hung mountains of the New Territories. Jake showed her how he could dive backwards and she, sitting on a sun-lounger, her face hidden behind dark glasses, laughed for the first time. Her teeth were small and pointed. He did it again for her and watched her image refract and distort as he rose to the surface of the water. He couldn't look at the way the circles on the pattern of her bikini stretched into ovals across her breasts.

By the time they got to the door of her room, he was shaking. He wondered if he should run or stay, but the idea of getting into the lift with the uniformed boy asking him, 'Which floor, sir?' scared him more than what might be expected of him inside the room.

But Leah took him by the arm and steered him in. As she leant against the door to shut it, she pulled him towards her by the collar of his shirt. She tasted of coffee and cigarettes and sadness. Jake had kissed girls before, after school, in the breathing dark of a cinema, but it had felt nothing like this. Her body was sinewy, febrile and insistent beneath his.

'My beautiful English boy,' she whispered, as she pushed him into a chair, unbuttoning his trousers, bending her head over him.

Leah is not something Jake talks about much – at the time, only Hing Tai knew. At first, Hing Tai flatly refused to believe it. Then he laughed hysterically. Then he pressed Jake for a detailed description of everything they had done.

The affair lasted for most of Jake's final year at school – eight, maybe nine months. He would bolt from the school gates, catch the Star Ferry across the harbour to wait in her suite. The doormen got to know him and, although they were obsequiously polite to his face, he was sure they sniggered about him behind his back. But he didn't care. Leah's suite was three times the size of his mother's apartment, had floor-to-ceiling windows, a Jacuzzi, the biggest bed he'd ever seen, and room service. Jake would sit at the desk in the bedroom and, as the light drained from the bowl of the harbour and the neon across the water came on, he would study for his A levels. When Leah appeared, she would pull off his school uniform, item by item.

'You know,' she said to him once, after the third time that evening, 'women don't reach their sexual peak until their thirties, whereas men reach theirs at eighteen. We match perfectly.'

He didn't tell his mother, and Caroline didn't ask where he was disappearing off to each evening. The only time he managed to shock Leah was when he let slip that Caroline was only four years older than her.

'Jesus fucking Christ,' she said, dropping ash over his bare chest.

Leah didn't think what she was doing was wrong but she knew it wasn't something of which she was proud. She'd never intended it to become a lasting arrangement – she'd thought of it as something that might happen once or twice. It had been years since she'd slept with a teenager; she was curious. But she loved him, envied him his youth. Her second husband, the last man she'd slept with, had been forty-nine: she was fascinated by the beauty, the flawlessness of the young, the way the muscles still clung close to the bones, the way the skin fitted the frame. She hoped that some of it might rub off on her, like pollen on a sleeve.

'I'm not taking you for ever,' she said to Jake over and over again, 'just for now.'

She told herself she was helping him. Men needed to be taught, especially young men. She was good for him in other ways too: she made him study, made sure he was prepared for his exams, nagged him about his revision, read over his applications to British universities and tossed them back to him, covered in her rounded handwriting.

When his exams finished, she got him a summer job as a runner with a new Hong Kong director, Chen. By the time his results came out and he found he had a place to study languages in London, he'd decided he wasn't going to university after all. Despite the cajolings of both Caroline and Leah, he refused to leave Hong Kong, and Chen.

Leah went back to LA at the end of the year. Jake went to the airport with her, even though she told him not to. 'I detest airport farewells,' she snapped. When she walked away from him, through the barrier, she didn't look back.

Years later, when none of it matters any more, he will start to tell the whole thing to Caroline, while they stand in her garden in Auckland.

'Oh, yeah,' his mother will say, flapping her hand dismissively, 'I knew about all that.'

'Did you?' Jake will be appalled. 'How?'

'I have my spies.' Caroline smiles. 'We met, you know.'

'You and Leah?'

'Mmm. We had lunch together once.' His mother will continue walking down her rows of beans, which are coiling themselves round and round criss-crossed bamboo poles. 'I liked her a lot.'

Stella slams the caravan door, releasing a shower of drops from the roof on to her hair and face. The caravan is behind the hotel, hidden by firs on the fringes of the

Rothiemurchas Forest. The smell of the trees around her is thick and pungent after the rainstorm, the earth soft, marshy and yielding under her boots. She ties a cagoule – a find from the hotel – by its arms round her hips and sets off up the winding, climbing driveway.

The road is empty, the intermittent white line swooping and curving before her. She walks along it, feeling the raised grainy surface of the paint through the thin rubber soles of her boots. A watery sun is straining through the clouds. A ginger, crescent-horned cow, scratching the underside of its chin on a five-bar gate, stops still and looks at her with soulful brown eyes as she walks by. A lone car passes, wheel-treads crunching on the Tarmac. She picks a tall frond of grass from the verge and strips it of its seeds, scattering them into a hedge. The conifer trees give way to tall, restless-topped beeches.

At the crossroads, she turns and, as she reaches the crest of the incline, suddenly it rises up before her – Loch Insh, a huge, silvery expanse of water, poured into the lowest dip in the valley. It's mirror-flat today, throwing back fragmented images of the trees, the mountains, the scattered houses of Kincraig.

Stella follows the road round. The loch disappears for a while behind a bank of dense-growing pines, but she can smell it on the air – that damp, fecund scent. At the church, she cuts off the road, past the new trees growing out of the wet, blackened stumps of dead ones, along the pebbled shore. The hotel boat is tethered to a rock. She slips off the knot and wades into the water, the boat rocking expectantly. Then, placing a hand on each side to steady it, she scrambles in.

Stella pulls at the oars, leaning back against the weight of the water, the prow of the boat cutting through its glassy surface, the wet wooden poles squealing in the oarlocks. Close up, the loch is less inscrutable – a rocky, lunar terrain slides below the curve of the boat. The water is clear but dark; peat has been picked up by the Spey river, which passes through the loch like thread through a bead. Beyond where Stella is rowing, through the low, narrow bridge to Kincraig, the river re-forms, pulling itself together again from the wide embrace of the loch.

She steers herself away from the shore, pulling on her right oar while the left hovers, drip-dripping, above the water. When she's half-way between both banks, she lifts the oars, swings them forward to rest in the boat and shuffles herself off the seat-plank, lying back among the lifejackets and tarpaulin. The scenery vanishes from view and clouds hang above her, held separate by snatches of blue. She listens to her pulse slowing down and the whir-whir of birds streaking over the loch.

A crackle comes from the pocket of her jeans. Stella reaches in and pulls out a card from her sister – forgotten and unread. She holds it in front of her face for a moment, gazing at the familiar writing. But her hands are still wet from the oars, and the ink dissolves and blurs, printing her fingers with lost meaning.

Francesca's parents, Valeria and Domenico Iannelli, came from a village in a high, wooded, mountainous area of Italy. If the country had been a booted leg, their village was where the ankle is at its slenderest, where the bone narrows down above the spread tendons of the foot. A stream flowed down from the mountains and in the main piazza of their village, where people congregated at night for *la passeggiata* and to talk over the day, there was a double-arched bridge where it split into two, one half flowing to the Adriatic, the other towards the Tyrrhenian.

Fifty years on, Valeria could still spot someone from her region, a skill that never failed to impress Stella. 'Agnone,' she would whisper to Stella, as a woman entered the café, 'definitely. Either that or Vastogirardi.'

Stella would peer up over the counter at the middle-aged woman, headscarfed, cardiganed and looking for all the world like any other woman in Musselburgh, then glance back at her grandmother who would be leaning forward and greeting her in hopeful Italian.

Valeria married Domenico in the church in the square where the stream split itself in two. She wore her mother's dress and her cousin's shoes. Her father, who owned the chemist's shop in the village, didn't smile once throughout the ceremony. He didn't want his daughter marrying a *contadino*, a man whose family had worked the land for generations. This Domenico had got himself work with a *padrone* overseas, and would be vanishing off to some place called Edinburgh in two days' time. Why any child of his would volunteer herself to be a *vedove bianche*, a woman abandoned by her husband for him to serve ice-cream to godless people, was beyond him.

After Domenico had gone, Valeria sat in her father's house, trying to learn the hard consonants of English from a book with pages fragile as onion skins, knitting shawls and cardigans and socks and gloves. People said Scotland was cold, as cold as it got here in the middle depths of winter when snow massed up on the mountains, but all year round.

'How do you do?' she intoned to the fireplace, the window frame, the shut door. 'My name is Valeria, Valeria Iannelli.' She paused to check her book, then returned to her mantra – knit one, purl one, knit one, purl one — as the body of her first child formed in her belly.

Every month, Domenico sent her money, which she tied into the silk scarf he'd given her when he'd asked her to marry him, as they stood under the canopy of his brother's olive trees. His letters, at first, were a disappointment. Valeria wanted, needed, love letters. She wanted pages of inked passion, adoration, descriptions of what he could see from his window, of the city she was saving to buy her way to, of how much he missed her, how much he longed for her, how he was desperate to see the face of his baby son.

Instead, Domenico told her that he worked a seventeen-hour day, that the *padrone* often lost his temper with him and the other man in the ice-cream parlour, that the people who came in were sometimes rude and called them 'darkies'. He almost had enough for their own café, where he would cook and she would serve – almost, almost. The *padrone* had agreed to let him buy one in a place by the sea called Musselburgh. When they'd made enough money, they could help bring out his younger brothers and cousins and anyone else from their village who needed to come. '*Campanilismo*,' he wrote, at the end of one letter, 'it's the way the whole world seems to work.'

Valeria waited two years, three years, the money for her passage straining at the frail fabric of her knotted silk scarf. When she finally shuffled down the gangplank of the ship after days and days at sea, her son clamped to her hip, she was gripped by a sudden fear that she might not recognise him, that she might walk straight past him and be stranded in this country of forcigners with nowhere to go. But when she saw him fighting his way towards them through the heaving throngs of people on the quayside, stretching out his hand to her, she almost laughed. She had remembered his face so exactly it was as if it had been her own.

Stella has never been able to give a simple answer when people ask her where she's from. She's unable to say just 'Edinburgh' or 'Scotland', but always has to add a qualifier, a codicil: '...but my mother's Italian' or '...but I'm half Italian'.

She doesn't know when she realised she was different from other people in this way. Maybe she always knew, maybe it was something she imbibed with the *fagioli*, *tortelloni*, *pollo al cacciatore* and *calzone* her mother fed them on. Other people were called Kirsty or Claire, spoke only English, and ate fish fingers, mashed potato, baked beans. She had stories from her grandfather about wolves in the woods around his farm, how they had to give half of everything to the landowner, how they had to eat horse-chestnuts when food was scarce; and stories from her mother about living in one room over the café, about having to pick up English at school, and how Domenico had been sent to prison during the war for being an 'enemy alien'. Stella never knew where this left her, a child who slept in a bunk-bed in a heated flat in Marchmont.

She was aware there was something about her that wasn't quite right: the way she looked, maybe, the darker hue of her skin, how she spoke or behaved, the things she said. She couldn't for the life of her pin down what it was. But when teachers and friends' parents asked her, curiously, loftily, 'What are you?' she knew the answer they were looking for: 'I'm Scottish-Italian,' she would say obediently.

Stella always thought that the two words didn't seem to go together, the hard sibilants of the first repelling the softer vowels of the second, like magnets set together. But it was a good phrase, a useful phrase, and she and Nina clung to it like a charm or a password. It explained, or at least gave a name to, their ever-present feeling of being not quite right, not quite convincing, not quite like everyone else.

Stella rested her chin in her hands, leaning on the counter, thinking about the homework she had to finish by tomorrow. The café was quiet today, the freezing, sleety weather keeping everyone at home. Their mother had said that maybe when the races finished they might get some customers.

Near the window, Nina was slicing potatoes into chip-sized pieces, scowling, her shoulders bent. Nina hated chopping chips. She complained that the knife slipped on the wet, uneven planes of the peeled potatoes, and she didn't like the feel of vegetable debris under her nails. Francesca had told her not to be silly and that she and Stella could swap if they wanted to. But Nina hated serving even more. 'I just can't be polite to people,' she said.

Francesca was sitting on the high stool at the till, going through the books, uncoiling the roll of receipts, a pen balanced behind her ear. In five minutes, possibly ten, Stella estimated, she could clear table six – a family with three horrible whiny children who had sprayed crumbs and soda stains all over the floor. Surely they'd be leaving soon. Stella sighed and began pleating a tea-towel into a fan.

'Hey,' Nina said.

‘What?’

‘By five o’clock we’ll have earned...’ Nina paused and did some calculations on her fingers ‘...six pounds each.’

Stella thought about this. ‘Nine pounds,’ she corrected.

‘Six.’

‘No, it’s nine. Because we’ll have done a total of–’

‘OK, OK, whatever,’ Nina said, lining up the knife with the centre of a potato. ‘Nine pounds.’ She grinned and lopped the potato in two. ‘Which means I have enough for that coat.’

‘Which coat?’

‘You know, the one we saw ages ago. The fake fur one.’

‘Where?’

‘In–’

‘Stella,’ Francesca’s voice cut across them, ‘table three, sweetheart.’

Stella put down the tea-towel and walked round the counter, hitching up her trousers. They were men’s suit trousers that had got separated from their upper half. A serious, heavy, grey material. She’d bought them in a charity shop. The hems dragged on the ground below her shoes but she liked them.

Half-way across the lino of the café floor she stopped. Her hands flew to her neck. A kind of tense, crushing feeling had closed about her. She suddenly couldn’t breathe, as if her apron was tied too tightly, as if her clothes were suffocating her. The clink of crockery and cutlery around her seemed deafening, booming.

At the table near the door sat a man. Stella looked at him for no longer than she needed to. He was alone, he was tall and burly, his frame folded down to fit into the booth, he had violently red hair.

She swivelled round. Her mother was looking up at her, questioningly, but her sister's head was still bent over her chopping. Stella walked back to the counter and placed her hand upon it. There was a sound like crashing water in her ears and she had the sensation that if she didn't watch where she walked, she might trip over a large drop.

'Did you get the order?' her mother asked.

Stella looked down at her shoes, at the hems of her trousers that had trailed through all the silty puddles of Edinburgh. 'No.'

'Why not?'

Stella moved round so that she was behind the counter. She wanted something between her and the man, something solid, something he couldn't see through. She held one elbow with the opposite hand. Her skin felt cold and slippery, like marble.

'What's the matter?' Francesca said, puzzled.

Stella saw Nina raise her head, saw her look at her, look at the man, then back at her.

Nina slammed down the knife. 'I'll do it.'

'What?' Their mother was really exasperated now. 'But Nina, I need you preparing the chips. If Stella's serving, she's serving. I can't have you both swapping over and swapping back, it's much easier if–'

But Nina was reaching into the pocket of Stella's apron and pulling out the pad. When Stella looked up, Nina was walking over the lino towards the red-headed man.

If there's one thing Irene Draper knows about it's running a hotel. When she found this place, twenty-five years ago, it was half derelict, decayed by neglect. The old man, the final relic of a line of lairds, was living in only two rooms on the ground floor, the rest of the house shuttered up. The staircase, when she took to it in her good leather shoes, was splintering and rotted, mushrooms were pushing their way out from between the treads.

The rooms on the upper floor were damp and mildewed, carpets curling, beds wet and sagging, the wallpaper peeling away from the crumbling plaster. There was no electricity – rusted gas-lamps dripped orange-brown stains down the walls. In a small corner room, Irene found a bath filled with what looked like old curtains, and an irate, spitting cat, guarding her litter of squirming, pink-footed kittens. Downstairs, the rooms in which the man lived gave off an airless, close, mammalian fog. From under the parquet floor of what would once have been a ballroom, the roots of the rampant laurel hedge had burst up into the light, thick, pale, fibrous and somehow obscene.

The estate agent had glanced at her as they stepped out again into the bright, sharp light outside and cleared his throat. 'It needs some work,' he began.

Irene ignored him, partly because he was annoying her just by being there, and partly because she didn't want to let on how excited she was. She knew a bargain when she saw one. This place smelt ... well, of rot and damp and lichen and filth ... but it also smelt of Potential. And Potential is something Irene has a good nose for.

All kinds of wastrels and undesirables were living in the outhouses and the gate-lodge. The first thing she did was serve them yellow-backed eviction notices. She stood over them with two policemen from Kingussie as they left on the final day of the demand, slinging their bags into the back of a rusting van. They made an emphatic rude gesture at her as they drove off. But Irene hadn't cared. She wasn't the type to let that rattle her. She had turned back to the building and begun rolling up her sleeves.

She'd been proved right, of course. It was a thriving, successful country-lodge hotel, these days. *A two-hundred-year-old crenellated, turreted, grey-stone country house, surrounded by acres of woodland and parkland,* the brochure reads. *Unparalleled service and luxury.* She'd installed power showers in the 1980s, whirlpool baths in the 1990s – she had a go in one once, when the honeymoon suite was empty for the night, but didn't think much of it. She's not sure of her next move. That's the secret of good hoteliering: improve, renovate, innovate. Always stay ahead of the game. It will come to her, whatever it is, she's sure of that.

Irene crosses her legs under her desk, enjoying the rasp of nylon against nylon. She has her own office, these days, in a former dressing room, with views out over the wood. She turns her head and looks out of the window. Something is moving among the emerging spring green of the trees. A figure, walking along the path. Stella.

That's another thing Irene had been right about. Stella Gilmore had arrived mid-morning on a day back in February, a day so cold that each leaf had encased itself in brittle white frost. Irene had had fires lit in the bedrooms and the heating on full, radiators rumbling and shuddering in every room. The cost had been hideous. And this girl had appeared in Reception, all of a sudden, asking for work.

February is slump-time for the hotel trade and Irene doesn't take anybody on in February. But, coming down to tell this person so, she changed her mind. As she stepped down her lovingly restored stair treads, she took it all in: the scarlet coat, the cropped dark hair, the bag at her feet. She heard the vowels of the Edinburgh voice. She saw the slightly wild eyes, the white, pinched look to the face. She saw the car outside, engine whirring from a long drive.

By the time Irene's court shoes had come into contact with the hall carpet, she had the situation assessed, and had already decided to give her a job. This girl would be worth it in the long run, Irene was sure. She'd recoup the extra outlay over the slack weeks with this one, as long as she stayed until after the spring. She heard the girl explain that she'd been working in broadcasting, which she knew didn't have much to do with hotel work, but she used to waitress when she was a teenager and she really needed a job for a while.

Irene didn't ask a thing. Sometimes, she knows, people just have to exit their lives. You get all types in the hotel trade. It attracts runaways like this. A husband, a lover, Irene guessed, with this one. Something like that. This girl was the type to incite passion and foolishness in men – those green eyes, that shut, expressive mouth, that coat. But Irene hadn't asked. She was no fool, and she was a business woman. If a well-spoken, easy-on-the-eye young woman turns up at your hotel in search of work, you don't turn her down. Who cares who or what she's on the run from? She'll be good for business.

As Irene sits in her office, watching the distant figure of her general assistant move along the path, she remembers something. She stands, unlatches the window and heaves it up. 'Stella!' she calls.

Stella stops in her tracks and wheels round. For a moment she can't locate where the voice is coming from, and she scans the building's facade. Irene waves her handkerchief in the air. 'Over here!' she calls. 'Yoo-hoo!'

'Oh.' Stella shades her eyes. 'Hi.'

'I have a telephone message for you.' Irene looks again at the slip of paper she'd written it down on. 'Nina called.'

Stella doesn't move. Irene waits to be told who Nina is. But Stella is silent.

'About half an hour ago,' Irene persists. 'She said that you should call her. It sounded quite urgent.'

From a long way off, over the grass and between the trees, Stella nods. 'Right,' she says.

'You can use the phone in my office, if you

like,' Irene offers graciously. Then adds: 'If you need privacy.'

'Er, no,' Stella shakes her head, 'thanks.'

Irene shuts the window, thwarted, peeved.

Francesca stands in the middle of her home. Out of the front window she can see the street, which is full of children – the boys riding bikes in circles, the girls on rollerskates or ducking in turn under a big skipping-rope. Some of the children she recognises as their neighbours or from the school; others she's never seen before.

She turns the other way and looks out of the back door, which she leaves open in summer. She likes the heat, the fresh, pollen-heavy air to drift in. Her daughters have spent all morning constructing a den with sheets and cushions, tying a rope from railing to railing and draping the sheet over it, weighting down the edges with stones. They have disappeared into it, their luminous cave, with books and crayons, the cat, jigsaws, drinks of milk. Nina came into the house half an hour ago, her face shining with exertion and pleasure, to ask if they could have their lunch in there, and Francesca had said, of course, what would you like?

Francesca glances out again at the gangs of neighbourhood children, then back at the billowing white sheets shielding her daughters. Somewhere, she knows, something has gone wrong. She doesn't know why her daughters aren't out there, as they should be, playing with the other girls, doesn't know why they spend all their time with each other. She watches them sometimes when they leave the house, or when they walk away from her across the schoolyard, Nina's hand encircling Stella's wrist, like a bracelet or a manacle. And she watches the other children as her daughters pass by. Groups tighten, turn inwards. Girls say things behind their hands. Boys kick footballs accidentally-on-purpose at them. It makes Francesca want to kill these children, to scream at them, to bang their stupid, ignorant heads together.

Stranded between the two windows, Francesca chews at her thumbnail. She's aware that it's her fault: she is their mother, she is responsible for everything. But she doesn't know what she's done, how she's managed to fail them in this way. Somehow, without meaning to, she has created two distinctly square pegs in a world full of round holes.

She moves towards the back door, looking speculatively at the den. Maybe she should take them a glass of lemonade, tell them lunch won't be long. But she carries on walking, past the fridge, through the kitchen and out of the back door. Her bare feet make no sound in the grass. The sides of the den breathe in the summer air, straining against the stones. Francesca sees the furred flank of the cat brush the taut cotton, then the point of an elbow-bone, close to the ground, and an ankle, high above it.

She knows she's spying, and that it's wrong, but she tells herself, as she crosses the lawn, that she doesn't know what else to do. Hasn't she asked them, again and again, separately and together, is anything wrong at school, do they want to invite anyone over to play, would they like a party for their birthdays, is there anything they want to tell her? The answer is always the same: no, said with an edgy look, a glance passed between the two of them.

Francesca crouches next to the den. If they discover her, she'll say she was just weeding the lawn. On the other side of the cotton the body of one of her daughters shifts and sighs. Stella? Or Nina? Francesca can't tell which. There is a low buzz of voices, like bees in a hive. Francesca leans closer.

'You must try not to think about it,' a voice was saying. Nina's, she thinks. 'When it comes into your head, you must just push it out again. That's what I do.'

The body closest to her shifts again, the juts of bones and joints appearing in the blank canvas of the sheet. It's Stella: Francesca can tell by the length of the limbs.

'But,' Stella whispers, so quietly that Francesca has to strain to hear, 'I can't. It just comes back.'

Francesca tenses, her mind racing. What? What just comes back? Their separation, their isolation? What is it? she wants to beg. Tell me.

Then Nina says: 'No one will ever know it was you, Stel. No one. I'll make sure of it.'

Francesca feels cold suddenly, as if a cloud has passed between her and the sun. She stands and backs away, brushing down her dress with sharp, swift movements. She'll make pizza for lunch. That's what she'll do. They'll like that, and this afternoon, she'll take them to the beach.

In the cool of the house, she shuts the door with a bang and gets down the flour, ready to make the dough.

Stella sits in the empty classroom, drumming the capped end of her fountain pen against the desk. Today is the final deadline to hand in her university application form. She's been working on it for weeks, filling it in with light pencil – her O Grade and Higher results, her extracurricular activities, her interests, the list of universities she's applying to – rubbing bits out and writing and rewriting them, over and over, until she has it exactly right. She's been spending this free period painstakingly copying over her pencil marks with black ink. She's done the whole form. Except for the list of universities:

1. Edinburgh
2. St Andrews
3. Glasgow
4. Aberdeen
5. London

She presses the pen into her palm, chews a strand of her hair. Out on the playing-field, the PE teacher is making a straggling crowd of first-years run round and round the hockey pitch. Every ten paces they have to drop to the ground and do press-ups. Stella shudders. She cannot wait to leave school.

'There you are.' Nina is walking through the classroom towards her. 'I've been looking for you everywhere.'

'Oh,' Stella sits up straighter, 'sorry.'

'What are you doing?' Nina slides on to the desk next to her. 'You're not still pissing about with that form, are you?'

'Mmm.'

Nina peers over her shoulder. 'I don't know what you're worried about – you're bound to get in everywhere.'

'I've nearly finished.' Stella eyes her sister. Nina looks flushed and a bit dishevelled. 'Where've you been?'

Nina picks blades of grass off her jumper, swinging her legs. 'Down the pavilion.'

‘Alone?’

Nina smirks. ‘Of course not. What would be the point in that?’

‘I thought you had biology.’

‘I did.’ She shrugs. ‘Couldn’t be arsed.’

Stella rolls the pen away from her, then back. ‘Neen,’ she murmurs.

‘What?’

‘Don’t fail it again.’

‘I won’t.’

‘You might.’

‘Oh, don’t start with me.’ Nina slides off the desk. ‘Are you coming?’

‘I just have to finish this.’ Stella glances at her watch. ‘I’ll find you at the gate in five minutes.’

‘OK.’ Nina moves towards the door. ‘But hurry up. I want to go into town before the shops shut.’

Stella waits until she’s gone, then looks down at the form. Edinburgh, first choice, St Andrews, second, London, last. She and Nina have had it planned for years: she will go to Edinburgh University and Nina to Edinburgh Art College. They’ll live at home, sharing the room they’ve always shared, and in the mornings will walk together to lectures. Perfect.

Stella’s never been to London. She doesn’t quite know why she’s put it there, in the last place. Does anyone ever end up going to their final choice? Stella doubts it. Her teacher told her that what she put fourth and fifth didn't matter. Stella has seen London on television and in films: funny squares with brick houses and trees and black railings, the porcelain-tiled underground railway, street markets, museums, pigeons. She knows it's about four hundred miles from Edinburgh, that it takes four or five hours by train, that it's huge, that it's filled with people talking in jerky voices.

The classroom is chilly, the radiators grumbling. German participles march across the board in chalk and dust motes swirl in the heatless winter sunlight. Outside, the first-years are being instructed to run backwards as the teacher hurls balls at them. Stella pushes her hair back and shuts her eyes.

When she opens them again the sunlight seems brighter, jarring, the walls of the classroom taller than before. She unscrews the cap on her fountain pen, leans over her form and writes in clear, black letters over the pencilled marks reading 'Edinburgh' the word 'London'.

Mel stands at the sink, filling a glass with water. Beyond the window, Jake is in the garden, looking down into the pond she and her father built together when she was about seven. Mel watches the cat crossing the lawn, tail held high, towards Jake. It stops a foot or so from him, looking up at his back, one paw raised. It miaows hopefully, but Mel knows that its miaows are not as loud as it thinks they are. Jake doesn't hear. The cat waits, tail curled into a question mark. Miaows again. Then, as a last resort, inches forward and rubs its head against Jake's shin.

He jumps and leaps sideways, pulled from whatever reverie he was in. He and the animal regard each other for a moment. Mel holds her breath. Will he touch it? Will he be nice to it? She knows he hates the dog, that he can't bear to be in the same room with it, but will he turn away the cat as well?

She sees him crouch, touch the cat's back, inexpertly run its tail through his fingers. He's never had pets, she knows. 'I don't know much about other species,' he'd said to her once. The cat circles him, surprised by this inept attention, but happy to take whatever it's given.

Jake is not like the other men who have passed through Mel's life. There is something about her that seems to match her with men who buy expensive presents but undress her impatiently, men who pay in restaurants but then drive home too fast. Jake doesn't have a car. She has no idea if he can even drive. She imagines that he would be at an utter loss if she were to ask him where he thought people bought jewellery or lingerie or hand-made chocolates.

Mel smiles. She knows that her family would prefer it if she were with a man who had a good overcoat, a degree, a heated car, a man who knew how to talk about the economy or where to ski or shrubs that grew in the shade or which wine to drink with dinner. Not that her parents or her brothers have ever said anything against Jake. But she's seen the way they look at him sometimes – that wondering, baffled, sidelong glance.

That's the other thing. There's an aloneness, a kind of completeness to Jake that intrigues her. Other men she's been involved with, and in fact every other person she's ever really known, have all been so enmeshed, so caught up in the criss-crossings of other lives – their families, their old lovers, their colleagues, their friends. The web was endless. But Jake has no family, or hardly any, never speaks about his ex-girlfriends, is private to the point of secrecy, and so elusive that she can never be sure he is really hers. Which only makes Mel more curious, more intrigued, more determined to attach herself to him.

Her own life can sometimes feel too heavy, too over-populated. She adores her family, of course, and all her friends – couldn't do without them. But she is fascinated by the freedom of Jake's existence, the lightness of it.

She rests both hands on the lip of the sink. Her legs shake beneath her, after spending so many months in bed. She should really sit down but she quite wants to stay where she is, watching her strange husband commune with her cat.

'What am I going to do?'

Jake held open the slats of the Venetian blind with his fingertips and peered out. In the acid sunlight, he could see a woman in the building opposite, searching for grey hairs in her bathroom mirror. On the floor above, an old man was putting his poodle out to pee in the window-box.

'Hah?' Hing Tai shouted from the kitchen.

'I said...' Jake began, in a loud voice, and then tired of the sentence '...oh, never mind.'

He let the blind fall back into place and turned round just as Hing Tai was appearing out of the kitchen with a smoking wok in one hand, tossing his *chow fan* with the circular wrist movement that Mrs Yee had taught them both, years ago, making them practise with a damp cloth standing in for the rice.

'What did you say?' Hing Tai said. 'Can't hear you with the fan on.'

Hing Tai lived on Kowloon side these days, in a tiny apartment in Mong Kok.

Much to the horror of all four parents concerned, he had, as soon as he'd got a job at the big broadcasting station, moved out of the family apartment and in with his girlfriend, Mui. Every time Mrs Yee saw Jake, she attempted to get him to talk Hing Tai into either moving back or at least marrying the girl (not that she particularly approved of Mui, who didn't fit Mrs Yee's idea of a good wife – she had a business degree, worked for a record company and spoke four languages, for starters). Jake tried unsuccessfully to avoid the subject whenever possible.

Jake slumped down into a chair. 'Nothing. It doesn't matter.'

'What?' Hing Tai demanded. 'Tell me. You know I hate it when you do that.'

He rubbed the underside of his chin. 'It was nothing.'

'Jik-ah,' Hing Tai said, still vigorously tossing the rice, 'if you don't tell me I'll kick you in the shoulder.'

Jake laughed, despite himself, glancing down at the sling shrouding his left arm. 'Well, in that case, I just said … no, moaned, actually … what am I going to do?'

Hing Tai regarded him for a moment, his head on one side. 'Hang on,' he said. 'Let me get the food. And the beer. We need sustenance for this conversation.'

Hing Tai clattered and crashed about in

the kitchen. Jake got bowls and chopsticks out of the cupboard and put them on the table. He struggled to open the beer with his one good hand, wedging the fridge-cold bottle between his legs.

'Give that to me,' Hing Tai said, as he sat down, reaching out to take the bottle and the opener. 'So,' he said, easing the tops off the bottles, 'how is she?'

'She...' Jake watched his friend pushing rice into their bowls '...not great. I mean, she's going to be OK but she's very ... down. Depressed. Panicky. Which...' Jake shrugged helplessly '...you know...'

'...is hardly surprising.' Hing Tai finished for him.

Jake nodded.

'What do the doctors say?'

'They say she's incredibly lucky. "Miraculous" is the word they use. It's miraculous that she survived. And that she needs to take everything very slowly. The whole thing of Lucy has made her much, much worse. Of course. They tell me again and again that she mustn't be upset at all, or excited, or ... or crossed in any way. Which is easy to say, but less easy to put into practice when you're looking after someone who has very nearly died and seen her best friend being killed.'

'Hmm.' Hing Tai upended his chopsticks and began picking out the best bits of prawn and dropping them into Jake's bowl.

'And–' Jake broke off, watching Hing Tai's darting chopsticks, and tried to cover his bowl with his hand. 'Will you stop that?'

Hing Tai pushed his hand away. '*Eiyah*, why so stubborn?' he said, in his mother's voice, making them both laugh. Then he pointed at him. 'You need to get your strength back, man. You look dreadful. Like a fucking corpse.'

'Oh, that's right,' Jake said, grinning, 'come over all racist, why don't you? Hit a man when he's down.'

'Shut up. And tell me–'

'Shut up *and* tell you?'

'Just shut up! And tell me what you were going to say.'

'When?'

'Before. You started saying "and"–'

'And?' Jake thought back. 'And?' He was raising food to his mouth when he remembered. 'Oh, yeah,' he said, lowering his hand, his good mood evaporating as quickly as it had come. 'She...' He sighed, cringing away from even saying the words. 'She wants to go home.'

'To her flat?'

'No ... no ... to–'

'England?

'Yeah.'

Hing Tai took a swig of beer. There was a pause. Jake pushed the pink comma of a prawn around his bowl.

‘And she wants you to go with her,’ Hing Tai said finally.

Jake nodded, without looking up. The fingers of his injured arm protruded out of the white cloth of the sling, pale, stiff and chalky-looking. He flexed the muscles in his lower arm and was almost surprised to see his fingers uncurl in response. It was as if that arm was no longer part of him, just a weight he had to carry, slung about his neck.

‘It’s such an insane situation,’ he muttered, still examining the hand. ‘It gets more insane by the day. Sometimes I look at her and think, who are you? what am I doing with you? And then it all comes back – what happened and what I did and–’

‘Jake, you had to do it.’ Hing Tai was insistent, forceful, the flat of his hand coming down on the table. ‘You had no choice. You did what anyone with an ounce of ... of conscience would have done. She was *dying*.’

Jake looked up at his friend, unconvinced.

‘You mustn’t be so hard on yourself,’ Hing Tai said, more gently.

‘But she’s so determined to believe we’re love’s young married dream and the idea makes me want to... I mean, I like her.’ Jake stopped for a moment and thought. ‘I used to like her. I know I did. I don’t know what

I feel now. Everything's got kind of ... swept away and ... and jumbled. But it's just that she's ... she's...' His hand whirled in the air.

'She's not the woman for you.'

'No.' Jake slumped in his seat with relief at having articulated something that had been worming its way around him, unspoken, for weeks. 'Not even close. And I just feel that ... that there's no way out, that I–'

'At the moment, maybe,' Hing Tai interrupted. 'You can't have this out with her now, obviously. But she will get better.' He gripped Jake's uninjured shoulder and shook it. 'She will. And then you can sort it out, and get back to normal and put it all behind you.'

Jake watched his fingers flex and retract, flex and retract, gripping and releasing empty air. 'You think?'

'Of course.' Hing Tai leant back in his seat, picked up his chopsticks and sucked on them meditatively for a minute. 'And as for going to Britain–'

'Oh, for God's sake,' Jake exploded in English, then went back to Cantonese: 'I have to go, don't I? I can't exactly just pack her on to a plane and wave goodbye.'

'Hmm.' Hing Tai shook his head. 'Not really. What about your job?'

'It would be OK. Chen's in development on a new script, so not a lot will be happening for the next few months. Plus he owes me about a year in holiday time anyway.'

'Well, it sounds like you've made up your mind.'

'Had it made up for me, more like.'

'Whatever,' Hing Tai said dismissively. 'You have to go, one way or another. It'll be fine. You might even enjoy it. Seeing your motherland, and all that.'

Jake grunted. 'I've never really been that curious about the motherland, as you call it.'

'Stop whining,' Hing Tai said, pushing his bowl away from him. 'You deliver her to her parents, you wait until she's better, then you take your leave. *Momantai*. It'll be great. I've always wanted to go to London. You could even go to Scotland.'

Jake looked up. 'What, and see the fatherland?'

'Exactly.' Hing Tai smiled at him.

'It had crossed my mind,' he admitted.

'There you go, then. You can't tell me you've never been curious about that.' Hing Tai looked at his watch. 'I've got to go. I'm going to the movies with Mui. In Yau Ma Tei. Want to come?'

Jake scratched his head, glancing at his own watch. 'I'd love to but I really should get back to–'

'The wife?' Hing Tai shot at him, pulling a simpering face.

'Fuck you.'

'Fuck you too, man.' Hing Tai stood up and stretched lazily. 'Haven't I always warned you about staying away from *gweilo* girls? They're trouble, man, trouble.'

Jake eases open the door and slides into the front room, as noiselessly as he can. The heat hits him like a wave. It's the dry, sucking heat of radiators, sealed windows, unventilated rooms. The dog, from its basket by the wood-burning stove, raises its head, alert, ears cocked, rumbling from its throat. It has never liked Jake. He sticks out his tongue at it. Horrible, stinky animal.

He edges round the side of the sofa but, seeing that Mel is asleep, starts backing away again.

'Jake?' He hears her voice, faint and croaky, just as he reaches the door. 'Is that you?'

He walks round and, sitting down next to her, sees with a sinking dismay that her face is as pale as flour, with delicate lilac hollows under the eyes. 'I thought you were asleep.'

'I was.' She yawns, her mouth stretching so wide that Jake catches a glimpse of the fleshy wet red part of her gullet. 'But I heard you come in.'

'I'm sorry. I didn't mean to wake you.'

'It's fine.' She shifts her weight. The sofa springs give out a long, low twang beneath them, like a harp. 'It's nice to see you.' She reaches out her hand to him; Jake makes himself take it. She starts making high-pitched murmuring sounds to the dog, who responds by thumping its tail on the side of the basket.

'Listen,' Jake begins, 'I wanted to talk to you about something.'

'Really?' Mel carries on with the flow of squeaky nonsense to the dog, who is now whining back to her at the same pitch. The noise is making Jake's ears ache.

'Mel?' He squeezes her hand. 'I had a chat with your parents the other day and–'

'Is this about the wedding?'

'Yes,' he says, surprised. 'How did you–'

'My mother is the worst person in the world at keeping secrets.' Mel smiles at him from her pillows. 'She's a pathological truth-teller. I'm not supposed to know. And Dad's not supposed to know that I know. It's all terribly complicated.' She puts her other hand over his. 'But we can talk about it. If you want.'

'The thing is...' he begins, and an image of Mel the morning after they'd first slept together flashes into his mind. He'd taken her for *dim sum*, to a place around the corner from his apartment. They had sat opposite each other and the table was so small that their knees kept interlocking, making it almost overturn, making them both laugh. She'd said she'd always been too scared to come into places like this, and he'd said, scared of what, and she'd said, I don't know, and he'd said, don't be scared. Which is exactly what he'd said to her the night before just as he was about to kiss her. Which made them both laugh again and she'd had to put down her chopsticks. Then she'd said, I'm not scared when I'm with you, and he'd said, good.

'The thing is,' he says again, 'I'm not sure–'

'You're not sure you want to do it.'

Jake stares at her. She looks back at him steadily, both hands wrapped around his. His heart seems to rise in him, like a bubble of air in water. Does she realise? Does she, despite all that's happened, know?

'Mel, I–'

'It's OK, Jake.'

'It is?' he says, barely knowing what he's saying, what this means.

'I know it's not really your style.'

'My style?' he repeats.

'The church, the big wedding, the white dress.' She puts her head on one side, smiling. 'I can't exactly picture you in morning suit.'

Jake doesn't know what morning suit is, but can make a pretty good guess.

'I don't know what we'll do.' She rubs her temple with her knuckle and looks out of the window. 'I didn't tell my mum this, of course. They're only trying to be nice. They think it'll be good for me. Something to look forward to and all that. I don't know what we'll do,' she says again. 'But we don't really have to worry about it now. We might,' she says, in a conspiratorial whisper, raising one eyebrow, 'end up having to do it anyway. Just to please them. You know what parents are like. Could you bear it?'

The airport bus leaves from Hennessey Road. Jake trudges away from his apartment, his head bent low, as if against wind, his mother's old rucksack on his back and Mel's two suitcases clutched in his right hand. She walks somewhere behind him, making conversation. He knows by now that his silent moments make her nervous, garrulous, make her fill up the gaps. She talks to his back about the traffic, how glad she is to be leaving and how she wants to get to the check-in desk in good time because she wants an aisle seat and is he sure, is he absolutely sure they shouldn't have taken the express train instead of the bus, and she is more than a bit worried about the traffic because even though it's only the middle of the afternoon, there's quite a flow coming from Causeway Bay and is he...

He cannot look at her right at the moment, so keeps her just behind him. His shoulder is aching from the straps of the rucksack; his cast covers his lower arm, which swings, pale and heavy, by his side. He hasn't let anyone write or draw on it. There is something about its white, hollow-sounding perfection that he finds oddly pleasing. He is beginning to forget what the arm underneath looks like.

She sits on the suitcase at the bus stop, her face ashen and spent with the effort of walking two blocks. She has lapsed into silence now, giving him the occasional anxious glance. Jake sees the bus coming from a long way off.

Once they are inside, it seems to travel incredibly fast. They are powering along, leaving Wanchai behind them, and he can see the slanting face of the mountains on one side, through the gaps in the buildings, and the flash of sun-scored water in the harbour on the other. The bus rises with the road, above ground, and the streets below them look narrow, the people foreshortened, and Jake can see their bus reflected in the sides of the buildings – fragmented, distorted – and, yes, he can see, for a split second, an image of his own face, staring back at him. Then it's gone.

Mel takes his hand, folding it into hers, Jake thinks that, before, when she was well, he liked the way she used to unbutton his shirts, intently, reverently, like a child unwrapping a parcel, and that perhaps he really does owe this to her, that it's the least he can do. Maybe it will be OK. Maybe he will find that he can love her. Maybe it won't be long until he can come back.

At the last stop before the tunnel a family takes a long time getting on, and just before the doors close, a dark shape flies into the bus with a flitting movement, as if jerked on a string. It swings towards the ceiling then changes direction, zooming towards the windscreen, where it crashes into the glass. Jake stares at it, appalled. It has webbed-leather wings and a short, muscular body. A bat.

A horrified murmur passes through the bus. Mel clutches his hand. The bat flaps away from the windscreen, stunned and disoriented, dropping towards the floor. It gains height again just as it comes towards the rows of passengers and manages to skim over their heads. Mel screams piercingly and ducks, her head slamming into Jake's shoulder so that, for a moment, he is so blinded by pain he doesn't see what happens next.

When he opens his eyes, a young Chinese woman in a beige suit is struggling to her feet, her hands clutched to the sides of her head. She isn't screaming, like lots of other people on the bus, but giving out small, crushed whimpers, tears blurring her makeup. Jake stares at her. Something is writhing and struggling in the silken black of her hair. With its clawed feet, the bat is clutching the strands near her scalp.

Jake starts to his feet. 'Open the window,' he says to Mel.

The woman is sobbing, her hair messed and sticking to her wet face. People are yanking open the windows, air roaring into the bus. Everyone is staring at him, wide-eyed. Mel is holding out a newspaper towards him.

'Use this, Jake,' she is saying. 'Use this.'

He has to hook his arm out of the sling to take it. He unfolds it and places its thick paper width across the woman's head. The action makes his arm ache, his fingers sting. Through the pages, he can feel the quick, feral beating of those leather wings and the clawing scratch of bone-tips.

At that moment, they enter the tunnel, sound and light sucked away. The bus and the swaying passengers are plunged into a lurid yellow-orange gloom. In one movement, Jake clutches the paper around the creature and pulls. The bat writhes and slips from the grasp of the newspaper. Beneath it, the woman sobs silently. He tries again and this time he feels the tiny form between his hands, stiff with panic, and he crumples the paper around it. Jake lifts his arms, pain hammering at his shoulder. Long hanks of the woman's hair fall from the bunched, convulsing newspaper. He turns and a middle-aged man is motioning him towards the window and Jake moves to it and flings the bundle through it.

The wind snatches it away greedily. Sheets of newsprint separate and float in the wake of the bus, falling gently to the grey Tarmac. Jake watches as a black, winged form rises from them, whipping away into the dark of the tunnel's ceiling.

His mother is doing yoga on the other side of the room. The Sun Salutation. Which means greeting, or saying hello. She spreads her hands out on the mat and her body flexes upward, the length of her hair hanging down, her heels flat on the floor. Sometimes Jake crawls through the arch of her body at this point, making her laugh and collapse on to the mat, but today he doesn't feel like it.

He kicks his heels against the chair legs and leans his elbows on the table. He rolls the black cylinder of a crayon away from him, then towards him, back and forth, back and forth. Outside, the sun is heating up the buildings, the street, the glass in the windows, the tops of the buses. The thermometer outside the kitchen window had said thirty-two when he'd checked it this morning. 'It's going to be a hot one,' his mother said, when he showed her. His mother is Caroline and also Mum. He's always called her Caroline but makes sure he refers to her as 'Mum' at school otherwise people laugh at him.

'What are you up to, Jakey?' Caroline is standing on one leg, her arms raised above her head, hands pointing like an arrow to the ceiling. 'Are you doing a drawing?'

Jake holds the crayon in his fist. If he closes his hand around it, it disappears. No one would know it was there. 'No,' he says.

'Oh. Are you writing a story?'

'No.' He can feel his mother looking at him but he keeps his eyes fixed straight ahead.

She appears opposite him, sitting down at the table. She moves aside the cups from their morning tea and the box of sugar. 'Taikoo', the box says. Jake likes the word.

'Are you writing a letter?'

He puts the crayon in the position Caroline taught him for writing, held slanted and firm between thumb and finger, resting on the muscle of his hand. He nods once.

'To Hing Tai?'

He shakes his head once.

His mother looks at him, puzzled. 'To who, then?' She reaches out and strokes the hair away from his forehead. 'Who are you writing to, love?'

'My father.' The words come out really

easily. Just two of them, Jake glances up at his mother, anxious. Will she be upset?

But she is just gazing at him, eyebrows raised. Her hand is frozen in an outstretched position, touching his hair. It feels heavy on his head. He wants to duck out from underneath it but doesn't dare. Then she moves again, starts stroking his fringe. 'Well,' she says, 'that's great, Jakey. How far have you got?'

Jake looks down at the rectangle of paper in front of him: *d e r e* is written on it in big, black letters. 'I don't know what to call him.'

'What do you mean?' she says quietly.

'Well.' He slides the sharp edge of his thumbnail up the side of the crayon. Tiny worms of wax wriggle out of the black and fall to the page. 'Do I say "Tom" or "Dad"?'

'Um.' She thinks, looking out of the window. 'I think ... either would be fine, sweetheart.' She reaches for the Taikoo and grips it before her in both hands. 'I think it depends on ... on how you think of him in your head. Do you think of him as "Tom" or as "Dad"?'

'I...' Jake frowns '...I don't know. I don't ... I just think of him ... as ... a person. A big person. Who looks like me.'

His mother nods. 'He did ... he does look like you. A lot like you.' She puts a strand of hair in her mouth. 'Just the same, in fact.'

'So, what do I put, then?' His crayon is

poised above the white page.

‘Perhaps ... perhaps “Tom” is best. What do you think?’

‘OK.’ He is already forming the straight, downward trunk of the *t*.

Caroline sits beside him, handing him the colours he needs and helping him with his spelling when he asks her to: *i wud like to see you*, he writes. Then he draws a picture of their apartment block, stretching up the side of the page: *we liv in hong kong. come soon. if you want. love Jake xoxoxo*. At the bottom he draws a picture of him and Caroline. He does her in her favourite dark pink flares and him in his green hat, although he makes sure that he colours in the hair, so that Tom knows he’s got black hair like his.

‘Jake, it’s splendid,’ Caroline says, when he lets her hold it in her hand. ‘Really wonderful. I love it. The only problem is,’ she says carefully, still examining his drawings, ‘that I’m not sure how we’re going to post it.’

‘I do.’ He goes into the kitchen and returns with the empty soy sauce bottle they finished last night with their dinner.

His mother stares at it for a moment, then laughs and claps her hands. ‘We have to wash it first,’ she says. ‘We don’t want soy sauce on your lovely drawings.’

They take a bus up and over the humpback

of Hong Kong Island, through deep-cut roads with concreted sides, through trees alight with fire-red blossoms, and down to Aberdeen Harbour, the road winding back and back on itself, the stretch of water getting nearer and nearer. The day is close and humid, hazy clouds swollen above them. Caroline haggles with the man over the sampan: she pretends to walk away twice but eventually the man spits into the water and motions for them to get in.

Jake clings to the green-painted side of the sampan with one hand and to the bottle with the other. His mother has to stop him throwing it over when they are two minutes from the harbour.

'Wait,' she says, putting a hand on his shoulder, 'wait till we're out a bit further.'

The dark, choppy water skims underneath the wide bottom of the sampan. The man sits at the tiller, a triangular hat hiding his face. The city looks tiny from here, a collection of uneven, upended boxes, loomed over by huge green peaks. When he's decided it's far enough, Jake holds the neck of the bottle in his fingers, draws back his arm and hurls it towards the blank stretch of the horizon. It travels in an arc and when it hits the glassy surface of the sea it vanishes for a moment. Then Jake sees its red screw top break through to air again and, inside, the white curl of his letter – safe and dry.

Mair had never recovered from rationing. Those government restrictions on food left their stamp on her until the end of her life. She would reach out and seize the wrists of her great-grandchildren as they buttered toast in her kitchen. 'Not too much, mind,' she would say, sliding the earthenware dish out of reach. Her daughters-in-law tittered to each other about the way she hoarded eggs in her pantry until they turned hollow and bad.

She lived in a valley in South Wales, in a town with a name that nobody from across the border could pronounce, their tongues stumbling and tripping over its paired Ls and Ds. And if rationing wasn't enough, Mair was sent evacuees from Swansea and Cardiff, urchin children the government informed her she had to house and feed.

They arrived filthy – the dirtiest things Mair had ever seen. They took her breath away, these three snot-nosed, smirch-faced hobgoblins on her doorstep. Mair stepped back into her hall, calling to her sons who were drawing aeroplanes in the kitchen: 'Upstairs. Both of you. Now this minute.'

When she heard the bedroom door shut, she marched the evacuees through the house, quick quick, to the backyard, where she burnt their clothes, the brown paper they wore instead of underwear, and their hair, which she shaved from their lice-infested heads with a cut-throat razor. She dressed them in her sons' patched pyjamas and lined them up in beds in the attic, head to toe.

Sometimes, when she couldn't sleep – and she often had trouble sleeping – she would hear them crying, a plaintive trickle of misery coming down through the ceiling joists, the plasterwork, the wallpaper put up by Huw on a spring day, several years ago, before this interminable war. But what could you expect? They were godless, these children. On the first night she had suggested they might like to say their prayers now and they'd looked at her as if she had two heads. Within a week, Mair had them kneeling at the side of their beds, stumbling through the Lord's Prayer: *Ein Tad, yr hwn wyt yn y nefoedd, sacteiddier dy enw, deled dy dernas*... It was her duty, after all, as a Christian. She had never, in all her life, missed a Sunday at chapel.

She had married Huw at eighteen and her friends' jealousy still gave her stings of secret pleasure. Huw did not, like most of the men in the town, work in the mine but in the mine's administrative office. So while her friends were scrubbing at the coal dust seamed into their husbands' bodies, she was serving dinner on proper china to a husband who wore a clean shirt every day.

Food was a magical thing to Mair, her reason for living, the thing that got her out of bed every morning. The simple alchemy of it never failed to enthrall her: a bag of flour, some eggs, a slab of butter, a dash of milk could be transformed, by her, into a cake or scones or pancakes or anything at all. Her mother had taught her how to make meringues from the viscous whites of eggs in a cooling stove. 'Leave them in until their tops are just beginning to brown,' she would say, as she handed Mair the wooden spoon to lick, 'then whip them out. Quick quick.' And golden sponges so light they were like beaten air. And soda bread, to be eaten with salted curls of butter, and shortbread, fruitcake, apple turnovers, jam tarts, oat biscuits, treacle pudding, steamed suet pudding, queen of puddings, and round, raisin-studded, sugar-dusted Welsh cakes. 'A man can tell your worth by the consistency of your Welsh cakes,' her mother had declared, rubbing clots of butter into the flour that fell from the sieve Mair was holding high above the bowl.

Mair loved eating – but only in secret. It was when she married and got her own house, her own kitchen, that she began to see food as an illicit pleasure, something women could lick or nibble or steal a mouthful of while the men were away. It was the only pleasure she allowed herself, those snatched hidden, private moments with her husband at work and her boys out the back when she could stand in her kitchen and fill her mouth, close her lips around the sweet, yielding mush of marmalade bread, the molten crust of a jam turnover. She found it difficult to eat if anyone else was there. Mair hated being watched, hated the idea that someone might count the number of flapjacks she was consuming or hear the small, constricted noises she made when she swallowed. The thrilling, transgressive secrecy of it was the best thing. If she was interrupted – by a neighbour appearing at the back door or a child coming down the stairs – she would shove whatever it was she was eating behind a handy jar or one of her ornamental teapots.

Huw was perplexed by the half-eaten sandwiches he came across occasionally, greened with mould, stuffed into a drawer of the dresser. He assumed it was one of the children. He would tell his wife and she would tut and fling them into the all-consuming mouth of the stove. He left her to deal with it, to talk to the child concerned: food and the family's consumption of it was her domain. It would never have occurred to him that the person who most often caused this paranoia and subterfuge was himself. As far as he knew, his wife, whose figure even after two children still fitted into the stays that had come into his home when they married, wasn't interested in food. She hardly ate a thing.

The war, though, ruined all this for Mair. Instead of beautiful orange-yellow yolks from the farm up the road, the government gave her powdered egg that she had to mix with water, slivers of butter with which she was supposed to feed her whole family, a mean paper twist of sugar the size of her finger. She was a wife, she was meant to provide, to cook, to feed – but how could she, with this dried, tasteless rubbish? And rationing made it impossible for her to make the extra for her to eat on her own. Even if she'd had a spare tray of scones and all the butter she wished, she could never have eaten them: the house was full of those horrible urchins, moping about in the kitchen all day, getting under her feet. It stole from her her very purpose in life, as well as her only pleasure. She had to put away her mother's beloved utensils. She would not insult them with this muck.

Even at the end of her life, when she was consigned to a chair in an old people's home near the Swansea docks, she could recall the feel of her mother's wooden spoon against her tongue, the grain of that damp, saturated wood, the taste of uncooked dough, the sticky, irresistible mix of egg, flour and water, the dry handle held firm in her fingers. Her mother had given her the things just before she died, almost, Mair always thought, as if she knew. 'My cooking days are over, *cariad*,' she'd said, as she parcelled them up in newspaper and string – the porcelain mixing-bowl with the cracked glaze, the wooden spoon, the brass-handled balloon whisk, the iron sugar cutters, the copper-bottomed milk pan.

From her chair with a view, if you sat up straight, of the restless, grey-brown waters of the Bristol Channel and the empty, shipless docks, Mair would ask her son, when he came to visit, 'What happened to my mother's mixing-bowl? Who has my mother's mixing-bowl?' When he evaded the question, Mair would turn to the daughter-in-law who always kept her coat on and say, 'Do you have it, perhaps? Do you use it? Do you?'

There was one day, when both of them had long since given up replying to this question, when she murmured, 'Perhaps Caroline has it.'

Her son had looked up, astonished, from the brochure of the car he was hoping to buy. His wife gaped her mouth at him in mock shock. Because Caroline's name was never mentioned by his mother – if anyone referred to her, she would make her face empty, rigid. But he was wise enough to leap at the chance. He was sick of hearing about that bloody bowl.

'Yes, yes,' he said hastily, creasing the brochure in his eagerness, 'that's right. Caroline has it.'

Mair sat back in her chair and thought about the mixing-bowl and the way it had a single, flat plane on the bottom for tilting it on its side, and how it was most useful for beating eggs into flour, and Caroline, her youngest child, her sin, her shame.

The clock unwinds. Two a.m. Three a.m. Four a.m. At four thirty, Jake gets up, leaving the bed, easing himself from the mattress so as not to wake Mel. The cold is making him shiver so he drags on a sweater and tiptoes out of the room, closing the door behind him.

The ground floor is freezing, the light blue-edged. The dog rumbles and groans from its wicker bed in the utility room. He checks that the door between him and the dog is shut firm, then he sits down at the table and pulls the phone towards him. The codes are unfamiliar to him from here. It takes him two fumbled attempts at dialling before he hears the click of connection and the miraculous pulse of a ring tone. Please be there, please be there.

'Yes, hello?' His mother's voice, clear and faintly distracted, sounds in his ear.

'It's me,' he says, as he always does. 'Hi.'

'Jakey,' he can hear the smile in her voice, 'I'm so glad it's you. I've been thinking about you all day. How are you?'

'All right. Not bad.'

There is a pause. He listens to the sound of distance, satellites, the vast roll of the Pacific Ocean.

'How's the arm?' It's as if she's shifted position. She seems closer to the mouthpiece. 'Are you still in plaster?'

'No. I had it taken off last week. It's fine now. It gets a bit stiff in the cold here, but it's fine. Almost back to normal.'

'And...' he hears her pause, selecting her words '...Melanie? How's she?'

'Um, well ... it's slow progress. She's getting better. But, you know, she's had a much worse time of it than me.'

'Yes.' His mother inhales sharply. 'I still can't believe you were there. When Lionel brought the papers in that morning, I–'

'Caroline, it's OK. I'm fine – remember?'

'I know, I know.' She gives a kind of shuddering laugh. 'I just want to see you, I think. Lay eyes on you.' She laughs again, properly this time. 'Only then will I believe that you're OK. Neurotic, I know.'

Jake picks up one of the medicine bottles on the table and reads the tiny print on it: Twice daily, with meals, M.J. Kildoune. He puts it down. 'How are things with you?'

'We're all great. I'm working lots. Lionel

isn't. The cats are well. But, look, I don't want to talk about that. Tell me how the land lies with you.'

'It's kind of...' he hesitates '...complicated.'

'What kind of complicated?'

'Just complicated.'

He's aware of his mother holding back all the things she wants to say. He pushes the pill bottles into a circle, their labels turned inwards.

'It must be the middle of the night there,' she says.

'It is.'

'Can't you sleep?'

'No. Not really. I can get to sleep OK, I just wake up a lot.' He glances at the clock above the Aga. 'Listen, I should really go. I'm on their phone.' Jake takes a deep breath. 'Caroline, I was thinking...' He stops, wondering how to go on.

'Yes?'

'I was thinking about taking a trip. To Scotland. While I'm here. Thought I might as well. You know, have a look around.'

Again, the booming silence of distance, punctuated only by his mother's breathing.

'We-ell,' she says, 'if you feel you want to, Jake. But I don't know ... I don't know what you'll find there. I mean, I've no idea what's ... there.'

'I won't know until I try, will I? I just thought if I'm here I'd be mad not to go and look at the place I'm called after. Don't you think?'

'Mmm.' She is reluctant. 'Maybe you're right.'

He's been on eight minutes already. 'I really must go.'

'Jake, call me again soon, won't you?' she says in a rush, trying to fit in as many words as possible at the end. 'Or write. Lionel's getting email. Let me know when you're going. And if you need anything.'

'I will.'

'Anything at all.'

'OK.'

'Do you promise?'

'I promise.'

Francesca and Stella surprise each other in the kitchen. Francesca had thought everyone was out and was about to take a guilty, indulgent mid-afternoon bath – something she does occasionally when she thinks no one else is around. Stella is standing next to the table, eating a sandwich and, Francesca is mildly disconcerted to see, wearing a floor-length scarlet plastic mackintosh. She has the cat, Max, draped round her shoulders like a fox fur.

'Hello,' Francesca begins pleasantly, trying not to mention or even look at the coat. Nina may be tricksy but Francesca thinks that she knows, that she's always known, where Nina's at, who Nina is. She feels increasingly that she's losing her handle on Stella.

Stella grunts through her food. Max purrs loudly, unscything his claws.

'I thought you and Nina were going for a walk.' Francesca thinks of the tank filled and ready with piping hot water.

'We were,' Stella mumbles.

'Ah.'

'But I came back.'

'So I see.' Francesca moves to the fridge, goes as if to open it, but then changes her mind. 'Why was that?'

Stella says something unintelligible, stroking the striped rings of Max's tail.

'Sorry?'

'I said, Nina wanted to go to the Camera Obscura.'

Francesca frowns. 'But ... but I thought you loved the Camera Obscura.' When Stella was a child, she had been fascinated by this magical trapping of the city in a wide, porcelain bowl. Francesca can feel herself smiling nostalgically for the small, dense-limbed being, leaning out of the pushchair to see. The mackintosh-clad, twelve-year-old Stella in front of her is eyeing her, scowling. Francesca makes herself stop smiling.

'I do,' Stella says. 'I just didn't feel like it.'

'Why not?'

Stella shrugs. 'Just didn't.'

'Well.' Francesca puts her hands on her hips, then takes them down again. She doesn't know what to say. 'When will Nina be back?'

'Dunno,' Stella replies automatically, and Francesca feels enraged and shut out by this autonomy of two, the kind of single doubleness, the way they always operate for and with each other – and usually against her. Her daughters changed and made her life. They allowed her to see the point of herself. They made her feel as though she belonged to this land where she had never felt any connection before. But they baffle her, frustrate her, drain her.

'I see.' Then Francesca remembers something. 'Stella, there's something I need to talk to you about.'

Stella twists her head towards her and stops chewing. She's picked up on some seriousness of tone. 'What?'

'I phoned your headmaster the other day and–'

'Mu-um.' Stella is furious already. Not a good sign. 'Why do you keep doing that? No one else's parents are on the phone every bloody day to–'

'Stella!' she shouts. 'Don't swear at me!'

'I'll swear if I bloody well want to,' Stella shouts back. Max flattens his ears to his head and leaps from Stella's shoulders to the floor, where he paces about, vexed and ruffled.

Francesca takes a deep breath and starts to count to ten. She gets as far as six. She had told herself she would try not to get confrontational with Stella any more. ‘He suggested, and I agreed,’ she continues, managing to keep her voice down, ‘that it would be best to put you and Nina in different classes when you go up to the high school.’

Francesca waits, trying not to cringe. She doesn’t say what the headmaster had really said: that her daughters never spokc to anyone other than each other, that they had no other friends, that the school was anxious about their extreme isolation.

There is silence in the kitchen. Stella stares at her. The silence stretches and Francesca becomes nervous. This is not what she’d expected. Rages and tears and sulks and explosions, yes. But not this. They’ve never been able to bear being apart.

‘I – I thought it might be better,’ Francesca stutters. ‘For – for both of you. Before you begin your new school. A new start. For both of you.’

Still no response. Then Stella puts down her plate and shifts to the opposite foot. She looks up at the ceiling. ‘You mean...’ she begins ‘...put Nina back up a year?’

‘No, no. She’ll still be in the same year as you. Just in a different class.’

Francesca waits, chewing at the skin surrounding her thumbnail. Stella appears to be considering the idea.

'Well, you'll have to tell her,' she says eventually, dumping her plate in the sink, 'because I'm not going to.'

Francesca is so relieved to have avoided a row she starts to gabble: 'Of course, of course I'll tell her. I would never, never expect you to do it. Naturally, your father and I will tell her as soon as she gets in and then maybe we could all sit down and…'

Stella has left the room. Francesca lowers herself into a chair. She and Max regard each other. She is amazed. Absolutely amazed. She'd expected a major row, a spectacular battle, floods of tears and rage. Maybe, Francesca thinks, hopefully, she might ask her to get rid of that dreadful coat.

An old jazz song was playing, a woman who died a tragic death crooning about there being no sun up in the sky, the pulse of her voice stretching at the thickened carpet walls of the studio. When this place had been built, someone told Stella once, the architects had been anxious about the noise of traffic in Portland Place and Regent Street being heard on air, so all the studios were buried deep in the centre of the building, like the tiniest figure in a set of

Russian dolls.

James was leaning back in his chair, one foot on the table, his headphones slipped down round his neck, chatting to the weather girl. Stella leant over the mike that connected her to the studio. 'Two minutes twenty-five, James.'

Through the glass she saw him sit up and reach for his mike. 'OK. We're ready.'

'Weather first and then we've got some calls lined up for you.' Stella kept her voice even, neutral. 'There's a woman who wants to talk to you about the benefits of kick-boxing.'

She saw him look up, searching for her. It was harder to see through the glass from his side. 'Tell her to go fuck herself.'

She laughed. 'You can tell her yourself. She's on line four. One minute fifty. She took exception to your assertion earlier that sport is bad for you.'

'Bloody cranks,' she heard him mutter.

'One minute forty.'

Stella turned back to the mixing desk. The door whumped open and a man from the production team leant in. 'Call for you, Stella.'

'What?' Stella jerked her head round. 'Not now.'

'It's urgent, apparently.'

'Who is it?'

'I don't know.'

She yanked the chair towards the phone and pressed the flashing line. 'Yes?'

'Stel, it's me.'

Stella raised her eyes to the ceiling. 'Jesus, Nina. I'm right in the middle of a programme. I can't–'

'I know. I heard you.'

'Then why–'

'Listen. I've left Richard.'

Stella sighed, tapping the end of her pen on the desk. 'Neen, is there any way–'

'Can I come and stay?'

'Er...'

'I'm at the airport,' Nina said threateningly. 'I'm–'

'Look, can you call back later? I'm – I've got plans for tonight.' The man Stella had been seeing had promised to pick her up from work, drive her home, and then ravish her. Which Stella had been rather looking forward to.

'If you don't want me,' Nina burst out, 'then maybe I'll just have to–'

Above her head, Stella saw the On Air light come on. 'Of course I want you,' she said, distracted. In the studio, the weather girl was reading from a script. Stella glanced at the levels and nudged one up with her knuckle. 'Of course you can come.'

Nina sniffed, slightly mollified. 'OK. I'll see you later. There's a flight that gets in at about quarter past midnight. So I'll get to you about one-ish.'

'Great.'

'I got a late one because I knew you were working.'

'Thanks.'

There was a pattern to Nina's occasional marital crises. Richard committed some misdemeanour (usually obscure and often incredibly minor), they rowed, Nina flounced out, not to return for several days, during which time she threw herself heart and soul into various types of outlandish behaviour – sometimes buying lots of expensive clothes, sometimes sleeping with someone else, or sometimes disappearing on a plane to a far-flung place. Richard either always forgave her or perhaps never knew the full truth, Stella could never tell which. Nina's freak-outs seemed to be part of the fabric of their marriage.

Stella finished the show, ignoring James's on-air digs about his producer always chatting on the phone, called the man to cancel, rushed out just in time to catch the last tube, stopped in at a twenty-four-hour Turkish store to buy supplies because Nina would be hungry after her flight. As the three brothers who ran the shop sat in the doorway on stools, Stella selected polished, bitter-skinned olives, a tub of creamy hummus and pitta bread, flat like shoe-soles.

At home, her answerphone was glowing

with a message: 'Stel, it's Nina, just wanted to...' a crackling interlude while there was some static and then some giggling '...calling on Richard's mobile. I rang him after I'd spoken to you and he came to the airport and got me. So everything's OK. We're in the car right now...' more giggling and rustling and the rumble of Richard's voice in the background '...not to see you. 'Bye.'

Stella picked up a glass – one of the tall, thick-based ones she loved – and hurled it at the wall.

Nina is sent to nursery. She is made to sit in a circle with the other children, her legs crossed beneath her. She has to speak English here, her mother told her, because they won't understand Italian. Sometimes Nina forgets this and asks for *latte* instead of milk and the teacher stares at her, eyebrows pulled down. They sing songs, play with water and sand, pedal round and round the narrow paths on tricycles, make collages of fish with glue and coloured lentils, and cut pictures out of magazines with scissors. The scissors are Nina's favourite thing. She likes the symmetry of them, the way they slice through the grain of the paper, the way the two identical blades work with each other and against each other.

Nina walks down the path, threading her

way through the tricycles, which the boys have left there. She is wearing her red tights and red kilt. This is her favourite outfit. Granny Gilmore gave it to her, not Granny Iannelli. Granny Iannelli gives her funny things – biscuits in thin, crinkly paper and mechanical wooden toys. Cradled in her hand is the snowman she has made: a toilet roll tube, covered in soft, pillowy cotton-wool with a red hat to match Nina's tights. Nina drew the face herself.

When her mother, who's waiting at the gate, sees her, she waves, her arm held aloft. Stella kicks her heels against her pushchair and screams. 'Dat,' she says, pointing at Nina, 'dat!'

Her mother is touching the soft white bulk of the snowman, praising it, telling Nina she is a clever girl, but Nina is not listening. She is looking at Stella. Or, rather, her hair. Instead of being brushed and held in a clip at the side of her head – like her own, like their hair always is – Stella's hair is held in bunches on top of her head in two green ribbons. Green velvet. Nina has never seen them before.

'…we'll put it on the mantelpiece when we get home,' her mother is saying. 'It'll be our first Christmas decoration and maybe later…'

'What's happened to Stella's hair?'

Nina sees her mother look down at Stella's

head, bisected neatly by the white line of a parting. She sees her mother's face blur and soften in something that looks like delight. Or pride.

'It's great, isn't it?' Her mother laughs as she manoeuvres the pushchair away from the nursery gate and down the pavement. 'I was doing her hair this morning and I suddenly realised that it's long enough to go in bunches. It's very pretty, don't you think?'

Nina looks across at her sister, who is sucking on a pine cone. The bunches and the ribbons bob up and down with the movement of the pushchair. 'Will you do mine like that?'

But her mother shakes her head. 'Oh, *piccola*, I can't. Your hair is too short. You and Stella have very different hair. She has my hair, you see.'

Nina thinks about this for a moment. 'Don't I have your hair too?' she asks.

'No, darling. Yours is more like your father's. Or maybe your grandmother's. Granny Gilmore.'

Nina grips the snowman to her. Granny Gilmore's hair is so white and thin the pink of her scalp gleams through. Nina sees that Stella's hair is black and thick and long. If she drew Stella, she'd have to use the black crayon for her hair. If she drew herself she wouldn't know which crayon to use – the brown or the yellow or the red? Or all three?

She watches as her mother reaches over and twines the length of one of Stella's bunches around her finger.

Francesca is breaking eggs into a bowl for an omelette, stacking the half-shells inside one another, when the phone rings. The girls are playing something in the corner, the running commentary from Nina interrupted by an occasional monosyllabic exclamation from Stella. Francesca goes into the hall and picks up the phone.

It's her mother, intent on detailing some imagined slight from one of Francesca's cousins, involving a letter dated two weeks before the postmark. Francesca half-listens for a few minutes, uttering, 'Mmm,' and 'Oh,' at intervals. She feels like Stella, under a verbal onslaught from Nina. Francesca takes a deep breath and tries to head her mother off: 'I can't talk now. The girls haven't had their lunch yet.'

Her mother scolds her, demands to know why Francesca hadn't told her the *bambine* were hungry and hangs up. Francesca rolls her eyes.

She goes back into the kitchen, but stops on the threshold. Nina is standing in the middle of the room, a curious gleam in her eyes. The floor is covered in uneven dark patches, like a shadow or something spilt.

Francesca stops where she is. Has Nina dropped something, some water or juice? She stares and the scene in front of her melds into sense. Scattered all over the lino are thick swatches of hair. Dark, soft, black hair. Just like her own. Francesca puts up a hand to feel it. It's still held away from her neck in a silver clasp.

Then a small figure comes lurching round the side of a kitchen unit. For a moment, Francesca doesn't recognise it – a strange-looking homunculus, it has bristly, tufty hair, shorn close to its wax-white scalp, and stubble all over its clothes. A hair-covered dwarf.

'Gone,' it announces. 'Hair. All gone.'

Francesca looks at Nina. She is clutching a pair of scissors. Her expression is calm, defiant, opaque. Stella bends over and starts foraging about in the strands of fallen hair. She regards Francesca for a moment, then offers her a fistful. 'Mummy,' she says, solicitous, 'hair?'

Francesca sinks to her knees. She accepts the severed lock from Stella and holds it for a moment, stretched between her fingers. She takes a deep breath. 'Nina,' she begins.

It is summer time again. The last, lazy weeks of term. Burst particles of pollen float in through the open window. It is double biology on a Thursday afternoon and the sun is angled high, pouring in through the blindless glass like heated syrup. They are supposed to have started next year's syllabus, but no one, not even the teachers, is taking that seriously. Stella, sucking on the tapering tip of her ballpoint, is choosing to ignore the uniform regulations, wearing instead a flowered dress she bought at a junk shop in the Grassmarket, thick woollen tights and some heavy-soled army boots. She is rather hot, but wouldn't admit it to anyone.

She looks up from her diagram of a human heart, where she is colouring arteries in red and veins in blue, and glances round the room. Louise, sitting at the front bench, is staring out of the window, one hand propping up her head, the other tentatively touching the crinkling skin of the packet of crisps under the desk. Felicity is mouthing something noiselessly and elaborately to her friend Rebecca – something that makes them double up in silent laughter, covering their mouths and leaning over the desk with the forbidden, subversive delight of it. The teacher, Miss Fowkes, sitting at the front, keeps loosening and pinning up her hair, over and over again, as if she can't get it right, or as if she wants to feel its warm, coiled length between her fingers.

There is a sudden knock at the door. The class shifts with interest. Stella takes the pen-end from her mouth. Felicity and Rebecca snap upright, mirth dying in their throats. A distraction. They all like a distraction.

'Come in,' Miss Fowkes calls. Nothing happens. 'Come in!' she shouts louder.

The door creaks open and Nina appears round it. She is wearing a skirt that is held together by an annoying buttonhole which is slightly too big. Stella wears it herself sometimes and she sees now that it's too long on Nina. Nina's hair is held away from her face with clips that Stella recognises as hers. The people who know that Nina is her sister are turning round to look at Stella, to assess – what? Their similarity? Their differences? Stella's reaction? Stella makes her face stony, impassive.

'Yes?' Miss Fowkes demands, and Stella flinches slightly.

'Mr Allen was wondering if you had a pipette.'

'Well, of course we do but we're using it just now.'

Nina glances at the floor then back at Miss Fowkes. 'He was wondering if you had a spare one,' she mutters.

Miss Fowkes sighs theatrically and gets to her feet. 'I'll go and see.' Then, addressing the class, she announces, 'I have to pop out for a minute. I want you to carry on copying the diagram on the board. And when I come back down that corridor I don't want to hear a peep out of you lot. Do you hear? Not a peep.'

She sweeps out, leaving the door open, a new, cool draught flowing through the classroom. There is silence for a moment. Then someone at the back – a boy – says, 'Peep.' Quietly but loud enough for them all to hear. Sniggers explode around him like fireworks.

Stranded at the front of the class, Nina hooks one foot around the back of the other. Her fingers fly to one of the hairclips. Her eyes travel over the class then lock with Stella's. The sisters stare at each other for a moment. Then Nina looks away. They don't acknowledge each other much at school. Stella looks down, looks at the diagram in front of her, at the lopsided shape of the human heart, its twin chambers, at the red and blue passageways flowing through it, seeing for the first time the way your heart is always full of two opposing elements.

'Hey! What's your name?'

The voice, brusque and insistent, comes from behind Stella. She turns. Stuart Robson is leaning forward on his bench, staring at Nina. Stuart is one of the more irritating boys in their year. He bangs against Stella outside classrooms, snaps her bra strap, draws obscene things on her jotters, and spits paperballs into her hair.

Once he wrote 'FREAK' on the back of her coat in felt-tip. She and Nina had had to scrub at it for ages to get it out.

'Leave her alone,' Stella says quickly.

Stuart glances at her, then back at Nina. A smile curls his lips. 'Hey, you,' he calls again, 'I asked you a question.'

'Leave her alone, Stuart.' Stella grips her pen, hard.

'Are you Stella's sister?'

Nina doesn't reply in that flint-faced, impenetrable way she and Stella have perfected over the years. Her mouth is clamped shut. You'd never know she was holding anything in. But Stella sees the violet-blue thread pulsing in her temple.

'Are you?' Stuart is on his feet now, sauntering down the aisle towards her. Nina gives no sign that she's aware of this. 'Is your name Ghoulmore, by any chance?'

A ripple of laughter passes over the class.

'Are you?' Stuart insists. 'Are you a freak-girl? A Ghoulmore?' He makes a whistling ghostie noise, like a child on Hallowe'en. Nina still doesn't react, giving the impression she is absorbed in something beyond the windows, her face turned away, her fingers laced into each other.

'If you're Stella's sister, Stella's older sister,' Stuart says, his face close to Nina's now, 'how come you're in the same year?'

Stella sees Nina swallow.

'Everyone says,' he leans close to her, 'that you're a bit of a spastic.'

Nina looks out of the window as if enjoying the view, her lips pressed together. Stuart reaches out and his fingers close over a hank of Nina's hair. Stella sees pain jag across those features as familiar to her as her own and she is on her feet and striding through the benches separating her from Nina. Her fists are curled and fury is raging through her, through every blood vessel webbed out in her body, and she feels she could do anything, anything at all to this boy who is injuring her sister, that she won't be answerable for the damage she's going to inflict on him.

Stella grabs his jumper and yanks him away from Nina. At fifteen, Stella is tall for her age, taller than Stuart.

'Get off her,' she hisses, through gritted teeth, ramming him up against the wall. There is a dull crack as his head hits brick. 'Touch her again and I'll–'

Stella stops, swallowing the words. Stuart is momentarily frozen, astonished by Stella's vehemence. Just as Stella sees that Nina is putting out a hand towards her – to help her or restrain her? – Miss Fowkes appears round the door, carrying a pipette. 'What's going on?' she exclaims. 'Get back to your seats.'

Stuart and Stella don't move. Blood is

pounding round Stella's body, making her head swim and pulsate. Everything seems too close suddenly – the walls, the people, the desks. She is holding on to Stuart almost for balance now.

'Immediately!' Miss Fowkes squeaks, handing the pipette to Nina.

Stella uncurls her fingers from the bunched wool of Stuart's jumper. Her sister's lips part, as if she wants to speak, but then she turns away.

Later, Stella finds Nina in their usual place in the canteen, right at the back, beside the window, at the table where they stack the spare chairs.

Stella puts down her tray opposite her sister. Nina is covering her nails with fluorescent marker, taking sips out of a can of juice.

'You all right?' Nina says, without looking up.

'Yeah. You?'

'Uh-huh.'

Stella picks up her fork, pokes at the crust of the pie on her plate, puts it down again. She sighs. 'I hate the canteen.'

Nina leans across and paints Stella's thumbnail yellow. 'Me too.' She recaps the yellow and gets out the pink, glancing, as she does so, at something over Stella's shoulder.

Nina clears her throat. 'Have you… I was

wondering if ... if you'd seen the new boy?'

There is something about the way she says this – carefully, thoughtfully – that makes Stella look at her.

'What new boy?'

'In the year above.'

'No,' Stella says. 'Why?'

'He's over there.' Nina points with her pen, keeping hold, Stella notices, of her wrist. 'Don't look now.' She checks the room. 'OK. No one's looking.'

Stella turns. There, in the dinner queue, is a tall, hulking boy with red hair. She turns back in her seat, forces herself to look out at the playing fields, at the jagged line where the roofs of the houses meet the glaring blue of the sky.

Nina is watching her, Stella's hand trapped between both of hers. Stella extracts it and folds her arms over her.

'He's not that like him,' Nina says, cautiously, 'is he? I mean–'

'Shut up.'

'He's quite good-looking.'

'Shut *up*.'

Nina puts all the caps back on her marker pens. The smell of the pie in front of Stella is making her feel nauseous.

'I just...' Nina tries to take her hand again but Stella won't let her '...I only wanted to to warn you.'

'I know.'

'I didn't mean to upset you.'

'I'm not upset,' Stella cries, near to tears. 'I'm not upset at all!'

Nina lines her pens up, then starts rearranging them in a star shape. Stella wants to leave, to run away. She can't bear the thought of that person, of him, behind her somewhere, but she can't look round either.

'When you think you see him,' Nina whispers, as she moves her pens about, 'what do you see?'

Stella stares at her, appalled.

'What do you see, Stel?'

Stella leaps up, dragging her bag with her, and runs through the canteen towards the door.

The library at school smelt of floor polish and damp paper. The dehumidifiers coughed and hummed from the corners, digesting the wet, mouldering heat of the rainy season. But you could still find circular bursts of grey-white mould on the pages of the books, still find your fingers flecked with spores after a lunchtime spent reading there. The other boys played football in the yard at break-time. Jake would have liked to join them but they all talked about football teams from Britain and Jake didn't know anything about that. He once asked the boy he sat next to how you know which team to support, and the boy had stared at him as if he'd asked what two plus two was. Then he'd turned round and started telling the other boys what Jake had said and they'd all laughed. Jake had puzzled over it for weeks – why was it so obvious to them which team to support and why was it so laughable not to know? – finally deciding that it must be something to do with not having a father. It was easier for him to come in here and pretend that he didn't want to play anyway.

Jake stood near the geography books, gazing up at a map of the British Isles. His mother never talked about where she came from. He'd asked her the name of the place several times and she would always say it quickly, from the side of her mouth, in an accent Jake didn't recognise as hers. She'd taught him a Welsh song once, all about a river, and drawn him a family tree in an exercise book. But when he went back to the book to find it, to put it somewhere safe, he found the page had been torn out.

His eyes travelled over the two uneven islands. The ragged, battered coastlines. The dog-shape of Ireland and the way you could see how Britain would have once fitted round it, before the tectonic plates shifted, easing Ireland free. The bulge of Wales, straining away from England, as if wanting to follow Ireland out into the water. He saw the way the roads and rails all rushed towards the big red dot of London, like streams of water gushing down a drain. He saw how Cornwall kicked out into the sea and how Scotland made everything look top-heavy, as if the narrow neck of northern England couldn't quite support its weight.

'Are you looking for anything in particular, Jake?' The librarian, a woman who wore her glasses on a chain round her neck, was standing behind him.

'No,' Jake fingered the frayed edge of his school shirt, 'thank you.'

'Are you sure?'

'Um,' he flushed deeply, 'no ... I mean, yes ... I was wondering where ... where Kildoune was.'

'Kildoune?' The librarian looked at him. 'Isn't that…?'

'I'm called after it. It's a place in Scotland.'

'Ah.' Her face broke into a smile. 'I'm from Scotland. Where is it near, do you know?'

'Er...' Jake tries to recall the word. 'Avie ... Avie-something. I think.'

'Aviemore?'

Jake nods quickly.

'I know it well! My sister has a house there. A beautiful place. Look,' the librarian stretched up above his head, 'it's right here. All the way up here.' Her fingertip rests in the middle of the widest part of Scotland, concealing most of the word: Jake can just make out the A and the V, but no more. He fixes his eyes on the point, willing himself to remember it, to be able to recall it when her finger drops.

The librarian moves away. 'Now, let's see if we can find that other place you were telling me about. Have you used the atlas before?'

Jake shook his head.

'Well, it's very easy. Let me show you.' She pulls a big, lean book down from the shelves. *Atlas of the World*, it reads, in faded gold lettering. 'At the back there's a list of all the places in the whole world, in alphabetical order.' Jake sat at her elbow, transfixed, his hands clenched together. It was almost as if this book might split open to reveal a picture of his father.

'Here are the Ks,' she said, and Jake saw a page crammed with tiny black words. 'K-i-l,' she murmured, as she ran her finger down the column. 'K-i-l, there'll be lots of these in Scotland, K-i-l-d ... Kildare, Kilden, Kildepo Valley, Kildonan. Oh.' She stopped. 'That's funny.'

'What?' He leant forward, anxious. 'What is it?'

'It's not there.' She turned to look at him, puzzled. 'Are you sure you've got it right?'

Mair's sons had been born in quick succession after her marriage: Alun when she was nineteen, and Geraint three years later. And that, Mair decided, was enough. She'd hated the sweat and the bawling and the blood of birth. It made her unrecognisable to herself: who was making that bellowing noise, she'd asked the midwife, and was disgusted, horrified, when told that it was her. She'd insisted that they clean and wrap the babies in a shawl before she would touch them.

As for that other thing, that other act, she'd never been fussed. It all seemed too base, too animal to her. Sometimes, during it, she had to struggle not to picture herself from the outside – a woman with her knees shoved up into her armpits and a man straining and heaving as he effortfully mined his way into her. After Geraint, the place where they stitched her nipped and ached if she stood too long on the kitchen floor, the cold from the flags travelling up the backs of her legs. When Huw came at her in the night, it was so sore she was certain that seam in her flesh would tear and unknit.

One morning, after a dream where a huge red stain was spreading from her into the white of the sheets, into the flowers of the carpet, out of the door and down the stairs into the street where all the neighbours could see it, she seized the heavy end of the feather bolster and rotated it forty-five degrees. Immediately, she felt better and she spent the rest of the day cleaning out her cupboards. When Huw climbed the stairs that night, he found the swollen weight of the bolster, the thickness of another body, down the middle of the bed, dividing him from the warm, soft flesh of his wife.

It would remain there for the duration of their marriage. Very occasionally, he would manage a successful foray over the Wall, as he privately termed it. Once when he'd particularly praised a pie of russet apples, another time when he brought home a Christmas bonus. Otherwise, the mattress would soak up his seed, like tears. Or he'd been known to release them himself as he stood in the toilet out the back, watching through a gap as his wife hung out the washing, her dress creeping up her body like a tide.

The last time Huw ever made it over the bolster was the evening after Alun's wedding. Mair was forty-one but still slim in a suit she'd made specially, sewing buttonholes with thread she'd had to go all the way to the next town to find. Thinking about the way her calves emerged from the hem of the skirt, Huw ventured a hand over the feather-packed bolster. When it was not pushed firmly back, he ventured a wrist and then an arm. Then he risked his head over the parapet.

Three weeks later, when the usual ache in her back failed to materialise, Mair thought nothing of it. You couldn't get pregnant at forty-one. It couldn't happen. Everyone knew that. Three months later, she was still firm in her conviction, dogged in her denial. It was impossible, completely unheard of. There had never been anyone in this town who had a baby in their forties. It just didn't happen.

It was Mrs Williams from next door who said something first. Maybe she'd noticed that the monthly rags were absent from the washing-line or maybe she'd guessed from looking at her. She came round the back one day and into the kitchen, where Mair was sitting at the table, motionless. She'd been scouring the wood, ready to roll out pastry, when she'd felt a quickening, a flutter, low down in her body.

'When are you going to go to the doctor, now?' Mrs Williams placed her knuckles on the table.

But Mair was defiant. 'Why would I need a doctor?'

Mrs Williams sighed and sat down. 'They say,' she began, covering Mair's hand with her own, 'there's a man down Maesteg who can give you something to...' she jerked her head sideways '...you know.'

'What?'

'You know,' she said again, and leant

forward to whisper: 'Bring it off.'

Her face, when Mair looked at it, was kindly, concerned. Mair drew her hand out from under hers. 'I don't know what you mean,' she said slowly. 'Why don't you get out of my house?'

They never spoke again, even though they lived next door to one another for the next thirty years.

Mair had never been ashamed of anything. Everything she'd ever done, she'd done in the full knowledge that what she was doing was right and good and justified. Yet suddenly here she was, a church-going, God-fearing woman of forty-one with two grown-up sons, and a rounded, full, life-stuffed belly. What would people think? The idea that anyone she walked past in the street could look at her and know that she'd done ... *that* ... and *recently* ... was more than she could bear.

When she started to show, she kept mostly to the kitchen, the backyard, and occasionally treated herself to a lie down in her front parlour. Anyone who called round was told through the letterbox that she was feeling 'poorly' and couldn't take visitors. When the nurse offered Mair the bundle containing her first daughter, she said, 'Take it away', and turned her face into the pillow.

Caroline was difficult from the start. Whenever Mair looked at her she just thought of the hot shame of Huw's fingers scuttling over the bolster. The way this baby regarded her was different, unsettling. Eyes round as pebbles, fists curled. Mair had the distinct sensation that the baby didn't believe a word she said. Huw said she was going daft but soon her own words started sounding hollow, even to herself.

'It's a lovely day today,' Mair would attempt, as she lowered the baby into its chair. The baby would glance at her, chewing sceptically on its teething ring. Mair would turn to the window and see that there were in fact sudden spots of rain falling on to her washing.

Caroline perplexed and enraged Mair. She was such a perverse, wilful child. If Mair called that it looked like rain so she should take her wellingtons to school, Caroline would go to the back door, remove the wellingtons she had on anyway and replace them with her leather shoes. If Mair remarked that Caroline should cut her hair, Caroline would spend hours cross-legged on her bed, brushing and brushing it so that it would grow more quickly.

The noise of her in the house set Mair's teeth tingling. The tinny rattle of the transistor radio Geraint bought for her sixteenth birthday, the clunk of those dreadful clogs she wore on the stone kitchen floor, the way she sighed all the time, the jangle of the many silver bangles she strung up her arms, the swish through the air of that long, straggling hair.

And Caroline turned up her nose at food – something Mair could never forgive. She said her potatoes were overcooked, her carrots tasteless, her meat stringy, her gravy fatty. She wouldn't eat puddings, wasn't at all tempted by gooseberry fools, refused all gingerbread, jam tarts, flapjacks, homemade fudge. She starved herself until her bones stuck out through her clothes. It was then that Mair started egg-hoarding. If Caroline wasn't going to eat them, she would wait until there was somebody who would. Then Caroline came home and said she was no longer going to eat meat. Mair threw the skillet at her, which missed and chipped the dresser door.

The waste enraged Mair. That a daughter of hers could consign to the bin an entire meal, a perfectly good meal, was beyond her. You never lived through the war, young lady, Mair would say and find that Caroline, hollow-cheeked, was reciting back to her the rest of the speech. You'll sit there till you eat it, she would shout, but Caroline was already up and out of the front door, hair swooping after her. Huw kept his head down, concentrating on his plate. When Caroline did permit food past her lips it was only in the way a prisoner might consume a meal so as to have the strength to escape the next day.

At eighteen, Caroline leaves. Huw finds the note, tucked into the butter-dish. Mair is inconsolable. She takes to her bed, lying alongside the bolster, crying and wailing into it about her Caro, her baby. After a week of this, Huw, out of his depth and unable to negotiate the kitchen on his own, calls Geraint, who calls the doctor.

When Mair descends the stairs again, she is dressed, her hair done, her sleeves rolled, her apron on, the pills the doctor gave her sporing into her bloodstream. She reads the note through once, then pulls open the stove and hurls it in – it's not alight, so Huw is able to retrieve it later.

'I will never,' Mair announces, 'speak of her again.'

And she doesn't, until that moment in the old people's home when her eye is fixed on a distant tanker, cutting its way through the oily waters of the Bristol Channel, heading for open sea.

Jake, who has no idea that he's inherited his insomnia from his grandmother, knows he won't get back to sleep again. After he puts the phone down from his mother, he wanders around the darkened lower floor of the house. Around the kitchen, out into the hall, through the sitting room, then back again, the half-lit garden disappearing and reappearing at different angles through the windows.

He feels vaguely transgressive, illicit, like a cat burglar or a spy. He eats an apple from the bowl on the kitchen table, he reads the various lists and memos and cuttings pinned to the board in the hall, he peers at all the photos on the window-sill in the living room: Mel at primary school with missing front teeth, Mel with her siblings, her elder brother's wedding at the church down the road.

Jake turns away quickly and finds himself facing a bookcase. Biographies of people he's never heard of – cricketers, politicians – a few novels, lots of gardening books, some self-help manuals, and three atlases. He hooks his fingers into the top of the biggest one, tips it towards him and flips it open.

The mantra is familiar to him now: Kildare, Kilden, Kildepo Valley, Kildonan. Right where it should be, smack between Kildonan in New Zealand and Kilembe in Uganda is nothing. Nothing at all. No trace of this supposed place that he is named after.

He once saw a Hollywood musical with Gene Kelly and Cyd Charisse about a mythical Highland village. Lots of fake Scottish accents, red wigs and extravagant dance numbers. You could only find this village on a certain day once every two hundred years, or something like that. Otherwise it just vanished without a trace. Sometimes he thinks Kildoune is like that and some part of him keeps willing him to check all the atlases he can get his hands on, just in case he's hit on the right day and it will be there right between Kildonan and Kilembe.

But not today.

Jake opens the book at the British page and locates Aviemore, roughly half-way between the fibrillated, fragmented west coast and the clear, sheer lines of the east. He looks at where he is now, then back at Aviemore, then at the dense tangle of London and he sees, rising from its confusion, a distinct black line, bristling with dashes. A railway. The line heads singlemindedly north, right through the centre of England, then along the coast, swerving left along the Firth of Forth, through Edinburgh, then on.

Nina was more than an hour late home from school. Francesca had been into the bedroom twice, demanding that Stella tell her where her sister was, but Stella had been forced to reply, honestly, that she didn't know.

Stella was lying on her bed reading when Nina burst into their room. She didn't turn round. Behind her, she heard Nina throwing her bag and her coat on to the floor. She felt the bed rock as Nina climbed on.

'Where've you been?' Stella said, to the bedhead.

'Out and about.'

'Did you see Mum? She's on the warpath.'

They lay head to toe, like sardines fitted into a tin. Nina's hand was curled around Stella's foot.

'I told her I had music practice,' Nina said.

'But you didn't.' Stella rolled on to her back but couldn't see her sister's face, just the white tilt of her jaw.

'I know.' Nina removed a clip from her hair with slow exactitude and laid it on the bedside table. 'I've made a decision,' she said, with a smile in her voice.

'What decision?'

Nina tipped her head forward and looked at her down the lengths of their aligned bodies. 'A big decision,' she said, her eyebrows raised teasingly.

Stella sighed. Nina could play these games all night. She fiddled with the silver ring encircling her middle finger, twisting it round and round. It was always looser when she was cold.

'Don't you want to know what it is?'

'Yes,' Stella said, impatient, 'but only if you're going to tell me now. This minute.'

Nina examined the nails on her right hand, almost as if Stella wasn't there. Stella sighed and slumped back to the bed, bringing her book up to her face.

'You know Chris?' Nina said immediately.

Stella knew exactly whom she meant but, for a reason she couldn't really fathom, made out that she didn't. 'Chris Davis?'

'No. Chris Caffrey.'

'Is he the one with a blue jacket?'

'No.' Nina flicked her nail against the sole of Stella's foot. 'He's got a black coat. Blond hair.'

Stella scowled, scanning the printed blocks of text, pretending to be reading. 'What about him?'

'I've just been for a coffee with him.'

This time Stella dropped the book to her stomach. 'You haven't. Have you? What, just now? Where? How come?'

Nina shrugged with supreme nonchalance. 'I waited for him after school. We went for a walk on the Meadows.'

Stella was aghast. 'Are you serious?'

'Yeah.'

'What, you just went up to him and said, hey, Chris, do you fancy a coffee?'

'More or less. Stel,' Nina leaned forward, as if eager to impart a secret, 'it was really easy.'

Stella stared at her sister. They were silent for a moment. Then she turned on to her side, pressing her face into the pillow. It smelt of the washing powder their mother used, of musty feathers, of shampoo. 'Isn't he ... I mean, isn't he–'

'The best-looking boy in the school?' Nina tossed her head. 'I know. That's the point. Because I've decided.'

Stella sighed. 'Decided what?'

'I'm going to seduce him.'

She liked saying the word 'seduce', Stella could see that. It pulled her mouth into a perfect bow.

'There has to be some way,' Nina continued, her fists curled, 'we can stop all the shit we have to put up with. And I think this is it.'

'What?' Stella scoffed. 'Shagging Chris Caffrey? Yeah, right, Nina, that's really going to–'

'I'm sick of it, Stel.' Her eyes were glittering. 'I'm sick of being the school weirdo. Aren't you?'

Stella didn't say anything.

'Aren't you?' Nina persisted.

'Yes,' Stella muttered, 'but I don't think that's the way to go about it.'

'Well, I do. Here,' Nina threw something on to the bed, 'have a look at this.'

Despite herself, Stella glanced at the book. *Sex: A How-to Guide*. Stella fanned the pages under her thumb; sketchy pencil drawings of a man and a woman, limbs entwined, in various positions, skimmed past. 'Did you buy this?'

'Nah.' Nina grinned. 'Nicked it.'

'Nina–'

'Don't Nina me. It's fine. I never get caught.'

'You will.'

'I won't. I'm too good.' She grinned again and slapped Stella's leg. 'Don't be a prissy pants. Come on, let's read it.' She lay down on her stomach next to Stella, so that they were side by side, and opened the book between them.

Stella touched the smooth grain of the paper with the whorled print of her finger. Nine of her fingers had matching, almost identical looped patterns, which slanted off to the side, like sand pulled by tides. The fourth finger on her left hand was whorled in concentric circles. The weakest one. Her wedding finger, Nina had pointed out.

'Oral sex,' Nina was saying. 'Yuk.' She stuck out her tongue. 'Foreplay,' she read. 'Let's start there.'

About the time Caroline begins school, Mair becomes obsessed with death. Not death in general, just her own. She wakes up one morning convinced that she is going to die – and soon. She decides to rouse Huw, reaching over the bolster and clutching his arm.

'Huw, Huw.' She shakes him. 'Huw, wake up.'

He opens his eyes in shock and stares at

the ceiling. 'What is it, love?'

'What will happen to Caroline if I die?'

'Eh?'

'If I die,' she repeats urgently, sitting up now. 'What will happen?'

Huw closes his eyes again. 'Go back to sleep,' he says, and turns over.

But Mair can't. She is pinned to the mattress with horror at the vision of this late child left motherless, uncared-for, unreared, a wastrel, a vagabond, a disgrace to her family name. She wouldn't trust either of her daughters-in-law with the task, or her sister, who married a man much beneath her and lives at the other end of the town. There is no one, she realises, that she could ask, no one who gives her peace of mind. She hasn't a minute to lose. Mair rips back the blankets and gets out of bed.

When Caroline gets back from school, her mother calls her upstairs. On the threshold of her parents' bedroom, she stops. Spread on the floor is a tea-towel. Which is unusual in itself. Tea-towels aren't allowed on the floor. And her mother's jewellery is arranged over it. Caroline lifts her eyes to her mother. Mair is standing in the middle of the room, one hand clutched at her throat. Her hair, Caroline sees, has been liberated from its perpetual curlers. Which can mean one of two things: somebody has died or this is in some way a Special Occasion.

'What it is, Mam?' Caroline asks, from the doorway.

'Come here.' Her mother beckons.

'Why?' she asks, unnerved by the spots of high colour on her cheeks, the sight of those tight, regular curls that grip her mother's head like a swimming hat.

'This child is sent to try me,' her mother addresses the ceiling. 'What did I do to deserve this? Don't ask questions,' she is speaking to Caroline again, 'just do as I say. Come here.'

Caroline crosses the room, her satchel clutched at her side. Her mother kneels down in front of her and takes her by both shoulders.

'Now, Caro, this is very important. Are you listening?' Caroline nods mutely, wanting to pull away. Her mother's fingertips are digging into her skin.

'I want you to look at the jewellery on the tea-towel. Look carefully, mind.'

She and her mother stare at the red-and-white striped Welsh linen. A brooch in the shape of a swan, a string of yellowing pearls with a gold clasp, her mother's engagement ring with its solitary diamond eye, a jet bracelet, an opal on a tarnished chain, some blue bead earrings that screw on to her lobes. They hurt her ears, Caroline remembers her mother telling her.

'Have you looked?' Mair demands.

'Yes.' One of her school socks is beginning a slow creep down her shin but she daren't stoop to pull it up.

'Properly?'

'Yes.'

Yes what?'

'Yes, Mam.'

'If I die,' she begins, looking into Caroline's face, her hands still gripping her shoulders, 'and your father marries again, the new wife will try to take my jewellery.' She leans closer. 'I want it to go to you. Do you hear? All of it. It's all yours. You mustn't let her have it. Or either of your aunties. Do you understand?'

Caroline nods, not really understanding at all.

'And the silver cream jug downstairs. That must be yours too. And the wooden love spoon your da gave me. Don't let the new wife get it. In fact,' Mair starts up, pulling her apron straight, 'we'll hide them. That's what we'll do. You and me. And we won't tell anyone, see?'

'Yes, Mam.'

When Huw comes in from work, his daughter is seated at the table with her school books spread out in front of her. The kitchen is freezing, Caroline's lips almost blue with cold.

'What's happening, love?' he asks. 'Isn't the stove lit? Where's your mam?'

'Hiding the jewellery from your new wife.'

Caroline can pinpoint the moment she realised her mother's grasp on the world was imperfect, flawed. After seeing a neighbour pushing a pram up the hill, she had turned from the window and asked how babies came to be born. Caroline watched with curiosity as her mother launched into a sentence, then stopped, began sketches, then scribbled them out, flushed, faltered, stuttered, and then muttered something about God's decree and a mam and a da.

'It's about love,' her mother declared, as if she'd at last lit on what she wanted to say. 'And it's only ever something that happens when you are married.'

Caroline remembers the idea unfurling in her mind, as if it had been there all along but she'd never paid it full attention: you are wrong. Her mother was wrong. About everything.

It was a bad thought, she knew, and not one she should ever say out loud. But she suddenly saw that whatever her mother said wasn't necessarily true, as she'd always thought it was, that what she said only related to a small, closed world that Caroline wanted no part of. She looked as her mother showed her photographs of her brothers in a stiff christening gown, she listened as her mother told her that her babies would one day wear the same gown and, even aged nine, knew for certain that it would never happen.

When Caroline leaves, she eases her mother's jewellery box out of its hiding place – behind a loose piece of skirting-board in the front parlour. She's going to take something with her, the swan brooch maybe, not because she'll ever wear it but because she wants it.

When it comes to it, though, opening the lid on those jewels she hasn't seen in ten years, something fails her. She can't do it. She can't take even one of those things her mother loves so much she hides them away and never wears them. She snaps the box shut and pushes it back into its secret place. She'll take nothing from this house, nothing from this place. Just herself.

She catches the bus to Cardiff. She cries the whole way, great gulping sobs, so noisy that the bus driver asks if she's all right. By Cardiff, she's stopped crying but she's scared, convinced that her mam will appear any minute, shouting that she's not too old to feel the dap on her backside. But she manages to hitch a lift to London, where she asks for directions to the King's Road. She walks up and down until, miraculously, she falls into conversation with two women who ask if she wants to crash at their place. She's not sure what they mean, but says yes anyway.

She schools herself to round her vowels, clip her Rs, swallow her Ts. She doesn't want to come from anywhere, doesn't want a particular place leaving its mark on her. A phrase that comes back to her again and again, during the discussions they have in their basement commune, is 'child of the universe'. She doesn't speak it aloud to the people around her because it comes from some prayer her mother had framed on the wall in the kitchen. She'd never realised that any of that stuff had embedded itself in her at all. But she remembers it as she maps the streets of the city, the geographies of her new life. 'Strive to be happy,' it ends.

She likes to think she remembers nothing, that it's all been erased from her head – the chapel, the prayers, the dreadful dinners, the steep-streeted town, the dual swirl of language at their table, in the shops, at school. But she finds, in those heightened moments of either extreme pain or extreme love, that it comes out of her, that long-buried vocabulary, her mother tongue: *duw duw* will spring from her mouth if she burns her hand on the gas flame. *Cariad fach*, she murmurs to her baby, as she strokes his sleeping head.

Jake sawed through the pinkish slab of beef on his plate and raised it to his mouth. Mel was helping herself to more roast potatoes and her father was stirring the gravy with a curve-handled spoon. The dog sat with its nose tilted to the smells of the table, long curds of drool hanging from its muzzle.

'…and I said to her that I always keep my receipts, always, always…' Annabel was saying. 'And she knows I've been going into that shop for over twenty years, so I really don't see what is so outrageous about me wanting to take it back. I mean, I must be one of her most loyal customers.' She shook her head. 'The one time. It had to be the one time I threw out the receipt.'

'But are you sure you threw it out?' Mel said, with infinite patience.

'Well, I don't know what I did with it. All I'm saying is–'

'So, Jake, tell me,' Andrew sliced through this conversation to address him, picking up his wine glass, 'what are your plans now, job-wise?'

The food felt suddenly cold and congealed in his mouth, coating his teeth. 'Sorry?' he managed.

'You were involved in film out in Hong Kong, weren't you?'

Jake gripped his cutlery. 'That's right.'

'What was it you did exactly?'

'Well, I used to build sets but now I'm a director's assistant.'

Andrew was looking at him, his face open but bemused. 'And you … and you like it?'

‘Yes,’ Jake nodded. ‘Very much.’

‘He loves it,’ Mel cut in, resting her hand on his leg.

‘I don’t know much about these things,’ Andrew began uncertainly, and Jake became aware of a very fine, almost imperceptible web being spun round him. Had Andrew been put up to this by Mel? Or was he just being paranoid? ‘But I do know a lot of it goes on in London.’

‘It?’

‘Films. Film-making. Soho is ... Soho is...’ Andrew floundered, waving his hand in the air. Mel and Annabel concentrated on what was on their plates, assiduously cutting and slicing their food, not looking his way. ‘It is what you might call the...’ He cast a glance at the curtains for inspiration. Jake felt almost sorry for him. ‘...the nerve-centre of the British industry, which is ... which is one of the oldest and ... and most renowned in the world.’ Andrew took a gulp of wine.

Jake felt he ought to say something to acknowledge this speech and came up with: ‘Right.’

‘So,’ Andrew rallied himself again, ‘what I would do if I were you is–’

‘Dad,’ Mel said gently, ‘don’t hassle him.’ Jake was surprised. Was she not in on this after all?

‘I’m not hassling him, darling. I am just trying to help. Maybe he,’ Andrew indicated

Jake with his knife, 'would like to get stuck into a new job rather than just sit about the house with you women all day.'

'Don't point with your knife, Andrew,' Annabel said.

'He doesn't sit about. He–'

'All I'm saying, Jake,' Andrew appealed to him, 'is that I'd be happy to take you into London at some point if you wanted to drop off your CV to a few people. You know. Network.'

Jake inclined his head. 'Thank you.' He saw Annabel and Andrew exchange a glance and realised that the plot, if he could in fairness call it that, was between them.

'And when the time comes,' Andrew lowered his voice and leant so close that Jake could see an uningested slick of potato on his tongue, 'I'm very happy to help you and this young lady here with a deposit on a flat in London. I know that's where you'll want to be – youngsters like you. So. Just tip me the nod whenever.'

'What are you whispering about, Dad?' Mel asked.

'More beef, Jake?' Annabel proffered a dish, which swam with fat and blood.

'Tip me the nod, eh?' Andrew winked at him, swilling his mouth out with wine.

'Actually,' Jake cleared his throat and put down his fork, 'I meant to say. I'm thinking of going away for a bit. A few days. Maybe a fortnight or so.'

'Really?' Mel was looking at him, puzzled. 'Where?'

'Scotland.'

'You didn't tell me that.'

'Well, it's only a vague plan. So far. I was going to tell you but–'

'But, Jake, I can't go to Scotland. I'm not–'

'No,' he said carefully, aware that Annabel and Andrew were trying not to listen to this interchange. 'No. I thought I'd go on my own.'

Mel put down her cutlery.

'If that's OK with you,' he forced himself to add.

Mel looked dismayed, almost tearful, but was struggling to hide it. 'Why Scotland?' she asked brightly.

'I've always wanted to go there. And ... I thought now would be a good time.'

'You're right, Jake,' Annabel chimed in. 'He's right, Melanie.' She laid a hand on her daughter's arm. 'It's his first time in England. He should be getting out and seeing the place. No point in sitting about the house, is there?'

'It's very cold up there,' Andrew said. 'Play golf, do you? Marvellous courses they have, marvellous.'

Mel's expression relaxed – slightly. She raised her napkin to dab at her mouth.

‘Well, as long as it’s not for too long.’ She curled her fingers round the back of his neck.

Francesca was the last of her parents’ five children, all of whom lived in the flat above the café on the main street of Musselburgh. It was a town stretched along the coast outside Edinburgh with only one other Italian family – the two brothers who ran the barber’s shop. Domenico would catch the bus with them up to Edinburgh once a week, to go to the social club for Italian men in Leith to play *scoppa* and drink wine. Francesca and her siblings were sent to Italian language classes in Edinburgh after school on Wednesdays, which, in truth, they didn’t really need – their parents never really mastered English so they always spoke Italian at home, among themselves. ‘My children are Italian, my family is Italians my friends are Italian, everyone who works here is Italian – why on earth would I need to learn English?’ her mother would shout whenever Francesca, reluctant to translate yet another letter from the council, the taxman, the school, begged her mother to learn.

Francesca’s brothers and sisters tried to teach her bits and pieces of the language spoken outside their café before she went to school, but none of it had stuck and on her first day she'd been unable to understand anything anyone said to her, or to stop crying. She'd been called a 'durty wee Tally' by her classmates and people laughed at her accent, her clothes, the food her mother gave her for lunch. Once, she approached one of her sisters in the playground and, forgetting, spoke to her in the language they spoke with their parents. Her sister had turned, her face white and scared, and hissed at Francesca: 'Don't ever speak Italian to me here.'

Her siblings left, one by one. Her elder brother married an Italian girl and went to work in her family's businesses in Edinburgh, her sisters both became nurses and slept most nights at the hospital. Her other brother went to America, married, divorced, married again, and later returned to help run the café.

Francesca drifted out of school, thought about applying to college but never got round to it, worked at the café, rolling the pastel colours of ice-cream into balls, went for long walks. Sometimes along the small, curving beach, or past the private school behind a high grey stone wall to the racetrack where the ground reverberated with thunder-hoofed horses looping round the bend. Sometimes she walked in a repeating figure of eight round and round the town's three bridges, crossing and recrossing the river, stopping on the middle stone bridge to gaze down at the slow-moving brown water and watch the swans that gathered there in the weeds, trying in vain to beat back against the current.

She felt a vague fear all the time. Her world had somehow shrunk around her. She knew nothing and no one, or at least no one outside her parents' sphere of influence. How could she decide what she was to do in the world if she knew nothing about it? Sometimes she was afraid that she would one day have to leave her parents, have to go away from them, and sometimes she was terrified that she would never leave them, never get away from them. She worried that people she passed in the street in Musselburgh were laughing at her: there goes that Italian girl with nothing to do. Soon she stopped leaving the café altogether.

It was her uncle who saved her. He and her father were sitting huddled down in a booth. Francesca served them coffee, then went back behind the counter and stood there, gazing out of the big window, shifting her weight from each foot every sixty seconds. She counted them in her head.

Her father and Uncle Agostino were murmuring in low tones. She saw, out of the corner of her eye, her uncle glance at her, then look away. She thought she caught the word *figlia*. Daughter. Were they talking about her? Francesca wiped the spotless aluminium counter with a heated cloth. When it had dried with the energy of its own heat, she wiped it again.

She liked her uncle, who ran a delicatessen in Leith with his wife who'd never, as her mother put it, 'been blessed with children'. But she didn't like him talking about her. She was running the cloth under the hot tap for a third time when her father called to her. 'Come,' he said, beckoning. 'Sit down beside me here.'

Francesca slid on to the plastic banquette. A hundred slit reflections of her face looked back at her from the mirrored walls. Agostino leant across the melamine table and pinched her cheek.

'You are looking so thin, *mia cara*. What has this brother of mine been feeding you?' He raised the espresso cup, which looked tiny, like a doll's house cup, in his huge hand, to his lips. 'Now. Francesca.' He took her hand. 'Appollonia and I were wondering if you could grant us a favour.'

'Sì, mio zio, senz'altro.'

'Well, hear what it is first. Appollonia and I, we are not as young as we were. The shop is big. Our legs are tired. We have one girl helping us sometimes,' he shook his head and laughed, 'a crazy English student girl, but it is not enough. I have asked your father here and he says he can spare you.

You see, Appollonia and I were wondering if you would come and work with us for a time. You can live with us above the shop. Maybe you'd like to be in the city for a while. A change of air, perhaps.' He pressed her hand. 'We would be so happy to have you.'

Francesca looked at her father, who smiled at her and nodded. She gripped Agostino's hand in hers and took a deep breath, down to the bottom of her lungs. *'Sì, sì, Zio Agostino, grazie. Mille grazie.'*

On her first day, Appollonia put her behind the counter with the crazy English student girl. Francesca had never seen anyone who looked quite like her: she had false eyelashes, great half-moons of blue eyeshadow and a skirt that barely covered her rear.

'I'm Evie,' said the girl. 'Your hair's amazing.'

'Oh,' said Francesca, thrown, touching the thick plait that hung round her neck like a noose, 'thank you.'

A woman appeared, wanting slices of *prosciutto*. Evie hooked the immense haunch of meat down from the ceiling and crashed it into the slicer. 'Have you ever tried back-combing it?' she continued, over her shoulder.

'Sorry?'

'Your hair.'

‘Um,’ Francesca glanced down at her hands, ‘no.’

‘But you should.’ In her excitement, Evie took her foot off the pedal for the meat slicer. It whirred plaintively, winding down. ‘It would look wonderful in a beehive.’

Francesca gazed at her, perplexed. ‘In a beehive?’ she repeated.

‘I’ll do it for you. I’ve got curlers and spray.’

‘Um…’

‘You don’t know what a beehive is, do you?’

‘Is it a hairstyle?’

‘My God.’ Evie snorted, her hands on her hips, abandoning any appearance that she might be cutting the customer’s ham. ‘Where have you been living, darling? In a bunker? I think–’

‘Excuse me.’ The woman was rapping the counter with her knuckle.

Evie rounded on her. ‘All right, all right, I’ll be with you in a minute. I think,’ she continued to Francesca, ‘you need to come over to my digs.’

‘I … er … I…’

‘What?’

‘I’ll have to ask my mother,’ Francesca mumbled.

‘Your mother?’ Evie was astounded. ‘What are you – twelve?’

‘So, darlings,’ Evie exhaled a lungful of smoke into the dim light of the department-store café, ‘I hear there’s a man on the scene.’

Stella, half-way through a sip of hot chocolate, coughed and choked. The first thing in her head was terror, terror that Nina might think she had told on her. But Nina was banging her fist on the edge of the table, furious. ‘How do you know? Has Mum–’

‘No, no,’ Evie cut across her, ‘not your mum. Your dad, actually.’

‘Dad?’ Stella was surprised. ‘I didn’t know you and he ever ... I mean...’

Evie looked at her and laughed. ‘No, you’re right. We don’t ever. Not usually. He called me yesterday. Said he’d seen one of you locked in an impassioned clinch. He’s in a terrible flap about it, poor man.’

‘So that’s why you wanted to see us,’ Nina said accusingly. ‘Because Dad told you to, because–’

‘I wanted to see you today because I wanted to see you.’ Evie uncrossed and recrossed her legs emphatically. Under a narrow black wool skirt, she was wearing a pair of boots with blade-like heels and criss-crossing laces that pulled the leather close to her legs. Stella wanted some like that so badly it made her feel weak. Could she ever be like that? Adulthood seemed an interminable time away. She didn't know if she could wait that long. 'No one tells me what to do, darling, you know that.'

Stella dipped the curve of a teaspoon in and out of the surface of her hot chocolate. She could kill Nina, who was sitting there trying to cry. That was a special trick of hers. It got her out of everything. Stella knew how she did it – she'd told her once: 'Think really hard about the time Max got run over,' Nina had said, 'really, really hard until you feel the tears. It's easy.'

'What cross faces you have,' Evie exclaimed. She stretched up from the table and waved her hand in the air. The waiter saw her immediately. Evie had always had that knack. 'Let's have some cake and you can tell me all about your paramours.'

She insisted on the sweet trolley being brought to their table and wanted to know the names of each and every cake. The waiter even got her a spoon so she could taste the profiterole sauce, before she rejected it as 'far too rich'. Three Morningside ladies watched, shocked, from the next table. After a close inspection, an éclair, a slice of chocolate gateau and a religieuse were placed before them with a flourish.

'Religieuse, for Chrissake,' Evie said, slightly too loudly, as she spooned a morsel into her mouth, 'I bet those poor bloody

French nuns never got to eat anything like this. Mmm,' she placed the spoon back on the plate, 'divine, no? So. Your boys. Come on, tell all.'

'I don't have a...' Stella began, infuriated '...a ... boy. It's nothing to do with me.'

Evie surveyed her, eyebrows raised. 'I see. Nina?'

Nina tucked her palms under her legs, her eyes huge and bright with unshed tears. 'I don't know what to say,' she whispered, coy and shy suddenly. 'What do you want to know?'

'His name would be a good start.'

'Chris.'

'As in Christopher?' Evie considered this. 'A good name, she pronounced. 'What else?'

'Well, he's seventeen. He'd be in the same year as me if it wasn't for...' Nina stopped short. Evie nodded. 'Um. He collects LPs. He wants guitar lessons. He's got curly hair–'

'Dark or fair?' Evie interrupted.

'Fair.'

'Blond? Good. Blonds are more dependable, I find. Dark ones break your heart.'

Stella glanced at Evie, wanting to ask more but not knowing how.

'And you like him?' Evie said.

'Yes.'

'Really like him?'

Nina shifted in her seat. 'I think so.'

'Good.' Evie smiled and dabbed at the corners of her mouth with a folded napkin. 'And are you sleeping with him?' she enquired, in the same tone of voice.

Stella turned to look at Nina, interested all of a sudden. Would she tell the truth? That she'd been trying to persuade him but so far he'd refused? Would she tell Evie that she had managed to part Chris from his underpants only twice, and both times his erection had shrivelled and flopped? 'Like this,' Nina had told her, and demonstrated with the limp tassel on her dressing-gown.

Evie was watching them across the table. 'Darlings, don't be embarrassed. I'm not your mother and I'm not going to tell your mother either.'

The sisters were silent, Nina glaring down in the direction of Stella's knees.

'Stella,' Evie appealed to her for the first time, 'you tell me. You must know.'

'Er,' Stella glanced at Nina then back at Evie, 'well–'

'No,' Nina said, through clenched teeth, 'we're not. I can't believe you're interrogating me like this. It's unbelievable. It's really ... really invading my ... my life.' The tears came now, perfect and silver, chasing each other down Nina's cheeks. God, she was good. 'I can't believe you don't trust me,' she sobbed, as Stella looked on, half in awe, half in disgust. 'I'm not going to sleep with him. I promise, Evie, I promise.'

'Darling child, don't make promises like that, I beg you.' Evie was utterly unperturbed by Nina's tears. Unlike Francesca would have been. 'Now, listen,' Evie rummaged in her bag, 'this isn't exactly the advice your father was hoping I'd give you but, believe me, this is the kind of advice you need.' She pushed across the table a small, flat, blue-and-white box. Stella looked at it. Evie's nails were blood-crimson, filed to a point. On the box was another one of those sketchy drawings of a man and woman. DUREX, it screamed, DUREX DUREX. Stella looked away, at the Morningside ladies, at the Scott Monument out of the window. When she looked back, Nina had her hand over it, trying to cover it, trying to push it back towards Evie.

'No, no,' Evie was shaking her head, 'you must take them. Really. You must.'

'But–'

'Nina, take them.' Evie gave a violent push and Stella saw Nina make a show of reluctantly giving up. 'And whatever you do, don't tell your mad Catholic mother I gave them to you. If she finds them, it wasn't me. Is that clear?'

Nina nodded. Stella nodded.

'You know how to use them?'

Nina nodded again.

'Make sure he has one on before he comes anywhere near you. Understand? *Anywhere* near you.'

Stella clamped her hands over her face, which was prickling hot. 'Evie,' she pleaded.

'It's important, darling,' Evie said to her. 'It's important that you both know this. Spermatozoa are persistent, devious little devils.'

'Yes,' Stella forced out.

'Are we clear?'

'Yes,' they said in unison.

'Marvellous.' Evie leant back and stubbed out her cigarette. Nina was already gathering up her coat and bag. 'Shopping time, I think,' Evie said. 'Shall we go?'

The day after Archie first takes Francesca for a walk in the Botanical Gardens, he sits in his mother's house watching the dog, Jinty. She is rubbing her flank along the edge of the sofa, her muzzle held close to the packed fabric. His mother is making tea in the kitchen; he can hear the gathering whistle of the kettle, the clatter of china cups. Outside, the afternoon is sinking into evening.

Once a fortnight, his mother baths Jinty in the big square sink in the kitchen. Jinty bears this indignity but not without shivering and sneezing, a mournful look in her brown eyes, and a slight moan escaping her lips, to which Archie's mother replies with a strict 'Shush!' After being wrapped in a towel and dried in front of the fire, always this pantomime: Jinty racing round the room in a frenzy, horrified by her scentlessness, desperately trying to pick up, to borrow, any smell she can. The dank, lanolin odour of the carpet, the pungent wax of the parquet, the animal whiff of the horsehair sofa – anything is better than nothing to Jinty.

Archie watches her wriggling around on the sheepskin rug until he can bear it no more.

'Come here, Jint.' He holds his hand out to her. 'Come on. It's no good, you know.' The dog trots over to him, her tail waving, looking up at him as if he might be able to help her.

Archie lays his hand between the dog's ears. He's been buying hunks of cheese off the black-haired Italian girl for almost three months now. He's been in the delicatessen every lunchtime, despite the scornful snickers of the blonde girl, each time trying a different tactic. The cinema? A coffee? Could he take her to tea? A recital? Francesca had shaken her head, her plait swinging from side to side, her eyes cast down. An exhibition at the art gallery? The theatre? A trip to the sea? A dance? He'd made up his mind to suggest church, even though he was sure she'd be a Roman Catholic and he'd never set foot in a Catholic church in his life and wouldn't know what to do, when she leant over the counter, her cheeks flaming, and said, 'Perhaps a walk.'

She turned up with her mother. And her aunt. The older women were dressed almost identically, in long black skirts and black cardigans buttoned to the throats, with their hair pulled severely away from their faces. Archie had to try very hard not to show his shock at the appearance of these Baba Yagas. They were both tiny, about half Archie's height. He had to bend his knees to shake hands with them. The mother clutched a large, furled umbrella in one hand and looked him up and down with thinly disguised disdain. Neither spoke any English, yattering what sounded like instructions – or maybe criticisms – to Francesca.

He and Francesca walked ahead, with the Baba Yagas arm-in-arm, bringing up the rear. They seemed to enjoy the gardens, pointing and exclaiming at everything, the mother, Signora Iannelli, stopping to sniff the flowers. The rose garden was a big hit, also the lavender banks, but they didn't like the hothouses. '*Troppo caldo*,' they complained, fanning themselves, in their woollen skirts, woollen stockings, woollen cardigans.

He asked Francesca questions, in between the incomprehensible shouts from behind, and had to stop himself laughing when she told him she'd been born in Scotland. She barely spoke English, he thought, and even when she did her accent was so strong it was as if she was speaking Italian.

Archie bought them all tea, which seemed to thaw the aunt at least, who for some reason seemed very taken with the teapot. Francesca sat with her hands in her lap. Signora Iannelli glared at him across the cakes. But Archie was not about to give up easily. He'd grown up the sickly, protected only child of a widowed mother, rarely allowed out of the house, let alone Edinburgh, and Francesca seemed to him a breeze flowing from a new direction. As they'd sat around the tea things, he'd had to resist the urge to lean over and sniff her hair, her skin, to inhale her foreignness, her scent of faraway places, of another world.

Jinty wanders away, her claws clicking on the parquet, and Archie's mother arrives in the room, saying something about the milkman leaving two pints instead of one. Archie wonders for a moment how she'd react if he brought Francesca here. A foreigner, an immigrant, a Catholic, an under-educated shopgirl. She would weep into her handkerchief, invoke his school fees, his dead father, his delicate health as a child.

But, like Jinty, he is bothered by his blandness, his scentlessness. A well-brought-up Presbyterian Edinburgh boy who does his job and lives with his mother, he feels he has nothing to him. At times, walking home in the evening fog, Archie thinks he might very easily fade into invisibility, incorporeality, so insubstantial, so ordinary does he feel. He wants something to give him definition, a smell, an edge, something that sets him apart, so that people might no longer say 'Archie who?' but 'Archie, him that married the Italian.'

In a sense, he falls in love as much with her family as with Francesca herself. He loves the way Valeria carries vats of water or sacks of flour on her head, the way she leaves the tap on in the kitchen because she is still so delighted to have running water. He loves the way cousins, sisters, uncles, brothers are always coming in and out of the café. He has always felt that he and his mother were too small, too confined a unit. He loves the pungent tastes of the food they sit round a crowded table to eat. He thinks of them like drops of oil in water: a distinct, cohesive presence, unchanged by the alien element surrounding them.

Archie goes to night school to learn Italian. His efforts make Francesca smile, and Valeria snort. Valeria has not taken to

Archie. She doesn't want this freckled, milk-pale Scot who persists in mangling her language getting his hands on her youngest daughter. She keeps telling Francesca that what she needs is a nice boy – which Francesca knows means a nice Italian boy.

But Domenico intervenes.

'If that is who she loves,' he says to his wife one night, as they lie in bed, 'that is who she loves.'

Valeria pummels her pillow irritably but knows better than to argue with Domenico. He'll only bring up her father and how he didn't want them to marry, and being reminded of that at this precise moment would only annoy her more.

Nina succeeded in deflowering Chris – and herself – on his bedroom floor while his parents sat downstairs watching the news and weather. 'I got rid of my hymen!' she whispered to Stella, across the black space between their beds. 'I felt it go. There was a kind of stretch and then a sort of pop.'

Three weeks after that, she ditched Chris and took up with a boy called Pete Gilliland in sixth year. She dumped him after a week and went out with Scott Miller, then Angus McLaren, then David Lochhead, Kevin Patterson and Patrick Caffrey (Chris's older brother).

Stella watched as her sister shrugged off

her old persona and stretched herself into a new one. Nina had been right. As her notoriety spread, the boys all suddenly wanted her, suddenly stopped taunting her or calling her 'Ghoulmore'.

Stella saw that Nina's life at school was easier now, saw that sex was a way of making yourself accepted, with certain people. Mainly boys. She also saw that it gave other people – girls – a different reason for hating you.

Jake gets on the train at smoky, rush-hour-jaded Euston Station. He's been on night trains through China and across Mongolia and the length of Vietnam, so he's surprised by the plushness of the compartment. He's more used to bare mattresses and a floor covered in fruit peel, nutshells, cockroaches and spit.

Jake lies on his stomach on the bunk and peers out of the window. A blackened brick wall, a flash of weak grey sky, rows of houses with identical chimneys, red buses, a playing-field, a block of flats, a huge advertising hoarding with an image of a woman, head tossed back and lips parted, the backs of houses, flitting by with giddying speed – a child at a piano, a woman taking down her washing from a rack, a man at a cooker, a couple embracing, a man with a baby on his lap. It seems extraordinary to him that he is travelling up the spine of the island whose shape he's spent so long gazing at, poring over, thinking about.

Last night, after he'd got into bed, he'd suddenly felt Mel at his back, the mattress bouncing as her body moved close to his. He could feel the cold rush of her exhalation on his shoulder-blades, the round bones of her knees pressing into the back of his thighs. He'd cleared his throat, edging himself fractionally towards the rim of the mattress. But she'd moved forward, draping her arm over him.

Jake had stared at it, dangling over him, the short fingers, the slightly squarish nails. It began stroking his chest in an insistent yet uneven rhythm.

'Mel,' he'd begun.

'Sssh,' her voice had hissed wetly in his ear and her hand dived down and started floundering about in his waistband.

'No.' The word had shot out and he jack-knifed into himself and he was sitting up, away from her, on the edge of the bed. 'No,' he said again.

Mel had been silent for a minute. He felt her gaze on his back. Then she turned over quickly, tugging the duvet after her.

Jake sighs and slides to the floor, pushes down the tap and rinses water over and over his face. Then he lies back in his bunk and stares out at the blackening world. He can't sleep, his mind churning over like an engine that cannot catch. The blue night-light buzzes. He hears a woman on the other side of the partition coughing, the shuffle of the guard down the corridor, the train groaning and creaking beneath him, pulling him sideways through the night, clanking through stations he will never visit.

Stella has cleared away the breakfast mess, set the huge dishwasher in motion, polished the tables and taken the hiking details of another guest before he vanishes up into the mist shrouding the Laire Ghru.

In the kitchen behind her, Pearl is energetically banging pots down from the shelves. Stella likes Pearl – a woman in her fifties who does a night shift at an old people's home before coming in to work mornings at the hotel. Pearl sleeps in the afternoons, then gets up in time to make dinner for her children and grandchildren, most of whom seem still to live with her. Years before, her husband had 'buggered off with the town bicycle'. When Stella asked her how many children she had, Pearl replied, 'Six or seven, hen, six or seven,' then laughed so much she made herself wheeze and had to reach for her inhaler.

Stella stretches out her legs under the desk. Outside, the sun is shining down on the trees, which hold green buds at their branch-ends. White alto-stratus clouds race each other across a blue sky. Beside her, the phone bleeps into life. She lifts the receiver. 'Hello, Reception, how may I help you?'

There is a slight pause on the line, then: 'Stella.'

With that single word, the sense of well-being, of calm, slips away from under Stella. It isn't said as a question, just a flat, unequivocal statement. She swallows, gripping the receiver to her ear. 'Hi,' she manages.

'Well,' Nina says, deadly cold, 'are you going to tell me why you're avoiding me?'

Stella twists her fingers in and out of the telephone's springy coil. 'I'm not avoiding you. I–'

'Stella,' Nina interrupts, 'I've left you seven ... no, eight messages in the last month. I've written you two letters and four cards. You don't reply to any of them. Not one. You vanish into thin air for weeks and I have to find out from Mum where you are.' She takes a gasp from her cigarette. 'What the fuck is going on?'

Stella's face feels tight. 'Nothing. Nothing's going on. I just... I've been busy.'

'Busy?' Nina snaps. 'Don't bullshit me, Stel. You may be able to spin Mum and Dad that line, but not me. You chuck in everything in London and just take off, you–'

'I didn't...' Stella stammers. 'I didn't chuck it all in, I–'

'You did, so.'

'I did not.'

'Stella. I phoned your work. They told me you left without giving notice.'

'Oh, did you now?' Stella decides the best course of action is to go on the attack. 'I can't believe you, poking your nose into my business. For your information, my contract was coming to an end and–'

'Mum tells me you're near Kincraig.'

It is her trump card and they both know it. Stella is silent. She presses her fingernails into the soft, fleshy parts of her palms. She doesn't know when she last heard Nina say that word.

'What are you doing there?' Nina asks, and the gentleness in her voice panics Stella more than anything.

'Nothing,' she whispers.

There is a pause.

'Stel, please,' Nina says, her voice low, 'what's happened? Why are you there? Please tell me.'

Stella cannot speak. She can hear Nina breathing, but not herself. She must be holding her breath. Nina, don't, she wants to say, don't. Don't do this, please.

'Stel,' Nina says quietly, 'you have to tell me what's going on. I've been going out of my mind. How could you do that? How could you go there, without ... without telling me? We both know what–' She breaks off, as if someone has come into the room. Stella can hear her scrabbling for her cigarettes. 'Look, I'm coming up to see you. I'll drive up at the weekend. It'll only take a couple of hours and–'

'No, you mustn't!' Stella bursts out. 'I don't think that's– I mean, I'm really busy. I don't have much time off.' She takes a deep breath. 'I have to go now, Neen. Sorry. 'Bye.'

She drops the receiver and bolts from the chair, bursting through the kitchen and out into the corridor. An image of Pearl, caught in the act of looking up, surprised, is smeared on to her retina. The phone is ringing again as she reaches the back stairs. It rings and rings and rings. There is a tableau stillness about it from here: she can picture the phone in the deserted lobby, the breath of quiet between each ring, the flowers beside it, the overblown petals scattered on the desk surface, the empty, pushed-back chair, the grass and the trees beyond the open door.

Eventually, she hears Pearl go through into Reception and pick it up: 'Hello... Yes... No, she's not around just now... No... Sorry... Aye, she was here a minute ago, right enough, but she had to pop out... That's right... Certainly ... right you are, then. 'Bye now.'

Stella, standing poised on the narrow back stairs, hears Pearl push her way through the kitchen and into the corridor. 'Stella?' she calls.

'Yeah.' Her voice, trapped in the small, enclosed wooden stairwell, bounces back at her, too loud, too soon.

'That was your sister.'

'Uh-huh.'

'She says can you call her.'

'Right. Thanks, Pearl.'

'No bother, hen. Are you away to do the rooms now?'

'Yeah.'

'OK. See you later, then.'

'OK.'

Nina looks across the dark space between their beds, and sees that Stella has gone. The blankets are pulled back, the exposed innards of the bed glowing white in the gloom. Nina sits up. 'Stella?' she says. 'Stel?'

Their bedroom is dark. Furniture crouches at the walls. Their school uniforms lie, limp and ready for tomorrow, on their chairs, cuffs and hems trailing to the carpet.

Something makes Nina look up, makes her heart leap in her chest. A pale figure looms above her in the dark. Nina has to stare at it for a few seconds before she realises what it is. Her sister is standing, poised and motionless, on the spar at the end of her bed, her bare feet curled round the wood.

Nina pulls back the covers and steps out of bed. The dark doesn't scare her. Nothing scares her any more. 'Invincible' is the word for it, Stella told her. She found it in a book. Nina tiptoes across the room.

Stella is perfectly balanced, like a swimmer poised for a dive. She doesn't sway, doesn't falter, doesn't even have to hold out her arms. Nina has no idea how she does it, how she manages to hold herself on this thin bit of wood.

'Stel?' she whispers.

She mustn't wake her. Never wake a sleepwalker. Stella is looking down, as if at a point far in the distance. Nina knows where she is. She can picture the drop of the precipice, the boom of water against rock. She doesn't like it that Stella goes there without her, doesn't like the thought of her sister there, alone.

'Hey,' she says, and reaches out her hand, curling her fingers into her sister's, slowly and carefully. 'It's me,' she says. 'You're dreaming. Come on. Come back to bed.'

Stella clutches at her hand, frowning.

'Come on,' Nina says, and tugs her arm. 'Back to bed. It's just a dream.'

Stella allows herself to be led down. As Nina is pulling the covers back over her, she starts to shake and shiver, her jaw clenched.

'It's all right, Stel,' Nina murmurs, as she tucks the blankets round her. 'It's all right.'

Stella's body is stiff and unyielding. Nina sits on the mattress next to her, stroking her hair away from her face, something she's seen her mother do. 'Everything's all right.' But her sister still shudders. Nina crouches down so that she can see right into her sister's sleeping face. She takes Stella's wrist in her fingers and grips it, hard. 'He can't get you now.'

'No, I'm sorry,' the woman has bright lipstick escaping into rivulets around her mouth, 'I don't know of any town around here called that.' As she finishes saying this she gives the stack of leaflets she's holding a smart tap on the desk, as if to punctuate her speech.

Jake is standing in a bookshop in Aviemore, the only place name he knows for sure, the only one he has, his mother's rucksack at his feet. 'How about a village? Or a hamlet or...' His hand circles wildly in the air. Is it just him or is this woman being spectacularly unhelpful? '...anything?'

She creases up her face, giving a short show of pretending to think, then shakes her head. 'I don't know of anywhere called that.'

Jake pulls his face into a smile as a way of stopping himself reaching over the desk and shaking her. 'OK.' He is not going to be downcast, he is not, he is not. He had known this would be difficult. Did he really think that by coming here it would magically materialise? 'I'll take this, please.' He lays the map on the counter and hands her a note picked at random from his wallet. She hands back two different notes and some coins with a sniff.

Outside, he struggles to unfold the map in the stiff wind. He's going to scour it for anything he recognises. It has to be here somewhere. He can't give up now he's got this close. It must exist: there was no possible reason why Tom would have lied about it to his mother. Maybe it wasn't the name of a town, like he and his mother had always thought – maybe it was a mountain or a valley or a river or whatever. Who knows what makes people give things names in this place?

The wind is too strong. The map flaps and strains for escape in his hands. The air is thin and icy clear. He needs to find somewhere to stay. But first he needs to find somewhere to have breakfast. Then he can lay out the map on the table and examine it properly – he will find it, he will, he will. And bugger Mrs Bookshop.

Jake looks up, along the street, and sees, for the first time, the peaks of mountains, denting the sky.

The windows are full of weather. Rain flings itself at the glass and clings on desperately as it slides down, buffeted by snatching grabs of wind. Stella sits on a stool behind the counter of the Buttercup Tea Room, her hands propping up her chin. She's driven into town for the puff pastry for tonight's beef Wellington. Pearl's cullen skink to start, the beef for the main course, and a choice of two desserts to finish. Passing the tea room, she'd been hailed by the Australian waitress, Moira, who'd asked her if she'd mind the place for ten minutes.

Cars plough up and down the length of the town, stretched like a ribbon along the main street. People cloaked in primary-coloured rainwear hurry along the pavements. The tea room isn't busy: a couple of tweed-swathed ladies bent in close conference over a scone, a blank-eyed woman with a baby in a bunny-covered high-chair, and a young guy. Black hair, plastered upright into spikes with rain, the shoulders of his jacket dark with water. An empty, crumb-studded plate sits on his table. A rucksack, battered and ancient, is propped on the floor next to him. He doesn't look like the kind of person this town usually attracts. He stands out. His clothes aren't right. Too impractical. They're not tweed or Gore-Tex or wool. They smack too much of the city. He looks like an urbanite, Stella decides, looks like he's landed here by accident.

He is sifting through coins, picking them

up one by one and examining them as if he's never seen them before. Must be foreign. American, maybe? No, Stella doesn't think so. He looks European. French, perhaps. He's hard to pin down. There's something about him she likes, though. The way he sits on the chair. It's a rather sissy-looking chair with a padded floral seat and an upright back, but he lounges on it as if it were a bed – his legs splayed and stretched out, one arm dangling loose by his side, his shoulders rolled back. He looks very ... post-coital. Stella smiles to herself. It's not every day you get someone like him to look at, especially round here.

As she surveys him from her vantage-point on the stool, his head jerks up, as if he's sensed her gaze. His eyes roam round the tea room until they meet hers. Stella blinks, unmoving. Is she still smiling? She's not sure. She has a horrible feeling that there's the ghost of a grin on her face. They stare at each other for a second. Then he drops his coins on to the table and shifts himself upright in the chair. 'Could I have another tea, please?' he asks.

Stella slides off the stool. 'Sure.'

She looks at the Gaggia machine next to her, which is sighing and shuddering like someone on the verge of tears. It's similar to the one in her grandparents' café. She finds a cup and a teabag on the shelf above her.

She runs her hands over the Gaggia levers, then eases one down. Boiling water jets into the cup, billowing the air with steam. His voice was odd. Accentless. He's a Brit, definitely. He's certainly not Scottish but he doesn't really sound English either.

She tips a milk-jug into the cup and white unribbons in the dark water.

The waitress walks towards him through the scattered tables of the tea room, a steaming cup held in her hand. Sunlight glows into the room briefly, the windows flaring with light. Jake glances out to the street. A sudden burst of sun is illuminating the wet buildings, the car windscreens. The weather seems so unpredictable here. It had been sunny and clear when he got off the train but then a squall had appeared, soaking him in seconds. His skin is clammy and chilled and sticks to his clothes.

He turns back to the table, to the strange coins lying there, to his empty cup and plate, to the tea room, to the woman walking across the room towards him with his name written across her breast. Kildoune, the starched cotton of her dress reads, Kildoune.

Jake stares at her. She has smooth black hair, which lies in a slant across her cheekbones, green eyes and skin so delicate he can see the blue thread of a vein travelling up her neck. Her colours assault his mind: the dark, the green, the blue, the white, the red of her mouth. And his name on her chest. Kildoune. In black, cursive letters.

'Your tea,' she says to him, and places the cup down on the table. He goes to move the coins out of her way and the back of his hand brushes against the soft, mushroom-pale skin of her inner arm, and as they touch there is a kind of humming vibration, like two messages meeting on a wire.

'What is that?' Jake blurts.

The waitress glances at him, his empty plate held in one hand, a slight frown dipping her brow. 'What?'

'That.' He points at her breast, the word written there. 'That,' he says again. 'What is it?'

She touches it, the raised embroidery. 'Kildoune?' she says, and Jake wants to shout, clap his hands, seize her by the shoulders, kiss her on the mouth that just uttered his name. 'It's a hotel.'

'A hotel? Where?'

She gestures in a direction behind her. 'Over that way. Beyond Kincraig.'

'Show me.' He struggles about inside his bag for the Ordnance Survey map. It refuses to behave, to open properly, to lie straight in his hands, its origami interleaves resisting separation. He is terrified that this woman – the only woman seemingly who knows where or what Kildoune is – will vanish into thin air. He has to stop himself grabbing her by the arm and handcuffing her to him. 'Show me exactly,' he insists. 'I have to go there.'

She is staring at him as if he's quite mad. Which is a pretty fair assessment at the moment. She shifts the plate into her other hand, throws a glance over her shoulder. 'It's quite…' She stops, her eyes straying over his battered rucksack. '…posh.' She finishes uncertainly.

'No, no.' Jake flattens the map to the table. He feels crumbs crunching under his touch. 'I don't want to stay there, I just want to…' He trails away, seeing the faint alarm in her eyes. Deep green eyes with long, curling lashes. She doesn't really need to know all this. Appear normal, he wills himself, take a deep breath. 'I just want to … see it.'

'Oh.' She leans over the map and Jake sees a warning in the neck of her overall: KEEP AWAY FROM FIRE. He gazes at it, at the knuckles of her spine disappearing down into the white folds. 'Right,' she says, the tip of her finger hovering over the map, 'well–'

At that moment the bell on the door dings. The first waitress, a small woman with reddened cheeks, hurries in. 'Stella, you're a star!' she exclaims. 'Thanks so much. Phew.' She comes to a standstill in front of them. Looks from Stella to Jake and back again. 'Was everything all right?'

'I was just showing this guy,' Stella gestures at him, 'where Kildoune is.'

'Oh.' The Australian girl elbows Stella out of the way. 'I can show you.' She beams at him, her face too close.

Jake doesn't look at where she is pointing on the map, but watches the girl. Stella. She crosses the room, away from him, towards the counter. She picks up a coat and moves towards the door.

'Do you work there, then?' he asks, as she passes by him, close enough for him to reach out and touch her. He can't think of anything else to say. He wants to detain her, delay her, keep her with him. He doesn't want her to disappear out of the door and into the outside world, never to be seen again.

She fixes him with her clear, green stare. Is she smiling at him? No.

'Yes,' she says, 'I do.' Then she turns to the Australian girl, who is talking about bus times and the possibilities of hitching. 'I've got to run, Moira, see you later.'

At the door, she puts her hood up over her hair and turns to close the door after her. Just as it is about to shut, she looks up, straight at him. They stare at each other for a split second. Then she pulls the door to and is obscured by rain and the condensation swarming up the windows.

Stella made a tent with her bedclothes, balancing a mallet from their croquet set in the middle of her bed – the lower bunk, because Nina always had the top – and she dived down into it, delighted. Where she slept prostrate and stretched out every night was suddenly a secret peaked space, with tapering, sloping walls, the light glowing red through the crocheted blankets.

It was early. Too early for her parents to be awake – they weren't allowed to go in to them before eight at a weekend. Nina was still asleep.

Stella wriggled out, feet first, and roamed the flattened carpet of the room, collecting armfuls of bears with nonplussed faces, dolls with eyes that rattled inside their hollow plastic craniums. These, she bundled into the tent and lined up in rows, straightening any that dared to lean drunkenly on their neighbour.

'This is our tent,' she announced to them, lying on her stomach. Her legs stuck out at the end of the blankets, but what did that matter? Most of her was in here, in this new, private space. 'Our secret tent.' The toys looked unimpressed.

After a while, she got bored with arranging and rearranging them, and her arm was tired of holding the croquet mallet upright. She emerged, hair mussed and static, let the tent collapse and it became just a blanket-covered mattress, lumped with the mysterious shapes of toys. Stella could make out a padded leg and the grasping, outstretched hand of a doll. She tipped back her head and looked speculatively at the swollen sag of the mattress above her. Nina couldn't still be asleep, could she?

Stella reached up and, slipping her fingers between the sharp wire meshing, pressed her hand up into her sister. Nothing. She did it again. Still nothing. She threw herself down on her back and, putting her feet against the hard metal knots of the mesh, pushed up. The weight of Nina's body rose and fell back. Stella waited, puzzled. Then she heard something, a soft, unintelligible noise.

Stella slid out of bed and climbed the wooden ladder, the creases falling out of her pyjama knees. She hooked her elbows into the edge of the bunk and looked at her sister.

Nina was lying on her side. Her eyes moved under her lids.

'What did you say?' Stella asked.

Nina's lids lifted, then fell again.

'Did you say something?' Stella whispered, breathing hard into Nina's face. 'Are you awake? Neen? Are you awake? I made a tent. Do you want to see? It's really good. There's room for both of us. Sort of.'

Nina mumbled something.

'What?' Stella leant closer.

Nina opened her eyes. 'Don't feel well,' she muttered.

Stella pushed at her parents' door, hearing it hiss against the carpet. The room was still and fugged with warmth. Sunlight cut in around the edges of the curtains. The carpet had dark blotches of flowers, twining into each other, all connected, and Stella stepped from one bloom to another until she'd reached her father's prone form. Half of his face was obliterated by the pillow. One arm was stretched back behind him, to touch the curve of her mother's hip. Tiny hairs were pushing out of his skin – millions of them. By the hairs on my chinny-chin-chin. Stella leant over, fascinated.

'Dad,' she whispered. 'Daddy.'

'Go back to bed, Stella.' His voice was clear and firm. Almost as if he was awake. But his eyes were closed.

Stella turned and walked back to the door on the petal clusters. In her room, she dragged a stool to the cupboard, stood on it and reached up to pull down their doctors and nurses set. She snapped the elastic of the hat with the red cross about her chin and climbed up the ladder again.

'Now, patient,' she said, as she knelt on the bed, 'I'm going to have to listen to your heart.'

Nina gazed at her, listless and inert, as Stella fitted the plastic stethoscope into her ears and pressed the disc to Nina's nightie. She could hear nothing at first, then the tubing picked up a distant, irregular thud, slow as the clock in their grandparents' sitting room. Stella whipped the stethoscope out of her ears.

'And now for your temperature.'

She inserted the thermometer into Nina's mouth. Nina's eyes closed and her head slid sideways. Maybe she wants to be left alone, Stella thought.

She spent a while unpacking and repacking the things into their case, her legs crooked at right angles over Nina's. She listened to the endless swish-swash of her own heart for a bit. She unravelled a crêpe bandage and rewound it into an even cylinder. Then a strange, gurgling sound came from Nina. Stella squashed the bandage into the case, snapped down its locks and crawled towards her sister.

Nina's eyes were shut. She'd gone back to sleep. The plastic thermometer with its inked red line drooped from her lips, which were pale and bloodless. Her hair was sticking to her scalp like seaweed. Stella leant closer and saw that her eyes were in fact half open and her eyeballs were turned upwards so that only the whites showed. Her breathing didn't sound as it always did when Stella woke in the night – it was too fast and shallow.

'Neen,' she began. She touched her hand. It felt damp and burning hot. 'Nina?' Stella gripped Nina's wrist and gave it a shake. The arm fell away to hang loose and slack off the side of the bed.

Stella climbed back down the ladder, through the room, across the landing to her parents' door. This time she didn't use the stepping-stone flowers.

'Daddy.'

'Mmm.'

'Dad.'

'Stella, I've told you–'

'Dad, there's something wrong with Nina.' Stella didn't realise she was frightened until she heard her voice, which was high-pitched and shrill. It made her burst into surprising tears. 'Please wake up,' she wailed.

Her father's eyes sprang open. He looked at his younger daughter for a few seconds, then swung his legs out of the bed and went into their room. Stella trailed behind.

'She – she said she didn't feel well,' Stella spoke through her sobs, 'and then – and then she went back to sleep and then–'

Her father looked at Nina, laid a hand on her forehead. 'Christ,' he muttered, then his voice rose to a shout, 'Francesca! Francesca!'

In the lobby, Stella shakes the wet from her hair and peels away the waterproof from her damp clothes. She is thinking that she must change her uniform because this one is damp and that the duck ornaments could do with a dust and that she should take the pastry straight to the kitchen, when Mrs Draper bustles past. She stops when she sees Stella standing there, dripping water on to the mat.

'Stella, there you are. Come with me. I want you to meet someone. A new member of staff. Remember I told you we needed some outdoor work doing – maintenance, painting, that kind of thing? Someone to help you when everything gets busy over the summer. I'm sure you could do with a hand...'

In Mrs Draper's office, a man stands at the window, his back to Stella. He turns round when they come in.

Stella hadn't realised how tall he was. She has to look up at him to meet his gaze. She is still holding the wet slick of the waterproof in her hands.

'Hello again,' he says to her, and smiles.

part three

Stella wakes with a jolt, her heart loud and urgent in the cave of her ribs. She is face down, blind, the linen of the pillow pressed to her mouth and nose.

She turns round and sits up in one jerked movement. The caravan is empty, the early-morning air arctic-cold against her skin, the tree tap-tapping on the roof. She can see all the way through to the door. Nothing. It's all right, she tells herself, it's all right. But her heart continues to pound.

She'd been dreaming she was a child again, standing near an edge where brackish dark water falls away to thunder against rocks out of sight.

She scrambles from the bed, fighting off the bedclothes, which clutch and cling to her, and goes to the mirror. The reflection that meets her there is adult. Definitely adult. Stella scans it. Skin imprinted with fabric folds, lips pale, the black of the pupils wide, depthless. It's all right. It was years ago. Years and years. But somehow it doesn't always feel it.

Stella turns away from herself. The light behind the slatted blinds is a dull white. It's early. She goes back to the bedroom, wincing at the cold of the carpet under the bare balls of her feet, and picks up her clock. 6.45 a.m. She won't sleep again so she drags her uniform over her head and pulls two sweaters over it.

The dog joins her as she is trudging to the old stables for firewood. It dives out of its kennel, straight as an arrow, tail waving, high-pitched yips escaping from its throat. Stella sleeks the fur between its ears before they set off again, together, the dog with its nose held to the ground.

Passing the old, renovated pigpen near the stables, Stella is momentarily surprised to see the curtains shut. She passes the wood-basket into her other hand.

'We'd forgotten about him,' she says to the dog, 'hadn't we?'

The dog stops and looks up, attentive, ears raised, scanning her speech for sound patterns it might recognise.

Jake is reluctant to enter the kitchen on his first morning. Mrs Draper had told him to come down for breakfast after nine when the biggest rush would be over. But he loiters in the lobby, his hands wedged into his pockets. From behind the swing door into the kitchen comes the sound of laughter, a brief shout, a radio playing and the banging of plates and cutlery – the noise of people used to working together.

The door is pushed open and he sees the

girl from the café emerge. Stella. She has her hair held back from her face in a wide band. She vanishes up the long, thin corridor and into a room at the end.

Jake waits uncertainly at the bottom of the stairs. He feels a bit overwrought, a bit wired. He didn't sleep a wink last night but lay awake watching the night count down on the luminous face of his digital watch, repeating to himself, over and over, you're in Kildoune, you're in Kildoune. It seems extraordinary to him. The proximity of it all, the physical connection with Tom, is overwhelming, unbelievable. Everywhere he looks he sees – objects the banister, the light switch, that stone threshold, the fireplace which might have been touched by the hand of his father.

From the kitchen comes a burst of hoarse singing, then a clatter, then a curse. He looks down: the trailing, complex pattern of vines in the carpet twists around his feet, as if willing him to trip and fall. He looks up: the stairs wind up to the next floor, and he is just able to glimpse a pair of forked antlers, hanging right above him.

'Do you want some breakfast?' a voice says. Stella is standing at the swing door, a pile of used plates in her hands.

'Yes.' Jake moves towards her. He can feel himself smiling. Is he smiling too much? Maybe. She isn't smiling at all. 'That would be great.' He takes his hands from his pockets and gestures at the plates. 'Can I give you a hand?'

Stella shakes her head, holding the door open for him with her foot. 'I'm fine. Go through.'

The kitchen is hot, cramped, overlit, and full of steam and the smell of ground coffee. At the sink is a small, stumpy-looking woman with a mouthful of broken teeth, and a man in chef's whites stands at the stove, a long, spiked implement in one hand. A pan spits and sparks on the hob, slivers of bacon shrivelling in fat.

Stella slides the stack of plates on to the surface and flicks open a pad of paper. 'Venison sausages for two,' she says, very fast over the noise, 'one with mushrooms, the other without, the one without with scrambled, the one with with fried, OK?'

The chef nods without turning round. 'Got it.'

'This is Jake,' she announces, 'who'd like some breakfast.'

'Got it,' the chef says again.

The woman at the sink is in front of Jake, flipping a sodden dish-towel over her shoulder. 'I'm Peril,' she says to him.

'Sorry?' Jake leans over the counter anxiously. She can't be called 'Peril', can she?

'Peril,' she insists, again.

Stella, standing at the toaster, glances at him, then back at the woman. 'Peeuurrllll,' she explains, flattening the vowels. 'Peuurl.'

'Ah.' The mists clear for Jake. 'Pearl.'

'Ha,' Pearl guffaws, 'Peurl. Peril. Peurl.'

They both laugh. Even the chef turns round and bares his teeth.

'Pearl,' Stella says, 'could you show Jake where all the paint and ladders and stuff are kept? Mrs D told me she wants him to start painting the windows today.'

Pearl staggers off down a passageway, still giggling. 'Come with me, laddie.'

By midday, the air is motionless and humid, the sky heavy with unfallen rain, Jake peels off his T-shirt and works in just his jeans, a blowtorch held in one hand. He is pleased to have something to do, a definite task to perform. Otherwise he'd probably just wander about in a daze. The paint blisters under the roaring jet of heat, pulling away from the window-frames and falling to the ground in shards. Sweat blooms on his forehead and itches at his scalp. He scrapes at the stubborn streaks with a metal spatula.

The rooms of the house are dark and fathomless from the outside, like looking down into a lake. Jake circles the building, hefting the ladder against the lumped stone walls, counting up the windows, calculating how much paint he'll need, checking for any rot. When Mrs Draper asked about his experience of painting windows, he hadn't mentioned that he'd only ever painted windows on film sets, windows that opened on to fake scenery, to digital hallucinations, to nothing. But he didn't think it mattered – how different could it be?

As he is turning the searing blast of the torch on to the dining room windows, he sees Stella inside, the pale oval of her face floating up to the surface.

Of course Jake didn't really expect his father still to be here. He hadn't pictured him standing at the gate of this mystic place called Kildoune with open arms, waiting to welcome him into his life. But there was also, of course, that small, disruptive part of him that kept whispering, he might be there, what if he's there, he could be there. No matter how logically he tried to think about it, no matter how convinced he was that there was no way he'd find him by finding Kildoune – he was still disappointed.

Jake hadn't realised how much he'd wanted to find him until he got there. He'd always told himself that it hadn't mattered, that his mother had been enough for him, that she had made up for any lack he ever felt. But here, standing in front of Kildoune, which is full of unfamiliar strangers, he can't tell that lie to himself any more. Motherhood is a clear, prescribed thing. Those nine months you spend with another being pocketed inside you are a lifelong, unwritten contract that can't ever be cancelled. But fatherhood is nebulous, undefined, and can be almost nothing, a mere tailed cell shot out into the void.

He doesn't know what he expected. He expected nothing and everything. He's thought about Kildoune all his life, imagining and reimagining it, building it and tearing it down in his mind. But he'd never expected this: a grand house in grey stone, a thicket of dank fir trees, a huge sky piled with clouds, and a long-necked woman who watches him with the grave, impenetrable gaze of a cat.

Stella comes out of the front door of the hotel, a plate in one hand with a sandwich on it. She has to shade her eyes against the glare – the sun has broken through and burned away the cloud. The air is filled with the sweetish, steamy scent of hot bracken and peat.

She looks about her, then sees, beyond the gravel and the curve of lawn, the right-angled triangle of a ladder against the house. The new guy, Jake, is perched at the top of a hypotenuse, energetically scraping at the paint on an upper window, his T-shirt draped over his head, Beau Geste-style.

'I made you a sandwich,' Stella calls, as

she reaches the bottom of the ladder, holding up the plate to show him. 'I'll leave it here.'

'No,' he puts down the scraper and yanks the T-shirt off his head, 'wait a sec. I'll come down.' The ladder judders and rocks as he descends the rungs. Stella puts out a hand to steady it. 'Thanks.' He grins as he leaps the final three to the ground. 'Fantastic,' he says, taking the plate. 'I'm starving.'

Stella forces herself to look away from him as he pulls on the T-shirt. The ground around her feet is littered with hard, dry paint curls. She waits for him to speak. Didn't he want to ask her something? He says nothing, though, just smiles at her as he lifts the sandwich to his mouth. It is an oddly personal smile – the corners of his mouth curving upwards with an easy slowness as his eyes skim over her face, her hair, her throat.

'How are you getting on?' she asks abruptly.

He nods as he chews and swallows. 'Not bad. Some of the windows are in a bit of a state, a bit rotten, but Mrs Draper says she's going to get someone proper in to fix those.'

'Proper?'

'Yeah. Not like me.'

'Why? Are you not proper?' she says, then immediately regrets it.

He eyes her, and smiles again. 'No, not really. Are you?'

Stella decides to ignore that. 'Whereabouts are you from?' she asks instead.

'Hong Kong.'

She laughs. 'Hong Kong?'

'Why's that funny?'

'I don't know.' She has to stop herself laughing again. 'It's just not what I was expecting you to say.'

'Why? What were you expecting?'

'Er ... I'm not sure. I don't know – London, maybe.'

He shakes his head and grimaces. 'No way. I've spent all of maybe forty minutes there. Didn't think much of it.' He fixes her with his blue eyes. 'What about you?'

'What about me?'

'You're not from round here either, are you?'

'How can you tell?'

He shrugs, as he pushes the last of his sandwich into his mouth. 'I just can.'

'How?' she demands, although she knows she should really be ending the conversation at this moment and walking away.

He takes a step back and pretends to survey her from head to foot. Stella flushes hot under her clothes. 'Your haircut,' he ticks off on his fingers, 'those shoes, your accent–'

'My accent?' Stella scoffs. 'And what would you know about that, Mr Ex-pat?'

'Not much. But I can understand you,' he

touches the centre of her thorax, 'which is more than I can say for most people around here.' He shrugs again. 'You just don't say Invernessshire to me.'

Stella glares at him. She feels obscurely and inexplicably furious. She's been here, alone and undisturbed, for months, and then this guy turns up from nowhere and starts asking her personal questions. Why are you here, she wants to say, why have you come?

'So are you going to tell me where you're from?' he says. 'Or is it a secret?'

'It's a secret!' she snaps.

'OK.' He seems unperturbed. 'Whatever.'

Stella turns on her heel, the gravel crunching under her, and walks away, fast.

'Hey!' he calls after her receding figure. 'Can you tell me something?'

'What?' She doesn't stop but flings the word over her shoulder. He's made her angry but he's not sure why.

'How long has this place been a hotel?'

This makes her stop, he notices, and half turn. In the bright sun, her shadow is a poised black shape at her feet, crouched and ready for her next move. 'Twenty-five years, I think,' she says. 'Something like that.'

Jake lays this mentally next to his own lifespan, like two tape-measures unrolled side by side. That leaves four years over for

Tom to go to India, meet his mother, conceive him and – what? What else could he have done in that blank stretch of time? God only knows. Come back here to his commune? The house seems an unlikely venue for a commune – too big, too grand. Did he go elsewhere? Move on? He's not here now, Jake's sure of that, but the possibility that Tom might still be in the area, in another commune, maybe, or leading a straight life in a semi, makes the fine hairs on the back of his neck rise and bristle. He wonders for a moment how Tom might react if he were to turn a corner and find an image of his youth, his past self, his doppelgänger, walking towards him.

'Twenty-five years?' he repeats.

'Yeah.' Stella has turned fully towards him now, her shadow double shifting with her. 'Why do you ask?'

He won't tell her. He won't. 'Nothing, I–' And then he changes his mind. 'Well.' He thinks. 'Someone ... I know might have ... lived here once. A long time ago. A ... a relative.'

'Oh,' Stella nods, 'right. You should ask Pearl. She knows everything.'

'OK. I will.' Jake gives her a small wave as he mounts the ladder again. 'Thanks.'

Stella doesn't go in the ambulance with Nina and her mother. She watches as the two men belt her sister to the wheeled stretcher. Nina's head is turned to one side and they have strapped something that looks like a plastic mask to her face. The elastic holding it there yanks her hair into a peak on the top of her head. Stella wants to smooth it straight. She is sure that Nina wouldn't like the feel of her hair pulled in that way.

Their mother is wearing trousers under her nightdress and has a coat of Archie's round her shoulders. Her feet are bare on the Tarmac of the road. Lots of people have come out of their tenement and the surrounding ones to watch the Gilmore girl being taken away. Stella wishes they couldn't see her mother like this. Francesca steps into the ambulance before the stretcher so she is waiting there as Nina is lifted in. Stella is glad about this. She wouldn't like to be alone in that dark space, hung with wires and straps and tubes. Then the men slam the doors closed.

Stella and her father follow the wail of the ambulance. Stella's place is behind her father, who always sits in the driver's seat. It seems wrong that half of the car is empty. She looks over at the vacant seats where her mother and Nina ought to be and worries that, without the ballast of them, the car might unbalance, tip over.

At the hospital, her mother, still barefoot

and in her nightdress, clutches her hand without looking at her and tells her, over and over again, that everything is going to be all right. Stella is put on a chair that wobbles when she moves.

Her father disappears first, then her mother, then both of them. A nurse comes by and leaves a basket of brightly coloured toys that Stella is too old for. Stella rocks the chair back and forth under her, looks at how the light from a window in the corridor ceiling gushes in to pool on the polished linoleum, and counts the number of noises she can hear. She gets to forty-two and gives up. She realises she is very hungry but doesn't know who to tell. She pulls both laces from her shoes, ties them together and starts playing cat's cradle, which is what she and Nina always do when they're bored. But there's no one to insert their fingers into the beautiful symmetry of the criss-crossing joins and lift it away from her and she can't remember what comes after the third move, and when she tries to make it up the skeins knot and tangle around her hands and eventually she drops it into her lap.

Her grandparents appear when the light from the ceiling window has slanted enough almost to touch her on the leg. Stella is surprised to see them. Her grandmother kisses her forehead a lot and squeezes her to her overall. Her grandfather disappears, then her grandmother, and then they reappear with her parents.

The four of them stand in the corridor and a great discussion goes on above Stella's head. The adults can't stop touching her – on the hair, the shoulder, the arm. Stella doesn't like this and wants to wriggle away. But then she looks up at her father's face and she can see that it's wet. His eyes are blurred, the lashes stuck into spikes. Her father's been crying. This horrifies Stella. Her father never cries. Never. Fathers don't. She knows that. She looks to her mother and sees that she, too, is red-eyed and clutching damp tissues in her hand.

Stella begins to weep, very quietly at first, tears rising up out of her eyes and spilling down her face. She holds the thick tangle of laces to her face and sniffs into it. She looks again at her parents' faces and panic surges through her body like an electric shock. She takes a deep, shuddering breath.

'WHERE'S NINA?' she roars. 'WHERE IS SHE? WHERE'S NINA?'

Within seconds, it seems, she is in the café at Musselburgh. She is sitting on the counter, her legs dangling over the side. Her grandmother is feeding her ice-cream with a long silver spoon and talking to her in soothing, soft Italian. The windows are steamed up but she can just make out the rain falling, beyond them. Her laces, strangely, are back in her shoes – not in the way she likes them, slanting over each other, but pulled in straight lines. Her grandfather is on the phone in the corner, a cigarette held in the same hand that holds the receiver. Stella wants to remind him that it's there because he seems to have forgotten it, ash falling in drifts down his waistcoat.

'Where's Nina?' she says.

Her grandmother's brown eyes regard her. 'You know where she is. I told you. Remember?'

'Dov'è Nina?' Stella tries Italian.

'You remember the hospital,' her grandmother says gently, and then says more things Stella can't quite understand. She can see her grandmother's lips moving and she can hear the sound but she doesn't seem to be able to separate it into words.

'Where's Nina?' she says again. *'Dov'è Nina?* Where's Nina?'

Stella had what Nina referred to as her 'flip-out' the summer she was nineteen. They had been out of school, and apart, for the best part of a year – Stella at university in London and Nina, initially, at art college in Edinburgh. Nina had lasted half a term: when the tutor had told her she was to spend four weeks building a loom on which she would spend next term weaving her own tweed, she told him he could go fuck himself.

She spent weeks mooching in her bedroom, listening to music, plucking her eyebrows, dyeing her hair different colours and writing Stella long, indignant letters, until Francesca marched her along to a secretarial college. Armed with a 'competent pass' in touch-typing (Nina had only managed this by bribing the girl on the next desk to do hers) she got a temping position at a GP's surgery. The young but ambitious doctor who ran the place was shocked at the state of her typing but decided he wanted to marry her anyway.

Stella returned from her secret new life in London to a house full of wedding brochures, dress patterns, seating plans, present lists, colour swatches and caterers' catalogues. Her mother was so tense the tendons in her neck stuck out under the skin. Her father hid at the office all day. In the place of her art-student sister, who wore paint-spattered dresses, chased boys, drank too many vodkas and forgot her medication, was someone who had manicures, talked to estate agents, discussed fabric for bridesmaids' dresses, and wore tailored skirts, high heels and silk scarves knotted at her throat. And every day for dinner there was this stranger in a suit who addressed her sister as 'My Tempting Temp'.

Stella went into town, withdrew everything she had in her savings account, accumulated from summers of waitressing for her grandparents, and walked along Princes Street to a travel agent where she bought a train timetable for Europe, a rail pass and a guidebook.

She left mid-morning, while Francesca and Nina were out having a fitting at the dressmaker, pulling out her bag from under her bed. Her handwriting was scrawled and unrecognisable as she wrote the note, 'Gone to Europe, I'll be back for the wedding', and she couldn't stop looking over her shoulder as she hurried down Arden Street to the bus stop, as she waited on the platform at Waverley for the train that would take her away to liberty, freedom, peace. She only relaxed when she was on the rolling, pitching night ferry to Calais, surrounded by drunk, snoring men, tartrazine-fuelled children, the smell of petrol and reheated food, and gangs of people with sleeping-bags. Stella had never been abroad before.

She caught a series of trains through France. She bought a tray of white-fleshed peaches in Paris and ate them, one by one, as she sped through maize fields and vineyards with the windows open, the scented, warm air swirling into the carriage. Reaching the south in the dead of night, she climbed quickly on to another train that said 'Marseille to Roma' on the side.

She arrived in the early morning, the

muscles in her arms aching from clasping the bag to her as she dozed. She stumbled down the train steps and walked through the station, towards the sunlight. She asked directions in the language her mother had taught her, unsure that it would work. But these strangers not only understood her but spoke back. It seemed unbelievable to her, magical almost, that anyone outside the microcosm of her family used these words, this grammar, this syntax.

In the wide, snag-toothed sweep of the Colosseum, she ate her last peach, a map of the city spread on her lap. She went to the pink-walled house where the famous young poet died, climbed up and down the Spanish Steps, soaked her feet in a fountain shaped like a boat. She kept wanting to stop passers-by, to hold them by the arm and peer into their faces. Everywhere she looked there were people with her jawline, her cheekbones, her brow. Don't you recognise me, she wanted to ask them, surely I must know you.

She was possessed by an urge to see everything. She went deeper into the country, catching more trains, climbed the spiralling steps up a striped *campanile*, went to a town that had been buried deep in volcanic ash for thousands of years, swam in the blue Adriatic, ate *stratiacelli* in tiled *gelaterie*, the taste of it so recognisable it made her smile.

In a town whose name she knew from her grandfather's stories about how he came to Scotland, she got on a bus that the man in the ticket kiosk told her would take her to her grandparents' region. It wasn't easy to get to their village. No one, the ticket man said, ever really went there. She changed buses in Agnone, then had to hitch a ride with a family who said they could take her close to where she wanted to go. Stella sat in the back, wedged between their children, her bag on her lap. Their car climbed higher and higher, the air thinning, crags of mountains looming above the road.

The family dropped her on the verge and she had to walk the path her grandfather had taken, sixty years before, in the opposite direction. When she turned the last hairpin bend and saw the village up ahead, Stella realised she'd never really believed that the place they came from, the place they'd told her about, was real and actual and had continued to exist without them.

She sat for an hour on the double-arched bridge above the split in the stream, and took a secret pleasure in buying a round tin of aniseed sweets at the chemist's shop. She walked around the empty cobbled streets, looking at the piles of neatly chopped wood, the geranium pots, the chickens scratching at the ground, the water fountain with its worn lip. She looked at the blank windows of the buildings that were abandoned, tumbledown, and wondered which one had been Valeria's. An old man coming slowly up the hill saw her in the doorway of a crumbling stone house and mumbled, '*Scozia*,' as he passed, 'they've all gone to *Scozia*.' Stella thought about running after him and asking if he remembered Valeria and Domenico – he was roughly their age, he must have known them – but she stayed where she was. She wanted to remain anonymous, not leave any mark.

She stood in a phonebox in the square, considering the way the light splintered on the water and where on earth she might sleep tonight and how noisy motorbikes were and what she should buy for lunch.

Nina answered on the second ring. 'You are in so much trouble,' she said.

'I know,' Stella replied. She kicked off her shoes and hoisted herself up to sit on the metal stand. Her body was warm to the core in this country, her joints pliable, loose. She might have felt more Scottish here than she'd ever done before but it was as if the very molecules of her being were responding, recognising the climate. In the café in Musselburgh she could hear her mother screeching, 'Is that her? Is that her?'

Stella hung up. She looked again at the trickling water of the streams, at the splintering and re-forming reflection of the sun, at the hazy shapes of the mountains. Jumping down, she discovered that someone had reached under the glass and stolen her shoes. She walked barefoot through the church, the frescoes casting gold and blue light on to her skin.

It seemed to have been agreed without anyone telling her that Stella would live with her grandparents while Nina was in hospital. She was given the back room and the bed her mother had shared with her sisters. It was a double, with a headboard so polished that it threw back a shadowed, indistinct version of your face, and a dipped sag in the middle of the mattress. If Nina had been in it with her, they would have rolled towards each other in the night.

Stella spent several weeks in what her father called a 'dwarm'. She sat on a chair in the kitchen, beside her grandfather as he cooked chips and peas and fish for the *scozzesi*, gazing into space, her legs dangling over the lino. She couldn't speak, wouldn't say anything, except for questions: where's Nina? when's she coming back? is she going to die? when am I going to see her? Without her, Stella had no idea how to behave, how to live her life, what to say, what to do all day.

Her grandfather made her favourite dish –

curls of potato *gnocchi* – and fed them to her himself, as if she was a baby. The tears dripped from her face into the *pomodoro* sauce and Domenico stirred them in, calling them seasoning. Her mother came to see her once a week, took her for walks round the bridges of the town, holding her hand too tightly, weeping into her handkerchief.

Valeria came back to the café one day with a navy apron, just like theirs but in a child's size, and tied it over Stella's clothes. It was the summer holidays, she explained to Stella, so the café was extra busy and they needed her help. Stella carried glasses of lemonade to customers, and was allowed to squirt the sauce on to sundaes. She translated the more elaborate requests of the customers so that her grandparents could understand. She sat up on the counter, telling her grandmother who had finished and who was still eating and who might like some more coffee. 'What would we do without you?' her uncle Giancarlo said, often several times a day. Then Stella only cried at night, when the room around her seemed empty and large.

It seemed as if she had been in Musselburgh for months, for years, by the time Valeria took her to see Nina in hospital. Stella was surprised. She had been asking to see Nina for weeks and her grandparents kept saying no, but why don't you write her a letter instead? Stella didn't know why her grandmother had suddenly changed her mind.

'Why can we go now?' she asked, as they sat on the bus.

Valeria pretended not to hear, fussing with tickets and putting the change back into her purse.

'Why am I allowed to go now,' Stella persisted, 'but not before?'

Valeria sighed. 'Just because,' she said, and Stella watched her turn away quickly and blow her nose.

Her grandmother held her hand in both of hers as they trudged through corridor after corridor, went up some stairs, along a glass walkway. They passed abandoned wheelchairs, shut doors, nurses with squealing shoes, people walking along in dressing-gowns, doctors with stethoscopes, a man holding two inverted bunches of orange flowers, a woman with no hair. Before they went through two heavy swing doors, her grandmother stopped to straighten Stella's collar.

'*Sei pronto?*' she said, touching Stella's cheek. '*Andiamo.*'

They were in a long corridor, one side of which was windows, the other a wall of sickly yellowish-green paint. It was very quiet. Stella suddenly thought she needed the loo but the set look on her grandmother's face told her she shouldn't ask. They came to a stop near the end.

Valeria bent down and hoisted Stella up. There before her, beyond the glass, as if on a television screen, were her parents, her mother sitting in a chair beside a bed, her father standing beside her, and on the bed was a stick-figure with hollow eyes and a shaven head, looking straight at her. Stella saw that it was dressed in a flowered nightgown like the one she had.

'Smile,' her grandmother was whispering, 'give her a smile.'

Stella pulled her face into a smile. The air in the hospital made her teeth feel dry and cold. She lifted her arm and waved.

'That's it,' Valeria encouraged. '*Brava ragazza.*'

Stella asked, 'Why isn't Nina waving back?'

'She can't move, my darling.'

Stella waved and waved. In the scene on the other side of the glass, her mother waved back and so did her father. The three of them waved frantically, as if something terrible might happen if they were to stop.

'Take a good look at her, won't you?' her grandmother whispered, so quietly that Stella wasn't sure if she heard right. 'So you can remember.'

The ceiling above her is a patchy grey-white. Nina knows off by heart the pattern of frail cracks that runs through it like rivers through mountains, seen from a plane.

Nina's never been on an aeroplane. But it's how she imagines it might be if she were flying high above the earth, just below the white wisps of cloud. She would look down and see the puckered earth passing far beneath her and the flickering shadow of the plane, printed there by the sun.

She moves her eyes inside their sockets. It seems to take a great deal of effort, as if they are weighted or as if a machine inside her is slowly cranking down.

The room is dark, the blinds lowered. The slats have been tilted towards the floor, but from where Nina is lying she can see the black slits of night reaching into the room. She is puzzled. Weren't her parents here just a minute ago? Or was that a long time before? She can't remember. She has a slight recollection of Stella. With their grandmother in the corridor, looking in at her. But maybe that never happened. She can't remember when she last saw her sister.

She lifts her eyes to the clock on the wall opposite the bed. She can see the second hand jerk and stop, jerk and stop, but when she tries to focus on the thicker arms they dissolve and jitter before her.

To her right, she is surprised to see, is a nurse. Sitting in a chair beside her. Eyes bright as mercury through the gloom. Nina doesn't know why there is always a nurse in her room these days, watching her. There never used to be.

Nina looks away, looks down the length of her body, draped in the hospital blanket. She could have sworn that her arms were folded over her, fingers tucked into the elbow creases of the opposite arm. But now she sees that they have been placed by her sides. Her feet fall away from each other in a symmetrical V, the blanket peaked over them.

Beyond the room, beyond the grimacing faces of cartoon characters daubed on the windows in colours that hurt her head, is a noise. Someone running down the corridor. Feet snap-snapping against the lino. Nina knows that lino. She remembers its dark red, pocked surface, the grainy, uneven feel of it under her slipper soles. On the last day that she'd been able to walk, she'd moved along it. All by herself. All the way to the bathroom. She wouldn't let them carry her, no she would not. She'd shaken and lurched and had to cling to the wall by the last joints of her fingers and it had taken her a long time and it had hurt. But she'd done it.

A small figure whizzes past. A boy from the ward down the corridor. Nina's seen him before. He came into her room at one point and asked her what her name was. Before she could answer, the nurse in the room shooed him away. He is running, pulling a drip-stand behind him like a train on a string. His laughter is torn off as he passes her open door.

Then she hears something else. Feet coming after him. Heavy feet with a broad sound. Adult feet. A nurse.

'Come back,' the nurse calls. 'I mean it.'

'You can't catch me!' the boy cries, and his voice sounds distant as if he's turned a corner. Nina thinks that there is a corner that way, beyond her room, turning off into a larger corridor. She used to see it when she used to leave the room.

Then the nurse outside hisses in a low voice, 'Be quiet.' *Be quiet.* Nina will hear it again later in her head. 'There's a little girl dying in there.'

For a split second, Nina feels sorry for the little girl and is wondering how old she might be, what age you need to be to die, and whether the little girl is frightened and if she will be lonely over there on the other side and Nina is turning her eyes on the nurse beside the bed to see if she is sorry too. But the nurse is looking cross and strangely ashamed. She is darting up out of the chair and slamming the door and making sure it's shut firm.

When she comes back to sit down again she won't look Nina in the eye. Nina stares at her, stares and stares. But she won't look up. And then Nina understands.

Pearl has been ordered to soak twenty-five electroplated nickel silver candlesticks in a vat of scalding water with a touch of ammonia. If there's one thing that gets Mrs Draper going it's globs of wax on her candlesticks. Not to mention grubby skirting-boards, dusty pelmets, old soap, scentless pot-pourri, scratches on table surfaces, cracked plates, crooked rugs, shoe scuffs on chair rungs.

The ammonia sweats from the steam, making Pearl's eyes smart. Hot, griefless tears streak down her face. Her hands are red and livid under the water as she chips off the wax-glue with her fingernails. Under her breath, she remembers the song her youngest grandson had been singing when she dropped him off at school this morning: 'He grew whiskers on his chinny-gan, the wind came out and blew them in again, poor old–'

'Pearl?'

A voice close behind her makes her jump, makes the candlesticks jolt together under the water. 'Christ!' she exclaims at Jake, one hand pressed to her chest. 'You scared the life out of me.'

'Sorry,' he says. He has paint in his hair. Which is a shame because it's nice hair. Lots of boys his age seem to be cutting it off these days, like her son, shaving it close to their skulls, but he wears his quite long and kind of messy-looking.

'Here,' she says, 'you'll need some white spirit for that.' She points at his head.

Jake raises his hand and fingers the stiffened white strands. 'Oh. Didn't know I'd done that.'

'In the cupboard there.' She hustles him towards it. 'At the back. You'll find a rag over there.'

Jake spills a stinking pool on to a scrap of old towel and checks in the reflection of the door-glass as he pulls his hair through it. 'Er, Stella mentioned...' he mumbles '...um ... I was wondering...'

Pearl looks up from smearing a candlestick in chalky silver cleaner. 'Uh-huh?'

'Do you remember a commune here?'

'A what?'

'A commune. Like ... like a house of people all living together. Young people, maybe. About twenty-five, thirty years ago.'

Pearl buffs the frilled lip of the candlestick, puzzled. 'Ehm...'

'It was here in Kildoune, I think.'

'A commune, you say?' She sees her lips say this new word in the polished silver shaft and then it falls into place. 'Oh, you mean the hippies.'

'Yes.' Jake starts towards her as if he's going to embrace her. 'Yes,' he says again, gripping the rag in one hand, 'the hippies.'

'Aye,' she says cautiously. The stench of white spirit is wafting off him.

'You remember them?'

'Aye.' She nods. 'Of course.' She laughs briefly. 'They were kind of hard to miss.'

He is staring at her now, his eyes large and intent. 'They lived here?'

'Aye. Well, not in the big house – out the back.'

'Right. Do you... I mean, what do you remember about them?'

'Well...' she begins.

His intensity is making her uneasy and, as if he senses this, he speaks again: 'You see, a relative of mine lived there,' he gabbles. 'Here, I mean. In the commune. And I'm just trying to – to find out more about ... him.'

Pearl frowns, thinking, then intones all she can recall, like she remembers having to do at school, a long time ago: 'The old boy, Mr Grant, he let them stay in the bothy out the back. They were here for quite a while. Four, maybe five years. Something like that. I was working for him then – cooking and cleaning but, frankly, it was a thankless task. The cleaning, that is.'

'And you used to see them? Talk to them?'

'Oh, aye. They were nice enough. Very young, most of them. Wore funny clothes, you know. Lots of folk up the town used to complain about them. But I always said they were harmless.'

'Can you show me where? The – the bothy, did you say?'

Pearl and Jake walk through the woods. Her hands are easier now, out of the ammonia. Jake keeps close by her, adjusting his step to whatever direction she takes.

'There you go,' she says, and points, where the trees thin out, to a long, low stone building. The corrugated-iron roof has part-collapsed, one of the windows gone. A tall, waving plant sprouts from the chimney. As they look, the empty hole in the roof explodes with birds, their wings whirring.

'It was an old clearance cottage that someone put a roof on at some point. The hippies dug a garden all round it, grew vegetables and the like. But it'll have all overgrown since.'

They reach the door and Jake vanishes inside.

'Haven't been up here for ages,' she calls after him, staying outside with her arms crossed. She doesn't like going into disused houses, especially clearance houses. Makes her feel a bit spooked. 'Mrs Draper keeps talking about renovating it. You know, putting in heating and all sorts, to rent out as a holiday home. But she hasn't got round to it yet. I'll believe it when I see it, personally. Is there anything much in there?

Any furniture?'

'Er...' Jake sounds far away, distracted. 'A bit.' There is a pause. A complete, still silence. The wood around her rustles and sighs, sunlight appearing and vanishing in patches on the ground.

'What like?' Pearl says, just to keep talking. She doesn't like this wood particularly, either, and certainly doesn't like standing about in it, waiting to be got by whatever it is that gets you in a wood.

'Sorry?' Jake says eventually.

'What like?' she shouts. 'Furniture.'

'Um, there's ... there's an old sofa.' His voice, through the thick stone walls, comes near her then fades away. He's having a good look, obviously. 'And ... and a bed frame and ... a mattress. But it's all rotted.'

Pearl is straightening her apron when he comes out of the door again. He has to duck his head and he puts up his hand to touch the lintel as if to judge the space, or protect his head, or just for the sensation of having the cold grain of stone against his fingers, she doesn't know but, as he does, everything – what they are doing here, what he is doing here, who he is, why he came – is suddenly clear to her. She has seen someone else do that very same thing in that very same spot in the very same way, someone who looked like him. Someone who, all those years ago, looked just like he does now. She'd forgotten all about him but when she sees Jake touch the lintel like that, a shutter somewhere in her memory opens. Pearl stares at Jake as they stand together outside the bothy in a clearing in the wood and she sees, she knows, she comprehends.

'What happened to them, do you know?' he is asking.

She clears her throat. 'They left, son, they all left. When she bought the place, Mrs Draper–' She breaks off, thinking that perhaps he might not want to hear that.

'Threw them out?' he finishes.

Pearl nods.

'You don't know where they went?'

She shakes her head.

'Any of them?'

'No. Sorry.'

As they walk back over the springy, needle-covered turf towards the big house, Pearl touches his shoulder, lightly, just once.

Stella is doodling, her feet balanced on a drawer of the desk, scoring the corner of a newspaper with intricate squares and triangles. She's on late duty, which means she has to hang about in Reception until after midnight, answering the phone and dealing with anything the guests might want. She doesn't mind it. What she hates is the walk back to the caravan through the black wood, which rustles and moves around her, and how, at night, at a certain point on the path, you can hear the river in the distance, rushing through the earth.

She is pulling her jumper sleeves down over her hands when she realises with a start that someone is standing behind her. She twists round. It's the new guy. Stella stares up at him, speechless, fingers still gripping her pen. He seems as surprised to see her as she is to see him, standing there with one hand raised, his mouth half open.

Stella rallies herself. Why is she staring at him? Why is he staring at her?

'Hi,' she says, taking her feet off the desk and laying down the newspaper. 'You OK?'

'Yeah,' he says, but doesn't sound as if he means it.

He looks a bit freaked, as if he's seen a ghost, his hair standing on end, his eyes wide. In his hand, she notices, he is clutching a twenty-pound note. Stella has to resist an urge to giggle. 'Is that for me?'

'What?'

'That.' She points at the note.

'Oh.' His face relaxes. 'Well, sort of. I was wondering if I could have some change. For the phone.'

'Sure.' Stella bends over and rummages about in the desk drawer for the petty-cash box. Jake stands close by her, she notices. A little too close. She allows the chair wheel to edge sideways, to clash against his foot. He lets out a small noise of pain and steps back.

'Oh, sorry.' She hooks a strand of hair behind her ear, suppressing a smile, and, from the top of the small heap of assorted notes in the box, picks up a scribbled note in Mrs Draper's handwriting: *£20 to Jake Kildoune as pre-wage float.*

Stella frowns and reads it again. Jake Kildoune? That's his name? He's called Kildoune? She turns to look at him, still holding the bit of paper.

'Is there a problem?' he asks. 'Because I can always–'

'No, no,' she says quickly. 'No problem. I was just...' She trails away. Jake Kildoune. It really isn't any of her business. She turns back to look at the piles of change and notes. 'I was just wondering how much you needed.' Stella starts counting out twenty-pence pieces. 'I can give you one ... no, wait a minute ... two pounds in twenties and fifties, and–'

'I'm phoning long-distance,' he says.

'Oh.' She shakes her head. 'Of course, I– Right.'

Their eyes meet once as she pours the coins into his cupped hands. He is the first to look away. She points out the phone, hidden behind a dried-flower arrangement in the hallway, and she has just picked up the newspaper and started on a new pattern of interlocked squares when she hears money clunking through the phone and Jake saying: 'Caroline, it's me.'

Stella skims an article about a cabinet reshuffle. Caroline? Must be his girlfriend. She twitches the jumper sleeves down her wrists again and shivers. It's freezing in here. She starts again with her squares, colouring in every second one. She isn't listening, she really isn't. It's a private conversation and, anyway, she's reading the newspaper.

She turns it over and stares at an advert for a memory aid. Jake is telling Caroline something about an overnight train and arriving in Scotland early in the morning.

'I found it, Caroline. I found it. I'm *here*.' His voice seems to strain and waver, and the sound of it makes Stella lift her head. 'No, no,' Jake is saying quickly. 'He's gone. Long gone, by the sounds of it... Yeah... Yeah... I know...' Stella hears him take a deep, shaken breath. 'It's a hotel... No... He was in one of the outbuildings... Yeah, today, this afternoon. I got someone to show me, someone who remembers them... Yes... It was so weird, much weirder than I thought it would be...'

Stella is hunched over her doodle, horrified. Whatever this is, she really should not be hearing it. She looks about her wildly. She is hemmed in on four sides by the desk, the filing cabinet, the electric heater and a heap of files. She cannot leave without him hearing her. She knows the door will squeal on its hinges, the chair springs will twang, that she cannot step over the files without moving the heater, which will make a crashing noise like a cymbal, and he will realise just how close she is and that she's heard everything. And all the time things are knitting themselves together in her head: the relative he mentioned, the relative who once lived here, that surname of his written on the petty-cash slip, seeing from an upper window him and Pearl walking out towards the bothy in the woods, the way he is talking is not the way you talk to a girlfriend, it's the way you talk to a parent, a mother, the incredulity on his face when he read the word on her uniform in that Aviemore tea room. Stella feels opened out with sadness for him. She doesn't know what she will say when he crosses the hall after this conversation, she doesn't know what to say at all because what can you say when you've overheard–

A loud, shrill noise makes her jump, makes her drop her pen. It's the hotel phone and Mrs Draper telling her something about a consignment of doilies arriving tomorrow and is Stella sure, is Stella absolutely sure, the cupboard was cleared out and dusted today because if it isn't, come eleven a.m. she's going to have a lot of trouble on her hands, three thousand paper doilies and nowhere to put them.

Caroline sits for a moment beside the phone, one hand still resting on the receiver. She turns her neck and looks out of the window. She thinks idly that she must clear the pumpkin bed, must dead-head the roses, should really mash some fertiliser into the soil around the peas. That's the thing about gardening, there's always something to do, you're only ever just catching up with yourself.

It's almost noon, the sun level, the ground shadowless. Thousands of miles away, her son is still in yesterday. *I found it*, he'd said. He had gone searching for it, just as she had always known he would, and he had found it.

She feels as though she ought to do something to mark this moment – make a note of the date and time, perhaps, get out a photograph of her son, burst into tears. But she feels no particular urge to do any of those. The moments that affect you are only ever the ones you're not expecting. The ones you know will arrive, the ones you've been waiting for, have almost an unreal, rehearsed air about them, because you've imagined them so many times.

There are things she never told Jake: that at Kathmandu she'd turned round and gone back to Delhi. That she'd gone about the city, fatigued but hopeful, asking at every ashram for a tall Scottish man called Tom. That she'd pinned notes to three motorbikes like the one he had. That she had felt overwhelmingly that he should know, and that as long as he didn't she'd feel deceitful, a thief. That she spent four days weeping in a room before getting up the strength to leave. That after Jake was born, she'd sent letters to Kildoune, near Aviemore, Invernessshire, but nothing ever came back.

Caroline gets up, pushes her feet into her clogs, gets her gardening gloves down from a shelf. She thinks, not for the first time, about that single, singular, single-minded spermatozoon propelling itself through her, spiralling upwards. It strikes her again as unaccountable that this thing took place while she was busy doing something else – sleeping, walking about, fucking, riding on the motorbike, talking to Tom. It seems mad, perverse, that something as momentous as the beginning of her son could go unheard, unfelt. You'd think there would be some immediate outward sign, that your eyes would change colour or your skin darken or the blood race hot through your veins. You'd think you'd at least hear the moment of impact – a boom, that collision.

Caroline thinks about this as she pushes her way out of her house in Auckland, swinging open the back door, coming down the steps in her clogs.

Jake knows he should phone Mel, that he really must, but he still spends five minutes fiddling with coins and change and another ten minutes or so sitting beside the payphone in the hallway, thinking about what he's going to say, how he should get some waterproof shoes from somewhere, the taste of venison as compared to beef, the way someone has painted half of the ceiling in the hall with a slightly different shade of white from the other half, how light British money feels in the hand, Stella's eyes, the sight of the rusted bed skeleton out in the bothy, how he'd quite like to murder Mrs Draper, the feel of the reflected, radiated heat of a blowtorch, the family whose luggage he carried up earlier, how Hing Tai won't have woken up yet but his mother will be eating lunch soon, the rounded swell of bunions at the sides of Pearl's feet and how she's had to cut slits in the sides of her shoes for them.

He picks up the receiver and holds the low buzz to his ear. He feeds in coins one after another. The machine immediately regurgitates them into a too-small metal cup and Jake has to get down on his hands and knees to retrieve some of them from under the stool. He starts again, hears the ringing but doesn't manage to get the money in quickly enough. The connection dies. The machine eats and digests a fifty-pence piece anyway; Jake hears it passing like a bolus through its system.

He presses his fingertips to his forehead, takes a deep breath and tries again.

'Hello?' Andrew.

'Hi, it's Jake.'

'Jake!' Andrew pronounces his name with delight, which must be feigned because there's a pause while Jake hears him trying to think of what to say next. 'How's the ... ah ... golf?'

'Er, well, I haven't really–'

'Must be wonderful. Having a good time, are you?'

'Yes, it's–'

'How's the weather? Awful, is it? Can be dreadful. Rained the entire time I went to Scotland.'

'Yes.' Jake stares at the small grey screen on the phone where his money is being counted down. He doesn't have that much change left – the call to New Zealand made the machine very hungry indeed. A light perspiration is breaking out on his brow. 'Is–'

'Well, I'm sure you don't want to be chatting to me like this. I'll get Melanie for you. Hold on.' Andrew puts down the phone with a clunk.

'Thanks,' Jake says, to nobody.

'Jake?' He hears the pleasure in her voice and it gives him a falling sensation in his stomach.

'Hi. How are you? How are you feeling?'

'OK,' she says. 'Missing you, though.'

'Oh.' He hears himself emit a nervous laugh. 'Um, what have you been up to?' He starts scratching his head and once he starts he finds he somehow cannot stop. It's a rough, grating feeling that he likes, the rasp of fingernail against scalp.

'I'm fine. I saw the specialist yesterday and he said I'm doing really well.'

'That's great, Mel. It's wonderful. I'm so pleased.' And he is.

'How are you?' she says quickly. 'I mean, are you OK?'

'Yeah.'

'You sound a bit…'

'A bit what?'

'A bit funny.'

'No, no, I'm ... everything is ... fine.'

She drops her voice. 'Mum's been putting on the pressure.'

'The pressure?'

'You know. For us to set a date.'

He is having trouble understanding what this means, and when it does percolate through to him he has to scratch his head even harder.

'I said we could leave it for a bit, couldn't we, but she seems to think that all the good dates get booked up in advance.'

'The good dates? Are there such things?' It occurs to him when he says this that he might be going mad. 'Ha ha ha,' he says.

'Well, apparently,' she says. 'Anyway, let's not talk about this now. Are you having a lovely time? Tell me where you are and what you've seen.'

'I'm in a hotel,' he blurts.

'Whereabouts?'

'Kildoune.' There seems to be a problem with the synapse that filters internal thought from actual physical speech. Where has it gone? He needs it back.

'Kildoune?' she repeats. 'But ... but that's–'

'My name!' he says manically. 'I know!'

There is a pause in Norfolk. He knows the doubtful expression she'll have on her face. 'Is that why you went there?' she says finally.

'Yes,' he says. He sits up straighter. Maybe that will help. Blood supply from the spine to the brain. Or something.

'Oh.'

Another pause.

'Listen, I'm going to be here for a bit–'

'In the hotel?'

'Yes. I'm doing some work for them and–'

'Work? What kind of work?'

'Er, I'm painting the woodwork–'

'Painting the woodwork?' she repeats, as if he's said *making a porn movie*. 'You're a guest in a hotel and you've offered to–'

'No, no, I'm not a guest. I'm a...' He has to stop and think. What is he? At this precise moment, he has absolutely no idea. 'I'm doing some work for them,' he finishes lamely. He has a feeling he's said that sentence very recently but can't be sure.

'But, Jake–'

There is a sudden and bossy bleeping on the line and she vanishes, abruptly, blissfully, as if some telecommunication fairy decided to intervene and whisk her away from him. Jake sits, still holding the receiver to his ear, staring at the grey screen, which is flashing '00' at him.

When Stella is finally allowed into Nina's hospital room, summer has leaked away and vanished down a hole. Stella is back at school but her grandmother made her change out of her uniform into a dress, and her legs are cold.

Stella doesn't look at Nina as she is ushered in by Domenico. She doesn't look as she steps over the square lino tiles – she only walks on the black ones, sideways like a crab, but doesn't do it obviously so that her mother notices because Stella knows her mother wouldn't approve and might tell her off later. She only looks when she's right up beside the bed and her hand is touching the crackle of the sheet.

Close up, Nina is shrunken, worn away like soap. Her hair is shaved close to a colourless scalp and the bones of her face stick up under the skin. It's her eyes that Stella recognises. They're the same as they've always been, the same as hers.

'We're getting a kitten,' Stella says.

Nina doesn't reply, just stares at her as if she's never seen her before. Stella is surprised. She and Nina have campaigned for a kitten for ages and ages.

'He's stripy,' Stella adds. She looks round at her grandfather. Domenico nods at her encouragingly and pushes her closer so that her elbows are pressed up against the bed. Why is Nina looking at her like that? Stella has an urge to wriggle out from between the bed and her grandfather's hand on her shoulder and run out through the door of this room that smells funny and away down the corridor. She doesn't like it in here. She doesn't like the way her sister, or this person they tell her is her sister, is looking at her.

Stella jiggles up and down on one leg. 'We can't have him yet because he's got to be able to lap up milk on his own.'

She sees Nina taking in the coat she's wearing. She remembers that it used to be Nina's, before. She tries again. 'What shall we call him?'

'Max,' Nina says.

'OK.'

She can feel the adults around them, watching them, listening to them, as if she and Nina are on a stage. She wonders what she should say next. Everyone seems to be waiting for her. She runs through the things her mother told her: remember she can't walk, remember she can't move, she's got a virus in her brain, a virus is an illness, and don't talk about school because it might make her sad.

She looks at Nina's arms, lying alongside her. They don't seem connected to her any more and look brittle, as if they might snap like glass rods. The skin on the inside sockets of the elbows is dark with purple-black bruises.

Nina sees her looking. 'They take blood out of my arms every day,' she whispers.

'Do they?' Stella is horrified. 'How?'

'With a needle. And a syringe. And sometimes the blood comes out in a gush and won't stop afterwards but keeps on coming out, and sometimes the needle misses the vein and they have to pull it out and do it again.'

'Does it hurt?'

'Yes,' Nina says, and her eyes spark, 'and sometimes–'

'Why don't you show Nina the book you brought her?' Francesca has appeared beside them.

The book is about a family of creatures

living in Finland, which, Domenico told her, is very cold and very far away. Her uncle's been reading it to her. Stella is just disentangling it from her pocket, when Nina asks a question. 'How's Miranda?'

Miranda is Nina's friend from school. Her best friend. She has lots of yellow hair that her mother does in ringlets. Stella glances quickly at Francesca, then back at her sister. Nina's head is propped upright by two pillows. Only her eyes move. How can Stella tell her that Miranda goes about with Karen now and hasn't asked about Nina for a long time, and that no one plays skipping any more – the game Nina was best in the whole school at – and that Nina's year have been on a trip to the Botanical Gardens and that Nina's gymnastics team are winning all their medals without her?

'Fine,' Stella says.

She thinks about all the veins branching out through Nina's body and how they must be empty and dried out like the bed of a river they saw once on holiday in the Borders. She reaches out and touches Nina's fingers, just to be sure she's real, to be sure she's the same. They feel stiff and clammy, and they twitch.

'When you do that,' Nina addresses her with her eyes shut, 'I feel it in the other arm.'

Stella finds this fascinating. She lets go of

Nina's hand, darts to the end of the bed and grips Nina's right foot. 'Keep your eyes closed,' she says. 'Don't peep. Which foot am I touching?'

Nina screws up her face, thinking. 'Um ... left?'

'No!' Stella squeals.

Nina opens her eyes. They both giggle. 'Again,' she says. 'Try again.'

Behind them, the grown-ups scrape their chairs against the floor and start to talk. Nina closes her eyes against the white glare of the tube-lighting and Stella reaches out to grip Nina's right knee.

Stella steers her car up the winding driveway of the hotel with one hand. With the other, she holds a half-eaten apple and fiddles with the tape machine, which, for no apparent reason, has died.

She's going for a drive. She would never admit it to anyone but she loves driving – not in London or Edinburgh, where driving is all about edging your car between the gaps left by other people and waiting at traffic lights. Here you can bowl along roads through forests, over rivers, around crags, branches lashing at your windows, sharp clean air filling the car.

Stella stabs at the tape-machine buttons but then gives up, sighing. She gives the steering-wheel a twist at the top of the drive, pulling the car out into the road. She's wearing her pink-lensed sunglasses and the scene bobs before her, lush, weird and purple-skied.

She hasn't driven half a mile when she sees a figure walking along the verge, where trees with peeling silver trunks crowd in next to the road. From far away she knows it's him, and as the gap between them telescopes down, she is debating whether to stop or not. Why should she, she hardly knows him, what is he to her anyway, just a wave would be fine, why should she stop, there's no point, she's not going to stop, she's not, she's not, she's just going to wave.

But the tyres screech against the asphalt and the car comes to a halt, flinging her forward then back against the seat. She looks down, amazed. She appears to have her foot down hard on the brake. From the other side of the window, Jake is looking at her expectantly.

She leans forward and winds it down. 'Hi,' she says, in her best attempt at indifference, tossing her hair out of her eyes. Again, he's standing too close. 'Have you been for a walk?'

He nods. 'What are those?' he asks, grinning at her in that way he has. 'Your rose-tinted spectacles?'

Stella laughs. She's never thought of that. 'They might be.'

‘And how does the world look from behind them?’

‘Rosy.’ She makes sure she meets his eye straight on. ‘How do you think?’

There is a pause, during which he conducts a full and detailed examination of her face, as if he’s about to draw it. ‘Where are you off to, then?’ he asks.

‘Just driving.’

He looks past her into the car. ‘Got room for a passenger?’

Without waiting for an answer, he is straightening up and making his way round to the other door. Stella is horrified. She doesn’t want him in her car, doesn’t want him anywhere near her. As he passes in front of it, she is seized with an urge to lean across and slam down the lock so he can’t get in.

But it’s too late. He’s there, right inside, leaning in, his shoulders filling the space, hefting the detritus on the passenger seat – shoes, a book, several maps, bottles of water, an umbrella – to the back seat. ‘It’s so beautiful here,’ he is saying. ‘But that’s not really the right word, is it? It’s wilder than beautiful. More violent, more extreme.’

Stella sees that his hair is almost as black as hers, that the backs of his hands are speckled with paint, that he has at some point chipped one of his incisors, that the cuffs of his shirt are slightly frayed. He folds himself down to fit through the door, then stretches out his legs and feels about under the seat for the lever to push it back, saying something about how he came to a river he wasn't able to cross.

'Seatbelt,' she says, because she has to say something. He seems to bring out in her a curious pitch, the way a tuning-fork can only be heard when set against a table.

'All right, all right,' he mutters, as he reaches behind him, 'keep your hair on.'

Stella lets off the handbrake and they slide into movement. The road curves round a field filled with bent-necked cows, a huge beech tree, a sign for bed-and-breakfast. A car coming in the other direction makes Stella slow and steer more carefully.

'So,' he says.

She glances over at him, then back at the road. He is looking at her, his head on one side.

'What?' she says.

'Tell me things.'

'What things?'

'Everything. Anything.'

'What do you mean?' She jabs her glasses further up her nose.

'Er ... how long have you been here? Let's start with that.'

'Are you always this nosy?'

'Yeah,' he is shifting about now, adjusting the headrest, opening and closing the glovebox, 'probably.'

Stella winds down the window with jerky movements, about to throw out the remains of her apple, which has turned brown and floury. 'Well–'

'Wait, wait.' He lays a hand on her arm. 'I'll eat that.'

'Really?' She jolts against him as they round a bend in the road.

'Yeah. Pass it over.' He takes the apple from her fingers, careful not to let it drop into the space between them, and she hears the scrunch as he sinks his teeth into it. It seems a strangely intimate thing for him to do, to press his mouth to where hers has been. 'So,' he says, through his mouthful, 'where were we?'

'You were interrogating me,' Stella says, 'and–'

'And you were being uncooperative.'

She smiles. 'That's right.'

'So, are you going to tell me how long you've been here?'

'No.'

'Why not?'

'I don't feel like it.'

'Why?'

'I don't know. I just don't.'

'You'd make a great spy, you know that? Do you ever give anything away?'

'No.'

'To anyone?'

'Not really.'

'Wow,' he murmurs, looking out at the passing scenery. 'A woman of mystery.'

The car mounts a hill, then begins running down an incline, freewheeling. Stella feels suddenly foolish. There isn't really a reason why she can't tell him how long she's been here. 'I've been here since February,' she says meekly.

He turns to her in his seat. 'And where were you before?'

'London.'

'Working in a hotel?'

'No. I was ... I'm a radio producer.'

'Really?' He sounds surprised and has to take a moment to digest this piece of information. 'So ... if you don't mind me asking – which you probably will – what the hell are you doing here?'

Stella looks over at him, eyes narrowed. 'What do you mean?'

'Well, you're a radio producer and you're cleaning toilets for a living.' Jake shrugs amiably as he devours the apple. 'How does that work?'

'Work?'

'I mean, are you not just a bit overqualified? And why here? This isn't exactly the kind of place you end up in by accident.'

'I don't really want to talk about it,' she says, checking her rear-view mirror. 'And anyway,' she counters, 'I could say the same thing to you. You were a film director, you said to Mrs Draper, and now–'

'A film director's assistant.'

'Whatever. How come you're painting windows?'

Jake scratches his head. 'I don't really want to talk about it,' he says, with a grin.

'Fair enough.' Stella indicates and swings into a left turn. 'We're quits, then.'

She drives him down a tree-lined track, at the end of which, stretched out between them and a steep, rocky incline, is a lake. The Lochans, she calls it. It is a silent place, hidden from the road by dense forest. If you didn't know it was there, you'd never find it. The water, sheer and glassy, is almost black with peat, the ground soft and layered with pine-needles, which have been pulled into neat, uniform directions by the water, like nails drawn by a magnet.

The sky is high and blue above them as they walk along the labyrinth of mesh-covered duckboards. Small, brown-winged birds arrow up, screeching, from the heather, as they pass. He asks her questions – more general questions – and, after a bit more wrangling, he gets out of her that she grew up in Edinburgh, that she likes working in radio, likes the idea of an invisible world out there, listening, that she's never been to Hong Kong, that she once trod on a sea-urchin in the South

China Sea and had to sit in the sand for hours, tears running down her face, pulling out the spines, one by one.

He asks her what the phrase 'clearance cottage' means and the question makes her stop in her tracks ahead of him, turn round and stare at him. You really don't know what the clearances are, she says. She is wearing a blue T-shirt and as she gives him a lesson in Scottish history, he notices she keeps pulling at the neckline to knead at a point in her neck.

It fills him with a curious, dragging sympathy, seeing her press her knuckle to this sore spot in her body. It makes him want to reach out, take her hand away and put his where hers had been. He imagines her skin would be warm and taut under his touch and, as he listens to her talking about mass emigration, he finds himself wondering what kind of scent it would leave on his fingers.

When the hospital had relinquished Nina to the outside world again, their father carried her in from the car. Stella watched from the front window, saw her father hoist the blanket-swathed form into his arms and down the front path. She looked so much smaller than she used to.

Stella had been so excited about Nina coming home that she hadn't really thought about what it would be like when she did. She hadn't realised that Nina would still be ill. She'd imagined that everything would be like it used to be. But her parents tiptoed about, and instructed her to do the same. Her mother carried trays in and out of the sitting room, and Nina lay motionless on the sofa, looking out at the street.

Twice a day, Francesca lifted Nina to the floor and did the stretching exercises the physiotherapists set. These hurt Nina so much they always made her cry; and Francesca, hating them as much as Nina did, cried too, but only when Nina couldn't see. Ever since Nina got ill, their mother had wept all the time – in the bath, in the kitchen with her back to the room, in the garden, in her bedroom, on the street when she and Stella met a kind, enquiring neighbour. But never in front of Nina. Stella kept tissues in her pockets to hand out to her mother whenever she needed them.

When Stella got back from school, she would turn the pages of books for Nina, sit with her while they watched TV, tell her what she'd done in class that day, and, once, when Nina asked her to, fetched the pair of shoes Nina had before she was ill. Stella had to rummage for ages at the back of their cupboard to find them.

'Here,' she whispered, because without saying anything they both understood that this was something they needed to do in secret, something difficult to explain to the mind of an adult, 'I found them.'

Stella placed the shoes on the blanket covering Nina. They were blue leather with punctured holes in the shapes of flowers, small brass buckles and a bar across the foot in the shape of a T. Francesca bought them both new shoes every spring, so these had had enough wear to hold the contours of Nina's feet, to be scuffed on the toe, to be eroded down on the heel, for the leather to be creased and scarred.

'Turn them over,' Nina said.

Stella pushed a hand into each, feeling the empty, inverted shape of her sister's feet, and turned them upside-down. She watched Nina's face as she examined the way the soles were smooth as pebbles, worn down by walking, by running, by the constant moving over pavements, over paths, over grass.

Stella turned them back and, as she did so, a trickle of sand emptied from the inside of one on to the blanket. She and Nina looked at it – a miniature sandcastle. Stella remembered that the day before Nina got ill, Granny Gilmore had taken them to the beach at Portobello and they had run together along the shore, trailing seaweed behind them like tails and their grandmother had shouted at them to watch out for the tide or the sea will ruin those shoes of yours.

Nina looked away, stared hard at the piled fabric of the sofa.

'Shall I take them away?' Stella asked.

Nina nodded.

The virus that Stella's sister caught, a virus so rare that medical books mentioned it only in passing, ate into her brain, making lace of her synapses, leaving her paralysed and immobile for months.

Nina had to learn again how to walk, write, climb stairs, swim, catch a ball, use cutlery, sit up, ride a bike, balance, skip, climb trees, hop, dance, stand, play the piano, feed herself, raise a cup to her lips, run, push buttons through fabric, dress herself, buckle her shoes, grip a pen or a fork or a knife in her fingers, butter bread, open jars, slide a key into a lock, brush her own teeth, comb her hair. Elementary stuff, but then most people only have to learn it once.

The school took one look at her – a shaking, stumbling, ghost-faced girl – and decided they didn't want her back. They said she belonged in a place for the handicapped. In short, they wanted her to be someone else's problem. Francesca and Archie, uncharacteristically, argued about this with the education authority, the council, the school, the obstinate headmaster, their MP. At the start of the new school year, they maintained, their daughter would be well enough and able enough for her old primary school: they would make sure of it. They were not going to shut her away in an institution and forget about her. At this point, Francesca stopped crying. Just like that. And Stella was determined that nothing should ever make her cry again.

When the school were finally forced to re-enrol Nina, they put her back a year, in a class of children almost two years younger than her. This was Stella's class.

Everyone is wearing a new jumper, has a new pencil case or a new pen. They're going to start writing in ink this year. Stella can see the sharp, boxy creases in the boys' shop-fresh shirts, the reflection of the high windows in the polished, scratchless toes of her shoes. A few people look different after the long holiday – Lydia's skin is brown, her hair yellow (she was going to Florida on holiday, Stella remembers her telling them all last year) and Anthony Cusk is suddenly taller.

Stella glances across at her friend Rebecca. Rebecca is the girl Stella has sat next to since Primary One – her best friend. Stella hasn't seen her all summer. Rebecca is now sharing a desk with Felicity and the two of them are bent over something together. Stella lengthens her back, straining to see. A book? A comic? She can't make it out.

She can feel Nina next to her. Nina has her hands planted in her lap. Stella knows that this is so they won't shake. Nina is wearing the green gingham dress Stella wore last year and staring down at the surface of the desk, scarred with compass marks and ink spillages. Her hair has grown back, but in uneven tufts that make their mother bite her lip as she tries to brush it.

Miss Saunders claps her hands together at the front of the class. 'Now,' she cries, 'everyone!' She smiles at them in an unfocused way, looking over their heads at the back wall. 'We're going to be writing about What We Did in Our Summer Holidays this morning. But first I want you all to give a big welcome to Nina Gilmore.'

The sound of her name makes Nina jump, Stella notices. Her right leg starts to shake involuntarily and Stella sees her grip it with her hand, trying to still it.

'Nina has been very ill, in hospital, with brain damage,' Miss Saunders announces from the front, 'and has been off school for a whole year. So we're all very pleased to have her back and we'll all be giving her any help she needs, won't we?'

All faces swivel to look at them. Under the

desk, Stella puts her hand over Nina's, feels the judder of unbiddable muscle and nerve, and presses down with all her might. The leg stops. Nina is trying not to cry, Stella sees, glaring down, her mouth pressed together. She grips her fingers. Don't cry, she wills, sending the message down her arm and into Nina's, please don't.

'Now,' Miss Saunders swings round to the blackboards, 'take out your jotters and on a new page, in nice, neat handwriting, write–'

Stella is distracted by Anthony Cusk turning round and staring at her. Or is it at Nina? She can't be sure. Her eyes flick back to Miss Saunders, trying to rejoin whatever it is she is telling them to do, but he is mouthing something now, his lips opening over his yellowish teeth. What is he saying? Stella tries not to look at him but she can't help it. He is mouthing something, pointing at Nina, then pointing at his temple. Stella recognises the word 'brain'.

She looks away, looks straight ahead of her. Has Nina seen? She can't be sure. Her sister is picking up her pen and starting to form letters in her uneven, jagged handwriting. Stella makes a grab for her own pen but she can't not slip one more glance at Anthony. Why is he saying that? He is making horrible faces now, twisting his features into grotesque, warped expressions, puffing out his bottom lip with his tongue.

Miss Saunders is saying something about paragraphs and nice, clear sentences, and Stella is anxious because she's missed the whole explanation and doesn't know what it is she's supposed to be doing and hasn't had Miss Saunders as a teacher long enough to know if she'll get cross if Stella asks her to say it again and why is Anthony Cusk mouthing horrible things about her sister?

Something comes whizzing through the air and strikes Stella sharply on the cheek, making her jump and gasp. It falls to the floor. A balled-up piece of paper, torn from a jotter. The fact that Stella jumped has made Nina jump and her writing arm is shaking, her pen rattling against the desk, a repetitive, persistent noise in the concentrated quiet of the classroom.

Nina drops her pen and grips her arm with her other hand. People are turning round to look at them, and Stella sees Felicity glance at her, then turn away to whisper something in Rebecca's ear and a titter is passing through the room like a breeze.

'Quiet!' shrills Miss Saunders. 'All of you!' She glares round the class. Then she says, in a different, patient voice: 'Nina, do you need anything?'

At break-time, Nina walks next to her, her head bent. She doesn't see the girls from her old class staring at her across the playground, she doesn't see people pointing at her, urging others to look, she doesn't see people laughing behind their hands, she doesn't see Miranda turn quickly away. Stella sees it all, though. Nina walks like someone with their ankles tied together – uneven, lurching, tentative.

Behind the shelter, Stella's friends are playing Grandmother's Footsteps, Rebecca with her face to the green-slimed stone wall, the others in various stages behind her, frozen in position. Stella stops at the edge of their game, bending to yank at her knee-socks.

'OK,' Rebecca is saying, 'you take four scissor jumps!'

Felicity is on her second when she stops, legs splayed like blades. 'Do you want to play?' she calls to Stella.

Stella glances at her sister then back at her classmates who, she sees, are all regarding her with new, guarded expressions. 'Yes,' she says, clearing her throat. 'Yes, please.'

Felicity abandons her marker and crosses the yard towards them, her hands on her hips. Stella watches her come, watches the bracelet on her wrist as it mirrors a bright sliver of sun, the way her eyes flutter half closed when they meet Stella's, the clean, shining bounce of her hair. She comes to a stop in front of them and looks from one to the other, thinking, considering. Then she opens her thin mouth, hardly at all but just enough to say, 'Well, you can play, but she can't.' And she points at Nina, her finger jabbing the air between them.

Fury flares up in Stella. 'If she's not playing then I'm not playing.'

'Fine.' Felicity flounces round, back to the game. 'See if we care.'

Stella turns to look at Rebecca. But Felicity is linking her arm through Rebecca's and the two of them are facing Stella. Even though Rebecca won't look up but stares down at the ground, her cheeks a scorching red, it is enough.

Stella takes Nina's hand. 'We didn't want to play anyway,' she mutters. 'Come on, Neen.' She turns, pulling her sister after her.

When Jake comes down to the hotel, dinner has been served and the guests are all on their coffee, the girl doing the washing-up tells him.

The monosyllabic chef bangs a plate of risotto in front of him and the girl finds him a fork. For a few minutes there is peace, as the three of them eat. The oven ticks as it cools, the dishwasher swish-swashes and rumbles, and Jake eats quickly. All this fresh air makes him starving. He is slightly dismayed to see no sign of Stella anywhere. He thinks about starting up a conversation, then decides against it. The chef scares him.

‘God,’ the girl exclaims, glancing at her watch, ‘is she still on the phone?’

The chef shrugs and makes an unintelligible noise. He arranges another plate of food, Jake notices, with more care this time.

‘She must be,’ the girl answers her own question.

‘Who?’ Jake asks.

‘Take this through, would you?’ She hands Jake the plate and indicates the door to Reception. ‘She’ll be starving to death out there. Don’t let Mrs D see you.’

Jake pushes the door and it opens, magically it seems to him, on Stella, sitting at a desk, saying ‘Mmm ... mmm’, into the phone. Her face lights up when she sees him – or perhaps it’s just the food. She motions for him to put the plate out of sight behind a vase. Jake hands her the fork. He wonders if he should go back to the kitchen but something makes him want to stay.

‘Maybe I could suggest...’ she begins, but the voice at the other end of the line rises, querulous, insistent. ‘I see,’ Stella says, rolling her eyes at Jake. ‘I see. Well, perhaps the answer would be to–’

Again she is interrupted. She pushes a forkful of risotto into her mouth and chews. She mimes someone chatting with her hand, then has to swallow hastily. ‘As I said, there are no twin rooms available for that particular weekend. I do appreciate your problem. But perhaps–'

The man has more to say about his problem. Jake shifts from foot to foot, glances round the desk, at the stacks of brochures, price lists, the vase of outsized daisies, the way Stella's fingers are drumming on the cover of a large diary.

'Well, as long as your wife doesn't mind sleeping on a camp bed, then...' She shakes her head as the voice twitters on and on. 'If a double bed really is out of the question, then maybe I could suggest a–'

Divorce? Jake scribbles on a piece of paper and holds it up. Stella has to turn away and hold her hand over her mouth.

'OK. Fine.' The conversation finally seems to be winding up. 'No problem at all. Stella,' she says, 'my name's Stella. Thank you. Yes. Thanks so much. Goodbye, yes, 'bye.'

She slams down the phone and buries her face in her hands. 'Oh, God,' she groans, 'I don't want him here! He's evil! Can you imagine being married to him? Do you think the wife was in the background, listening to him telling a complete stranger that he could not, under any circumstances, sleep in the same bed as his wife, even for one night?'

'Maybe she was busy plotting her escape,' Jake says. 'Tying the bedsheets together. Or lacing his food with arsenic.'

'Let's hope.' Stella tucks into her risotto,

ravenously. 'I'm starving. I thought I was going to expire from low blood sugar. Imagine if I'd died. The last thing I would have heard was his voice.'

'Asking you for a camp bed for his wife.'

Stella giggles. 'Marriage,' she says, and shudders.

Jake looks down, passing a hand through his hair. She has kicked off her shoes, he sees, her feet bare, her toenails painted the red of newly oxygenated blood. He imagines her doing it, crouched over in that caravan of hers, loading a brush with caramelising, liquid lacquer and daubing it on in careful, straight strokes.

She is eyeing him, her face puzzled, slightly suspicious. Has she seen him staring at her feet? Possibly.

'I can tell a lot about you from your feet,' he says quickly, so that she doesn't think he's a perverted foot-fetishist.

'Really?'

'You see this?' Jake crouches in front of her and points at her second toe. 'My mother's reflexologist boyfriend told me that–'

'Wait a minute,' she interrupts. 'Your mother has a reflexologist for a boyfriend?'

'Had.' Jake grins. 'Among others.'

'Oh.' He can see her making some mental adjustment about him or about his mother or something.

'Anyway,' he continues, still in a kneeling

position, 'I can reveal to you that you have Roman ancestors.'

She laughs and he feels the movement of it on his face. He tries to stop himself from thinking that she is within arm's reach. If he wanted to, or dared to, he could raise himself up and kiss her, in one single, swift movement.

What was he saying? Jake tries to focus his mind. 'At some point...' he launches off again, uncertainly '...a relative of yours consorted with the enemy and–'

He breaks off because she is still laughing, more hysterically than is strictly necessary. 'What's so funny?'

'I have Roman ancestors? Well, thanks for letting me know.'

'You knew already?' he says, a bit crestfallen.

'Er, yeah.' She finishes her final mouthful and puts down her fork. 'My mother's name was Iannelli.'

'Ah.'

'Her parents emigrated here in the 1930s. She's a fully paid-up member of the Hyphenated People. And so am I.'

'The Hyphenated People?' Jake repeats, sitting back on his haunches.

'My mother's phrase. You know, Scottish-Italian. Anglo-Irish. British-Chinese or … or British-Asian or … whatever it is you are.'

'The Hyphenated People.' Jake tries it out.

'I like that.'

There is a pause. They stare at each other.

'So, tell me about my Roman feet, then,' she says abruptly.

'Well, Tang told me–'

'Tang?'

'The ex-boyfriend. One of.' As he says this, Jake is wondering how she might react if he touched her. Could he do it?

'He told me…' he begins, and then he does it. He sees his right hand reach out and curve around Stella's ankle, where veins pulse near to almost translucent skin. He sees a look of doubt, of panic almost, pass over her face and he's certain she's going to pull away. But she doesn't. She allows him to lift her foot to his knee. He feels the bones of it adjust and curve around his kneecap. Her skin is surprisingly warm under his hand.

'Tang told me,' he says again, and he's aware that his voice sounds slightly different, slightly lower, 'that having second and third toes as long or longer than your big toe is a typically Roman trait.' Jake touches each toe, to demonstrate, feeling the hard surface of that scarlet varnish. 'And those dastardly centurions went about spreading their seed all over the world. Giving lots of people defective feet.'

'Defective?' She pounces on the word.

'Yeah. I'm afraid so. Having extra-long second toes makes you roll sideways on the balls of your feet, damaging, in the long term, the tendons and nerves.'

Stella is quiet for a moment. All he can think is that he has her ankle wedged between both of his palms.

'That's interesting,' she says, her head on one side. 'But obviously bollocks.'

Jake feigns outrage. 'How can you say that?'

'You're trying to tell me that a race of people who conquered a huge empire and had armies marching all over it on foot had congenital foot disorders?' She withdraws her foot and stands up, lifting her plate. 'It's bollocks,' she says again. 'And anyway,' she says, as she passes through into the kitchen, 'there's nothing wrong with my feet.'

Stella and Nina stand in the big assembly hall. Every morning the entire school comes in here and sits in cross-legged rows to sing hymns and watch the children in trouble being dragged to the front. But now it's empty – just their class waits in a snaking line, dressed in shorts and plimsolls, and Miss Saunders, in starch-white plimsolls herself, under her long, flowered skirt, is busy arranging a long line of rubber mats to lead them, one by one, to the gym-horse.

Stella likes the gym-horse. It's solid, packed with wiry hair, covered in leather worn smooth in patches. When you leap over it, just your hands come into contact with it, your feet vanish and, just for a split second, as you clear it and reach the other side, you can see what it would be like to be able to fly. Stella would like to put her arms round it and hug it.

Behind her comes the sound of stifled, snorting giggling. Stella strains her ears but doesn't turn round. She hears someone – Felicity? Emma? – whisper something about butterflies. Stella's mother sewed a patch in the shape of a butterfly on to her shorts after Stella climbed some railings she shouldn't have. Her mother brought the patch back from one of her days out shopping with Evie, and Stella loved it the moment she saw it – its wings are purple and orange and it has deep blue antennae. And now they are all laughing at it.

Stella doesn't care. She lifts her chin to show them she doesn't care. There is the sound of shuffling and more giggling behind her and there is a cold, clammy hand in contact with her arm and she is turning round to see that Anthony Cusk is pressing the flat of his hand to her skin.

Anthony turns round to the people behind him, brandishing his palm at them. 'Gilmore germs!' he shouts. They duck and shriek and dart away from his reach. They are playing their favourite game, a game that Anthony always instigates: a kind of tag with the supposed infection you got from touching either her or Nina.

Stella hates Anthony Cusk more than anything else in the universe. Her grandmother says that hate is a very strong word and that it's wrong to hate people, but Stella hates Anthony. She imagines her hate like a ball of black tar, lodged in her chest. Last week she went to the toilet during break and when she'd come back to the yard she'd found a circle of children around Nina, who was sprawled on the ground. Anthony Cusk had been pushing her back to the ground every time she tried to get up, with just his finger. It didn't take much to overbalance Nina – sometimes Stella thought the wind might blow her down. Stella had burst into the circle and smashed her hand into Anthony Cusk's face and it had hurt her knuckle and Anthony's nose bloomed roses that dripped petals to the floor, and Stella had been in trouble and had to go and sit outside the headmaster's office all afternoon.

'Nina, dear,' Miss Saunders is calling from her position beside the horse, 'you should probably sit this out.'

Stella watches her sister shuffle to the side of the room, almost unable to bear her being that far away from her, and Stella is alone in the line with laughing enemies on both sides.

'I'm not standing next to her,' someone says. Stella doesn't see who because she's staring down at the interlapped parquet that screeches if you rub your plimsoll along it. People are peeling away from the line around her, running round to the back, just so as not to stand near her, and suddenly she is stranded at the front of the queue.

'Come on, Stella,' Miss Saunders calls, 'you first. Stop messing about, you lot,' she says to the children behind her, who are jostling and fighting and laughing.

Stella sees the long runway of mats, laid end to end, stretching to the hulking mass of the horse. She sees Miss Saunders with her arms held out, ready to help her over. She feels the back of the room, the crowd of their tormentors, fall away from her as she runs. Her legs move under her and she can hear the tugging crinkle of her clothes.

As the orange-brown flanks of the horse loom closer, something falters in her stomach. But she makes herself do it. She can't stop in her tracks, can't fail, not with those people behind her. She pushes herself up, springs forward, but as soon as her palms are pressed against the worn leather, she knows something is wrong. The floor wheels up too soon, too acutely and she feels herself dropping, feels the room twist around her and she is wondering if this is what it's like to be Nina when her forehead and shoulder hit the stinking rubber of the mat.

Miss Saunders is scolding her, saying she's done this lots of times and that she must get straight up and do it again, and her head is throbbing, pulsing with pain. She can hear far-off gales of laughter and Miss Saunders shouting at them to be quiet. Stella doesn't think she can do it again, doesn't want to do it again. She wants more than anything to be curled up somewhere dark and still, somewhere far away from here, because she just feels so tired, so unbelievably tired. She has to press her hands together to distract herself, stop herself crying and maybe Miss Saunders sees this because the next moment she is pulling her up by her arm and telling her to go and sit with Nina and, as Stella walks across the acres and acres of squeaking parquet, she touches the butterfly that Evie and Francesca chose for her, just once.

Jake doesn't see Stella for days. She's always out or having a day off or elsewhere in the hotel, doing the rooms or cleaning or seeing to difficult guests. Occasionally, Jake hears her tread, catches a few snatched syllables of her voice, sees her shape through an upper window, finds a piece of paper scored with her handwriting – a shopping list, a drinks order – but nothing more. If he goes in pursuit of her, he finds only empty corridors, deserted rooms, but with doors swinging shut, curtains moving in the breeze, as if she's always just out of reach.

It makes him impatient, he notices. He catches himself thinking about the red scarf she uses to tie her hair back, how she presses her teeth into her bottom lip when she's concentrating and the sound her shoes make when she walks. A girl from Aviemore does several evening shifts in a row and she slaps Jake's dinner on to a plate with a brusque swivel of her wrist.

He goes to the bothy most days. He walks the rooms, touching the door handles, the rusted window catches, the stone mantelpieces, looks up at the sky through the collapsed roof, gazes out of the windows. If he looks hard enough, he reckons, he should be able to memorise the view from each window. He wants to imprint himself with this place, with this dilapidated house, so he can remember it, keep a reserve of it, for a time when he's no longer here.

Jake is aware that coming here and being here aren't enough. Since arriving, he's realised that he carries within himself a lack, a vacuum, a vacancy. That he always has carried it, and always will. But if he feels it rising inside him, expanding like gas, he has to tell himself what he's gained by coming to Kildoune. Jake cannot get over the fact that he is living among people who have spoken to Tom, interacted with him, had contact with him, known him, just by being here, Jake is at only one degree, one remove from his father. Whenever he feels that desolation, that lack threatening to engulf him, he has to remind himself of this.

The weather splits and cracks open, and the rain comes down. It is soft, feathering wet, not like the downpours in Hong Kong. This rain is almost invisible and seems to drift sideways. Jake has to leave painting Kildoune's windows for fairer weather. He digs the vegetable garden, taking the iron prongs of the fork to the dense clods of soil, ripping out the snaking, gripping weeds by their roots, driving in stakes for the peas to hook themselves round as they grow.

He gets filthy, his palms mapped out in dirt, his boots heavy with mud. But he likes the work, enjoys the heated sweat it brings, learns how a landscape that appears empty is, when you look from the corner of your eye, teeming – rabbits, foxes, blackbirds, sheep, pheasant. The ground and the forest rustle and shiver with life. Sometimes Jake puts down his fork and looks round, thinking something or someone is there, but finds nothing, just bracken waving in the wind.

Stella pushes the head of the vacuum-cleaner

around her in big, wide arches. She hums as she works and the virulent pattern of the hall carpet bristles and stands to attention under the suction. Two guests pass; the wife nods at her. She ate mushrooms and toast for breakfast, Stella thinks, drank two kirs last night, wears nylon slips and beside the bed has a book about how to time ovulation.

Suddenly, and without warning, the vacuum-cleaner cuts out, the dual pitch of its engine winding down into silence. Stella turns and looks at it, squat and round on the carpet, its neck held in her hands. She gives it an experimental kick – her usual method with wayward machinery – but nothing happens. She reaches down and shakes it. Still nothing.

Sighing and cursing under her breath, Stella follows the extension lead to where she's plugged it in. Maybe the plug's come loose from the socket. She's just about to turn in to the lounge when the vacuum starts up again, behind her.

Stella turns round and goes back. She has picked up the neck and has pushed it away from her once across the carpet, when it dies on her again. She throws it down, cross. 'What is the matter with you?' she demands, and stomps again towards the socket in the lounge. 'Stupid, useless thing,' she mutters.

Again, just as she reaches the door, it quivers into life. This time Stella stands motionless, her head cocked to one side. The sound of stifled laughter is coming from somewhere. She pushes at the door with her hand and moves into the room.

Jake is crouched by the socket and when he sees her says, 'Do you often talk to household appliances?'

She looks at him, amazed, her hands on her hips.

'Was that you doing that?' she asks. She hasn't seen him for days. She has, she half admits to herself now, been avoiding him.

'You should see the look on your face.' He collapses into laughter.

Infuriated, Stella seizes a cushion from a sofa. 'You bastard,' she says, laughing herself now. 'You horrible, horrible man.'

She makes for him, across the room, the cushion held before her. She thinks of the satisfaction of those stuffed, packed feathers glancing off his shoulders, his head. But as she reaches him, he grabs at the cushion and wrenches it effortlessly from her grasp. She is left weaponless, unarmed, her hands empty. His shirt is half unbuttoned, she suddenly notices, loose, and he smells of the outside, of the rain earlier, wet leaves, the soil he's been digging, and there is something about the way he is looking at her that gives her the sensation he can see right into her.

Stella turns on her heel and crosses the room.

Pearl is in the kitchen, top-and-tailing gooseberries, when Stella bursts in.

'All right, hen?' Pearl says.

Stella makes a small noise but doesn't stop, running through the kitchen and out of the opposite door. Pearl hears her footsteps crunching away through the courtyard.

A micro-second later, the boy Jake appears. 'Did you see Stella?'

'When?'

'Just now.' Jake dashes to the window and peers out. 'Did she come through here? Which way did she go?'

Pearl examines him. He looks peculiar, a bit panicked, and has a cushion clutched in one hand. She points in the opposite direction to the one in which Stella had gone.

'Thanks,' Jake says, and vanishes.

Pearl brushes the minuscule sharp hairs from her fingers and tips the fruit into a dish. 'Whatever next?' she says to the air, as she reaches for the ball of pastry.

But, dusting the rolling-pin with flour, she shakes her head. She knows exactly what comes next.

Jake is mowing the grass according to Mrs Draper's instructions – in even, level, contrary-motion strips – when the postvan crunches on the gravel. The postman doesn't get out, just hurls the bundle, held together by elastic bands, into the open doorway of the hotel. 'Post,' he yells at Jake, turning his van in an arc and disappearing off down the drive.

Jake switches off the lawnmower, the abrupt stop of the noise creating a momentary stasis. He walks over to the bundle, bends to pick it up and, stretching off the elastic bands, shuffles through it. Some catering magazines, mail-order uniform firms, one or two booking letters, a few for Mrs Draper, a couple of letters for Stella, redirected from an address in London, and a postcard. For Stella. Jake doesn't mean to read it but it's in huge, red capital letters: CALL ME OR DIE, Jake frowns. No name. No return address.

Leaving the rest of the post on the front desk, Jake sprints up the stairs two at a time. The landing is quiet. Sunlight lies in oblong patches on the carpet. He strains his ears, turning his head one way then the other. 'Stella?' he calls.

Nothing.

He walks towards the north turret. The rooms are all shut and silent. The corridor carpet moves under his feet. The severed heads of deer stare down at him from the walls; a stiffened, balding grouse stands, poised for flight, wired to a branch. Call me or die. Who on earth would send such a thing?

Where the corridor splits, turning off towards the laundry cupboard and more rooms or the steep staircase to the north turret, Jake stops. 'Stella?' he calls again.

Still nothing. He listens out for anything – footfalls, the whine of a vacuum-cleaner, the crack of bedsheets. Nothing. He is turning to go back the other way when he hears a noise, a shifting of the building, a creaking of a floorboard or a wainscot, nothing more. He turns back.

'Stella?' he calls. 'Is that you?' He climbs the last few steps towards the thick oak door and shoves at it with his shoulder.

The room is filled with a blazing white light, all the furniture and carpets and objects leached of colour and dimension, Jake instinctively brings a hand up to shade his eyes. He's never been in this room before. All the windows are open, the curtains writhing into the room. The sheets and counterpane and pillows have been ripped from the bed and thrown to the floor. Dead flowers are splayed, up-ended, in the bin. A fox crouches, glaring, in a glass box. Stella stands in the encircling curve of the turret, her back to him, looking out to the glen.

'Stella,' he says again.

She turns and blinks, as if surprised to see him. 'Hi, Jake,' she says. She touches the stone wall with one hand; the other is pressed to her neck.

They stare at each other for a moment across the bright, wrecked room. Jake can't think what it was he came here for. His mind is filled with the idea that she is there, in front of him, six paces from him. All he would have to do to reach her is step through the churned-up sheets and pillows and then he'd be standing next to her.

A cloud must be passing over the sun because the brightness of the room fades suddenly, acquiring dimension, depth. Objects around them rise up like images into photographic paper. Jake clears his throat. 'I brought up your post.' He is stepping through the mess of sheets and towels on the floor but when he nears her she has her hand out. He puts the letters into it and without them his fingers feel empty and stiff.

'Thanks,' she is saying and shuffles through them, Jake watches her face as she comes to the postcard. CALL ME OR DIE. Her eyes flick over the red ink, scored into the cream-white card, then to the address, written in a rounded disjointed hand, then back to the capital letters. She moves it to the back and looks instead at one of the forwarded letters. The second makes her grimace. 'Oh, God,' she says.

'What?'

She sighs as she lifts the envelope flap. 'It's

just this–' She breaks off, scanning the closely spaced words on the page. She laughs, briefly, then moves to the bed and sits down. 'Oh, for God's sake,' she mutters, reading on.

'What is it?' Jake lowers himself next to her and lies back, his hands clasped behind his head. 'Bad news?'

'Not really. It's from this guy...'

'Your boyfriend?' Jake says this quick as a flash.

'No, no, this guy I used to work for.'

'Ah.' Jake stares at the four-poster canopy above him and tries not to smile.

'He wants to know if I'm coming back.' Stella gives a short, impatient sigh and shoves the pages back into their envelope. 'Can't be arsed to read it now.' She tosses the scrumpled envelope on to the bed between them and lies back. Jake grins to himself. The mattress bounces slightly as she comes to rest beside him.

'I'm really tired today,' she murmurs.

He glances down at the letters, then back at her. Her eyes are closed, her chin tilted towards the ceiling. He's never realised before how long her eyelashes are. He can see the rise and fall of her ribcage as she breathes, and the swell of her breasts beneath her uniform. He sees how close they are, lying together on this huge four-poster bed. He feels the magnitude of the house, the glen, the country around them. If he were to stretch out his arm, he could touch her brow, her cheek, her shoulder. It would be so easy, so natural. He imagines the heat of her mouth under his, the feel of those breasts crushed against him.

He reaches up and rubs his face instead. This is terrible. He wants to kiss her so badly. How would she react? Would it really be a good idea, under the circumstances?

Jake decides, in a split second, that he doesn't care. He doesn't care about the circumstances. He doesn't care whether it's a good idea. He doesn't care about anything at all. He just has this overwhelming, towering feeling that he should, he must, he has to kiss her right now, and that if he doesn't he might never get the chance again. He rests his hand on the bed between them to brace himself as he leans over.

Stella pulls herself upright, into a sitting position. She is humming, pushing her hair behind her ear. 'If I lie here any longer,' she is saying, 'I'm going to fall asleep.' She kicks her legs against the end of the bed, picking up her letters.

No, Jake wants to shout, no, come back. He rolls over on to his stomach, wanting to punch the bed, the pillows, anything. In the effort of not doing so, he accidentally emits a small moan.

Her head snaps round and she looks at

him, a slight frown on her face. He has to say something, he has to. Otherwise she's going to think he's a weirdo. Quick. Say something. Anything. Anything at all. Something normal, Jake racks his brain for things to say but it only comes up with things like, kiss me, come here, I want you. For God's sake. Think, man, think.

'Who was the card from?' It comes out in a garbled rush, a burst of inspiration.

Luckily she has understood. She gives a short laugh. 'You saw it, then?'

'Sorry, I didn't mean to, I–'

'It's OK. It's kind of hard to miss.'

'Who's it from?' Jake asks again.

'My sister.'

'I didn't know you had a sister,' Jake says, mildly outraged by the omission of this information.

'Well.' She shrugs, unapologetic. 'I do.'

She gets up and starts unfolding the new sheets, her back to him. Jake raises his head to look at her. What did he do? He's got the distinct feeling that he's said something wrong. Stella has done that thing she does sometimes, and closed herself up like a fan.

'What's she like?'

She shrugs again, still facing away from him.

'Is she older or younger?'

'Older.'

'How much?'

‘Two years.’

‘What’s she like?’

‘I don’t know.’ She shakes out a sheet, which cracks against the air like a whip. ‘She’s ... like herself. Any further questions? Or have you finished now?’

Jake gets up and wrestles the soft, swollen bulk of a pillow into a new case, stiff with washing. ‘So ... er ... how come she’s sending you death threats?’

Stella looks at him, the bed between them. ‘It’s a long story,’ she says, and bends over to pick up the box of cleaning things, ‘a very long story.’ And she heads for the bathroom.

A rap on the door made Stella raise her head from the pillow. She tightened her arm round Sam’s shoulder as she eased herself up, so as not to push him off the narrow, unyielding university-issue mattress. He was asleep, his face buried in her shoulder, his leg thrown across her ankles, pinning them to the bed.

‘Who is it?’ she called.

Suddenly, unbelievably, her sister was in the room, right there, standing beside the rust-stained washbasin, the lower half of her caught in a slanting beam of light, wearing a coat that had been Evie’s. The lavender suede, Evie called it.

Stella stared at her, astonished. It seemed so unaccountable, so strange to see Nina here, in this context, in her London room that it took a moment for her brain to catch up, for her to convince herself that she wasn't imagining things. Nina here? It just didn't fit.

'Hi,' Nina said, and she looked round the box of a room, over the desk, the floor littered with clothes, the posters on the walls, the books lined up against the wall, toppled like dominoes, and down the length of Sam's naked, sleeping body, entwined with Stella's.

Stella watched, paralysed, as Nina took in the life Stella had made, away from her. 'What are you doing here?' she managed.

'I've left art college.'

'Left?' Stella struggled upright, easing her arm out from underneath Sam, who was stirring now and turning over.

'Dropped out.' Nina pointed at the body wedged into the bed. 'Who's he?'

'He's ... er...'

Sam chose this moment to come fully to life. Realising someone was in the room with them, he thrashed around – an impossible thing to do in a single bed. He slid away from her, alarm filling his newly awakened eyes. Stella made a grab for him but she was too slow, and he fell to the floor with a thud.

'Fuck,' he said. 'Ow.' Then he looked up at Nina. 'Oh.'

‘Hello,’ she said, making no attempt to hide that she was having a good look at his naked form. ‘I’m Nina. Stella’s sister.’

She was even offering him her hand, for heaven’s sake, when Stella leapt out of bed, dragging the sheet from the mattress and dropping it over him. ‘Nina meet Sam, Sam meet Nina,’ she gabbled, as she collected what clothes she could find on the floor and yanked them on. As Sam staggered upright, Nina sat down in the chair beside the desk.

‘It’s very nice to meet you,’ Nina said. ‘Stella didn’t tell me she was...’ Nina picked a hair off her coat ‘...seeing anyone.’

‘Really?’ Sam shot Stella a surprised look.

‘I...’ Stella began, ‘I hadn’t ... had the chance... I...’ She ground to a halt, stared at the ground and, seeing a used condom reclining, slug-like, beside a book, kicked it under the bed.

‘She’s so secretive,’ Nina said. ‘Don’t you find, Sam?’

He was standing in the middle of the room, draped in a sheet like a Roman statue, his face unsure. Stella wanted one of them to leave. At that precise moment, she would have given anything for that. But him or her? She didn’t know. All she knew was that both in the room together made her light-headed, dizzy, as if there wasn’t enough oxygen in there for all three of them.

‘Let’s go and have breakfast,’ she said.

They walked down the road, an awkward threesome. Sam, as usual, took her hand and Stella saw Nina looking sideways at this, and it made her feel uncomfortable because the only person she ever held hands with was Nina and here she was, walking along beside her, but holding hands with someone else. Stella, under the guise of scratching her nose, extracted her fingers from Sam's. Which made her feel so guilty she couldn't look him in the eye.

When they set out she was between them, but she found this position too over-significant, too much. So as they passed the bus-stop, she skipped round to be next to Nina. But this made her see how, after almost eighteen years of walking along together, she and Nina were in perfect, rhythmic step, whereas Sam was hopelessly out of kilter, his feet hitting the pavement at irregular intervals between their precise, metronome strides. Which was bizarre because she could have sworn that when she and Sam walked together normally, they were in exact synchrony. How could that be?

The café was run by a Greek family, and cheap. When they arrived, there were several people Stella knew at a table and more chairs were brought, then another smaller table, so they could all eat together. Nina sat between two students from Stella's eighteenth-century seminar group. Two boys, Graham and Neil. Nina didn't order any food for herself but, as she regaled them with a story about a life-drawing class, she reached over, in turn, to take chips from their plates.

'...and he had the smallest, and I mean the smallest, cock you have ever seen...' she was saying, as Stella watched her pierce the perfect yellow eye of Neil's fried egg, yolk drooling out over the plate into the nest of chips. 'It was like this.' She held up the chip. 'No, wait,' she bit off the end, 'it was like this.'

They were bowled over by her, Stella could see, the two of them gazing at her as if they'd never seen such an exotic, wonderful creature. Stella saw the way she played them off against each other, taking food first from Graham's plate until he felt secure, assured, then turning to Neil and, after just the right amount of time, turning back.

'Hey, Stel,' Nina leant over the table and addressed her in Italian, 'you don't have that kind of problem with him, do you?' She jabbed the truncated chip in Sam's direction.

'What did she say?' Sam said, anxious, laying his hand on Stella's thigh.

'Nothing,' Stella muttered. 'Doesn't matter.'

'So you speak Italian?' Graham was saying, keen to get Nina's attention back.

'Yeah.' She looked at him, puzzled, then glanced over at Stella. 'Didn't she tell you?'

She looked round them all. ‘We speak Italian at home.’

‘I didn’t know that,’ Graham said, looking from her to Stella as if they were interesting specimens. ‘Did you, Sam?’

Sam had both his hands clutched around his empty mug. ‘No,’ he said. ‘No, I didn’t.’

Stella pushed back her chair with a scrape and went to the counter. She stared at the rows and rows of cans, the boxes of sauces in bright, full sachets, the heap of wooden forks, the stripes on the apron of the Greek woman. She would buy ... something. Another cup of tea. Or a glass of water. Or some chocolate? She didn’t know what she wanted. All she really wanted was to slip through the door of the café, start running and not look back. This collision of her worlds made her feel insubstantial, weakened, unsure of who she was supposed to be, how she was meant to behave. She had the sensation, when she got close to Nina, that her sister exuded a force like gravity, pulling her back to Edinburgh, to her parents’ flat, to everything she thought she’d left behind.

Suddenly Sam was there beside her, his hand in the small of her back. ‘Are you OK?’

His face was flushed, unsure, when she turned to face him. ‘Yeah. I’m fine.’

‘Your sister...’ he began.

‘What?’

‘She’s really...’ he looked over at the table

'...really weird ... and mad.'

Stella closed her eyes and had a vision of herself hurtling down towards earth, like a skydiver, and laid out in front of her were two fields, in one of which was Sam, his head tilted back to watch her descent. In the other was Nina. Whose field would she choose to guide herself towards? There was no choice to make, of course. It would always be Nina.

'Don't say that.' Stella pulled away from him. 'Ever.'

Jake grips the pitchfork, hooks the chair through the rotted netting of its seat and heaves it to the top of the bonfire. The fire spits out a firmament of sparks, then claims the chair rapidly, flames curling round its structure.

He's clearing out the smallest barn. Mrs Draper has been down here all morning, a mac over her clothes, a handkerchief over her nose, directing him as he disentangled ancient Lloyd Loom chairs from the embraces they'd been in for years, disinterred collapsed chests of drawers, an old showerhead, stacks of mildewed and stinking curtains.

She ordered him to burn everything. The fire took a long time to catch, smouldering at him sullenly, refusing to burn until Jake splashed it with paraffin, and it exploded, roaring, sucking at the air around it.

He's found a couple of treasures. An old storm lantern, which he thinks he might give to Stella for her night walks back to her caravan, and a bicycle, chain arthritic with rust and tyres flaccid, but it's a good one. It has an iron frame, a sprung saddle and solid, spoked wheels. There's something about it he likes, the way the wheels tick-tick when they move, the arch of the upright handlebars, like a pair of antlers, the bell still gripped to the metal.

With one eye on the fire, Jake rubs down the bicycle with an old rag, groom-style, and pumps up the tyres. He upturns it, working the pedals first one way, then the other, easing oil into the links of the chain, into any part where metal works against metal, the wheel whirring in space.

He is cycling round and round the yard in a circle when he hears a voice, close to his head.

'That belonged to the hippies, you know.' Pearl has appeared from nowhere, like a genie, her hands wrapped into her apron.

Jake puts a foot against the ground. 'The bike?'

'Uh-huh. Find it in the barn, did you?' She looks him up and down, as if considering buying him. 'There was one in particular used to ride it. All the time. Young guy. About your height, your colouring.'

She moves off towards the vegetable plot, vanishing as quickly as she came, leaving Jake staring after her.

When the bonfire has burned out, consumed itself to a smoking heap of ash, Jake rides his father's bike down the track. This simple act fills him with such unadulterated delight that he has to stop himself laughing out loud, or pounding his fist against the handlebars. This seat, these pedals, this rusted bell – all touched by Tom. He feels as though the single degree of separation between them has collapsed. He feels he never wants to get off it, never wants to be parted from it, that he'd like to just cycle off and never stop.

Jake has always wondered if it would have been easier if his father had abandoned them, moved on, run off with someone else. There would have been a clarity, a finality to it. He has never been able to get over the fact that his father doesn't know, that he has no inkling of there being an offspring of his out there in the world. Jake feels a kind of sympathy for him sometimes. He has always felt that he knows enough of Tom to be sure that Tom would have wanted to meet him, to see him. It's a peculiar cruelty that his father slipped out of their world, like Alice through the mirror. This bike is the closest he has ever got – the closest he'll probably ever get. And that, in itself, should be celebrated.

He passes some guests and has to turn the wheel to avoid a collision with them. He is always surprised to encounter guests, as if he forgets that's what Kildoune is for. They stare at him – a cinder-flecked man on a bicycle – as if he's dropped from Mars. Do you know who this bike belonged to, he wants to yell at them, do you have any idea?

He is thinking that there is something wrong with the steering, some imbalance, or that the handlebars are misaligned when he curves round a bend in the drive and suddenly Stella is there in front of him, next to a rhododendron weighty with red-black blossoms.

Jake squeezes the one and only brake. Nothing happens. He careens past her and comes to a stop only when the front wheel hits the ditch at the side of the drive. He topples over, into the wet bank of flowers, banging his forehead on a branch, crushing petals and leaves beneath him.

'Are you OK?' She sounds anxious, Jake is pleased to hear.

'Yeah.' He rubs his forehead, picking himself and the bike out of the ditch. 'I think so.'

'Where did you get that?'

She is dressed in jeans and a black sweater, and looks more as he imagines she does when she's not at the hotel – in that other life of hers to which Jake has no access.

‘I found it.’ Jake pulls burrs and twigs out of his clothes. ‘And resurrected it.’

He grins at her, unspeakably delighted. She looks from him to the bike and back again, puzzled.

‘Come for a ride,’ he says, on impulse.

‘Er, no, thanks. It’s clearly not been a very successful resurrection.’

‘Come on.’ He reaches out and seizes her by the wrist. ‘It’s strong enough for two.’

She tries to pull away from him. ‘There’s no way you’re getting me on that thing.’

Jake manoeuvres her round to the front of the bike. ‘Jump up,’ he says. ‘It’ll be like that film – what’s it called?’

He sees her think about it, survey the bike, then relent. ‘What film?’ she says, as she levers herself up on to the handlebars.

Jake pushes off with his foot. ‘You know, it’s really famous. It’s got Paul Newman and–’ The bike wobbles and lurches to one side. Stella screams and leaps off, stumbling to her knees on the driveway.

‘Sorry,’ he says, concerned. ‘Are you hurt?’

‘No. But no thanks to you.’

‘Let’s try again.’ He holds out his hand to her. ‘Come on.’

She considers him and the bike, brushing off her knees. ‘I’ll sit at the back,’ she says, ‘on the pannier thingy. It looks safer. You set off and I’ll jump on.’

‘Will that work?’

'Yes. My sister and I used to do it all the time. Go on,' she motions with her hand, 'off you go.'

Jake presses the pedal and the bike cranks into motion. The rhododendrons shake their red fists at him and he hears Stella's footfalls crunching on the gravel and then he feels her weight hit the bike, which swerves slightly, but it's easy to keep the wheel steady and then her arms are passing round his body and he looks down to see her feet dangling over one side, skimming along above the ground.

'Whole families travel like this in China,' he says, directing his voice under his arm.

'Really?'

He seems to feel the vibration of her voice through her touch.

'Which way?' he asks, as they reach the top of the drive.

'Right ... no, left.'

He pushes down on the pedals, hard, as the ground rises.

'Come on,' she says, and slaps him between the shoulders, 'put your back into it.'

They clear the slope and they are moving fast, past silver birches, horses behind a fence, a stone house where a woman is swinging a child round and round. Stella is shrieking and laughing, shouting about the brake, but all Jake is conscious of is her arms round him – the world they are rushing through is indistinct and blurred, as if the two of them are the only real, breathing, sensory beings within it.

He steers the bike along the curves of the grey road, but they seem to fly above it. A car passes, dragging at their hair and clothes, and Stella is saying something about the place she learnt to ride a bike for the first time and how she thought her uncle was still holding on to the saddle, but then she looked round and saw him standing, arms folded, a long way behind her and she was so shocked she fell off.

The road dips again and they are rushing down towards a wide stone bridge straddling a gully. As soon as he sees it he knows he wants to stand there with Stella, that it is the kind of place where things happen, where things begin. He wants to stand with the river below them and the sky above them, with her, on the bridge, Jake puts his foot down, feels the road scraping the underside of his sneaker, and grit flies up, clattering against the bike's machinery.

They come to an abrupt and unbalanced stop. Jake leans the bike against the bridge wall and peers over the edge. Raging black water boils through striated rocks, whitening and frothing.

'My God,' he says, spray coating his face. 'What river is this, do you know?'

'The Feshie,' she mutters.

Jake turns to look at her and he sees that it's happened again. Her face is closed, set, her hands clenched together.

'Are you all right?'

'Of course.' She won't look at him.

He stares down again at the churning river. Its roar reaches up to them, bouncing off the gully's stone sides. 'It's amazing,' he says, hoping to draw her out of her mood. 'We could walk along it, if you like. There's a path.'

'No. I don't want to.' She sounds desperate, almost childlike.

'Really?'

'No.' She shakes her head. 'Let's go. Please.'

'OK.' Jake follows her, mystified, back to the bike.

'Anyway, so I said–' Francesca broke off and turned her head, listening. There was the sound of the front door opening, the draught excluder swishing against the tiles. 'Here come the silent twins. I'll tell you later.'

'Why do you call them that?' Evie ground her cigarette butt into a convenient teacup (a dreadful thing, garlanded with tartan bows and something that looked like sheaves of wheat – probably some clan heirloom from Archie's family).

'Sssh.' Francesca held a finger to her lips

and twisted round in her seat. ‘Hello!’ she called.

Nina appeared around the kitchen door. She was looking better all the time, Evie thought, more colour in her cheeks, more flesh on her bones. She would never win any more gymnastic medals, but her balance and mobility were improving. She could almost pass for normal, Evie decided, if you didn’t know.

She watched Nina embrace Francesca, then Nina moved to link those thin, wasted arms round Evie’s neck. Evie pressed her cheek to Nina’s head and inhaled. Evie loved the smell of children: not any children, just these two, she didn’t like any others. They smelt of soap and air and innocence. There was a hint of school today – pencil shavings, floor polish, the blunt scent of ink – but she could still detect it. There was, she thought again, very little of the Gilmore in them. The Iannelli genes had emerged triumphant both times, especially in Stella.

Stella was lurking in the background, grave-faced. No kisses from her today. Evie surveyed her. Something was up. She could tell. She looked from Nina, seated now at the table with a glass of milk, to Stella and back again. There was something new about them, a kind of consciousness, an archness, as if they were pretending somehow, covering up. They were behaving not like schoolgirls but like two people acting being schoolgirls.

'Cesca, you're not still cutting their hair, are you?' she asked, raising a new cigarette to her lips.

Francesca nodded, her hand flying to Nina's curls, which were also beginning to look more normal.

'For crying out loud.' Evie touched the snipped ends of Stella's hair – an excuse to draw her close – and sparked her lighter. 'You two are going to have to come to the salon with me,' she said, cigarette gripped between her lips, 'are we agreed? Take your scissor-happy mother out of the equation.'

Stella gave a wan smile.

'How is the dread Miss Saunders?' Evie hugged Stella's body to hers. 'She's not still wearing those elastic-waisted skirts, is she?'

Nina nodded, not looking up from her milk.

'I still haven't recovered from the one she had on at the Christmas concert,' Evie continued, glancing from one sister to the other, 'the one with poodles on it. Remember?'

Nina nodded again, smiling now.

'Promise me something both of you. Never wear dogs. Do you hear me? Our Miss Saunders should be arrested for fashion crimes against the young and impressionable, eh, Stella?' Evie turned to look at her, seeing for the first time that the buttons on her school shirt had been ripped away from the material, leaving ragged-edged holes. 'Darling, your shirt's torn,' she exclaimed.

'It's not, is it?' Francesca murmured. 'Oh, Stella, that's the third time this month.' Francesca started pulling the shirt over Stella's head. 'I've told you not to play those rough games. We can't afford a new uniform at the moment, you know that.'

'What's that, sweetie?' Evie pointed with the glowing tip of her cigarette at an aubergine-coloured bruise mottling Stella's inner wrist. She saw the two sisters exchange the briefest of glances and she saw Francesca, bending over the shirt, miss it.

'I fell,' Stella said, without looking at her.

'On to the inside of your wrist?'

'Uh-huh.'

Evie took a draw of her cigarette. 'Must have been quite a fall.'

'It was,' Nina jumped in. 'It ... was.'

Evie blew the smoke out in rings for Nina, who usually liked to reach up and poke them with a teaspoon. But not today.

'Haven't you two got a letter for me?' Francesca was saying. 'Stella, this shirt is ruined.'

Again, Evie saw them look at each other, then away.

'How do you know about the letter?' Nina murmured, licking out her milk-smeared glass.

'Don't do that, it's disgusting.' Francesca took the glass from her and put it out of reach. 'I was on the phone to Rebecca's mother today and she said she'd had a letter about a school trip.'

'We don't want to go,' blurted Stella, standing in her vest and school skirt, one hand covering her bruise.

'Can I just see the letter, please?'

'We don't want to go.' Stella spoke with real terror in her voice. 'Don't make us go, please.'

'I would like to see the letter,' Francesca repeated, with infinite calm.

The letter was produced, after much scuffling about in the hallway, the unstrapping of satchels and frenzied whispering. Francesca put on her glasses to read it. Evie crossed and uncrossed her legs, reaching down to straighten the back seam of her stocking, thinking of the lover she would be meeting later, her latest conquest. A lawyer. Married, of course, but that was how she preferred them. That way they didn't start interfering and encroaching. She eyed Stella, who was sitting with her head bent over her undrunk milk.

'It sounds lovely,' Francesca said brightly. 'Wouldn't you like to go?'

No response. Stella gripped her glass between two hands, condensation radiating out from her fingers.

‘“We will be staying in a residential teaching centre in Kincraig, Invernessshire,”’ Francesca read aloud and Evie could see how, in another life, she might have made a teacher. ‘“The children will have an opportunity over the week to take part in a range of outdoor sports, including canoeing, hiking, orienteering–”’

‘Sounds ghastly,’ Evie barked. ‘I’m with them, Cesca. Don’t make them go.’

Stella remembers hearing her mother, a few days later, on the phone in her bedroom: ‘Evie, you know I always appreciate your input... I know you love them... No, no, I don’t think so…’

Even from where she was, loitering in the hall, noiseless in her socks, she could hear the tinny rattle of Evie trying to persuade her, trying to save them. But it was no use. When their mother made up her mind, there was no changing it.

‘…Their teacher told Archie that they were having “integration difficulties”... That was the exact phrase... I don’t know what else to do, Evie... You know what they’re like. They’ve only ever had eyes for each other... The trip might help them to socialise a bit more... It’s not normal, or healthy, the way they are... They’ll have fun, I know they will.’

Near Loch Insh, they go over a bump in the road and the chain comes off the bicycle. They spend ages struggling with its oiled, slippery links, their fingers turning black. Jake is dogged, determined that he can mend it, and wrestles with it for three-quarters of an hour before he's ready to admit that they are not going to be able to repair it without tools. It is, Stella tells him, the last time she'll ever go out on a bike with him.

By the time they reach the hotel, dinner is over and everyone gone, the kitchen empty. Stella hadn't realised how late it had got.

'That was good,' Jake says, stretching. He shrugs off his jacket and the buttons rattle on the counter as he puts it down.

Stella stands at the sink, scrubbing the oil off her hands. 'Apart from the bike falling to pieces,' she says, 'and you being a stubborn bastard and us having to walk miles in the dark – yeah, it was great.'

'OK, apart from it being a disaster, it was good, you have to admit.'

'Do I?'

Jake is silent. Then he says, very softly, 'I had a really good time.'

Stella glances at him and sees that he is looking at her. She looks away, scrubs diligently at her fingernails. She feels light-headed and slightly crazed, stretched like a violin string. She doesn't know, cannot see what might happen next.

'Me too,' she attempts to say, but it comes out too loud. The surface of her, in the unnatural glare of the electric light, seems calm and even and white; but the blood, muscle, water and bone of her is blazing, acute.

'We should do it again another day.' He moves as if he's about to come round the sink towards her. 'When I've mended the bike. Don't you think?'

They stare at each other. Stella counts four thuds of her heart, so hard they are almost painful. 'That,' she forces, and her voice comes out as terribly formal, terribly Edinburgh, 'would be nice.'

Jake seems to hesitate, puzzled, examining her face. Whatever it is he sees there makes him cross his arms and look down. 'Right,' he says, reaching for his jacket. 'Well. I'll see you later, then.'

The kitchen door closes behind him, swinging back and forth. She listens to his footsteps recede down the corridor. Then she collapses on to the sink and clutches her head in her hands. 'Oh, God,' she says aloud, to the kitchen. Part of her wants to laugh, with relief that he's gone, that whatever it is between them has been put off, that she doesn't have to deal with it right this minute, but part of her wants to run after him. 'Oh, gggggodddd,' she groans, and, hearing the well of the sink repeating her word back to her, distorted and atonal, she giggles.

She straightens up and looks about the kitchen. Everything looks very stark and hyper-real: the row of knives above the chopping-board, the mixing-bowls fitted inside each other, the cluster of cafetières, a pile of laundered tea-towels, folded into squares, teacups stacked in a toppling tower. A plastic container of indeterminate vegetables lies beside the kettle, smothered in clingfilm. Without really knowing why, she picks it up and goes through into the storeroom. It is dark and moist and insulated. She doesn't snap on the light because she's just going to dump the box on the table and come straight back.

But suddenly Jake is there, right behind her, taking her by the arm and swinging her round. 'Nice?' he is saying. 'That would be *nice?*'

Stella is pushed up against the table-leg. In the soft dark she can just make out the side of his face – the curve of his brow, the indentation of his eye. His breath is hot on her cheek.

'OK.' She pretends to think for a moment. Her body is vibrating, ringing, like a glass played by a fingertip. 'Quite nice,' she manages.

He points at the plastic box. 'Put that down,' he says.

Stella shakes her head without really knowing why, clutching the box to her.

'Put it down,' he says again. And when she still won't, he takes it from her and places it on the table. He moves nearer again and because she is right up against the table there is nowhere for her to go and she can feel his stubble catching in her hair and it is almost more than she can bear.

'Maybe...' she begins, addressing the region of his torso. There is something snagging in a deep recess of her mind, a half-remembered thing, a reason why she shouldn't be doing this. 'Maybe ... this isn't such a good idea ... I think that...'

But with a swift movement his arms are round her and his shoulder is pressed up against her face. There is really nowhere for her arms to go but round him and it is so simple, yet such a glorious relief, that she cannot think why they haven't stood like this before. She is sure there is something she wanted to say and she opens her lips to speak, but he leans forward and presses his mouth to hers and the kiss seems to explode into her, like the first gasp of air after a long dive. Stella clutches him to her in disbelief. He is filling his hands with her hair and she finds that he touches her as if he understands her skin's Braille.

Suddenly, a sound interrupts them. A loud, persistent shrilling. She knows he hears it too: there is a small jolt in his movements. But he carries on, pretending he's heard nothing, pretending it's not there.

'Jake,' she says.

'Mmm?'

She is arched against him, her fingers tangled in his clothes. She breathes in and the scent of him fills her body. She imagines the molecules of his particular smell pulled deep into her lungs and mingling and dissolving with the blood flowing through the alveoli, then rushed away into her system.

'That's the phone.'

In the dark, she sees his eyes lift, then close. His mouth meets hers again, silencing her.

'Jake,' she pulls away, 'we'd better answer it.'

He holds her to him tight, so tight she can barely draw breath. He is kissing her neck, one palm cupped round her cheek. 'No,' he says.

She runs her hands down his back, her legs twined round him. 'I think we should.'

'No,' he mumbles again, 'we're busy. Very, very busy.'

Something occurs to her and she stiffens. 'Jake, it might be Mrs Draper. She phones from the gate-lodge sometimes.'

He rests his forehead on hers and looks straight into her eyes. 'This may come as a surprise to you,' he says, 'but right now I don't care.'

The ringing continues, sharp, drilling. Jake laces his fingers, one by one, between each of hers. 'For God's sake,' he mutters.

There is another pause.

'It's going to disturb the guests, isn't it?' he says reluctantly.

Stella slides off the table, away from him, disentangling her limbs from his. He kisses her once, twice, three times before letting her go. 'Come back quick,' he calls after her. 'I haven't finished with you yet.'

Stella staggers through the blazing light of the kitchen, pulling her clothes straight, disoriented and giggling. 'If you stop now,' she is muttering at the phone, as she pushes through the door, 'I'm going to kill you.'

She lifts the receiver and the noise that has been dominating the past few minutes of her life stops. For a split second she is so relieved she forgets who she is and what she is doing.

'Um.' Then it comes back to her. 'Kildoune House Hotel, good evening, how may I help you?' Her voice sounds distinctly hysterical and joyous, she notices. Hopefully the person on the other end won't notice.

'Hi.' A female voice. Soft, hesitant. 'Is it possible to speak to Jake Kildoune?'

'Sure,' Stella says. 'I mean, yes.' Come on, get a grip. 'Who shall I say is calling?'

‘It’s his wife.’

Stella holds the phone away from her ear. The colours of the flowers in front of her seem very bright. She looks down and sees that someone has put all the brochures in the wrong place. They are stacked haphazardly on the shelf where the registration forms should be. She’ll have to sort them out. At some point. Not right now, though. She places the receiver on the desk carefully, as if it’s made of very fine, thin bone china.

She stands in the stark electric light of the kitchen. ‘Jake,’ she says. The single syllable of his name sounds explicit and very final, like the slamming of a door.

‘Come here,’ he shouts, from the storeroom.

‘Jake,’ she says again. There is a peculiar feeling in her solar plexus, as if it’s filled with a heavy, damp gas. She rubs at her lips, her neck, her cheeks with the back of her hand.

‘Come here now!’

‘It’s for you,’ she says. She inhales. The air seems very cold. ‘It’s your wife.’

There is a long silence from the black oblong of the storeroom door. Then Jake appears in it, dishevelled, his hair standing on end, his shirt half hanging out, and one hand clamped to his forehead.

‘Stella, listen...’ His voice is low, appalled.

She drops her gaze to the floor. ‘She’s on

the phone. For you. In Reception.' She points. Then she remembers that he knows where Reception is. But she still says, 'Through there.'

Jake swears under his breath and steps towards her.

'Don't,' she says, 'just don't.'

He swears again, then bashes his way through the door to Reception. Stella ducks out into the corridor.

'Hello?' she hears him say, hurriedly, then call: 'Stella, wait a sec, would you, just wait.' Then, in a rush: 'Mel, hi, how are– Right... Good... Listen, can I call you back?' Mel presumably isn't very happy about this because the last thing Stella hears as she runs down the corridor is the electronic buzz of a voice.

She slips through the darkened shapes of furniture in the lounge and out of the French windows. The cold forces itself immediately between her skin and her clothes. She hurries away from the hotel in a straight line, without any sense of where she is going or why, stumbling down the bank and across the lawn. By the time she reaches the flower border, she is shivering convulsively and her teeth are rattling in her skull.

There's a wife? A wife? He's married? Stella clenches her fists. She has strict views about falling in love with married people –

you just never do it, never even get close to it, never get embroiled. But him, this one, he doesn't behave like he's married. Not at all. So how was she supposed to tell? She feels edgy, close to tears, deflated, as if someone has skewered her through the chest. She bites her lip, willing herself not to cry. She has an urge to thump something. Really hard. Preferably Jake.

She hears the front door bang open and feet crunching through gravel. The pale of Jake's shirt streaks across the courtyard. 'Stella!' he calls. 'Stella?'

She steps behind a large stone urn. Jakes sprints towards the top of the bank.

'Stella?' he shouts into the dark. 'Are you there?'

She holds her breath, watching as Jake spins round and runs up the side of the hotel, in the direction of her caravan.

Stella turns towards the river, towards the loch, and presses her back to the stone urn, latticed with moss. She sinks down to her heels, huddling herself into a ball, and waits, her jaw set with fury.

They were wrong for this, Stella saw. All wrong. The other girls were dressed in identical outfits, as if they'd all agreed on it beforehand: a towelling tracksuit in some pale, sugary colour, white trainers and a matching backpack. Felicity's was marshmallow pink, Rebecca's sherbet yellow.

Both she and Nina were in the smocks Francesca had made from patterns she sent away for by post, cardigans knitted for them by Valeria and buckled shoes that clattered on the steps of the bus as Stella helped haul Nina aboard. Stella loved the brushed nap of her smock material, the twining pattern that Francesca had made sure met properly at the seams so as to continue without interruption. Nina's was a bit different, with less red in it. They had spent an hour leaning over the catalogue with Francesca, choosing which pattern they would have. That kind of decision their mother took very seriously. She'd said the red would bring out the green of Stella's eyes, and the green would bring out the red of Nina's hair. Stella had liked the inverted symmetry of the idea.

Everyone on the bus was getting out their lunchboxes. Miss Saunders hadn't said they could but she didn't seem to be telling anyone off. Even there, Stella saw by looking round, they were wrong. The girls around them had proper plastic boxes with a carrying handle and a matching flask, filled with crisps, chocolate and white sliced-bread sandwiches with the crusts lopped off. The box Nina was pulling from her bag was an old ice-cream tub from their grandparents' café – it had 'Iannelli Ices' scored into it in swirling script – which would, Stella knew, be filled with a flat, olive-studded ciabatta, some dried apricots and perhaps some of the almond biscuits her mother had made last night. Those she would give to Nina. She didn't like almond; her mother always forgot this. 'I can't remember which one of you dislikes what,' she said, if they complained.

Stella was just reaching down to her bag to get out her own identical box, when out of the corner of her eye, she saw Anthony Cusk coming down the aisle towards them. His crowd of friends was cheering him on. His hair was violent against the floury white of his skin, his eyes sunk deep into the pudge of his face. Stella hated everything about him – his large, fleshy-lobed ears, his clammy, bitten fingers, his pale, colourless lashes.

'Hello,' he said, in his nice voice, which made Stella quail. He was leaning on the back of Nina's seat and Nina was looking straight ahead, out of the window at the bare-topped mountains flashing by. Stella began to fear that letting Nina sit in the aisle had been a mistake, but they were quite close to Miss Saunders's seat so Stella had thought it would be all right.

'What do you want?' Stella hissed. 'Go away.'

'That's not very nice,' he said, leaning closer over her sister. 'I've just come to see how you are. How's the shaky girl getting on?'

Before Stella could do anything to stop him, he reached right over Nina, seized her by the wrist and started shaking her arm. It was a horrible parody of how Nina used to shake.

'Still shaking, I see,' he said, turning to receive and acknowledge the laughter of the rest of the class.

Nina's lunchbox and all its contents flew from her hand. Stella saw the foil-wrapped packet of biscuits skid across the bus floor, far out of reach.

'Let go of her!' Stella leapt up and gripped a handful of Anthony's hair and yanked. He yowled, still shaking Nina who was crying now. Stella tugged harder and she felt Anthony's other hand grab her round the throat and squeeze. The air was trapped in her neck like a cork in a bottle and everybody around them was watching and laughing. She felt her face going red, her lungs full and burning. In recent weeks, what Anthony did to her had been getting worse and worse. What started as taunts and the odd pinch on the arm had, ever since Stella made his nose bleed that time, become headlocks, arm twists, painful kicks in the shin, body-crushing thumps. She had begun to really fear him, to have nightmares about him, to shake if he came near them.

She had no idea how far it might go, or where it might end.

Suddenly Miss Saunders was there, holding on to the ceiling rail.

'There's always trouble wherever you are, Anthony. Go back to your seat this minute!'

Stella felt his hand slide from her throat, felt the noise of laughter subside around her.

'Did you drop your lunch, Nina?' Miss Saunders was asking, in the low, melodious voice she always used when she talked to Nina, as if anything louder might injure her. Stella despised that voice. Why couldn't she talk to Nina properly?

Nina nodded, wiping at her tears with the back of her hand.

'Dear dear.' Miss Saunders picked up the Iannelli Ices box and put the half-eaten ciabatta back into it. 'Here you are. Would you like a tissue?'

'No, thank you,' she muttered, without looking up.

'What did she say?' Miss Saunders looked over her, at Stella. 'Would she like a tissue?'

'No,' Stella said. 'She wouldn't.'

The morning is grey and moist. Mist hangs heavy on the chimneys and turrets of Kildoune House, as if the clouds have given up and slumped, exhausted, to earth. The rooks exclaim and groan overhead.

Jake watches the brindled dog trot along the path with its funny sideways gait, distracted now and then by smells. When it sees Jake, standing by the edge of the forest, it flattens its ears to its head and bounds towards him, pushing the wet nub of its nose into his hand, yelping with pleasure at finding someone not only outdoors at this hour of the day but so obviously purposeless. It licks his fingers with a long, hot tongue and looks up at him with yellow eyes.

Jake runs his hand along its sleek body, feeling the rhythm of its ribs, its muscled torso, quivering with warmth. He is folding and unfolding the velvet of its ear when he sees Stella appear through the trees.

She is wearing wellingtons, her uniform held up away from the wet and dirt of the track, shoes clutched in her other hand. The dog gambols towards her, wriggling with pleasure, unable to contain itself at the idea of not one but two people out and about. Jake sees her bend, offer it a hand and murmur some words to it as she marches towards him.

Jake moves down the track to meet her. Her face is set, steely. 'I've been up for ages,' he begins, 'waiting to see you. I wasn't sure if–'

She sidesteps him. 'I know,' she says, without stopping. 'I heard you outside the caravan.'

'Oh.' He hurries after her. 'Right.'

She hasn't looked at him, hasn't lifted her face to his.

'Look, Stella,' Jake tries again, 'I tried to find you last night but–'

'I know,' she says again. She is walking fast, her wellingtons making an empty sucking sound. Jake strides behind her.

'Stella, please. Can you stop for a sec? We need to talk about this. I know I should have told you but–'

'Yeah,' she cuts across him, 'you should have.'

'It's not what it seems, I promise. If you'd just let me–'

'Piss off, Jake,' she snaps, increasing her speed.

'Listen.' He takes her hand, and his touch seems to startle her so much that she whips round.

Their eyes meet briefly and, as she snatches her hand out of his, Jake is appalled to see that she is on the verge of tears. She wheels away from him. Jake stays where he is, fixed to the spot. What has he done? How can he have let this happen?

He watches her shape, receding from him through the trees, and suddenly knows that he cannot let her leave his sight, that for her to go away from him now would cause such a rift, a scar in his life, that it might never heal over.

'Stella, please!' he shouts, and the forest seems to shift, to absorb his words. 'I can explain. Just listen to me, for two sentences. That's all I ask.'

She takes a step, then another step, then stops. She is standing, Jake sees, by the fork where the path splits in two, one half leading up to the bothy. Around them, the trees fill like lungs.

'One sentence,' she says, without turning round.

'One? OK. Done. One sentence.' He bites his lip, seven feet from her, thinking. 'It's meaningless,' he says. 'Meaningless.' His words come out with effort. 'I don't–'

'That was your one sentence!' she interrupts, walking on again. 'That was it!'

Jake ignores her. 'I don't love her,' he says, stumbling after her, 'and I never have. Do you hear me?'

Stella strides on. 'You married her, didn't you?' she retorts over her shoulder.

'I had no choice.' Jake breaks into a sprint. 'You have to believe me.'

Stella gives a short laugh, also starting to run. 'Oh, yeah, right. She forced you, did she? Very convincing, Jake. She–'

Jake and Stella burst out of the thicket of trees at the same moment. The light is very bright and Mrs Draper is standing in front of them, her arms folded and her high heels wobbling on the uneven stones.

‘What on earth are you two doing?’ She surveys them both, a frown strung over her face. ‘Running a race? It’s rather early in the day for that. I’ve been looking for you everywhere, Jake.’

Stella pulls her uniform straight and slips away towards the back door. Jake’s body makes an involuntary move towards her, but he recalls himself in time.

Mrs Draper is watching him, eyebrows arched. ‘Well, now,’ she exclaims. ‘I won’t ask what’s going on. No, I won’t.’

There is a pause while she waits for Jake to speak. Which he doesn’t. He rubs a hand over his face, watching Stella walk away.

‘So,’ she snaps. ‘I have plans for you today, Jake. I want you to finish clearing out the barn, get rid of all the–’

‘I thought I was helping St–’ He stops. ‘I mean, I thought I was doing the rooms today.’

‘No. I want you to do some outdoor work. If that’s all right with you,’ she adds, pointedly.

Jake swallows. ‘Yes. Of course.’

The centre was a cluster of pebble-dashed white buildings on a high piece of heathland. The land around it had been recently deforested, so all you could see from the window were the severed stalks of trees and a steep, forbidding shale-face of a mountain.

Even indoors, the air rang with cold.

Stella turned back to their room, to where Nina was sitting on the lower bunk-bed, laying out her clothes. It had six bunks in it, but only two others were taken, by Fiona and Sally. Fiona was a large-limbed girl with eczema and Sally her mostly silent, small and stunted friend. Stella had often wondered if they were real friends, like she and Rebecca had been, or if they just put up with each other because it had fallen, in the great pairing-off that happens early among girls in the same class, that they had both been left without a partner.

Stella was trying not to think about how, if this trip had come a year ago, she would have been sharing a room with Rebecca and Felicity and all that lot, who had been planning midnight feasts all the way up on the coach – who would be invited, whose bed they would be held on, and who would be on look-out. She tried not to think about it at all.

Stella sat down next to Nina on the bed.

'Have you got them?' Nina whispered.

'Yes.' Stella pulled the teddy they had brought with them on to her lap. He had a doleful face, velvet paws and a belly that could be unzipped at the back, for the hiding of secret things. This morning, they had taken both of the brown-glass bottles of Nina's medication from where their mother had put them, in Nina's washbag, and pushed them into this soft, flannel-lined pouch. Stella eased them out, unscrewed the caps, which were childproof and needed an extra shove down before you twisted them, and was about to count out the right number (a pink one three times a day, two yellow ones twice a day, Stella had repeated it over and over in her head the night before as she lay awake) when Nina said: 'Let me do it. I want to do it.'

Stella hesitated. The last time Nina did it she was gripped, as she often was when it mattered most, by a violent spasm that sent the pills flying all over the room. Stella had had to get down on her hands and knees with her father to find them all again, rolled under the table, into the gaps between the floorboards, one in her mother's slipper.

Stella handed over the bottle and watched, nervous, as Nina tipped out the pills. Then she handed her the soda-water bottle Francesca had filled with water and watched her sister's throat constrict as she swallowed down the pills that smelt how Stella imagined gunpowder might.

'What's she doing?'

'Taking her medicine,' Stella answered, so quickly she wasn't sure if it was Fiona or Sally who had asked.

But Sally was watching them from her top bunk opposite, her elf-eyes narrowed, hands laced behind her head. It must have been her.

'I have to take medicine too,' Fiona said, with a shy smile. 'But Miss Saunders has got mine.'

'Oh,' Stella nodded, 'right.' Fiona's wash-bag stood on the floor between them, stuffed with medicinal-looking bottles.

Sally slid, snake-like, from her bed. 'I'm going to dinner,' she muttered.

Stella and Nina were the last in the queue. Stella took Nina's plates on her tray because she didn't think Nina could manage and she thought how upset she'd be if she dropped anything. She had to walk extra slow, so as not to drop them herself, putting one foot down in front of the other, following Nina, who was carrying their cutlery.

They sat down at the end of a table, leaving a gap of two seats between them and the other girls. But there was a flurry of tray-lifting, giggling, chairs scraping back, and they all left, moving to another table. Fiona was left behind, blinking, red-faced, then she picked up her tray and slunk away, without meeting their eyes.

'We don't want to catch anything, do we?' Stella heard Felicity say.

'You won't,' Stella shouted at her, half standing. 'She's better now!'

Nina was whispering behind her, 'Stella, don't. Don't, Stel, sit down.'

'If she's better,' Felicity met her gaze, calmly, 'how come she's taking medicine?'

Stella looked at Sally, weasel-featured Sally with skinny arms and mottled skin. She was sitting near Felicity, laughing but in a way that was wide-mouthed, too eager, too mirthless.

Stella turned and sat down again. She hooked and unhooked her feet round the chair legs and felt in her pocket for the stone Evie had picked up for her from their garden on Saturday. 'Keep this in your pocket at all times,' Evie had said to her, as she handed it over. 'And if anyone is ever horrible to you at school, you hold it in your hand and think of me.'

Stella touched it now, the surface worn smooth by the sea, but she couldn't imagine Evie here in this bright-lit canteen that smelt of old food and too many people, she couldn't imagine it at all.

'I want to go home,' Nina muttered, across the table.

Stella thought for a moment about what reply she should give. Should she force cheerfulness? Say that everything was going to be fine? Say that she loved it here?

'So do I,' she said.

'Do you think if we phoned Mum, she'd come and get us?'

'No.'

'What about Dad?'

Stella thought about this. 'Mum wouldn't let him.'

'Evie?'

'I don't know,' Stella said, and she touched the stone again with her thumbprint. 'Maybe. Yes. She probably would.'

'But Mum would be cross with us.'

'Yes.'

At the front of the hall, Miss Saunders, in a blue tracksuit, was clapping her hands: 'In a minute, I want all of you in the main room, where we're going to talk about the orienteering trip tomorrow up the Feshie river. OK?'

Stella is attacking dirt with a vengeance, scouring bathtubs with bleach powder, vacuuming violently, stuffing the faces of the washing machines with soiled linen, sweeping dirty plates into foaming water.

'Heavens,' Pearl remarks, looking at her sideways, 'you're full of energy today.'

Stella doesn't answer, just starts scrubbing at a black hand-mark on the kettle. She's keeping away from Jake. It's a full-time occupation. She's made sure she's been out of the kitchen all day, up in the bedrooms, or in the games room or stocking the bar. She had to hide in a shower cubicle mid-morning, when he'd come upstairs to look for her. It's a perfect building for subterfuge and avoidance – lots of nooks and cupboards, secret stairways hidden behind drapes, rooms leading out of other rooms, trapdoors up into the attic – and she knows it much better than him, knows every route through it.

Late afternoon, she stands in the turreted room, looking down to where he is stacking the skeletons of old sofas, pollarded branches, broken chairs, on to the bier of a bonfire. She can catch the scorched scent of it, or is it just her imagination? The bonfire coughs and sparks and she sees him swat at his sleeve. An early midge? Or did a glowing cinder land on him? She looks at the curve of his neck, the shape of his shoulders as he stands, leaning on his pitchfork.

You should leave, she tells herself. It's time you were going. Or is it? She doesn't know if she can face life elsewhere. Doesn't know if she can shrink herself down to slot into it again. Could she? Can she see herself somewhere else, a city, working on a radio show? It doesn't seem like a life she once had, a life she could ever fit into. Stella doesn't know precisely what it was she came to do; all she knows is that she hasn't done it, it hasn't happened. Why should she let some man drive her away? Bugger him, she thinks, and turns away, trying to pretend that her heart doesn't feel fractured, sore.

That night, she finds a piece of paper folded and pushed under her door.

Stella
You're avoiding me, I know, and I have to say you're quite good at it. Where did you learn to be so devious?

I need to talk to you. If I don't get a chance to explain myself within the next few hours I may go mad. My sanity is in your hands. Come round to my pigpen. Now. Please.

Jake x

His writing isn't how she would have imagined it. She looks at the way he signs his name, the upward stroke of the *J* smaller than the *k*. The single kiss. Stella reads it through twice, then crushes it into a hard pellet and aims it into the rubbish.

A few minutes later she comes out of the bedroom and leans over the bin, looking at it. Then she pulls it out, unpicks it from its dense ball and irons it flat against the wall. She puts it into her pocket.

She is coming down the narrow, low-ceilinged corridor in the oldest part of the house, heading for the farthest room, where she has to do a change.

Suddenly, and without any warning, something leaps out of a recess where a deerhead hangs impaled on the wallpaper and grabs hold of her. Stella lets out a shriek and falls sideways into an occasional table, sending a china vase flying to the floor. She is being held from behind, an arm firmly round her waist, and she recognises, if not Jake himself, then the scent of him, the density of his body.

She twists and kicks, struggling to free herself. 'What are you doing?' she shrieks. 'Let me go.'

She feels her feet leaving the ground and she is being lifted and carried in the opposite direction to the one she'd been going in.

'Jake,' she batters at his arm, really angry now, 'put me down!' She curls her fist and sends flailing punches behind her. 'Jake!'

'Stop shouting, will you?' he says, close to her ear, as they stagger their way through the corridor. The repeating pattern of the wallpaper slides past Stella's eyes, giddying her. 'You'll deafen me.'

They reach the door to the laundry cupboard, which Jake kicks open with his foot. Stella grips the door jamb as they pass through, hanging on to it, stopping them in their tracks.

'For God's sake,' Jake mutters, as he prises her fingers from the wood, 'you are actually the most bloody-minded woman in the world. Do you know that?' He manages to loosen her grasp and slams the door behind him before putting her down.

The second she is free, Stella launches herself forward, letting out an inarticulate growl, towards the door – and Jake. He catches her, pinning her wrists together with one hand and turning the key with the other.

‘It’s true what they say about fiery Italians,’ he is saying, as he draws the key out of the lock. ‘And fiery Celts. Jesus, what a mix.’

Stella thumps him, hard, on the arm. ‘Let me out.’

‘No.’

‘Let me out!’ she shouts, enraged.

He shakes his head.

‘Give me the key, Jake.’ She holds out her hand. ‘Give it to me right now or – or I’ll scream.’

‘Scream away,’ he says, ‘there’s no one around. Mrs Draper’s at the cash and carry. Pearl’s left for the day.’ He slides the key deep into the front pocket of his trousers, right down by his groin. ‘If you want this, come and get it.’

Stella kicks a pile of clean sheets, which topple to the floor. ‘God,’ she grinds her teeth, ‘I hate you, I hate you, Jake Kil–’

‘OK. Enough about that. I tried to talk to you like a civil human being but you weren’t having that. I told you I was on the brink of insanity and you obviously didn’t care. So. Desperate times call for desperate measures. This,’ he waves his arm round the neat, pale stacks of towels, tablecloths, sheets, pillow cases, ‘was my only option.’

Stella stands in front of him, her fists clenched. 'If you think that abducting me and imprisoning me in a laundry cupboard is going to make me forget what a spineless shit you are, I can't–'

Jake smiles at her. 'Spineless shit. I like that. Now listen–'

'No,' Stella says, stepping right up to him, 'you listen. I am not the kind of woman who does the married man thing, OK? And if you think for one minute that you have any chance of changing my mind about that, then–'

'She was dying, Stella.' He says this very quietly and very deliberately. She almost doesn't hear him, but the words reach her, stilling her voice in her throat. 'Right there in front of me.'

Stella frowns. At their close proximity, he can see the dark, liquid pupils of her eyes widen, like the aperture of a camera.

'What do you mean?'

Jake passes his hand through his hair. 'There was this ... this thing ... that happened ... in Hong Kong. A few months ago. At Chinese New Year.' He breathes in then out again. He hasn't spoken to anyone about this for ages, and he's never had to describe it to anyone from the beginning. 'It might have been on the news over here, I don't know. It was–'

'The crush?' Stella says.

He looks at her. 'Yes. How did you–'

She takes a step away from him. 'I read about it in the newspapers.'

'Well.' He takes another deep breath. These words seem to be taking up more oxygen than normal ones. 'I was there and ... she was there. Her friend, her best friend, died. Was killed, I mean. And Mel ... Mel was very badly hurt. And she was lying there on this bed in Intensive Care and she said to me that...' Jake rubs his face with his palm '...it sounds so weird to just say it like this, but she said that she couldn't bear to die without ... without marrying me.'

Stella eyes him. Is she wondering if he's telling the truth? He can't tell.

'So you married her,' she says.

'Yeah. That night. The whole thing was completely ... surreal. I'd just been in this terrible, hellish ... unbelievable thing, the kind of thing you can't even imagine happening, let alone happening to you, and I'd broken my arm and this girl I'd been seeing for a few months is dying and ... and I knew I didn't love her but all these doctors were saying she wasn't going to last the night and–'

'But she did.'

'Yes.' Jake nods. 'She did. And there I was, married to this girl, this ... this stranger, practically, and I brought her back here to her parents ... which is why I'm here, in this country and...' he suddenly feels emptied out '...that's it. The whole story of ... of my marriage. My so-called marriage.'

She doesn't say anything, still scanning his face. 'How is she now?' she asks finally.

'She's all right,' he says. 'Better. Much better. She'll be fine. I wanted to tell you this so you'd understand ... so you'd see that I'm not...' he shakes his head, trying to work out what it is he wants to say '...I'm not the kind of person who would try it on with someone while I was married.'

'But you did,' she insists. 'You did exactly that.'

'Yes, I know, I–'

'While you were married to someone who was seriously ill.'

'Yes, yes.' Jake sighs. 'I know. And I can't tell you how much I regret it.' Realising how that sounds, he falls over himself to add: 'Not telling you before, I mean. About my situation. I regret that. Not ... not what happened.' He looks at her steadily. 'I don't regret that at all.'

Stella seems to have developed an intense interest in the carpet pattern.

'I'm not really married,' he insists. 'You have to see that. Not really. I mean I am, officially, legally or whatever, but I mean not in the sense that I have any kind of–'

'Does Mel know how you feel?' Stella

interrupts him, her arms wrapped round her body like chains.

Jake presses his lips together, checked, silenced. Why is it women have an innate ability to cut to the chase? To sniff out the germ of a situation? How do they do it?

'Hmm,' he elects to play for a bit of time, 'not exactly. I mean–'

'Not exactly?' she demands.

'Er,' he decides to be straight, 'no. No, she doesn't.'

'Right.' Stella holds out her hand. 'The key. Give it to me.'

Jake doesn't move.

'Jake! Give me the fucking key.'

'No,' he says, a childish urge flooding him. 'I don't want to, I–'

'I don't give a damn what you want.' She springs at him again and Jake is momentarily stunned into immobility by the feeling of her breasts jouncing against him through the combined material of their clothes. 'You may not think you're married but if the person you're married to thinks you are, then you are.'

They tussle. Stella fights to put her hand down into his pocket, he holds her wrist away from it.

'You're probably right,' he says, feeling the heat coming off her, 'but–'

'There's no but about it,' she says. 'If you think I'm going to have anything to do with you while you have a wife, let alone a sick wife, then...' her fingers enter his pocket '...you must be mad.' He feels her hand sliding deep into his trousers and he groans involuntarily. She pulls out the key, triumphant, incensed. 'Pervert,' she spits.

'OK,' he says, as she shoves the key into the lock. 'OK. You're right. Of course you're right. I'll deal with it. I promise you. I'll talk to Mel.'

Her eyes flash as she looks at him. 'Don't do anything on my account.' The lock clicks and she yanks open the door. 'Pervert,' she says again, as she slips into the corridor.

As she comes towards him on the platform at Waverley Station, Jake thinks she must know something is wrong. She must.

But maybe not. She is waving at him, her hand high in the air, a wide smile on her face. She is clutching a magazine and her expression is lit up, hopeful. He feels the cruelty he is about to deal out twist inside him, like something he cannot digest.

He'd called her to say he needed to see her and would come down to Norfolk. But she had suggested a weekend in Edinburgh. She was feeling much stronger and could do with a change and Edinburgh was so lovely, they would have a really good time.

She throws her arms about his neck and is kissing him, on the mouth, on the cheeks, on the neck and he cannot put his arms round her, yet he can't not, and all the time she is marking him with traces of herself, her saliva, her lips. Jake has to stop himself flinching away.

They go to a café across a side road from the station and he buys her a coffee and a yellow triangle of shortbread, crusted with sugar. Petticoat shortbread they call it, she tells him, as she sips her coffee, looking round at the leaflets in a rack, the people going into the art gallery next door, a child drinking from a straw by the window.

'Mel,' Jake says. He has to get this over with but has no idea how to begin. How do you say something like this?

She puts down her cup. Looks at him. He sees her examine his face carefully, as if committing it to memory. An image of Stella flashes, unbidden, into his head. Stella cracking an egg with one hand into a basin of flour, her head bent in concentration. He's in Edinburgh. Stella's city.

Jake clasps his fingers together under the table. 'I wanted to see you today because–'

'We could go to the gallery later, if you want,' Mel blurts and Jake sees the tiniest flicker of panic cross her face like lightning. 'You'd like that, wouldn't you?'

'I have something I need–'

'Or the castle!' she exclaims, leaning to touch his arm. 'I haven't been there for years. That would be nice, wouldn't it?' She is almost pleading now, her face creased, as if she might cry.

'Mel, I can't marry you.' He says it very gently. He puts his hand on top of hers. He tells her he is sorry. Somewhere behind them, a waitress clatters cups on to a tray. A door bangs and two men breeze past them, saying something about a lost bus ticket.

She looks sideways and down, towards the empty chair at the table with them. 'But we're already married,' she says.

'I know.' He finds himself staring at the ring she has worn since that night in the hospital. He realises he has no idea where it came from. Someone, one of the nurses, perhaps, produced it from somewhere and he's never thought about it before. 'What I mean is,' he says, 'I can't be married to you.'

She eases her hand out from under his. Tears spring from her eyes almost instantly, as if they were already there, behind her lids, waiting. They spill down her cheeks and she wipes at them quickly with her napkin, her face turned away.

'Please, Mel,' Jake says, anguished. 'Please don't cry.'

He lifts the curtain of hair away from her face, presses his head to hers. She doesn't pull away. People are glancing over now, looking away, then pointing them out to their companions.

'I'm sorry,' he whispers. 'I never ... I never meant for this to happen ... for me to ... to hurt you like this. It just–'

'Can I ask you something?' Her voice shakes slightly.

'Of course. Anything.' He sees that she is clenching her hands together, nails pressing into the flesh around the knuckles.

'Do you...' tears start flooding down her face and she scrubs at them angrily with a sodden napkin '...did you...' she gets out '...did you love me?'

Jake is silent. This conversation eddies and churns around him like dangerous water. What should he say? He knows that truth isn't always the best thing. But is it better in this circumstance than a lie or a half-lie? He has no idea.

'Did you? I need to know.' She gives him a small, brave smile through her tears.

Jake stares down at the fake teak of the table surface. 'I did,' he says carefully, 'at the beginning. Or at least I thought I could.' He looks at her, into her reddened eyes, at her streaked face, and sees that she is trembling with the effort of not sobbing. 'The thing was, it was all still so new and recent by the time we ... by Chinese New Year. It was such a massive thing to happen to us that it ... it kind of made it...' Jake grinds to a halt. 'It's not that I feel nothing for you and it's not that I regret what ... what we did that night.

I mean, I would do the same again if … if…'

'If I was dying in a hospital bed,' she supplies. 'Thanks a lot.'

'No,' he says. 'No, no. It's not that. Mel, you mustn't ever think that I did what I did out of pity or … or–'

'What are you going to do now?' She is sitting back in her chair, looking at him with narrowed eyes, toying with the tissue, ripping it into shreds.

'What? This afternoon?'

'I mean now in general. Are you going back to Hong Kong?'

'No. I'll go back up to–'

'This hotel place?'

'Yes.'

There is a silence. She is staring at him, raking his face, her mind churning over. Jake is puzzled. As well as discomfited by this sudden change in her.

'Why do you–'

'You've met someone else,' she says. The sentence comes out with a peculiar precision.

Again, Stella makes an unwarranted appearance in his mind – the way she tugs her fingers through the ends of her hair.

'No,' he lies, 'no, not at all.'

'You have.'

'I haven't.'

'You have.' Mel leans over the table, her face contorted with grief. 'It's that girl who answered the phone, isn't it? I can see it. It's written all over your face. You … you shit.'

He doesn't see her draw back her arm. All he's aware of is her hand cracking against his face, his head jerking sideways on his neck and a screaming ache in his cheek.

'Jesus, Mel,' he says, bending over the pain, his fingers pressed to his face, and he's amazed at how mild his voice sounds, 'what did you do that for?' He pushes his tongue round his mouth, feeling for loose teeth. Nothing. But when he looks at his fingers, he sees they are touched with blood. She must have caught him with one of her rings.

'You're a shit,' she bursts out, 'a complete and utter shit. All that – that crap you gave me about wanting to see Scotland and all the time you were just on the look-out for–' Mel stands up so quickly her chair crashes to the ground behind her.

'No, no,' he tries to protest, but his mouth feels numb and rubbery.

She whisks her coat off the back of a chair and slams her way out of the café, leaving Jake standing at the table, clutching his face.

Stella is up on the battlements, lying on her stomach in the lee of a chimney-stack. There's a fire-escape that leads here through the attic and up a ladder. No one ever comes apart from her. She loves the jagged teeth of the crenellations, the way the lead warms up in the sun, the way the breeze that snaps and cracks the saltire flag above her can't reach her if she lies low, how everything on the ground – the cars parked in rows along the hotel, the people walking away from them, Pearl making her way across the lawn – looks tiny and miniature as if she could reach down and pick them up in her hand.

It's late afternoon, almost time for her shift, almost time for Jake to be back. But maybe not. Maybe he'll need to stay longer. Maybe he'll decide–

Stella turns resolutely back to her book, reads through a paragraph. Stops. Goes back, reads it again, and then again. She fingers the note from Jake she found that morning, slid into the pocket of the apron she always wears for breakfast, which she is using as a bookmark. She doesn't need to look at it again. She knows it by heart: *Gone to meet Mel. I'll be back tonight. Get ready*.

She closes the book with a slap and sighs. She can't stop thinking about him. Not in any constructive, intelligent, coherent way. But whatever she is doing or supposed to be thinking about, her mind slips sideways and just repeats *Jake, Jake* to her, over and over again. She's never fallen for anyone the way she has fallen for him. It's almost like a disease, an altered, weakened condition. He deprives her of herself, makes her exist in a kind of stupor, a daze, a state of Jakeness.

It's ridiculous, Stella decides. How can it have happened so quickly? How can it have reduced her to such mindless idiocy? This has never happened before. It shouldn't be allowed, she thinks, as she hears the drone of a car in the distance. A taxi, perhaps? From the station?

Stella scrambles to her feet and leans against a battlement, looking out along the line of trees where the car will appear. The engine whines on and Stella thinks she catches a flash of red through the trunks but can't be sure. It's Jake, her mind is telling her, it's him, he's here. Is she ready? She doesn't know. Ready for what?

Then the car bursts out into the light travelling fast, a little too fast for the curves of the track. It sprays grit in its wake. Stella knows the car, recognises it, but it takes her Jake-confused mind a few seconds to catch up. There is a single person in it, sitting at the wheel.

Stella blinks and thinks for a moment how easy it is to shut out the world with your eyelids. She looks down to the ground and it seems miles and miles away, as if she's looking at a satellite image of another planet.

It was inevitable this would happen, she sees that now. Inevitable. But she'd thought herself safe here, hidden from the world, she thought that nothing could touch her if she cloistered herself away. She turns and sinks to her knees, crouching behind the battlements.

Jake hurries down the back steps. It would be quicker through the lobby but he knows Mrs Draper doesn't like staff using it as a short-cut. It's still early, just before six. Stella will be in the kitchen, preparing whatever vegetables the chef needs that night. He can catch her alone. Maybe drag her into the storeroom again.

Jake bursts into the kitchen, grinning to himself, which makes his injured mouth throb and hammer but doesn't stop him grinning. OK, he doesn't exactly have divorce papers to show her but surely the fact that they–

He stops short. There, in front of him, is a smaller, sharper-faced Stella, looking at him with the dead flicker of non-recognition.

'Jake, hi.'

He looks to his right and sees Stella, the real Stella, his Stella, standing behind the counter. There is something suppressed or agitated about her face, the expression taut, the colour high. She is gesturing to the woman. 'Jake, this is my sister. Nina.'

He doesn't really look at Nina as she takes him by the hand. No one speaks for a few seconds.

Then Nina says, 'I'm visiting.'

Jake nods. There is something strange in

the air between the sisters, something close and secret, like the inaudible screech of a bat, something as fine and brittle and twisted as spun sugar. He almost wants to put his nose in the air and sniff to ascertain, seek out its smell.

'Just for tonight. Although,' she turns to look at Stella, 'I might stay longer. Haven't decided yet.'

'Don't you need to get back for work?' Stella says stiffly. Her hand, resting on the counter, is curled into a fist, he notices.

'No.' Nina smiles and takes in Jake, from his feet all the way to his face. 'The joys of freelancing. What do you do here?'

'I ... um... Lots of different things. Maintenance, digging the garden, that kind of thing. Stella?'

'All sounds very manly,' she is saying, as Stella lifts her eyes to his.

'Have you got a minute?' Jake feels he might very easily burst if he doesn't get to talk to her, alone, right now.

'Er,' Stella looks at her watch, then looks back at Nina. 'I think so. I just need to–'

At that moment, the chef bangs open the door. He looks round them all, one by one.

'The fuck's going on here?' he growls. 'Some kind of party?'

They scatter out of his way as he walks through the kitchen.

'Nice for you if you can stand about

chatting but we've got eighteen for dinner tonight and if those veg aren't in the roasting tin in, let's say, ten seconds there's going to be trouble. And you two,' he jabs a ladle towards Jake first, then Nina, 'can get lost. I don't know what you think you're doing in my kitchen, this time of night.' He glares at Nina. 'I don't even know you.'

Stella rolls her eyes. 'All right, all right. Jake,' she turns to him and he has to stop himself reaching out to touch her, 'could you show Nina where the caravan is? Neen, I'll come and see you if I get a chance, otherwise I'll be off around ten-ish, I've got to...' She trails away, gazing at Jake, her brow creased. 'What happened to your face?'

He shrugs and grins. 'Tell you later.'

'My God,' Nina says, as they step out of the back door, rummaging for something in her bag, 'is he always that charming?'

'Who?'

'The chef.'

'Oh. The chef. Yeah,' Jake says. 'Pretty much.'

As they walk through the yard, Nina puts a cigarette to her lips. At the start of the track into the woods, she stops, as if waiting for something. She looks at him, fixes him with those oddly familiar eyes. 'Do you have a light?' she asks.

'No.'

She rummages again in her bag and brings out a box of matches. She leans away from the breeze as she strikes one. 'Big place,' she says, cradling the flame in her cupped palms. 'Very chi-chi.'

'Yeah. It is.'

'Have you been here long?'

'Couple of weeks.'

'Not as long as Stella, then.'

'No.' Jake points. 'The caravan's just this way. I'll show you – you can't see it from here.'

They set off again, Nina shaking out her match and flinging it into the moss-draped stones. As they walk along together, Jake notices that she moves in a strangely emphatic way, like someone who's learnt to do it by following diagrams in a book.

'Which way is the river?' she asks suddenly.

'Er...' Jake has to think about this for a moment. 'That way.' He points beyond the caravan.

Nina takes a deep drag on her cigarette. 'How far?'

'Half a mile or so. Maybe less.'

This information makes her shake her head.

'You know the area?' Jake asks.

'Kind of. No.'

'Kind of no?'

She gives a short laugh. 'Kind of yes.'

There is a pause. Jake waits for her to

elucidate. He doesn't know why but he gets the sensation that he is brushing close to something he's wanted to know for a long time.

'We were here once before,' she says, and Jake finds that he is listening to every syllable, afraid he might miss something. But as she says this she seems to pull herself straighter, toss back her head, as if shrugging something off. 'I've just had a big row with my husband,' she confides instead.

'Oh.' Jake is surprised by this admission. Then he laughs. 'So have I, actually. Except not my husband, obviously, my ... um...'

'Wife?' Nina supplies, turning to him.

It is a very simple scenario, almost like the start of a fairytale. Two sisters are walking beside a river. They are hand in hand, in matching dresses. The path is winding, embracing the curves and bends of the river. The river is dark, deep and fast moving. There are signs, as they walk, that the river has been higher, swollen by flood, swallowing up the verge and the path. But at the moment they are able to walk along, holding on to each other's hands.

The wood breathes and sighs around them. They have been left behind, far behind, by the people they set out with. The taller sister, who's not in fact the elder, helps the smaller sister as the ground becomes steeper, rockier, looser beneath their feet. They don't know exactly what lies ahead, but they are beginning to guess. There is a dimmed roar, a muted thunder, and the water pools out on the far side, fathomless, dangerous.

The taller, younger sister picks up a stone, pulls back her arm and tosses it in an arc into the river. The waters accept it with a gulp.

'Did you hear that?' she says, without looking round.

'What?'

'An echo. Listen.' She bends down for another stone but this time the stone flies further from her hand and hits the deep, slow-moving current on the far side and the river swallows it without a sound.

Not far away, at some parallel point in history, the same sister is in a hot, steam-filled kitchen, slicing carrots along their cortexes and tipping them into a steel dish. She leans up and away from the cutting-board, wiping the inside of her wrist against her forehead just as the other sister is knocking on the low, wooden door of an old pigpen, a stolen bottle of vodka clasped in her hand.

Jake had been so sure it would be Stella at the door that the sister's face is, again, a shock.

‘Oh,’ he says, stopping in his tracks. She is so strangely like yet unlike Stella. ‘Hello.’

‘Hi.’ She flashes her teeth at him.

‘Did you ... could you not find the caravan?’

‘Yeah.’ She nods. ‘I found it.’

‘Right.’

‘What are you up to?’ she asks, trying to see past him into his room.

‘Me?’ Jake begins to feel alarmed. What is she doing here? Didn’t he just say goodbye to her? ‘Not much. You know. Well, actually, I was waiting for–’

‘Mind if I come in?’

‘Er ... the thing is–’

‘I don’t like that caravan much. A bit spooky.’

‘Yes.’

‘That funny wood.’ She shivers, Stella’s sister, on his doorstep. ‘Don’t know how Stella stands it. I’ll just come and sit with you for a bit. If you don’t mind.’

The thought that he would be refusing Stella’s sister company if he were to say no registers in his mind. What would Stella say about that? ‘OK,’ he relents. ‘Sure.’

He steps aside and Nina enters his room, walks to the bed, sits down and kicks off her shoes. ‘I brought this,’ she says, holding up a bottle swinging with clear liquid.

Stella drops a tray of glasses on her way

across the dining room. She's not sure why. It just seems to slide from her grasp, as if she hasn't got it balanced properly, as if one of her arms is weaker than the other.

The glasses splinter and fragment on impact into thousands of tiny blades. She has to get a dustpan and sweep round disapproving feet, then carry the whole crunching, lethal bouquet to the kitchen.

It seems odd to her, this transformation. Two minutes ago they were wine glasses and now they are slivers of clear glass, to be wrapped and wadded in newspaper and thrown away.

'The thing about Richard is,' Nina is saying to him, leaning close and touching his shoulder with the hand that carries a burning cigarette. Jake doesn't like cigarettes. Why is he letting her smoke in his room? He doesn't remember her asking.

'What was I saying?' she says, looking at him intently. She seems very close to him, curled up on his bed. He can smell the nicotine and vodka coming off her.

'Richard,' Jake reminds her. He should stand up. It's very stuffy in here. Maybe he should open the door, get some air in. He struggles away from her, to the edge of the bed. Without the prop of his shoulder, Nina falls forward on to the mattress. She giggles.

Jake hoists himself upright and it is only

then that he realises how drunk he is. The pigpen tips and veers around him and his head feels thick and clogged. How can he be drunk? He looks round at the vodka bottle on his bedside table, puzzled. Still half full. Then he remembers the joints Nina had rolled. How many of them were there? She'd been asking him about Mel, all the while crumbling the resin into beds of tobacco. It was stronger than he's used to, he remembers thinking at the time, much stronger.

Isn't glass made from sand? Stella thinks, as she takes down the dessert order for a family from Glasgow. Another weird transformation, that. She breathes in deeply and tries to focus on what the woman at the table is saying to her – something about a dairy allergy. Keep it together, she tells herself, just for now.

He seems to be back on the bed. His head is sunk into a pillow, at any rate, and that appears to be the ceiling above him. Nina's voice goes on and on, like a river. She's talking about her job, about the people she works with, the patients she visits, how weird it is to be back here, how it all looks just the same, and in between there is a lot of stuff about her flat.

Jake wants nothing more than to go to sleep. His face aches dully where Mel hit him. His mind keeps sliding towards drowsiness and just as he is about to drop off, each time, something pulls him back. Some corner of him is aware that there was something important he had to do. Something very important. But right at this moment, he cannot quite recall what it was. All he knows is that it's stopping him sleeping.

Stella is running through a wood at night, the cone of a torch-beam bobbing and arching around her. She knows the way, but it still scares her.

The caravan had been empty, cold, the lights off. She rounds the grey bulk of the hotel, coming into the car park. Has she left, gone without telling her? No. Nina's car is still there.

Stella turns. Where can she be? She can't be in the hotel because Stella's just come from there. Did she go for a walk? But Nina would never be out at this time of night in the middle of nowhere on her own – she hates the dark.

Stella wants to shout her name at the top of her voice. How could she just disappear on her like this? She's been avoiding her sister for months but right at this moment she would give anything to have her here, next to her.

She has to be somewhere, Stella reasons with herself. She walks round to the other side of the hotel, past the patio, past the pot plants and up towards the barn. The air is full of minuscule circling insects, which adhere to her face, her hair, her hands. She is still walking when she sees the pigpen, the single window with the curtains drawn, the frame of light round the door. Stella stops.

She clasps and unclasps her hands, thinking. Then she tiptoes slowly, slowly up to the door and presses her ear to the grain of the wood.

At first she hears nothing. Just the muted roar of blood in her veins, like the sea trapped in a shell. She is cold, she realises, with just the cotton of her uniform between her and the night air. She'll go back to the caravan and get a cardigan. Then she hears something – a shift, a movement, like fabric against skin. And a sudden drawing-in of air, a quick sigh or an exclamation or a gasp.

Stella flinches away from the door. She turns and walks, ten maybe eleven paces. Then she starts to run, her hands over her ears, stumbling every few steps.

If you share a room with someone for eighteen years, you can recognise every cry, every movement, every breath, every sigh they make. That was her sister. Without a doubt.

Her sister and Jake. The idea is like red heat near a burn.

Jake looks down at himself, vaguely surprised. He is lying half in, half out of the bedcovers. He turns to see the clock and pain splits his head.

'Shit,' he mutters, putting his hand up to it. He eases himself into a sitting position. His eyes are stinging and his mouth is upholstered with fur. 'Oh, God,' he moans, 'I'm dying. I must be dying.'

Just then, he catches sight of a woman's shoe by the door. Black leather. A high heel. He stares at it and the more he stares at it the stranger it seems, as if it's some antiquated object he's never seen before and can't work out its purpose.

He twists round, making the bed – and the body, with its back to him – bounce. There is a woman lying in his bed. His mind informs him of this fact very calmly, as if this is a normal and acceptable state of affairs. For a moment he is unable to compute what has happened. Is it Mel? he thinks, baffled. No. This woman has short brown hair. Who could it be?

Stella. His brain supplies him optimistically with the name. But Jake knows it's not her and just thinking about her makes him remember.

'Oh, fuck.' Jake leaps from the bed as if it's contaminated. 'Fuck, fuck.'

He is so angry with himself, so utterly and purely furious, that he is unable to put on his shoes. He fights and wrestles against himself for a few minutes, trying simultaneously to stamp on himself, injure himself, and to shove his foot into the shoe.

With one lace done up, he bolts through the door. The light slams into his brow like a hammer on an anvil and he shuts one eye as he runs down the track towards the hotel. At the point where the paths intersect, he has to decide. Caravan or hotel? Caravan or hotel? Where will she be? Jake squints at his watch which is, miraculously as it seems at this precise moment, still round his wrist. It's seven something. Can he wake her up? Yes, he decides in a flash, he has to.

'You fucking idiot, you fucking, fucking idiot, what is wrong with you?' he is muttering to himself, as he sprints up the path into the woods. How can that have happened? One minute she was at the door, then she was inside with her vodka and her weed and then–

Jake comes to a standstill, his breath heaving in his chest. Pearl is standing in the middle of the path, arms folded across her apron, blocking his way.

'You won't find her there,' she says.

He feels very cold. 'Why? Where is she?'

'She's gone.'

'Gone?' The word hits Jake like a blow to the stomach. 'Gone where?'

'Gone. Left. Skedaddled.' Pearl comes

towards him and Jake backs away. Pearl is not someone Jake wants to mess with. He imagines she would know how to smite him with black arts or whatever you call them. 'And I for one don't blame her.' She sidesteps him and walks away, surprisingly fast for someone so small.

'Pearl, wait–' Jake wheels round, tripping on his loose lace, stumbling to the forest floor. 'Hang on a sec.'

Pearl carries on walking away from him. Jake, hauling himself from the ground, has to run to catch up with her.

'What did she say, Pearl? What did she tell you?'

She shakes his hand off her arm. 'She said nothing. Didn't need to.' She turns on him, this woman who is almost half his height, and she is scaring him more than anything else in his life. 'I see things. Doesn't take a genius to work things out, you know.' She shoves her face up close to his. 'You should be ashamed of yourself, laddie.'

'Listen,' Jake is forced, by the narrowness of the path, to walk behind her, 'it's not what...' He tries to formulate what it is he wants to say, what he needs to say. 'It's not what you think,' he finishes lamely.

Pearl snorts.

'Where has she gone? Pearl, please tell me. Please.'

'I don't know.' She stops so abruptly Jake

almost falls into her. 'And even if I did, I wouldn't tell you.'

Jake watches Pearl walk away through the forest, her shape receding down and down until she's no bigger than a goblin. He kicks the nearest stone, once, twice, with all his might. Then he sinks down to sit on it, clutching his foot in his hands. He doesn't think he has ever felt more desperate. What is he going to do?

Suddenly he raises his head. The trees above him writhe and toss, sunlight glowing through the branches. Something, some recollection from last night, is breaking through. He frowns and looks at his hands, spread out on his knees. His foot throbs vaguely. And then he can picture it as if seeing it on a screen: Nina, leaning over him and whispering into his ear, 'She killed someone, you know.'

part four

As Jake walks away, he tells himself he won't look back. Not until the end of the drive. That's the best view, the one that takes in the sweep of the lawn, most of the house and the trees behind. From there, Kildoune is turned to face the loch, but you can still see its turrets, the opacity of its windows, the battlements, and the track coiling away from it into the forest.

But when he reaches the gate, he can't do it. He can't turn round. He stands for a moment, the house behind him, the road in front of him, gripping the straps of his rucksack. Then he walks on, putting one foot in front of the other, his eyes on the ground.

He walks the cross-section of the valley, along the winding road, past the church, along the bridge, over the loch, under the railway. At the main road, he stands beside his rucksack, edging from foot to foot. He has this image of Stella getting further and further away from him with every passing second, of the thread between them stretching to breaking-point.

He doesn't have to wait long for a ride. A middle-aged couple take him as far as Pitlochry where they are going, they tell him, to buy their daughter a wedding present. They drop him on the A9 and Jake shades his eyes against the sun, looking down the silver-skinned Tarmac, his thumb outstretched.

When a car slows down and the driver, a man with a scorpion tattooed on his forearm, asks, 'Where to?' Jake isn't sure. Edinburgh or London? London? Edinburgh? Where would she go?

'South,' he says. He'll decide on the way.

It's only when he's swung his rucksack into the back seat that he realises he's left the bicycle behind. It gives him almost physical pain, just below his sternum. He has to stop still, leaning out of the car, caught in the act of pulling the door closed. He bites his lip and yanks the door to. He could never have taken it anyway.

'South it is,' Scorpion Man says. 'Anywhere in particular?'

Nina slams into the flat, flinging car keys, bag, coat to various bits of furniture. She pauses to check the answerphone for messages – none – then stamps into the kitchen.

Richard is sitting at the table, a triangle of toast in one hand, a medical journal in the other. 'Sweetheart,' he says, 'you're back!'

'Evidently.' Nina pushes her hair off her face. 'Listen, have you seen Stella?'

‘Stella?’ he repeats. ‘But I thought you were with–’

‘I was, I was. I mean today. This morning.’

He blinks, dazed. ‘I ... er–’

‘Yes or no?’ Nina shrieks. ‘It’s a simple question.’

‘No.’

‘Has my mother called?’

‘No.’

‘My father?’

‘No.’

‘Grandparents?’

‘No. No one.’

‘Shit.’ Nina holds her hand to her forehead. Her eyes light on a cup sitting on the kitchen surface. She thinks about hurling it to the floor. She imagines the noise of shattering china, the way the pieces would skitter apart on the flagged floor. It would make her feel a lot better but she probably shouldn’t do it in front of Richard. She decides against it. ‘Shit,’ she says again, and sinks into a chair.

Richard puts down his toast and comes towards her. ‘What’s up?’

Nina can’t answer him. She’s thinking, furiously turning over options. Where would Stella go?

Richard kneels in front of her. ‘What’s the escapologist done now?’

Nina laughs, despite herself, then despair overtakes her again. ‘Oh, God, Richard.’

She allows herself to bury her face in the front of his dressing-gown. His arms fasten round her, as she knew they would, and she inhales the metallic sleep-smell off him.

'What happened?' he murmurs. 'Did the two of you fall out? You can tell me.'

'No.'

'You can't?'

'I can't.'

He strokes a hand up and down her back. 'Well, don't worry. Whatever it is, it will all be fine.'

'I'm not sure it will,' she mumbles.

He pulls away from her, looks at her steadily, his hands round her waist. 'I'm sorry we argued,' he says.

'So am I.'

'I'm glad you're back.'

'Me too.' She smiles at him, then says: 'I need a shower.'

Jake is quite impressed with his sleuthing. He got himself to London, found his way to a phonebook, looked up Gilmore, S., wrote down her address, bought a street map, found the address, navigated his way there on the Tube, and here he is, walking down Stella's street.

As he nears the number of her house, he feels a dizzying mix of excitement and fear. She is there, probably, behind one of those windows. What will she say to him? How will she react? Will this be the second time in two days that he's been hit by a woman?

Her apartment building is a large house with steps up to the front door. Jake stands on the pavement looking up at it. He has no idea what will happen once he's inside – if he's allowed inside. But surely turning up like this will persuade her of his ... his seriousness about her.

Jake shoves the map into his back pocket and takes the steps two at a time. He peers at the array of bells and locates the middle one, which says 'Gilmore', in green ink that's been blurred and dispersed by rain. He presses it. Far off in the building there is a tinkling noise. He strains for the sound of footsteps, of voices, of anything, running over in his head the speech he's prepared.

Nina waits, surveying the cars lined up at the pavement. The door swings open. 'Darling,' Evie says, throwing her arms wide, 'it's about time I had a visit from you. How are you? I was thinking about you only the other day because–'

'I can't stay,' Nina interrupts.

'Oh.'

'I'm looking for Stella.' Nina allows a small pause in which she examines Evie's face. It is blank of all expression, unmoving, eyebrows arched. 'You haven't seen her, have you?'

Evie rests a bangled arm on her hip. 'Not for months, sweetie.'

Nina leans her weight against the stone door jamb. On a wire overhead, two birds fuss and squawk. 'And you haven't heard from her?'

'No.'

'Are you sure?'

The two women look at each other. They are almost equal height.

'As sure as sure can be,' Evie says. 'Why? What's happened?'

'Nothing.' Nina turns. 'Got to go.' She brandishes her mobile. 'Call me if you hear anything.'

Jake presses the bell again, this time for longer. Still nothing. He shifts from foot to foot and steps back to look at the building. A leaking gutter has spread an orange-brown stain down the wall. A plant leans out, waving, from a window-box.

Maybe she's out. She must be out. Jake lowers himself to the top step, his rucksack beside him, and leans his elbows on his knees. He'll wait.

He scratches a bite on his leg, pulls off his jacket and lays it over his bag. Maybe it's sitting in the warmth of the sun, but he feel a great wave of fatigue hit him. He's also, he realises, incredibly thirsty. Hangovers always do that to him. But he can't risk going to find some water – not now, not when he's come all this way.

Jake leans against the low wall, glancing up and down the street. A child beats a stick against the pavement, a woman wheels a bike along, a car tries to reverse into a too-small space.

Evie climbs the stairs back to her flat. She really must get the entryphone fixed so that she doesn't have to do this unseemly hike every time her doorbell rings. Inside, she snaps the dead heads off some flowers on a table, fiddles with a radiator setting, straightens a cushion.

'That was your sister,' she says, to the person huddled in the armchair.

Francesca is in the kitchen, peeling potatoes into a bowl, when Nina appears at the back door. Francesca jumps then laughs, still holding the peeler as she goes to open it. 'You scared me!' she says, as she hugs her daughter to her. 'Come in, come in. Why are you creeping about like that?'

Nina's body feels limp and her face, when Francesca pulls back to look at it, is paler than normal.

'What?' Francesca says immediately. 'What's wrong?'

Nina puts her bag on the table and grimaces. 'It's Stella,' she says.

‘What about her?’

She utters a single word: *‘Scarpata.’*

Francesca raises her eyes to the heavens. ‘Again?’ she shrieks.

‘Yeah.’

‘Where?’

‘Don’t know.’

Francesca sits at the table, banging the peeler down. A second later, she stands again. She has given up trying to decipher the relationship between her daughters, but it can still infuriate her. ‘I don’t understand,’ she says. ‘I thought you went to see her.’

‘I did.’

‘So, why this? Why–’

‘I don’t know!’ Nina cries. ‘Don’t ask me!’

Francesca crosses her arms. What is wrong with her family that this kind of thing happens again and again? Where did she go wrong? Motherhood, it seems to her, never ends. She gave birth to the child in front of her thirty years ago: long enough, you’d think, for you to be able to stop worrying about them. But no. They still do things, completely out of the blue, to disrupt your life, to surprise you, to make you anxious.

‘There’s no point in getting cross with me,’ Nina continues. ‘I was just letting you know. Putting you on the alert.’

Francesca nods, eyeing her daughter.

‘I have to go.’ Nina jiggles the keys in her pocket.

'OK.'

'I'll tell you if I hear anything.'

'Sì, sì.' Francesca waves her away.

She listens to Nina's car starting up, then walks to the phone. As soon as her mother answers, she announces: *'Stella scarpata.'*

From the street below, Stella can hear the rattle of a radio, the sound of someone hurrying along the pavement in high heels. In the corner, the TV screen is blizzarding, a videotape finished. The cat lies on its flank on the hearth, the tip of its tail flicking.

She raises her head, looks out at the blank, indeterminate sky. She's not sure how long she's been here. Days, perhaps. Or maybe just a few hours. She turns on to her side, drawing her knees up. Her body feels dull and heavy with inactivity.

She'd arrived on Evie's doorstep early in the morning, just after dawn. If Evie had been surprised to see her she didn't show it. She took one look at her and pulled her inside. She led her to the sofa, heaped duvets and blankets on top of her, supplied mugs of scalding coffee that Stella suspected were laced with whisky. She brought pyjamas, a hot-water bottle, lavender-scented handkerchiefs. She sliced buttered toast into tiny, crustless pieces and didn't say anything when Stella let them grow cold, spotted and unappetising. She put a black-and-white film on the video and Stella watched, dumbly, as a pale woman with over-pencilled eyebrows waited for her lover in a railway café, an invisible orchestra surging in the background.

Evie asked only one question: 'Is it a broken head we've got here, darling, or a broken heart?'

'Don't know,' Stella said. 'Heart, maybe.'

'That's good,' Evie had said, drawing an emery board along one side of her nail as the woman on-screen ran down a platform. 'Hearts are easier to mend than heads.'

Evie enters the room, dressed in an apron Stella has never seen before. 'I have broken the habit of a lifetime,' she announces.

Stella raises her head from the cushions. 'Really?'

'I,' Evie continues, handing her a cup of tea, 'have cooked. I made soup!'

Stella struggles to sit upright. 'What brought that on?'

'The sight of your pale little face, darling. I just couldn't bear it. You're going to have to eat it now, you know.'

'I will,' Stella says, blowing on the scalding tea. 'I promise.'

'If you don't, I might have to feed it to you through a piece of rubber tubing, suffragette-style.'

Stella smiles. 'I don't think it'll come to that.'

‘I should hope not.’

Evie sits down opposite her. There is a long moment of silence. Evie pulls off the apron and lays it over the sofa arm. The cat leaps up and settles itself on Evie’s lap.

‘I do have to tell you, darling,’ Evie says, kneading the cat’s ears, ‘that your entire family is going crazy. And I mean crazy, in the way only they can.’

Stella starts needlessly fiddling with the flex of a lamp next to her.

‘I haven’t told them you’re here,’ Evie continues, ‘but I think we need to let them know you’re OK before your mother starts getting the bishop to say a mass for you and your father hires a private detective.’

Stella doesn’t say anything.

‘Darling Stella, I’m not saying you have to see them, face a clan gathering or anything like that. Just let them know that you’re alive and haven’t driven off a cliff-edge somewhere. You don’t have to see...’ Evie pauses, choosing her words ‘…anyone ... if you don’t want to.’

Stella is relieved to hear the ringing of the phone. Evie gets up and goes into the other room to answer it and Stella is left in the room with the cat, who is ruffled and annoyed at being moved off Evie’s lap.

Evie returns quite quickly.

‘It was Nina,’ she says.

Stella puts down her teacup. She seems

unable to swallow and, for a moment, thinks she is about to choke. 'What did she say?' she manages.

'She knows you're here.'

'But ... I thought you said–'

'I didn't tell her. She said she had her suspicions that this was where you might be, and then she drove around the streets today and saw your car.' Evie points a finger at her. 'Remember that next time – hide the car. Anyway, there's a message. I wrote it down.' Evie holds the paper at arm's length. '"I didn't sleep with him,"' she reads expressionlessly, as if reciting a shopping list.

Stella sits motionless, transfixed by the steam wreathing up from her tea.

'Oh,' Evie says, 'and she's at the café in Musselburgh and wants to see you. Shall we go? Your car or mine? I thought we'd drive over. Mine, I think. Yours is probably caked in sheep shit.'

Stella sits opposite her sister in one of their grandparents' booths. They have sat like this so many times Stella gets the strange sensation that she can't be entirely sure what point they are at in their lives. Are they six and seven, with knickerbocker glories in front of them? Or are they teenagers trying to like espresso? Evie perches at the counter conversing with Valeria and Domenico as she always does – in French with an Italian accent. It seems to work somehow.

'Why didn't you tell me, Stel?' Nina is furious. Her default setting for most situations. 'Why didn't you just say?'

'Say what?'

'That you liked him. I wouldn't have gone anywhere near him if you'd said. You know I wouldn't.'

Stella shrugs, looks down at the jeans she's wearing. Evie had produced them, saying some man had left them behind and they were the only things in the flat that would fit Stella.

'Not that it made any difference.' Nina snorts. 'Nothing happened.' She leans over and touches Stella's hand. 'Nothing. He wasn't having any of it. I tried my entire repertoire,' she says, with a grin, 'physical, narcotic, verbal, alcoholic. No joy. You might draw the conclusion,' she says heavily, 'that he was in love with someone else.'

Stella says nothing, avoiding Nina's eye.

'He talked about you in his sleep.'

Stella looks up. 'What did he say?'

'Oh, I don't know.' Nina gestures, smoke wisping after her. 'You can't expect me to remember that. I was off my face. But he was murmuring your name at some point.'

Stella tries not to wince. The thought of them sleeping side by side is still a little too much for her to cope with.

‘How’s everything with Richard?’ she asks.

‘Oh, fine. The same. You know.’ Nina takes a sip of her coffee. ‘So, what are you going to do?’

Stella tugs at the ends of her hair. ‘I don’t know, Neen, I don’t know. I could go back to London and everything, but...’ she sighs ‘...I just feel–’

‘I meant about Jake,’ Nina interrupts.

‘Oh.’ Stella attempts to think, to make her brain operational. What is she going to do about Jake? She has literally no idea. Her brain comes up with nothing, just starts doing that repetitive *Jake, Jake* thing again. Should she ring him? What would she say? She’s having trouble keeping up with events. The man she loves is married. Except he isn’t. He slept with her sister. Except he didn’t. But they still spent the night together. In the same bed, by the sound of it.

‘I don’t know,’ she says again, hating the pathetic edge to her voice. She would like more than anything to be able to wind back time to the point where she was sending Jake to show Nina where the caravan was, where she could reach over the kitchen counter and prise them apart.

‘Because ... um...’ Nina pulls nervously on her cigarette ‘...there is something I ... I have to tell you.’

‘What?’

Nina is jiggling her leg, picking at the edge

of the table. 'There was one thing that happened.'

'I don't want to hear about it,' Stella snaps, afraid now.

'No, no, not like that. I think ... I think...' Nina stops and then the rest of the sentence comes out in a rush: 'I think I might have told him.'

Stella frowns. 'Told him what?'

'It.'

'It?'

'You know. It.' Nina leans across the table. 'The Thing.'

Stella hasn't heard Nina use that expression for so long that for a moment she can't recall what it refers to. But something in her remembers because the scalp shrinks on her skull and a cold sensation spreads through her.

She sits in Evie's lover's clothes and stares at her sister. Sometimes when she looks at her she can see the ghost of herself in her face. But not now. Nina looks weirdly unfamiliar to her, as if she hardly knows her. It's as if she's never looked at this face ever before. She sees a place where her mascara has smudged, the arch of her brows, that she has a few freckles over her nose, the rapid flutter of her eyelids. 'You are not serious,' she hears herself whisper. 'Nina,' she has to gasp to draw breath, 'why?'

'I don't know.' Nina jiggles her leg up and

down again, making the teaspoons shiver against the china. 'It just came out. I – I don't know why. It was an accident.' She rubs her fingers over her brow. 'It was just so weird being there. I'll never understand what made you want to go back. And I – I was drunk.'

'You've been drunk before,' Stella says, and she is getting up from the table, 'and managed to keep it to yourself. So why now? And why him, for God's sake, Nina? Why him?'

I am Stella Gilmore. I am twenty-eight. I have green eyes and black hair. I am five foot ten. I have a sister. I am half Italian. I own a car and a flat. I have lived in eleven different countries. I have never broken a bone in my body but once had pleurisy. When I was eight years old I killed someone.

These are the facts of my life.

Stella bolts through the café. In the mirrors she sees a gallery of Stellas, wild-haired, running towards her. She sees her grandparents, her uncle and Evie turning to stare at her. She yanks at the door and she is out in the street. The air is thin and cold after the warm fug of the café.

Nina is next to her, holding on to her sleeve.

'Where are you going, Stel? Don't go,' her

sister is pleading, ‘I’m sorry. I’m so sorry. Please don’t go. I’m sorry.’

Stella shakes her off. ‘I can’t believe you’ve done this,’ she manages to get out from between her teeth. ‘I can’t believe it. You have – you have broken me.’ She pushes Nina away from her and staggers further down the pavement.

Her legs feel weak and boneless, the sky above the stone buildings of Musselburgh too bright, too white, jarring on her retinas. Stella’s vision seems to be closing in at the sides, the scene melting and waving like the horizon line in a desert. She told Jake. Jake knows. This she cannot take, she really cannot take. The thing that she has kept secret, folded up small inside her, has been yanked out. That this knowledge could dry out Jake’s love for her is unbearable. For what else could it do? He knows. The worst thing. How could he ever bring himself to look at her again?

Putting one foot in front of the other suddenly seems the hardest thing she’s ever done. Then she is tripping and falling to the ground and it’s a relief because she doesn’t have to keep standing upright, and somewhere she can hear Evie’s voice saying that she hasn’t eaten a thing for days, and Stella is thinking, is it only days since I saw him, and she can hear her sister crying and saying her name over and over. Nina. Before there was anything, there was Nina.

'What will we do if we can't find them again?' Nina was asking.

Stella used the branch of a tree to haul herself up. 'We will,' she said.

They were climbing the steep path up the side of a waterfall. Misted, air-borne spray floated towards them, damping their faces, their hair, their clothes. Stella could taste the river on her lips.

As she turned to help Nina climb the final step of the incline, something whizzed past her ear like a bullet. Whatever it was landed in the gorse next to them. A loose stone? A landslide? Another missile came hurtling through the air and something struck Stella on the arm, sharp as an arrow.

She whipped round. There was a figure standing in front of them, legs straddling the path, next to where the water started tipping and sliding over the drop. Anthony. Flipping stones at them as casually as someone tossing coins. She saw him raise his arm and pull it back behind his head.

'Don't!' she cried. 'Don't! Don't hit her on the head. You mustn't!'

She shielded Nina's cranium, crouching over her. If she got a knock on the head, she relapsed, sometimes for days. It would be awful, unthinkable, if that happened here. The stone landed beside Nina's shoe, then another, further away.

Anthony stood looking at them, his arms folded. The path behind him was empty. Where was the rest of the class? Anthony liked an audience. But it was just him and her and Nina and the trees and the waterfall. She felt Nina's hand creep into hers.

'Where is everyone?' she heard herself say.

He smiled slowly and Stella saw the wolfish yellow of his teeth. 'Gone.' He jerked his thumb. 'Up that way.'

She didn't like the way he was looking at Nina, his eyes small and slitted, his head on one side, she didn't like it at all. Stella edged closer to her sister.

'What do you want?' she said.

'That's not very nice.' He loosened his arms so that they hung by his sides. 'I came back to look for you.'

'Why?'

He didn't answer but lunged towards Nina. Stella saw it coming. She stepped in front of her just in time, feeling the mass of his body hit hers. She would not let him get Nina, she would not. Fury was filling her head, roaring in her ears like water. Nina was screaming and clinging to her but Stella felt herself wrenched away from her sister, pushed so hard that the world was pitching sideways.

She hit the ground with a dull crack. Pain

spread from her back down her legs and she was momentarily winded, her lungs aching with emptiness, her hands muddy, the sun white and glaring above her. Somewhere, she could hear her sister sobbing.

Stella turned her head. Anthony was standing over Nina like an executioner, the collar of her dress bunched in his fingers.

'So I shouldn't hit her on the head,' he was saying. 'Why? What'll happen?' His other hand was raised high in a fist, Nina's head bowed beneath it. 'Let's see, shall we?'

Stella scrambled to her feet. She looked at the precipice and she looked at him. She saw that Anthony's lace was loose, snaking away from his shoe along the ground. It made very simple sense. Stella lifted her foot and stepped on to the lace. She could feel it there, trapped beneath her sole, and she placed her hands against the chest of Anthony Cusk and she pushed.

It was quite deliberate. She will never be able to convince herself otherwise. He was driven back, away from Nina, his hand coming loose from Nina's dress, his arms wheeling for balance, the raised fist uncurling and jerking back. The lace tugged itself free, slid out from under Stella's foot. She and Nina heard his small grunt of shock. They watched him stagger back, crashing into the river, the bed of wet, slimed stones making him slip and lurch.

They saw the black waters claim him, swirling round his legs.

He seemed to teeter on the edge for a long time. His eyes were wide, his lips stretched, his face strangely blank. He kept his grip on the earth with one foot, like a dancer or a man seeking flight. Then he tipped, his arms still circling, and fell.

There was a long moment, between him vanishing from the scene and the sound of his body hitting the rocks below, when Stella found herself thinking that maybe it hadn't just happened, that maybc he was playing a trick on them, that he was bound to be holding on to the lip of the waterfall, and any minute now he would reappear, a grinning jack-in-a-box.

But there was the deadened thud, another pause, then a splash as he fell into the water. And she and Nina were alone again.

Miss Saunders sees them coming from a long way off. They run over the expanse of green, which is wavering and brightening in the uncertain light. Something about them makes her stand, makes her shush the child talking to her, makes her strain her eyes into the sun.

The Gilmore girls are running over the glen. Stella is in front, her legs moving, her arms flying loose behind her like wings. Nina is in the distance, trying to keep up, and is it Miss Saunders's imagination or is she screaming?

Miss Saunders looks at the sisters, from one to the other. It will only be a few seconds, a minute maybe, until she finds out what it is, but she cannot bear it. It's the feeling all teachers dread. Nina's screams reach her in staccato bursts, as if by intermittent radio connection.

'What is it?' Miss Saunders shouts, somehow knowing that it's already too late. 'What's happened?'

Stella had looked. Nina hadn't. Stella had inched her way on her stomach right to the very edge – her dress would be soaking later, all down her front, but no one would ask her why – and peered over.

All her life she's wished she hadn't.

He was looking back at her, his eyes clear and open and seeking out hers. There he was, lying under the thick weight of water, staring at her.

Stella is lying on a bed with her sister, head to toe. Nina has made everyone else disappear. For a while there was flapping and fuss and her mother on the phone and people bringing cups of tea and tissues and advice. But Nina had managed to get her out of the café, into the car and back to her flat in what seemed like minutes.

Nina is stroking her ankle and telling her how she and Richard have decided to have a baby. 'He thinks it will calm me down.' She snorts. 'Weigh me down, more like. Stop me going off. What do you think?'

'I think...' Stella says, and her voice still sounds a bit funny to her, a bit hollow and far-away. She can't quite comprehend how she arrived here, in Nina's bedroom. It's as if she went to sleep in one life and woke up in another. 'I think if you want a baby, you should have one.'

'But that's the thing, isn't it?' Nina says. 'I don't know if I do. How can you know, if you've never had one?'

Stella shrugs. It always surprises her, the way rows and schisms with your family can pass over, drain away so quickly. One minute you can be screaming that they have ruined your life and the next you're curled up on a bed together, as if nothing has happened.

'That's the problem with babies,' Nina continues. 'The only way to find out if you want one is to have one. And by then it's too late. You can't just shove it back up, can you? There ought to be a kind of centre where you can–'

'Test-drive motherhood?'

'Exactly.'

Nina presses her hand to the sole of Stella's foot. 'So, what about you?'

‘What about me?’

‘What are you going to do? Stay in Edinburgh?’

‘I don’t know. Probably not. I don’t really want to be here.’

‘You’ve never really wanted to be here.’

‘I know.’

‘And Jake?’

Stella pushes herself up and swings her legs off the bed. Her head stutters slightly but clears. Through Nina’s bedroom window, she can see a woman with a red umbrella, pushing a leaflet into the letter-slit of a house opposite.

‘Jake ... is a lost cause, I think.’ She lowers her head to pick cat hairs off her sweater, letting them float away on the air.

‘You don’t know that, Stel.’

‘I do.’

‘You do not.’

‘Oh, really?’ Stella turns round and faces her sister. ‘Would you want someone after you’d found out they–’ She stops, biting off the words, remembering Richard is somewhere in the flat.

‘You have to at least give him a chance, find out if that’s what he thinks, which I don’t believe it is. It was so long ago, Stel.’ Nina shakes her by the arm. ‘Years and years and years. You have to put it behind you.’ She chews her lip. ‘I have.’

‘Nina, you didn’t do it,’ Stella whispers,

her voice hoarse, as if with disuse.

'But it was as much my fault as yours.'

'No, it wasn't.'

'It was,' Nina insists. 'If it hadn't been you, it would have been me.'

Stella turns to look at her. She cannot get over the fact that they are talking about it. The Thing. 'That's not true,' she says. 'And you know it.'

They are silent for a moment. Nina looks away, starts twirling a strand of hair around her fingers. 'You know what your biggest problem is?' she says suddenly.

'No. What?'

'It's not that you can't forget about it,' Nina begins, 'or that you see him everywhere. It's that you don't think you should be allowed to have a normal life, to have the things normal people have, to–'

'Bollocks.' Stella rounds on her sister. 'It's not that at all.'

'It is!' Nina stands up and starts pacing about. 'It's exactly that! I know that's really why you can't face Jake. It's not that you can't bear the fact that he knows. It's that you think you need to be punished for something you weren't punished for – something I made sure you weren't punished for.'

'Nina,' Stella interjects, but her sister talks over her: 'You have some stupid, pig-headed notion that depriving yourself of him is going to absolve you. You know what?' She comes to a stop. 'I may have even done you a favour.'

There is a pause. Stella stares at her, aghast. 'A favour?' she repeats.

'Yeah.' Nina lifts her chin, defiant. 'In telling him. You would never have told him and – and you'd have carried on being all closed up and shut off. This way you're going to see that it won't make any difference to how he feels about you. You might even begin to realise that you are allowed to be happy, that–'

'Oh, spare me the psychoanalysis.'

'I will not. And I will not let you throw a chance like Jake away. Stella, please,' she urges. 'It was an accident. It happened. Get over it.'

Stella picks at a loose thread in the bed-cover. 'Look, none of this matters anyway,' she mutters. 'I mean, I don't see him here.' She gestures around the room. 'It's not as if he's exactly desperate to speak to me.'

'He doesn't know where you are,' Nina points out, with sarcastic patience.

'There are ways he could find me. There's ... well, Mum and Dad are in the phone book for starters ... and ... er...' She grinds to a halt.

'I didn't even know where you were till this morning.'

'Well, maybe,' Stella says, 'but–'

'Stel, can't you see?' Her sister crouches in

front of her suddenly and takes both her hands in hers. 'You've let yourself get stuck. You've got to stop hanging on to this. Jake loves you.' Stella sighs and tries to pull away but Nina tightens her grip. 'Listen to me. He does. He's not going to give a shit about something that happened twenty years ago.'

'You don't know that.'

'I do.'

'You do not.'

'I do so. If you throw this away because you're too scared to move on, to – to let him into your life, then you're a fool. You'll have fucked up for good.'

Stella extracts her hands, stands up and walks to the window. She presses her forehead to the cool of the glass and looks up and down the street for the woman with the leaflets. She's disappeared.

Behind her, Nina throws herself on to the bed with an exasperated noise. 'I don't know why I bother,' she fumes, thrashing about, thumping pillows into shape. 'Might as well talk to the fucking wall. I know what you'll do. I know exactly what you'll do.'

'You do, do you?'

'You're going to run away again. And you'll keep on running away, just like you've always done.'

Stella thinks about this, watching her breath form and fade on the pane. 'Probably.' She nods. 'Yes.'

In the middle of a huge station, Jake pushes his bank card into a machine, shading the screen so that he can make out the green lettering.

He's been staying in a travellers' hostel, a grim place with twelve beds to each windowless cell and where the choking scent of disinfectant doesn't quite cover other, more ingrained smells that Jake doesn't want to think about.

He watches as the machine considers his request. He imagines the coded, electronic information being exchanged between this machine in a London railway station and his bank in Wanchai. Will it let him have it? He needs eighty pounds, minimum – enough to pay his bill at the hostel, where they have his passport held to ransom, and to buy a train ticket to Edinburgh. Jake glances round at the departures board. There's a train leaving in fifteen minutes. If he gets it he'll be in Edinburgh by late afternoon, and by evening, who knows? Stella's house, the café? If he doesn't find her, then he's in real ... but Jake doesn't want to think about that.

He checked his email yesterday, for the first time in weeks. There were nine messages from Chen, in ascending degrees of panic. The script they'd been working on had suddenly got the green light and he needed Jake back. Now. The most recent one was from Chen's PA, saying that if Jake wasn't coming back, he should let them know because they had found someone to take over Jake's job, if necessary. Jake had sat in the internet café with his head in his hands for minutes on end. Then typed: *Don't give my job away to anyone. I'm coming back. Give me three days – four at the most.*

Jake has exhausted everything he could think of in London. The woman in her flat wasn't Stella. She was a friend of hers, she said, one hand on the door, she hadn't heard from her in weeks. The girl he'd spoken to at the radio station had had the same peeved tone in her voice: Stella used to work there but not for a while now and, no, she had no idea where she was.

He turns back to the machine. His card is being regurgitated and a message is flashing at him: Request Denied, Insufficient Funds.

'Eighty measly fucking pounds,' he is muttering to himself, as he yanks a second card out of his wallet. 'It's not much to ask.'

He pushes this card into the narrow slot, sending a silent prayer to the god of autotellers. Please, please. Eighty pounds. That's all. I'll pay it back, I promise.

The machine has a long think. Jake shifts from foot to foot, watching the minutes to the Edinburgh train count down on the station clock. Then there is a horrible grinding noise as the machine gulps down his card. Request Denied, Card Confiscated.

'Shit.' Jake bangs his fist against the wall. 'Shit, shit, fuck.'

He closes his eyes for a moment. He finds it hard to fathom, the way his life has become so precarious. He drifted for years through school, through various jobs, various women, with nothing much to surprise or wrong-foot him. And all of a sudden he's almost killed, he's forced into marriage with someone he hardly knows, he moves half-way across the world, he goes in search of the father he never knew but finds a girl instead, he messes up in a shocking variety of ways, the girl leaves, and he runs after her. Which would have been quite enough for several lifetimes. But then someone tells him that this girl, the girl he loves, killed someone.

Jake opens his eyes and surveys the semi-lit chaos of the station: people running for trains, people gazing up at the departures board, people sitting on suitcases, waiting. What Nina told him that night flashes at him intermittently, like the beam of a distant lighthouse. He feels as though he should be more shocked by it, more affected. But he finds he is curiously unsurprised. There is so much about Stella he doesn't understand.

Jake tries to picture Stella at eight. He sees a thin child with an anxious face and small, clenched hands. 'She did it,' Nina had whispered to him, 'for me. Can you imagine?' Jake finds that he can't, he can't imagine it at all. He cannot for a moment even begin to appreciate what must have made her do it – he's not sure he could ever bear to know. The class bully. It makes him furious for her, makes him want to fold her hands in his and take her somewhere far away.

But he has to find her first. He shoves his wallet into his pocket and walks out of the station.

He stands outside a phonebox. People flow past him, on their way to the mouth of the Underground. The sun is hot, much hotter than in Scotland. Men are in their shirtsleeves, jackets held over their arms. The smell of rotting garbage reminds Jake fleetingly of Hong Kong.

He turns away from the phonebox. He walks off. He stops. He comes back. He stands for a moment, chewing his lip. He cannot do this, he cannot. He's nearly thirty years old – how can he have come to this? But his stomach is growling at him, he's eaten nothing today yet and he has just under a pound in his pocket. He could always hitch, but the massed tentacled roads of London confuse him. He wouldn't know which one to take and, anyway, he'd be scared of being picked up by an urban serial killer.

Jake presses his hands to his temples. What other option does he have? It'll be almost a fortnight until he gets his paycheck. He can't survive that long.

He pulls at the door of the phonebox and steps inside. Hearing her voice saying that of course she'll accept reversed charges from the UK makes him almost lose his nerve and hang up.

'Jake?' his mother is saying. 'Is that you?'

'Yeah. Hi.'

'Are you all right?'

'Yes.' He presses the receiver close to his ear. 'Actually, no. Caro, I need some money.' He hates the sound of his voice as he says it. 'I am so sorry to ask you this. Especially as I know you and Lionel can't exactly–'

'Where are you?' she interrupts.

'London.'

'London?' Caroline is incredulous. 'What are you doing there?'

'I can pay you back,' he continues, 'in a couple of weeks. I'll give it all back to you, I promise. I just need enough for a ticket to Scotland.'

He scuffs his sneaker against the filthy metal wall of the phonebox and listens to her thinking.

'What's going on, Jakey?'

Jake takes a deep breath. 'There's this girl. And if I don't get to Edinburgh today or tomorrow, then–'

'How much do you need?' his mother says immediately.

There was never any question about where Stella would be staying. Nina had swept up her bag from Evie's, slammed it into the car and dumped it in her boxroom. 'Towels in the cupboard,' she said, 'clean underwear in my drawers,' and started showing her how the electric blanket worked.

When Nina goes out to meet Richard for lunch, as she does most days, Stella is left in the flat. She has a long bath, half submerging herself in scalding water, watching her skin turn livid pink, the blood leaping close to the surface. She listens to songs on Nina's favourite radio station, stares up at the ceiling, soaps herself with the products arranged along the shelves. Later, she sniffs her skin and finds that she smells of her sister.

When she's dressed, her hair still wet, she wanders the empty rooms, sipping from a mug of tea. Nina's home is curious. Stella has never spent stretches of time alone here. Everywhere she looks are objects she recognises from the house they grew up in – ornaments, cushions, a chest of drawers, a vase, a picture. On the mantelpiece sits not only Nina's silver christening bowl, but hers. Their names are there, engraved inside the rims: Stella Giuditta Gilmore and Nina Maddalena Gilmore. By Nina's bed is one of the matching lamps they had beside their bunk-beds. Its pair, when Stella looks for it, is on the dressing-table. She is surprised by how much Nina has of their parents' house. She took nothing, kept nothing. Most of these things she'd forgotten about.

In the hallway, Stella sits on the stool next to the phone and gazes at some china mice Valeria once gave them for Christmas. Stella reaches out and picks them up, one in each hand, remembering the instant she touches them the feel of the hard, slippery glaze, their hollow fragility, their roughened bases.

'Hi,' she murmurs, 'remember me?'

The mice look back at her with an intent, preoccupied stare. She wonders what on earth she's doing, talking to china ornaments. She puts them down again quickly, in the same confidential huddle Nina had them in, and slides open the drawer.

Inside, she's amazed to find a cache of ancient things – school jotters, some Nina's, some filled with her own handwriting, ancient, discoloured photographs of the two of them, their old pencil cases, leather dry with disuse, but still filled with half-eroded pencils, compasses, greying rubbers. Stella unpacks the whole drawer and examines everything, running her fingertips over the jotter covers, the inked pages, the pen shafts, photos of them in the garden, outside Evie's flat, leaning against a car. She lays them all out on the floor, in an arc around her, and sits for a while looking at them.

Nina, she realises, is a kind of curator of their joint past. It gives her a peculiar ache in her throat that Nina wants these things. That, even though Stella disregards them, her sister saves them, looks after them, keeps them together.

There will be a time, Jake thinks, when he is not racing about Britain looking for people. He has to keep promising himself this – that his life will not for ever consist of mad dashes up and down a country in search of people who do not want to be found.

He shifts from one foot to the other and looks again at the café across the road. 'Iannelli's', the sign reads, in square gold letters. It has to be the one. He's walked around the streets, along the river and back again, asking random people where he can find a café run by Italians. A few of them looked him up and down suspiciously and walked on – he's no idea why – but the ones who did reply said there was only one. Iannelli's. On the high street. Stella definitely said Musselburgh was the town. Or perhaps it was something else. Is he sure it was Musselburgh?

Jake pushes himself away from the wall

he's leaning on. This is madness. All he has to do is go in and ask. It's very simple. This, after all, is his only lead. He crosses the road in a straight line, his jaw set. It's going to be fine. It'll be easy. He's just going to say he's looking for Stella, and do they happen to know where she might be. Simple.

As he nears the café, something fails him. Through the window, he can see two men, one older than the other, conversing with a customer. They are big, burly and they look like ... well, extras from a Mafia movie. Oh God, he thinks, you have messed about with not one but two of their family. He is going to end up at the bottom of the river in concrete boots. Or get a horse's head in his bed. His mother will never know what happened to him.

Jake swivels away and walks past, very fast. Then he walks back again. This is ridiculous. He has to stop faffing about. This café is the only link with Stella he has left. It has to work, it will work. He pushes the door and goes in. The men behind the counter nod at him, one smiles. There is an old woman as well, standing at a coffee machine, a cup in her hand. She smiles, too. Jake feels like an informer in the enemy camp. They all seem to be waiting for something.

'Um,' Jake says, 'er ... I was wondering...' Something makes him glance to his right and he sees, behind the counter, also looking at him, the woman Stella will be in twenty years' time. Are all families this identikit, or is it just this one?

'If I could...' His nerve fails him. 'Could I have a coffee, please?'

'Francesca?'

Francesca stops and looks at her friend across the counter. 'What?' She is annoyed. She's in the middle of a story about a curtain-maker in Joppa and Evie is craning round, obviously thinking about something else entirely.

'I think that's him,' Evie hisses at her, ducking down.

'Who?' Francesca is mystified by this behaviour.

'Him. You know.'

'I don't know what you're talking about.'

'Yes, you do. *Him*.'

Evie is winking significantly, and the penny drops. Francesca puts down the sundae dishes she's been wiping.

'Him?' She points at the dark-haired boy sitting at the back, hunched over a coffee. She has managed to glean only the vaguest sense of the recent ruction between her daughters but she's sure of one thing: it's all the fault of some boy. 'How do you know?'

'Nina described him to me.'

'But I thought he was, you know ...

Chinese.' Francesca whispers the last word.

'No, no.' Evie shakes her head. 'He's white.'

'Oh.' Francesca peers over Evie's shoulder to have another glance. 'He looks Italian.'

'Do you think?'

'Yes.'

'What? He's registering on your Roman-radar, is he?'

'Definitely.' Francesca has another quick look. 'Part-Italian, at least.'

'Well, he could be, I suppose. I'll tell you this, though,' Evie smirks in a rather lascivious way, 'your daughters have good taste. If you're going to fight over a man, then you might as well make sure he's–'

'Be quiet!' Francesca snaps. 'I'm going over.' She whips off her apron, muttering, 'Give him a piece of my mind.'

'Cesca,' Evie tags behind her, holding on to a corner of her apron as she marches through the café, 'do you think that's a good idea? Perhaps we should–'

'Is your name Jake?' Francesca bellows.

Jake starts, scattering sugar granules across the table, and looks up to see the older Stella woman bearing down on him.

'Yes,' he says, 'yes.' He leaps to his feet and almost salutes. There is another woman standing behind her, as if ready to restrain her. This doesn't look good. It's not quite the discreet chat he'd had in mind. 'Hi. It's very nice to meet you.' Caroline's lessons in manners seem to be asserting themselves. 'Are you–'

'I am Stella's mother,' the woman announces, drawing herself up. 'And Nina's,' she adds pointedly.

'Right. It's nice to meet you,' he says, and wonders why he's repeating himself.

'May I ask what you're doing here?'

'Actually, I'm looking for Stella. You don't happen–'

'Just Stella?' she snaps. 'Or Nina as well?'

'Er...' Jake founders. What would be the right answer here? 'Well...'

The blonde woman is murmuring, 'Francesca, perhaps we ought to–'

'If you think you can just come in here and start disrupting things between my daughters again, you've got another thing coming.' Francesca is waving her fist at him in what is definitely a threatening manner. 'How dare you slink in here? Haven't you done enough damage? My girls are–'

The people from behind the counter have arrived at the table. The older woman says something to Francesca in Italian and Francesca gives a short reply. Jake has no idea what it was, but it doesn't sound flattering. It contained the word *'brutto'* for a start.

'It's him,' the small blonde woman says,

very much in the kind of voice you'd reserve for saying, it's the devil.

The older man speaks and the woman Jake presumes is his wife turns to him to argue. Jake wants to close his eyes. Is this where he gets bundled into a back room? He wants to ask if he can make one last phone call. Is he letting his imagination run away with him? Probably.

'He just wants to know where she is!' the blonde woman is saying. 'That's all! We have to tell him. If she finds out that we–'

'Evie,' Francesca turns on her and starts arguing, saying something about him being unreliable, a game-player, and how they know absolutely nothing about him.

'Well, it doesn't seem to be stopping you making all kinds of judgements about him,' she retorts, and Jake decides that he likes her, that she's wonderful.

The old man is pointing at him, and his wife is nodding. The other man is leaning against the counter, his arms folded, staring at Jake. Jake doesn't like him. Not one bit.

He feels a hand on his arm and he flinches. But it's only the blonde woman, leaning towards him. 'I'd go if I were you,' she whispers.

Jake walks through the café. It's suddenly very long, seems to take him an age to get to the door. He glances one way and sees bits of himself reflected again and again in lots of angled mirrors; he glances the other and sees a collection of postcards pinned to a board behind the counter.

Then he is outside and the noise of their argument stops. He is, he realises, near tears. A woman walks by, glancing back at him, and he has to press the heels of his palms to his eyes. He moves off, without really knowing where he is going.

He has just reached a side street and is about to cross when he hears a voice behind him: 'Hey!'

Jake turns. Stella's grandfather is hurrying towards him his shirtsleeves.

'Hey,' he says again, and Jake waits for him, nervously. What now?

'Stella?' the old man questions.

'Yes.' Jake starts nodding, like one of those toy dogs people have in their cars. 'Stella, yes.'

He leans close to him and says something. A single word. Jake has no idea what it is.

'Sorry?' Jake says.

The old man says it again. Twice, each time looking closely at Jake to see if he has understood. Jake strains to hear but the accent is thick and not one he is used to.

It begins with a P – that much he can make out. The idea that he is being given a clue but can't comprehend it makes sweat break out on his brow. The old man pronounces the word again and again, slapping one hand against the other, then pointing down the road. Jake looks in that direction, bemused, then looks back. What can it mean and why the hell did he never learn any Italian? The man grips his arm, willing him to understand and, suddenly, something emerges from the run-together sounds.

'Portobello?' Jake seizes on the word. He remembers seeing it on a railway-station sign on the way here, and thinking that it was a strange name for a Scottish town. 'Stella's in Portobello?'

'Sì, sì.' The grandfather smiles. 'Portobello. Stella in Portobello.' He has Jake by the elbow and is hustling him towards a bus-stop. *'Capisce?'* He checks as the bus approaches. 'You understand?'

'Yes,' Jake grins, as he climbs on to the bus, 'thank you. Thank you so much.'

Stella's grandfather dismisses his gratitude with a single, short gesture. Jake says the magic word to the driver, pays, gets his ticket and sits down in the front row before he thinks of something. He jumps up and yanks open the window.

'Where in Portobello?' he says.

The grandfather nods and smiles. 'Portobello, *sì*.'

'Yes, but where?'

The bus jerks into movement and the grandfather waves goodbye. Jake asks the driver – twice – to tell him when they reach

Portobello, then watches the road spool out before him. The traffic gets denser as they near the city and more people get on: an elderly man, a woman with a dog in a basket, two teenagers who look like they should be at school.

Jake stares out of the window, hands gripping his knees. They are passing through what looks like a suburb. Large, sandy-stone houses with big, sloping gardens, flashes of the sea through the gaps, clipped hedges, white-painted signs for Bed and Breakfast. He sees, moving along the pavement, in step with the bus, two women.

At first it strikes him that they are walking very close together. He sees that their arms are linked and their hands intertwined. They walk together like old biddies who need the support of each other. Then Jake sees that there is something familiar about the nape of the neck of the taller one.

He leaps upright, cracking his head on the ceiling. 'Stella!' he shouts.

Everyone turns to look at him. The woman with the dog jumps and Jake presses himself to the window, banging on it with his knuckles.

'Stella!' he yells. 'Stella!'

People on the pavement stop and turn their faces up towards him. But not Stella or Nina. They are deep in conversation. Stella is saying something to her sister, and Nina is nodding. The bus picks up speed, leaving them behind. Jake bangs on the window once more, then lurches towards the bell. He jangles it, trying to keep the sisters in view.

'Can you stop?' he says. 'Please?'

The driver glances at him in the rear-view mirror but the bus rattles on, houses and people and streets flashing past.

'Please let me off,' Jake begs, jangling the bell again. 'Please.'

The driver utters a curse under his breath but, at the next lights, pulls the lever for the doors.

Jake leaps from the bus and, the second his feet hit the ground, runs in the opposite direction. He sees the faces on the bus swivel to watch him go. He estimates that he should reach them soon – he is running and they are walking in his direction, after all – but there's no sign of them. He glances over the road, in case they've crossed, then over his shoulder, but nothing. At the place where he'd first seen them, he stops, turning first one way then the other. The road stretches out in both directions, but the only figures he can see are lone people: a mother trailing a small child, a man carrying a carpet, a girl pushing a bicycle. No pairs of people walking arm in arm.

They've vanished. Jake's pulse is so fast, his heart beating so hard, he has to put up a hand and lean against a wall. Where can they have gone? Have they disappeared into one of these houses? Did he imagine it? Is he going to have to wait here in the hope of them reappearing? He would, he decides, he'd wait all night, rooted to this spot beside a lamp-post with an outdated flyer for a bring-and-buy sale taped to it, if that was what it took.

He has to resist the urge to shout her name at the top of his voice. He checks the road again, both ways. Still nothing. He looks speculatively at the side-street in front of him. It cuts between two rows of stone houses, and at its end is the sea. Jake looks at the strips of colour facing him: the grey slice of promenade, the ochre of the sand, the green-grey sea, touched with white, the jagged brownish mass of the opposite coast and, on top of it all, stretched right up from the horizon to arch out over where he is standing, the blue sky.

He hurries down the middle of the road. As he rounds the corner on to the promenade, the sea hurls a salt breeze into his face. Jake stops. He is standing outside a big red-brick Victorian swimming-baths. The beach is a huge expanse of pebbled sand, reflecting snatches of the sky. Groynes of blackened wood run along the beach, sinking themselves into water.

Descending some concrete steps to the

beach is Nina. Jake sprints towards her. She is struggling to light a cigarette, turning her back to the sea, holding her coat round her lighter.

'Hi,' Jake says, when he's close enough for her to hear him.

She looks up. She takes the cigarette slowly from her lips. She opens her mouth as if she's going to say something but instead she just points, with the cigarette, towards where the concrete lip of the promenade falls away to the beach.

Jake moves to the railings. Stella is ten yards from him, walking along beside the groyne, one hand trailing against the wood. He vaults over the railings and down to the sand in one movement. Pebbles and shells crunch under his shoes. He is sure she'll turn when she hears him but she doesn't. She is looking at something out to sea, her head on one side, and just as he is about to reach her, he hears her say, 'So, do you think we should–'

'Stella?' he says.

She turns. She has a pebble in her hand. Jake can see the emerald filigree of seaweed on it. He doesn't know what to say, where to begin. Her eyes travel down to his feet and back up to his face, as if checking it's really him. The relief at having her there, in front of him, within arm's length, is so great that he realises the tears he fought down earlier are threatening to rise again. Jake panics – what on earth is wrong with him? – and has to stare at the ground, at their feet, which face each other, at the way stones have stencilled patterns on to the sand.

'I want to apologise,' he says. 'For ... Mel and...'

He gestures inarticulately behind him. 'I've been an idiot.'

He curls his hands inside his pockets. He's been rehearsing this speech for so long you'd think it would come out better, but just being here with her makes him lose all sense of what it is he needs to say. He'd forgotten that she has that effect on him, draining his head of all rational thought.

'I know...' he soldiers on '...that there's no excuse ... that ... that there's nothing I can say to ... to... The thing is, ever since I met you, I ... I...'

He gazes at her. She is looking at him, a little perplexed, her hands clasped round the pebble. The mobile, angular beauty of her face he'd forgotten that too. 'What was I saying?' he asks.

'Ever since you met me,' she prompts.

'Ah.' He looks at the horizon for inspiration. 'Yes. Ever since...' he hears himself begin again. Then he sighs, his shoulders slump and he takes a step towards her. 'God, Stella,' he says, in his normal voice, 'I've been looking for you everywhere.'

‘Have you?’

‘Yeah. All over. In London and–’

‘You went to London?’

‘Yes.’

‘But I wasn’t there.’

‘I know that,’ he says, ‘now.’

She is silent for a moment. She shifts the stone into her other hand and he is aware of her looking over his shoulder at something. Her sister? Possibly. Jake doesn’t turn round to see. ‘Look,’ he says, ‘will you walk down to the sea with me?’

She glances behind him again, just once, but says, ‘OK.’

They walk side by side. Every few steps, he feels her sleeve brush against his. He wonders if she’s aware of it too. He still can’t get over the fact that she is here, that he found her, that they are together on this huge beach under the wide expanse of sky.

‘So how long were you in London?’ she asks.

‘A couple of days.’

‘And did you like it any more than last time?’ She looks at him sideways.

He smiles. ‘Not much. I was staying in a place that stank of bodily fluids and I couldn’t find my way about and I ran out of money. And the only person I wanted to see turned out not to be there after all.’

She lifts a hand to brush a few stray strands of hair away from her eyes. The breeze blows them back immediately and she has to turn her face to the wind to get rid of them. Jake stops walking and she stops too, looking at him expectantly.

'Stella,' he says, and he touches her arm, 'it's madness, us not being together.'

She looks up at him, scanning his face. 'I...' she begins, then, dropping her eyes, says, 'I think I'm going away.'

'Away?' Jake is exasperated. 'Away where?'

'I don't know,' she murmurs. 'There's this job in Boston that–'

'Fuck Boston. Stella, please. I want ... I just want…' What does he want? He has to think. Then, suddenly, he knows: 'I want you to come back to Hong Kong with me.'

She laughs. 'What?'

'Hong Kong,' he repeats, the idea unfurling in his mind. 'I want you with me, in Hong Kong.'

'You're not serious.'

'I am,' he insists. 'I've never been more serious in my life.'

'You think I'd come to Hong Kong with you just like that?'

'Why not? You just said you're going away anyway. You'll love it. It's like nowhere else you've ever been. It has everything you could possibly want – a city, mountains, beautiful beaches, national parks. Um. What else? The food is the best you'll ever eat. It's not too hot yet, or humid. Er. My best friend works at the big broadcasting station – we can talk to him about getting you a job.'

Stella, staring at him, shakes her head in amazement.

'Are you convinced yet?' he says. 'You can go on day trips to China. There are these great trams. You can go on night-time rides, from one end of the island to the other, to look at all the neon. You'll love it,' he says again. 'And, anyway, you have a moral obligation to come.'

'A moral obligation? How come?'

He shrugs. 'If I'm not back there in two days I won't have a job and I'll get kicked out of my apartment and I can't leave without you. So you'd be saving me from destitution and ... and disgrace.'

She leans against the salt-saturated wood of the groyne, running her fingertips over the pocked barnacles.

'You have to come,' he says.

She turns her gaze on him. 'Do I?'

'Yes. Because if you don't...' Jake moves towards her. Without thinking about what he is doing, he folds his arms round her and there, on Portobello beach, he lifts her off her feet. 'Because if you don't,' he says tightly, into her neck, 'I'm going to have to spend the rest of my life looking for another you. And I don't think there is one.'

She is struggling and laughing and saying

his name, saying she can't breathe, but her arms are round him, her fingers laced behind his neck. Jake kisses her cheek, her forehead, her ear, her lips, any part of her he can reach, and his mouth is full of her hair and for a moment he thinks that everything is fixed, that everything will work out.

But she twists in his grasp, turning her face aside, tugging herself away from him. 'There are things,' she says, 'I have to do.'

'What things? There are no things.'

'I promised.' She presses her hand to her cheek, distractedly. 'I promised my grandmother I'd work this week.'

'Fine. We'll go in a week.'

'But you said you have to go in two days.'

'A week, two days, what difference will it make? Just promise me you'll come.'

She looks down, her toe sketching curves in the sand. She shakes her head.

'Promise me,' he urges.

'I can't.' Her voice drops low into her chest. She lifts herself up so that she's sitting on the groyne and covers her face with her hands. 'I can't.'

Jake leans on the wood, a hand either side of her. 'Why not?'

'I just can't. I'm sorry,' she whispers, and she reaches out for him, curls her hands round his neck and pulls him towards her. His face is pressed to hers, resting on hers, her forehead against his cheek. Jake can't say anything. They are both shaking. He feels as though the sand underneath him is live, quick, that he might slide sideways or down. He puts his arms round her and holds on to her, tight. They stay like this for a while, her fingers straying through his hair. He can feel the fluttering thud of her heart through her clothes.

'I'm sorry,' she says, in his ear. 'I'm so sorry. Don't be angry with me.'

'Stella,' he breathes in the smell of her skin, 'tell me why you can't. Is it ... do you not...' He has to force himself to say it. 'Do you not feel ... anything for me? Is that it?'

'No!' She clutches him to her. 'Don't think that, don't ever think that. I just ... I just don't think I'm cut out for this.'

'You are,' he insists. 'You definitely are.'

'I'm not. I'd make you miserable.'

'You wouldn't.' He pulls away and cups her face in his hands. 'Quite the opposite. Can't you see I love you?'

Tears spring from her eyes and slip down her face and he rubs them away with his thumb. 'I love you,' he repeats. 'I really do.' Jake thinks of something. 'Stella, does this have anything to do with – with what your sister told me? About ... what happened when you were young?'

He sees her cheeks flame beneath the tears, her eyes widen, and he cannot believe it. 'If you think for a minute that something like that could change how I feel about you,' he gives her a shake, 'I can't tell you how wrong you are.'

She sniffs, her face agitated, panicked, brushing roughly at her cheeks. 'Really?' she says, almost inaudibly.

'No!' He lets out an incredulous noise. 'Jesus, how could you ever think it would? It's ridiculous, it's almost insulting.'

'But, Jake–'

'Well, how about if it was the other way round? If it was me? Would it have any effect on how you felt about me?'

She is silent.

'Would it?' he persists.

'No,' she says, in a small voice.

'Right.' He slaps his hand against the barnacled wood. 'Thank you. Now, are you coming to Hong Kong with me?'

She shakes her head.

Jake sighs and grits his teeth. 'Are you coming to Hong Kong with me?'

She looks at him, then looks away. 'No.'

'Stella Gilmore, you're driving me mad. Why not?'

She sits hunched, her hands in her lap. There is something about her expression – a resignation, a closedness – that tells him her mind is made up. He knows enough about her to see that nothing he could say will change a thing. She's not coming. Jake pushes himself upright, away from her, and moves off down the beach. The wind tugs and strains at his jacket. Several feet off, he stops. 'I don't know what to say to you,' he yells. 'I don't understand. This is what you want, is it? I go back to Hong Kong and you stay here, and that's that?'

He leans down and picks up a handful of pebbles and hurls them, one by one, into the wind. The sand is patched with pools of water and he throws the pebbles towards them, wanting to shatter the glass-perfect blue.

After a while, Stella appears at his elbow. 'I...' she begins, tentative '...I could call you. If you want.'

Jake throws another stone, furious, arching his arm back behind him. 'In Hong Kong?'

'Yes.'

'And what would be the point in that?'

She doesn't say anything, just bows her head. Jake sifts pebbles from one hand into the other. He lets one fall and catches it squarely with his toe, kicking it towards a bank of desiccated seaweed.

'Is that,' he says, trying to keep his voice even, 'all you can give me to go on?'

She nods. 'I'm sorry.'

Jake stands in his apartment, looking down into the street. Everything is so exactly the same it's as if he never went away. Or, rather, that he's stepped back in time. In the kitchen, when he arrived, he found a silver bracelet of Mel's, and in the bathroom cabinet, folded up, one of the slings he had for his arm. He feels as though he might, at any moment, turn a corner and bump into the person he was before Chinese New Year.

He unlatches the window and the white, burning heat of summer hits him in the face. Jake smiles. It's thirty-five degrees out there today and he loves it.

He's been back three days. Four if you count today. The haze of jetlag is lifting – he slept for seven solid hours last night – and he's beginning to get back into the mindset of being here. He needs to go to the market, buy some vegetables, should really give the apartment a sweep. He might get the ferry later to Kowloon, meet up with Hing Tai for *dim sum*. Hing Tai said Mui wanted to go for a swim later and did Jake fancy coming too? He spent yesterday in a meeting with Chen and the locations manager, discussing the places they could shoot the opening sequence of the new film, and Chen had wanted him to see various screen tests.

He is surprised by the ease with which you can slot back into a life. People tend to ask him a few questions about 'his trip', as they call it, then move on. Hing Tai had been a bit more insistent. Maybe he'd been talking to Caroline. He'd asked about Mel, then narrowed his eyes and demanded, 'And what else?' Jake had shrugged. They had been at Hing Tai's mother's and the room had been filled with people, relatives, colleagues, and Jake hadn't felt like going into it just then.

Jake closes the window. He'll go to the market now, before getting the ferry. She hasn't called. But it's only three days. Four, if you count today. Which Jake isn't. Yet.

Stella sits at the till, her knees drawn up. Behind her, her grandmother is talking to her uncle. Something about needing to stir the ice-cream in five minutes and how they have to fix a couple of the chairs and something else, in between, about a letter from Italy.

From her vantage-point, she surveys the room. Nina and Richard sit in a booth, the weekend paper between them. The café is full, as it should be on a Saturday in summer. Stella finds it peculiar sometimes: all these people, eating. By the window, at the back, along the wall, tables with people slicing food into pieces, raising it to their mouths, closing their lips round it, chewing and chewing, then swallowing, pushing the food down into their stomachs. She imagines the hordes who have passed through the café today, spreading out through Musselburgh and Edinburgh and Lothian, going about their business, Iannelli food filtering through their bodies.

A woman approaches the counter and Stella writes down what she wants. A toastie and a cappuccino. She takes the food order through to her uncle, then she gets down the cup to make the cappuccino.

As she stands at the coffee machine, she sees that the sun has come out. The door bangs and someone is entering the café. Nina is putting a cigarette to her lips and pressing down on the lighter. Richard is stirring sugar into his espresso. A young girl is running backwards past the window, laughing, clutching two loaves of bread to her chest.

Stella thinks: there are some things in life that will always be indissoluble, indigestible. The girl outside collides with a man carrying a saddle and she drops one of the loaves, still laughing. The smoke from Nina's cigarette uncurls to the ceiling.

Days later, she is in Nina's car.

'I want to make it quite clear I'm only doing this because I'm your sister,' Nina says.

'OK.'

'I want you to understand that I completely disapprove.'

'OK, OK.'

'That I think it's a stupid, crap, ridiculous idea.'

'All right, Nina, I get it.'

Nina accelerates up the Royal Mile, the tyres snapping on the cobbles, and soon they are swooping down the curved hill, the New Town laid out before them. Stella almost sighs. It's a shame she can't bring herself to live in this city. Maybe one day.

'I don't agree with what you're doing,' Nina continues, her steering made erratic by the fact that she's unwinding the Cellophane from a packet of cigarettes.

'You've made your point.' Stella flinches as they only narrowly clear a traffic bollard. 'Do you think you could keep both hands on the wheel?'

They wait in line at the lights to cross Princes Street.

'All I'm saying is–'

'Quite a lot,' Stella mutters.

Nina ignores her. 'Call him.'

'No.'

'Just call him.'

'No.' Stella shakes her head.

'Why?'

'I...' Stella tries to think of a reason. Then gives up. 'I can't.'

'I'll call him, then.' Nina flashes her a malicious grin. 'I can pretend to be you, easily.'

'Don't.' Stella looks across at her sister.

Nina shrugs and smiles.

'Nina, I mean it.' Stella is fierce. 'You must not.'

‘I might. It’s for your own good.’

‘If you do – I’ll – I really will never speak to you again.’

‘Yes, you will.’

‘No, I won’t.’

‘You will.’ She blows smoke over Stella’s face.

Stella winds down the window. ‘I will not. Don’t you dare.’

Nina sighs and drums her fingers on the steering-wheel. ‘Please.’ She changes tack, begging.

‘No.’

‘Please?’

Stella sighs. ‘Neen, just drop it, will you?’

‘Why not?’

‘Because first of all, I don’t know what to say, second of all, he’s probably still really angry with me, and–’

‘Third of all, you don’t know that.’

‘Well, you don’t know that he isn’t.’

‘I do.’

‘You do not.’

‘I do. The man adores you. It’s obvious. Sisterly intuition.’

‘Yeah, right.’ She shoots Nina a look. ‘Your sisterly intuition’s been great recently.’

Nina stubs out her cigarette in the ashtray. ‘I thought you weren’t going to bring that up again.’ She tosses the butt out of the window.

Stella holds up her hands. ‘I wasn’t. Look,

all I'm saying is, it's my life so let me handle it.'

'By running away to America?'

'Just ... let me be.'

Nina screeches to a halt outside the travel shop, on a double yellow line. 'I'll wait here. Don't be long. We have to be over at Mum's in twenty minutes.'

Stella gets out of the car and runs over the pavement. She glances at the lists of flights in the window: Madrid, Barcelona, Sydney, Prague, Los Angeles, Miami, New York. Return or one-way. She gets the light-headed feeling she always gets when faced with a world map, that dizzying scope of the possible. She could go anywhere, be anyone, rewrite her life just by getting on a plane. All she has to do is hand over some money. Travel strikes her sometimes as an almost suspiciously easy bargain: a new life in exchange for cash. Surely there should be something more Faustian, more binding about it? How can it be that easy?

She turns and looks at her sister, who is glaring balefully at her through the windscreen, smoke wisping from her mouth like a dragon.

When she comes back, she puts the shiny packet of an air-ticket on to the dashboard. 'Have a look,' she says.

'I don't see why I should.' Nina jams the keys into the ignition. 'As I've said, I completely disapprove of this whole scheme.'

'Just have a look.' Stella jiggles the packet invitingly in front of her sister. 'Go on.'

Nina sighs, flicks it open and scans the close type. Stella sees her frown, lean closer, frown again, then turn to look at her.

'Oh, my God,' Nina says slowly.

Jake has decided that work is the antidote to misery. He's getting to the office before eight and not leaving until about eleven at night. He's involving himself in everything – locations, rewrites, screen tests, rehearsals, costumes. He even sat in on a meeting with the caterers. Chen laid a hand on his shoulder yesterday: 'Slow down,' he said, 'you might crash.'

He's had the phone line tested twice. He got his mother to call him back, just to make sure it worked internationally. He bought a new answerphone, just in case. But it's been two weeks. Just over. Jake is beginning to realise that she might not call.

Maybe he's an idiot, but this scenario had never occurred to him. He doesn't know what to do. He wants to fly back to Britain, or Boston, or wherever it is she's got to, to see her again, to try to persuade her. But he hasn't the money at present and Hing Tai had said that if he heard Jake had so much as made enquiries about air tickets, he would confiscate his passport. Don't chase her, he'd said, let her come to you. But what if she doesn't, Jake had asked, and Hing Tai didn't have an answer to that.

Jake lifts a spoonful of *congee* to his mouth, then puts it down. He's having breakfast in a place near the office. It's a long, overlit room with rows and rows of tables. Steam obscures the windows and a long queue snakes from the counter to the door. The tables are full of people eating and drinking tea. The man behind the counter calls orders through to the kitchen, then shouts at the boy pushing a greyish mop around the tiles. Music spirals out of a radio. Four men sit at Jake's table, crushing him against the wall. One of them is expounding the faults of their boss while the other three listen. In the corner, an ancient woman on a stool picks her teeth.

Jake tunes into the conversation about the boss then, tiring of that, tunes into the one behind him. Two teenagers talking about their mobile phones. He eats some more of his *congee* but his heart's not in it. He wonders what he is doing, coming into the office on a Saturday. He'd told himself there were lots of things he could get done while it was quiet, but now he's here, he can't remember what any of them were.

He sits, his hands resting on the table. People swim past the windows, some glancing in at him. The boy with the mop reaches up and retunes the radio. The traffic on the flyover rumbles and shakes. The men next to him pour and sip tea, still talking. And suddenly Jake is sitting bolt upright.

He can hear Stella' s voice.

He tilts his head, disbelieving. It's her. He would swear his life on it.

He twists on his stool to look behind him. Nothing – just tables of people having breakfast. He leaps up, his stool clattering to the floor. It is her. Talking. As if she's there in the restaurant somewhere, or trapped in the walls, or has invaded his head. Jake turns wildly one way, then the other, trying to find the source.

People are staring at him now, the mad *gweilo*, looking about for something or someone, but Jake doesn't care. Where is she? The idea that she is somewhere near to him but he can't find her makes him feel as though he might lose his mind. Is he imagining it? Has she finally robbed him of his reason? He peers out of the window at the people on the pavement. Then he turns and starts weaving his way through the tables.

'Three suspects have been detained today,' she is saying, 'but police have not as yet issued a statement.'

Jake stares at the radio screwed into the wall, a small black and chrome box. Stella is speaking from it, talking to him about a drugs bust. He has to stop himself reaching up and kissing it.

Jake hurtles across the room, towards the phone sitting on the counter. For a moment he can't remember the number. Then it comes back to him. He hears the phone being answered on the first ring.

'*Wai-ee?*'

'It's me, listen–'

'Jik-ah?'

'Yeah, yeah. Now–'

'I'm glad you've called,' Hing Tai says chattily, 'because I was having this argument with my brother last night and–'

'Listen, I can't talk now, I–'

'Oh, thanks. Thanks a lot. For ringing me up and then telling me you can't talk. I mean, that's really nice. If I rang you up and–'

'Shut up, shut up a minute. This is really important.'

'What? What's more important than–'

'Hing Tai. I mean it. If you don't shut up and listen to me, my whole life could fall apart.'

'Shit,' Hing Tai says, unmoved. 'You'd better tell me, then.'

'OK.' Jake takes a deep breath. 'Somewhere in your building someone is reading the news.'

Hing Tai makes an impatient noise. 'Is that what you're calling to tell me?' he demands.

'Has your brain gone soft in–'

'I want you,' Jake carries on regardless, 'to do me a huge favour.'

As Stella steps out of the studio, the news pages in her hand, easing the buffered, soundproofed door closed, there is a man standing behind the producer. He is wearing jeans and a large-collared shirt, and the very tips of his hair are bleached white. Stella is wondering how you'd do that when she realises he is speaking to her. 'You are Stella?' he is saying.

'Yes.'

'Come,' he beckons, 'come with me.'

She follows him, puzzled, away from the studio, down a long corridor, through a lift lobby, into a stairwell, down a few flights of stairs. Every few steps, he turns round – to check she's still with him? Stella's not sure. He seems to be assessing her, looking her up and down, considering her.

'Can I ask what this is about?' Stella ventures.

'Come,' he replies, 'follow me, please.'

The building unravels before her. She hasn't got the hang of it yet, can't orientate herself within it. But that goes for the entire city at the moment. They arrive in a room where hundreds of people are sitting in sectioned booths. The man beckons to her again as he steps into a cubicle. When she comes to a stop, he is holding out a phone to her.

'Call for you,' he says.

'For me?' Stella won't take the receiver. 'Who is it?'

The man puts the phone to his ear, grinning to himself, and says something into it in Chinese. Then he holds it out to her again. 'He says you must stop being stubborn and take the phone.'

Stella is so shocked she does as she's told. 'Hello?'

'I've been waiting by the phone for weeks.' Jake's voice is close to her ear.

'Have you?' she says, and she worries for a moment that she won't be able to hear his answer because her pulse is deafening her.

'I can't believe it,' he says. 'I can't believe you didn't call me, and I can't believe you're here.'

'Well,' she says, 'I am.'

'I heard you on the radio.'

'Did you?'

'You were good. I think. Although I'm probably not the best judge right now. But I wanted to kiss it, if that gives you any idea–'

'You wanted to kiss it?' She laughs. 'The radio?'

The man in the cubicle is pretending that he's not listening, she sees, fiddling with his computer, but he's smiling and shaking his head.

'Listen, I'm coming to find you. You're not going to vanish or disappear anywhere, are you?'

'Jake, you don't need to come here. I can always–'

'No, no. Stay exactly where you are. Hing Tai's under strict instructions not to let you out of his sight. Just stand still, don't move and don't go anywhere.'

Jake bursts from the restaurant. Rain has just started to fall, dark circles spotting the pavement. He runs down the road, his sneakers slapping the concrete. As he turns the corner, the rain suddenly doubles, the spots on the ground merging until the whole street is slick and polished like sealskin. Owners of street-side noodle bars pull canopies over their tables and men are holding folded newspapers over their heads and people are dashing into doorways or under trees or into the MTR station.

Jake runs. The muscles in his legs burn and the rain slides in channels down his hair and on to his face. He gasps for air and drops fall into his mouth. He dodges men in suits, a woman dragging a steel cart, a family running in the opposite direction, a man weighed down with a bucket of crustaceans, two girls laughing to each other as they wring out their long ropes of hair.

As he runs, he sees the way the city copes

with rain. Water ribbons from pipes and gutters, from roofs, down the sides of buildings, bubbling across the tilting pavements and into the street, where it swirls round and down the drains, to be hurried away under roads, along invisible trenches. Buses and taxis plash through the lakes collecting against the kerbs, throwing tidal waves of water over the pavement, over people's ankles.

The rain is stinging his skin and he pushes himself to speed up, moving into the road, off the crowded pavement, water soaking through his shoes, his jeans, his socks. He goes under a big bridge where crowds of people are sheltering and when he comes out again into the light he can make out the radio station building up ahead and, in the doorway, Hing Tai and, behind him, Stella.

Hing Tai is looking the wrong way, across the road, but Stella sees him. She steps out into the street, into the rain, and raises her hand, like someone shielding their eyes from light, like someone answering a question.

acknowledgements

My thanks to: William Sutcliffe, Victoria Hobbs, Mary-Anne Harrington, Ruth Metzstein, Kate Jones, Beatrice Monti della Corte, The Santa Maddalena Foundation, Bill Swainson, Alessandra Gnecchi-Ruscone, Mary Lewis, Adam Sutcliffe, Dewi Davies, Elizabeth Ingrams, and my family – Patrick, Susan, Catherine and Bridget.

I am indebted to the following books: *Emigration in a South Italian Town: An Anthropological History* by William A. Douglas (Rutgers University Press, New Jersey, 1984) and *Multiculturalism in Practice: Irish, Jewish, Italian and Pakistani Migration to Scotland* by Suzanne Audrey (Ashgate, 2000). Also to Elizabeth Grant's *Memoirs of a Highland Lady* (Canongate, Edinburgh, 1988) – and to my mother, for giving it to me in the first place.